ALSO BY JANET NEWTON:

IN THE CHURCHYARD SPILLED

BEYOND THE PALE

GATE OF IVORY, GATE OF HORN

OVER THE WHALES' ROAD

BOOK FOUR OF THE LLANGYNOG MURDERS

JANET NEWTON

KINDLE DIRECT PUBLISHING

This is a work of fiction. Names, characters, organizations, events, and incidents are either a product of the author's imagination or are used fictionally.

Cover photo of the Irish Sea by Janet Newton

For Mom and Dad —

You gave me the gift of a family like Bronwyn's! I miss you every day, but you live in my heart always.

Note to readers:

The Welsh language is a Celtic language which is still spoken by about 30% of the population in Wales, along with English. Road signs are in both Welsh and in English, with Welsh being in the primary position. To my tourist eyes, Welsh words tend to be much longer than their English equivalents, with fewer familiar vowels. Names in Wales are often spelled the Welsh way.

Many of you have asked for a pronunciation guide for the names I use in my books, so here are the most common ones:

Llangynog	lang GA nog
Pennant Melangell	pen nant me LANG geth
Caernarfon	care NAR von
Twlwyth Teg	tell with teg
Pysgotwr	pes NOT wur
Cwn Annwn	sin ann win

OVER THE
WHALES' ROAD

Chapter One

"See me." The hand-written note lay waiting on Will Cooper's desk as he sidled in – only fifteen minutes late – past his co-workers in the Caernarfon major crimes unit of the North Wales Police Force. He ignored the gloating look of his colleague Sean Notley, who he despised, and the concerned glance of another partner, Beth Holway, who he actually liked. What he couldn't ignore, though, was the summons from Chief Superintendent Bowers, his immediate boss.

He considered fifteen minutes late acceptable, allowing for the fact that an accident had blocked the west-bound lane of the A4088 into Caernarfon, but that was today's excuse. He'd slipped back into his habit of arriving late to work again more often than not, now that he spent his free days at the cottage he'd rented in the little village of Llangynog, an hour and a half's commute on a good day and longer if an accident or inclement weather held him up. He'd nearly always arrived late when he'd first taken the transfer to Caernarfon from Cardiff drugs and alcohol, a transfer he hadn't wanted, but as he'd learned to enjoy his work in major crimes, he'd tried harder to conform to expectations. Then he'd met Bronwyn Bagley, and since she refused to move to Caernarfon, he'd given in and moved to Llangynog to share a house with her, creating his current problem.

He supposed a dressing-down would be the extent of Bowers' disapproval, but his stomach clenched at the thought nevertheless. He liked Bowers, who had always been fair with him. *No, more than fair*, he corrected himself. Bowers should have seen him off the job after he'd started seeing Bronwyn behind his partner's back. She was, after all, a suspect in that first big murder case. It was true that he'd used her for the information that had ultimately solved the case, but his methods were beyond unethical, and he'd been lucky to end with a two-week

1

suspension without pay. Notley, his partner on that case, had never forgiven him for solving the case without him and making him look the fool in front of their colleagues.

Bowers' open door beckoned. He stopped at the threshold and knocked, breathing steadily as he gathered himself for whatever awaited him inside. He really couldn't imagine what he'd done wrong this time.

"Come in." Bowers looked up. As always, his face was inscrutable, impossible to read. His dark hair was liberally sprinkled with gray these days, but his slacks were pressed and his white shirt brilliant against a blue and red striped tie. He gestured Will to a chair pulled up in front of his desk. "Tea?"

Will nodded as he slid into the chair. Unlike the chairs in the outer room where Will's desk competed for space with all the others, this one was padded leather, soft and comfortable. For some reason, it made Will feel even more guilty about his lackadaisical attitude of late. He ran a hand through his unruly hair and then tamped it down on his lap, wary of looking unprofessional.

He waited, his nervousness growing, while Bowers made the call for tea. Maybe he'd done something more serious than just coming in late to work? He tried to think back over the past few days. Things had been slow lately, no murders or really serious crimes where a misstep might cost a conviction in court and allow someone guilty of something heinous to go free. No, it had to be his tardiness that had landed him in trouble this time, a problem that could probably be banished with some subservience on his part. He steeled himself to apologize.

Bowers turned his gaze on Will. "I've had a call from Cardiff drugs and alcohol," he began.

Will couldn't help a confused frown. "My old stomping grounds," he mumbled.

"Yes," Bowers agreed. He allowed a slight smile to twerk his lips. "No, they haven't asked for you back, if that's what you're wondering. That door is closed, I'm afraid."

"I'm happy here, but what happened there wasn't my fault," Will blurted, to his dismay. "None of what happened was my fault." He needed to get control of himself. He sat up straighter in the chair, which was difficult considering how soft it was. The situation that had prompted his unwilling transfer had truthfully not been his fault, but it would earn him no credit to keep pointing that out.

"I know that. In fact, you came with the highest accolades."

That surprised him. "What did they want, then, if not to demand my return?"

Another slight twitch of the mouth indicated Bowers' attempt at a smile. "There's been an increase in drug activity in Liverpool, Manchester, and other major cities northeast of here. Drugs and alcohol have increased patrols of the southern English ports. You might have heard about a couple of recent drug busts?"

"I saw on the news about the one in Dover last week. Nearly a million pounds' worth of opioids, if I remember right. It was a major bust, must have delivered a huge blow to that network."

Bowers nodded. "We would hope so. But according to what I've been told, that was just a fraction of what's coming in, and Cardiff suspects – it's not confirmed, though – that whoever's bringing them in is diverting away from the southern English ports and bringing them in along the coast of Wales instead."

"Entering the country at Cardiff?"

"They tell me it isn't Cardiff," Bowers said, "but further north in an effort to bypass the more intense security of the southern ports."

"The ferry ports, then? Fishguard or Holyhead?"

"It's possible it could be either, but I'm told they've had a credible tip that a big shipment is coming in through Holyhead sometime in the next two weeks. A shipment can enter Ireland from the European mainland without a lot of questions being asked, and then if they drive it through to Northern Ireland, they can bring truckloads in on the ferry without much scrutiny there. Holyhead's further out of the way than Fishguard, less likely to be watched."

"Holyhead's a long way from the European mainland," Will pointed out. "Their costs would be higher if they're diverting through Ireland and Wales on their way to the bigger English cities. Holyhead's about the furthest north you can get unless they go all the way to the Scottish ports."

"Maybe they're willing to pay the price rather than risk the loss of a big load in a more obvious port, like they did in Dover. As I said, it's just supposition at the moment, but Chief Superintendent Matthews tells me their source is reliable."

"So, they come in through Holyhead, then across Wales and into England. South to Cardiff, too?"

"They don't seem to be worried about Cardiff at the moment."

Will grinned. "I guess my old pals must be doing their jobs, then." A mental picture of his friend and former partner Edward Smythe popped into his memory for a moment. He missed Edward. He'd been the best of partners.

Bowers had been watching him, silent for a moment. "You miss the job there."

"I liked what I was doing back then, but this is just as satisfying….as long as I don't end with Notley as a partner on a major case." He tried to keep his voice light, joking, but he hoped Bowers would catch his drift.

Bowers chose to ignore the comment. "I need your help with this, some advice before I meet with the force and ask them to keep an eye out." He looked up as a young woman knocked lightly at the door and then entered, setting mugs of tea on the desk.

He waited for her to leave before continuing. "I'm far from being an expert on catching drug smugglers. Ask me about murder, and I can tell you exactly how to proceed. But drugs…I've no experience there."

"No, sir," Will agreed cautiously, wondering where this was going. He reached for the mug of tea and sipped, then set it down.

"You, of all the people in the department, have the most expertise with investigating how and where drugs are being brought into the country and moved across it. I thought you could share some ideas with me about what to ask of my people so I don't appear a bloody fool in front of them." Bowers reached for his mug of tea, watching Will.

Will let out a breath he hadn't known he was holding. So that was it. "I'd be happy to share what I know, sir, but keep in mind that when I was working drugs and alcohol, I was often undercover, and I had contacts and informants I could use to help move my investigations on."

"Yes, I'm aware." Bowers watched him now with some impatience on his usually amiable face.

Will took a moment to think. He didn't want to appear a 'bloody fool' either. When he felt he had to offer something, he blurted, "Incongruities, sir." At Bowers' puzzled look, he elaborated. "Tell them to look for things that don't fit. A boat coming and going that hasn't been noticed before. A truck on and off the ferry, maybe arriving just in time to load and then being first off in port."

"A lack of time to check the load thoroughly."

"Exactly, sir. And then, beyond that, activity at an abandoned site, maybe a warehouse or an old factory, something like that. Evidence of wealth where it wouldn't be expected, like a dock worker suddenly having money for a vacation abroad or a…I don't know…a garage owner with a new, fancy car. That's something everyone can keep an eye out for when we're out working cases." Will reached for the mug of tea, holding it in his hands to keep them steady.

"They've said they're primarily interested in the port and the initial distribution afterwards, but the other possibilities would give them leads back to the port, I'm guessing."

"That's it, sir. Best to catch the big load as it comes in or if you can catch it when it's being divided for transport through to its destinations, that's even better." He thought for a quick second, sipping at the tea again. "The reason you want to catch it being divided is that you catch more of those involved at that point, and it's still the major players. If you notice something off in port, the best thing is to follow along as the drugs are being transported to their meeting site. They won't take a big truck across to the various cities. They'll divide the load into smaller vehicles, trucks or vans, and then stagger the arrival times. That means some of them will pull into out-of-the-way places and sit for a week or two before going on to their destinations. You try to plant someone undercover or put a bug on a truck or…or track them somehow without them knowing. You don't want word getting out to the suppliers; that's who you want to catch, not the little guys who work for them. It's harder to catch the big fish in the pond, but that's who you want most. Anything that leads back to the importers, that's a success, in my opinion."

"You don't bother with the dealers?"

"They don't have much idea, most the time, where their product originates and how it comes to them. It's a waste of time and manpower to pursue that line. All the major players have to do is recruit more workers to sell the product for them, and that's never hard to do."

"They've asked us to set up a checkpoint at the port."

"It's a good idea, sir."

"But it'll tie up a lot of people, divert them away from other places we might need them."

"You're talking constables, sir? Not detectives?"

"They want us to flood the area with general policing. They're sending undercover to help find the loads and DI's to take over when they do."

"The kind of thing you're talking about, sir, wouldn't be given up without a fight. I mean, if it's really big…"

"That's what I thought, too. They say they'll send teams up, and all they need from us is eyes on the ground."

"How sure are they that Holyhead is the port to watch?"

"They seem to be pretty sure there's a big shipment coming in there in the next couple of weeks."

"A big time span…"

"Yes, so you can see what I meant when I said it would tie people up."

"If they asked us to man checkpoints, then I think you have no choice but to comply, sir. Step up the traffic stops, especially on lorries. It wouldn't hurt to tell everyone else to keep an eye out for other irregularities as we're going about our business."

Bowers nodded, his face thoughtful. He set the tea mug on the desk and shifted in his chair, leaning nearer to Will. "Thanks, Cooper. I don't like it, but I think we have to help them out. With luck, we won't have anything too pressing elsewhere while we're short-handed."

"In the end, sir, catching loads of drugs when they come into the country helps with our other problems anyway."

Bowers sighed. "Yes, you're right."

Will hesitated. "Do you want me to do some undercover work up there, sir? I might be able to get some information that would pinpoint when that shipment is expected."

Bowers shook his head. "I was specifically told to keep you away from it. Chief Superintendent Mathews thinks the whole drug problem became personal for you, after your sister's death. He's afraid you might compromise the investigation, going after them too hard."

"I wouldn't, sir."

"I want to believe you." Bowers looked at Will intently, nodded to himself, and, without preamble, diverted to a different topic. "You were late today."

Here it comes, the dressing down. "Yes, I apologize, sir. There was an accident that held me up." Best not to be too specific about where the accident was.

But Bowers already knew. "I hear you're living in Llangynog on your free days. That's quite a commute."

Will nodded, mute.

"I hope she's worth it."

"She is, sir." Will let out a breath he hadn't known he was holding. It was probably better anyway to get this out in the open, to face Bowers' knowing. Then he wouldn't have to feel that he was sneaking around with it. "I know you haven't always approved of my relationship with Bronwyn, but as you've said before, I think I'm entitled to a personal life." He hesitated, chancing a glance at Bowers who was watching him enigmatically, with no indication of what he was thinking. "Relationships are hard in our line of work, sir. You know that as well as I do. We get called out at all hours, we get involved with a case and have to abandon whatever other plans we've made, we even leave home not knowing if we'll return, truth be known." He glanced at Bowers again and then focused all his attention on him. "We all think of that. But Bronwyn, she's different from other girls I've known, sir. She never complains when we have to change our plans. She just makes me a sandwich and wishes me luck. If she worries or resents me having a case, she keeps it to herself. She's the most unselfish person I know." He paused, knowing it had been a long, defensive speech. "I fancy her a lot, sir, but she lives in Llangynog, and I live here. The distance between us was a problem, and we couldn't figure out another way for it to work. I didn't think the commute would be a big deal and it isn't, except when there's an accident blocking the road."

"Or bad weather, or just a late start." Bowers suggested, a wry smile teasing at his lips.

Might as well admit it. "Yes, sir, or those things. I stay here in town when I'm on rotation. I still have my flat."

"It's the off-duty time I'm interested in."

What? Wasn't his personal time his own? "Sir?"

"It occurs to me," Bowers said, "that Llangynog is on the far side of the district." He paused, and then went on, his voice thoughtful. "The department would benefit from having someone nearer when a crime is committed on the far side of our territory rather than waiting an hour or two for someone to drive across the country to whatever little village has had someone murdered. Don't you agree?"

"Yes, sir, I can see that, but we have substations scattered around in that area to handle the immediate stuff."

"But no detective inspectors nearby."

"No," Will agreed. "It does take us some time to get to that side of the district."

"My thought is that it would benefit my department if I could, maybe, have you work from there some of the time. Not that you'd be officially on duty twenty-four seven," he hastened to add. "You'd be free to make personal plans on your days off, of course, but if I could call on you when you're there to check out crimes that occur in that part of the district, I think that would offset any tardiness I'm observing these days." Bowers seemed diffident, as if he were hesitant to ask. "Of course, any time spent investigating on your off-duty days on the far side of the district would be compensated with other time off, if that were to happen. You'd still have to come here for coordinating with your partners, paperwork, and so on, so you won't be able to live full-time in Llangynog. But you'd probably be there more often than you are now. What do you think?"

Will nodded, trying to contain excitement that left him a little dizzy. Bronwyn liked to watch *Midsomer Murders* in an evening sometimes; she was used to the idea of a detective husband being called out at inconvenient times, so she probably wouldn't be bothered. And it might mean more nights he could spend with her, if he were to be assigned to work cases nearer to Llangynog most of the time. "You're saying that I'd be more or less based on the east side of the district. I can see how it would be beneficial to assign those cases to someone who lived nearer.

It'd save time, but it'd also save money if we didn't always have to drive that far or pay for lodging when a case needs someone on scene. Would I stay in Llangynog while I work the cases that are located there?"

"You're playing on my good will here, Cooper," Bowers told him. "I was thinking that it'd put you closer for a quick response, not that you'd be based there all the time. As I said, you'd still need to be here for paperwork, and of course whoever you're partnered with would have to travel back and forth, and that travel time gives you a lot of time to review the case and make plans." He studied Will, and then gave in. "If it's within a 20-minute drive, I'll approve it some of the time. That's if it looks like the case will take more than a day to solve, of course."

"Nothing's within 20 minutes of Llangynog," Will groaned.

"Okay, then, a half hour. You're right that it would save the department some money if we don't have to put you up in a hotel or have you driving back and forth."

"Now if you'd just let me choose my partner…"

"Don't push it. You know my philosophy is that we're all working toward a common cause, that being ridding North Wales of crime, and we all work together on it – everyone from constables to me." He looked thoughtfully at Will. "You are entitled to a personal life, though. You're right about that. I really hope you can make it work with Miss Bagley."

A flutter of surprise caught Will unawares. "Thank you, sir. I think if there's a chance at a long-term relationship with someone, Bronwyn is the kind of girl who'd make it work."

"You broke a lot of hearts in the local forces when you decided she was the one."

Will shook his head in denial. "I'm sure that's not true, but thank you anyway, sir."

"I hope to get to know her better."

"We'll try to make that happen, sir. She does come here to visit sometimes, so we could try to arrange something."

Bowers hesitated, then took a breath. "I don't know if you're aware, Cooper, but I've managed to make my relationship work through the years."

"How many years, if I may ask, sir?" Will had always been curious. Bowers tended to keep his personal life, personal.

9

"Thirty-two, so far, and we've raised two children who are now successful adults. It can be done, Cooper. It just takes work and the right sort of woman. I hope you've found her."

"You give me hope, sir." Hope, yes, but certainty, not yet. He liked Bronwyn, liked her a lot, but the thought of committing to a lifetime with her still scared him silly. She often talked about living in the moment. He'd taken that idea to heart because it meant he didn't have to think about the next step their relationship might take. He was a coward and glad to admit it.

"I take it she likes the facial hair?" Bowers wasn't done, it seemed.

"She does, sir." Will grinned, rubbing a hand across his stubble. "It contributes to my untamed look."

"As long as it contributes to your professional look, as well..." Bowers murmured. He waved his hand. "Remember, you don't share details of your cases with her." Bowers obviously knew that Will got information from Bronwyn, but he had to say it, to keep himself in the clear in case it someday came to light. He let the smile flirt with his lips again. "Now you must have work to do."

"Yes, sir. Thank you, sir."

Back at his desk, he turned his chair to face the other detectives on duty, making sure that his computer faced back-side to them, and then he opened a game of solitaire. Things were slow. He was caught up on paperwork and ready for two trials scheduled to start that next month. Everyone was feeling it, the boredom that set in when there were no major cases to occupy their time. He glanced out over the open space where they had their desks. He'd bet pounds to pumpkins that everyone else was doing pretty much the same as he was, catching up on email, playing games, or looking up random topics on Google. Hopefully no one from tech support would check to see how they spent their long days.

While he moved the cards around on his screen, he let his mind wander, as it usually did, to Bronwyn. At first, moving into the cottage with her felt awkward. She'd only stayed with him twice at his flat in Caernarfon, and when he'd stayed in Llangynog it'd been at her parents' house, in their spare bedroom, which felt a lot more like a B&B than shared space with her. They weren't used to each other's habits, and living in the outskirts of Llangynog was a far different world than living in the city centre of Caernarfon. Shopping together for the few furnishings they could afford helped a little, as did moving half of his wardrobe and a few of his personal items into the house. The biggest help had been treating himself to a new leather chair and a bottle of Famous Grouse to sip in the evenings, as he did in Caernarfon. Still, he often felt more like a guest than not.

He'd met some of the neighbors and liked them: Graeme and Maeve next door with their two young children and Nick across the street with his new wife Dilys, a couple he felt they had much in common with.

He closed his eyes and stifled a chuckle, remembering earlier in the month when Bronwyn had decided the lawn needed mowing. He'd never mowed a lawn in his life so he had no idea what to do with the well-used old mower Bronwyn's dad had passed on to them. He'd stood there in mortified silence as she'd shown him how to put the gas in and pull the cord to start it. He still wasn't sure he was accomplishing the task to her standards. He only hoped she hadn't told her brother Maddock about his lack of experience. He'd think it hilarious. It was things like this that made him wonder just what he'd gotten himself into.

Not that he didn't enjoy it; he did. He'd told himself firmly not to overthink things, and if he didn't let himself delve into the future or think about all the work involved in keeping up a home, he had to admit that things were working out as he'd hoped they would. But now, Bower's suggestions might mean that he could be there more full-time than had been possible these past three months. Would that make him happy? Or would it be too much, too fast? Spending only his free days there had, so far, enabled them to ease into a shared household. He honestly wasn't sure about doing it more full-time. He enjoyed Bronwyn's company. He'd told her he loved her, and he thought it was true. But was it all leading toward a long-term commitment he wasn't quite ready for? And, the bigger question, would he ever be ready? He'd promised Maddock that their living arrangements would eventually lead to a "more permanent situation," as Maddock had termed it when he'd given his blessing to their living together. Thinking of what that meant still scared him silly.

11

Bowers called a general staff meeting a half hour later, detailing a plan to divert patrols toward Anglesey in an attempt to stop what they were calling a major drug shipment. Will watched him steadily as he incorporated Will's ideas into his instructions, but only once did Bowers let his gaze fall back on Will, a blank look that didn't single him out. It didn't matter. Will hadn't expected to be credited for his contributions. He was happy simply to have been consulted.

Afterwards, he went back to his solitaire game, trying to look inconspicuous as he clicked on the cards. He let his mind wander, wondering one moment if Beth's son Liam had been behaving himself and the next if he and Jay Mehta, his favorite choice of partners, could slip away for some lunch.

Just before noon, though, his desk phone rang, never a good omen. Maybe it was something simple, a domestic issue or someone reporting a robbery. He crossed his fingers on his left hand, picking up the phone with his right.

"Sir," the duty sergeant said crisply, "we have a suspicious death up by South Stack. Someone fell from the cliffs near the lookout. Do you know where that is?"

"I can look it up," Will offered. A fall from the cliffs, and it was always wet and slippery on those rocks, he was sure...*maybe this one will be just a fall and not a push, an easy and quick case.* Notley was on rotation with him at the moment, and he really didn't want to get stuck with Notley on something complicated. "We'll head up there and check it out. Is there a doctor on scene?"

"It's up on Anglesey, near Holyhead. Forensics have been sent for," the sergeant told him. "I'm not sure if a doctor's on scene yet or not. The scene's been secured, as best it can be with the surf along there, and the road into it is closed off."

"All good," Will responded, his mind busy. It was – what? – a couple hours' drive along winding, narrow roads, but most of it barren and free of traffic. Not a bad case to land, really. It'd be a pretty drive on a spring day.

He stood up and turned, only to see Bowers striding toward him through the desks. What now?

Bowers stopped and pointed at Will, Notley, Beth, and her partner of the day, Ian O'Flynn, in turn. "I need to see you four in my office before you go." He turned and strode away.

Will chanced a look at Beth. "What's this about?" he mouthed.

She edged closer to walk beside him toward Bowers' office. "Did you get a case? I heard your phone."

"Yeah, a fall from a cliff up at South Stack."

"We got one, too, just after yours. A welfare check in your favorite village turned up a dead woman."

"In Llangynog?"

Beth gave him a look as Notley's head swiveled his way. "Yes."

Will's heart skipped a beat. When he'd left Bronwyn, he'd told her to go back to bed, to sleep another hour before she had to be up and off to work. She didn't need to be up before dawn like he did on days he had to make the commute.

Beth touched his arm as they slowed to enter Bowers' office. "It looks like a case of domestic abuse, Will. Her parents called for the check as they hadn't heard from her and she didn't answer their calls. It isn't Bronwyn."

He nodded, giving her an embarrassed grin as they settled into the room, standing in a line across from Bowers' desk. There weren't enough chairs to go around.

"There've been two reported cases in the past few minutes," Bowers said. "Good timing, them being together."

They waited.

"I'm asking you to switch them."

"But, why?" Notley sputtered, obviously put out at being denied what looked like an easy investigation. He didn't like partnering with Will any more than Will did him.

"It's a financial decision," Bowers told him, watching their puzzled frowns. "Cooper, here, has a place he can stay for free in that area if that case gets complicated. Saves us the cost of a room, maybe for days or weeks, if he takes that one and it takes some time to solve."

And it keeps me away from Anglesey, from Holyhead, Will thought. *Mathews asked that I be kept out of the drug situation.*

13

Bowers waved them toward the door. "Go and get the information you need and then get on the road." He paused. "Cooper, a word if I may before you go? And Notley, you after Cooper, please. Wait outside and it'll be just a minute."

"Okay." Will hung back as the others took turns exiting. With Notley on rotation with him, it was not a good time to land a major case. Bowers was probably worried about that. Maybe Bowers would let him stay in Llangynog, though, if the investigation took longer than a day or two. It'd be better if he and Notley didn't have to spend all their time together, and surely Bowers would realize that the two of them driving back and forth would only create friction and do nothing positive.

Shoving his chair back from his desk, Bowers stood up. "You have the luck, don't you, Cooper? I just talked to you – what – not even three hours gone, and already there's a case right there in Llangynog. How big's that village, a hundred people?"

"I think five hundred, but that's still not a lot when you think about it. It really is a coincidence. Maybe meant to be? Fate?" Will grinned. "And you didn't want me in Anglesey, did you, sir?"

"You saw through that." Bowers let a smile flirt with the edge of his mouth. "If we needed one, could you find a place to set up a temporary incident room? That's if this turns out to be a major case, not just a simple domestic?"

"We've got a spare room," Will told him, wondering how Bronwyn would handle having Notley hanging around the house. "Or a garage, which might be better. More access."

Bowers nodded. "I was thinking more of space in a common building. Nothing there?"

"There's a community centre, of sorts."

"Could you check to see if they have a space we could use? Something we could make secure with a door we could lock up?"

"I'll see what I can do."

"That sounds workable. It may not be necessary." He gave Will a direct look. "I don't want you making this into more of a case than it should be, just so you can stay over there."

"No, sir, of course not."

"And Notley might need to stay there, too. Is there lodging in the village at all?"

"Some B&Bs and rooms at one of the pubs."

"That would probably suffice." He looked up, out the window of his office to where the detectives' desks were arranged, along with those of other staff. "I'll talk to Notley, fill him in on the situation with you living there."

"Yes, sir. It's okay if I drive myself then?"

Bowers nodded, the wry twist to his mouth barely apparent. "Just this once. You and Sean might need to drive together if the case gets complicated down the road, but for now there's no reason for both of you to make the commute back and forth to the station." He shook his head. "Don't be too eager, Cooper. This case may turn out to be something simple, after all."

"I hope it is," Will assured him. And he did hope so. Any time he ended up with Notley as a partner, he prayed for an easy case, something that wouldn't stir up the old animosity between them. "I'll call to talk it over with you before we decide whether we'll need to stay, right?"

"Yes, that's right." Bowers told him, waving him out the door. "You'd better get on the road. It's quite a drive, as you've told me not two hours ago. You might wait, though, so Sean can follow you there. I'd imagine you know all the shortcuts."

It sounded like a joke, but Will suppressed a laugh. He wasn't sure whether Bowers ever intentionally joked or not, so better to be on the safe side.

He couldn't help a saunter in his step as he strolled between desks toward the door, passing by Notley as he entered Bowers' office in turn. Will hoped Notley wouldn't figure out the real reason they'd been told to switch cases. Better if he thought it was a financial decision.

Beth grabbed him as he headed toward the door. "Lucky you," she whispered, with a glance around to make sure no one was listening. "Bowers must really like you if he's favoring you with cases that keep you close to Bronwyn."

Will leaned in close to her. "He was told to keep me away from the drug case," he confessed, wishing he didn't have to. He thought, though, that he owed Beth the truth. She'd always been good to him.

"Oh, so that's it," she murmured. "I wondered."

"Yeah, Bowers is always more than fair with me, but he can't go as far as to assign me to all the cases in the east part of the district, can he?" He didn't tell her what Bowers had said earlier, about him being given cases that opened up in the east when he was in the area. She'd hear of it soon enough; coming from him, it'd sound like bragging.

"Good luck with this one, then," she wished him with a smile. "I don't know whether to hope you solve it quickly so you don't have to spend more time working with Notley than you have to, or whether to hope it gets complicated so you can stay with Bronwyn while you're working."

"I don't know either," Will said as they parted ways and headed toward their separate cars. He didn't, truly, know which to wish for. If it was Beth or Jay he was working with, he'd hope it took months, but with Notley? Better to keep it short and simple.

Chapter Two

Bronwyn hadn't gone back to sleep after Will left. She never did on the days he had to rush off on the drive back to Caernarfon, unwilling to let him pamper her and make all the sacrifices so that they could be together.

She sent him off with a bag of his favorite raspberry scones and a flask of coffee, kissing him goodbye in the driveway after he'd put the top down on his little MGF convertible and climbed in. It'd be cold driving with the top down that early in the morning, but she knew that using the convertible as it was meant to be used was his way of celebrating the first nice days of spring, just as hers was to get out into nature and hike, if she could.

And today she could do just that. With two extra hours before she had to be at work at the counseling centre at Pennant Melangell, she'd have the time to brave the trail rather than just walking up the lane. It'd take her the entire two hours to make the hike and she'd be muddy and bramble-dotted by the time she got there, but she kept extra clothes in her office to change into, and getting outside would allow her to start her work week off in a mellow mood despite the stress of having the St. Melangell's Day celebration looming in a few weeks' time.

She locked up the cottage and walked up the lane until she could access the trail where it roughened and started to climb uphill through the old quarry workings. The trailhead was closer now that she had moved into the cottage that Will rented for them than it had been when she'd lived further up the road with her parents on the farm. It made it easier for her to talk herself into the hike on work days, not that she was reluctant.

She let her mind wander as she worked at the ascent, watching her yellow Labrador Daisy frolic on the hillside ahead. So much had changed in the past year, and all for the good. A year ago, she'd been lonely, wondering what she was meant to do with her life, committed to staying in Llangynog where she had her roots because that was where her secret life lay. In no other place did she have contact with the Twlwyth Teg, Welsh fairies, or Pysgotwr, the Green Man of mythology. She knew that because she'd tried to move away. She'd gone off to university in Wrexham as her parents had wanted, but homesickness had driven her back to Llangynog before she got very far into her studies. Life in a small and isolated village offered little in the way of a social life, but she'd thought then that she had the will to live a solitary life if that was what it took to satisfy her need to stay. Yet, despite these dark thoughts, she'd longed for more, and then she'd met Will Cooper.

Now, a year later, Will had become the center of her life. They pooled their money to rent a cottage they could share, and she was slowly becoming accustomed to enjoying day-to-day life with him when he could be at home with her and to living alone when he wasn't. Although living with him had seemed awkward at first, she now looked forward to his free days in Llangynog even more than she'd thought she would. They had fun together, hiking when weather allowed, sharing a glass of wine on quiet evenings at home, and talking over his cases when he shared the details with her. She'd never let herself dream of a life like the one she was now living; she still marveled at it every day. Her only wish was that Will could be with her full time. In the ten weeks since they'd moved into the cottage, his job had kept him away for three. She knew his job was an essential part of who he was, but she couldn't help feeling resentful, although she tried not to let him know it.

Her life's purpose, too, was coming into focus. As she explored new ideas for the Saint Melangell Centre, she felt she was helping to maintain the place as the sanctuary it had been for over a thousand years. There was a mystique there that had little to do with the modern world and everything to do with something spiritual that she could not define. Although she was not a counsellor herself, nor a psychologist like her friend Janice Hatcher, she did have opportunities to help occasional drop-ins, pilgrims they called them, to organize their lives so as to enjoy more peace and less stress. Now, too, she had been experimenting with nature meditation, guiding small groups and individuals to open their senses to experience the natural world, and she found it brought most of them a sense of tranquility and oneness with the larger world around them. It seemed a natural expansion of what the centre could offer.

She took the path's turns automatically, having walked the trail hundreds of times. When the ascent leveled out, she paused to catch her breath and looked out at the view, now resplendent in spring greens. Wildflowers dotted the hillsides up Cym Pennant and over toward Craig Rhiwarth. Above her, a dark cloud loomed threateningly, but she hadn't seen rain in the forecast so it didn't worry her much. As she gazed at it, a pair of rooks flew across the darker grey, and she watched them as they soared playfully, black until their wings flashed silver when they occasionally caught a beam of sunlight. She lost herself in their flight until they disappeared into the distance. She took a moment then to breathe in the sweetness of the air, unable to distinguish one flower scent from another but reveling in the sweet perfume of spring. She reached down to pick a bluebell, tracing it with her finger and then rubbing the leaf and stem between her fingers, and listened intently, hearing nothing in the silence except Daisy as she dashed through the brush.

She couldn't linger too long, though. Work meant a schedule to be kept.

At the centre, she slipped through the unlocked door and grabbed Daisy's collar to pull her into her office. She shut the door quickly and told her to stay in the doggie bed beside her desk, then changed into work clothes – brown tweed trousers and a light blue blouse. She pulled on comfortable flats and then stepped out the door to place her wellies outside to dry in the sun.

Back in her office, she sat at her desk and opened the mail left for her by Reverend Wicklyff. The registrations for the pilgrim's walk she put in a pile and then she frowned over the remaining two letters before deciding that neither needed to be kept. She opened her computer and checked the website, finding more registrations there. The pilgrim's walk seemed to be attracting more participants in this, its second year, than it had the previous year, which made her happy. It had been her idea to commemorate St. Melangell's saint's day with the trail walk and an accompanying mountain bike ride, bringing much needed funds into the centre and the church, but also bringing people to the site so they could see all it had to offer.

Daisy snored as she started entering tee shirt sizes into her flow chart. She liked to keep track of them as they came in so it would be easy when the time came to call in the order for the shirts – one big thing to cross off her to-do list. Having the experience of the previous year's walk in her memory helped her stay organized. She still had plenty to do, but nothing loomed.

A knock on her door made her jump, so absorbed was she in her work. Daisy woke with a start and leapt to her feet, tail wagging, and Bronwyn turned to see Janice Hatcher, the centre's psychologist, peering around the doorjamb.

"Janice, hi," Bronwyn greeted her as she pushed her chair back from the computer. She gestured to a folding chair she kept in a corner for the rare times she needed it. "Want to sit?"

"Thanks." Janice reached for the chair and unfolded it, sitting down gently as if afraid it would collapse. "Are you busy?"

Bronwyn laughed. "I'm always busy, but especially now with the celebration coming up." She eyed Janice curiously. "What's up?"

Janice waved a paper at her. It looked like a page torn from a newspaper, jagged on the edges. "This is what's up, and I think you're going to find it very interesting."

"What is it?" Bronwyn leaned toward her, trying to see the flapping paper. "A news article?"

"It's about something called 'forest bathing,' and it's what you do, Bronwyn. It's almost exactly what you do, and now it's an official thing, with a name. You were talking about getting some training in meditation. Well, this is it. It's nature meditation, like you do, but now you can get certified and be official."

"Slow down…I'm not following. Forest bathing?"

"It's what you do with some of our clients. It turns out that the Japanese were doing something very similar in the 1980s, and it's spread across the world as research shows the benefits of getting away from technology and big cities and learning to interact with nature. Guides get certified now, and it's becoming a recognized natural health care option." Janice consulted the remnant of newspaper. "According to this article, it helps lower levels of stress hormones and improves mental health and even immunity." She looked up at Bronwyn, her face animated. "If you got certified, it'd be another professional way we could attract clients here. What do you think?"

Bronwyn frowned, taken aback. "It sounds like a good idea," she began hesitantly, "except if it's what I already do, then I'm confused about needing training. That training isn't something that's offered locally, is it? Where would I have to go?"

"If you're certified, you'd have more credibility." Janice's face was set. "There's a course in the Brecon Beacons week after next. I know the board will give you the time off to attend."

"But that'd mean a week away from home," she protested, thinking of Will. She would hate to miss out on their time together. "With St. Melangell's Day coming up right after that, I don't know if I can afford the time away." It sounded like a good excuse to her.

Janice noticed her hesitation and saw through her little deception. They'd become good enough friends that Janice wouldn't be easily fooled. "It's just a week, and I'd imagine Will could get along without you for one visit. Maybe he could visit his niece while you're gone. I know he likes to see her when he can."

Bronwyn clamped her mouth shut. That was a sore point between them. She thought it only natural that he would take her along when he visited Lark so that she could finally meet his parents, but, somehow, he always found a reason to avoid that. "Let me think about it," she said, trying not to let Janice see her agitation.

But Janice was not to be daunted. "I'll get the board to pay for it. Then we could advertise nature walks for small groups and individuals, and that might attract more business to the centre, as well as helping our pilgrims who come seeking help. It could be a part of a package when they book the conference room, too. If you get certified and it brings in more paying customers, the board would probably give you a raise." She looked at Bronwyn hopefully. "Don't you think it's a great idea?"

"I…" Bronwyn tried to process it all, "yes, I can see that it would be good to get certified, that it would make what I do more professional." She tried to put enthusiasm into her voice. Leading groups in anything wasn't really her forte. But she would be helping people, helping them find the peace they sought at Pennant Melangell. Wasn't that what she felt compelled to do, to carry on the mission begun by the saint so long ago? She didn't want to allow fear, or insecurity, or whatever it was that made her shy in front of strangers, to stop her fulfilling her potential. "But the St. Melangell's celebration is coming up fast, and there's a lot to do to get ready. I can't see getting away for a week just then."

"By then, main registration will be closed, and you'll have the shirts ordered. You're always so organized that I bet it won't make a difference at all."

Bronwyn closed her eyes. It'd add some stress, but she was feeling better organized this year, so it'd probably be okay. "It does sound like something worth doing," she conceded.

"It does, doesn't it?" Janice smiled happily. "We could put it in our advertising before the pilgrims walk so more people would be aware that we were offering it. 'Coming soon – forest bathing!' something like that?"

"We could," Bronwyn agreed, wondering what she was getting herself into. But if a door opened, she must be meant to walk through, right? "Give me the information, and I'll check on it." Maybe they'd have another session later in the summer when things weren't so busy.

"I'll talk to the reverend about it," Janice offered. "I'm meeting him this afternoon to discuss another matter, so I could bring it up and see what he thinks."

Bronwyn nodded. "Thanks, Janice. You're a good friend." Janice would be pushier than she would and probably get a better result.

"Together, we make this centre work to help people so we can go home at night and feel good about ourselves and the world." Janice stood and folded the chair. "Speaking of which, I've got to get back to my office. I have a session starting in a few minutes."

"See you at lunchtime?"

"In the sensory garden at noon."

Bronwyn had a hard time concentrating on her work after Janice left. She finally turned her chair and reached down to fondle Daisy's ears, absently stroking her head while thinking it over. She understood the importance of having a certification if it was available. She really believed in what she did, and being certified would make it all official. Natural health options were a trend, and maybe more people would come to Pennant Melangell for help if they thought her qualified.

It was also true, though, that she desperately wanted to make her personal life her priority. She'd dreamed of a life where she had a partner she loved and a job she enjoyed, and at the moment she had both. But she'd also vowed to make it her life's work to try to keep Pennant Melangell relevant in the modern world, continuing its mission of sanctuary and peace, so she supposed there was nothing for it. She spun around in her chair and reached for the phone.

A quick call informed her that only one training session was planned for the time being, and that there'd been scant interest in that one. Did she want to put her name down for it, in case it started to fill up? She reluctantly supplied her information, having been assured that she could cancel without being charged if for any reason she couldn't attend.

It was scheduled for a Monday through Wednesday, the first week of May, which meant she'd have the two weeks after for final preparations for St. Melangell's Day. It also meant that she'd be away for all the time Will would be there that week, his current schedule generally permitting a Saturday evening arrival in Llangynog and a Tuesday morning departure if no major case loomed. The course included local lodging, so she wouldn't need to arrange anything other than transportation there. Of course, she'd have to present the idea to the board of directors to see if they'd approve her absence, and maybe even pay for the course. She didn't know how she'd afford it otherwise, having scant funds available after pooling her money with Will's to furnish the house in the most budget-minded way possible.

The board wouldn't meet for another week, but that would be too late for her to register. She decided an email was in order to explain her request. She put her fingers on the keyboard and thought for a while, then typed a proposal that she ended up feeling proud of. It emphasized what an asset a certified forest bathing guide would be to the centre, with the potential of bringing in more clients and enhancing the experience for those who reserved space for meetings or workshops. She ended it with a reminder of what St. Melangell's mission had been through more than a thousand years, and she felt that it would be hard for them to deny her request with that final thought in their minds.

She hit "send" and then sat back, satisfied. It was nearly lunchtime, and she'd accomplished little beyond worrying about the workshop. Nevertheless, she decided to take Daisy out for a short walk before lunch She'd devote the afternoon to her other tasks.

Daisy loped ahead of her toward the foot path, her obvious delight in being outdoors contagious. Bronwyn watched her slide to a halt to smell the lych gate before continuing her journey across the parking lot to the trailhead, and she shook her head, amused. Daisy was a very different dog than her old Nan had been. The sheepdog had been focused and serious, while Daisy was very much a free spirit. She'd have to get Daisy signed up for classes, too, if she wanted her certified as a therapy dog. She sighed. There was so much to do, things that would keep her away from her time with Will, and she couldn't help resenting it all. She wasn't sure where classes were offered for Daisy, but obviously they wouldn't be in isolated little Llangynog.

She stood at the trailhead and waited for Daisy to stretch her legs and empty her bladder. A light breeze had sprung up, but the earlier clouds had blown away. Muddy ruts and puddles marred the trail itself, but standing at the edge of it brought a smile to Bronwyn's lips. She closed her eyes and listened, hearing the slight rustle of grasses and the patter of Daisy's feet. An insect buzzed her and her eyes sprang open, but she missed whatever had passed near to her ears. She took a breath and breathed in the scent of mud that overwhelmed the other scents of spring. Smiling ruefully, she opened her mouth, but nothing tickled at her taste buds. Lastly, she concentrated her senses on feel: the coolness of the breeze tickling at her bare arms, the suck of mud on her shoes – she should have changed to her wellies.

With a shrug, she dismissed the thought and started back toward the door of the centre. Soon they'd start getting a trickle of walk-in pilgrims to deal with, a trickle that would hopefully grow as summer warmth enticed people out to hike or bike the local trails. Perhaps she should advertise a daily nature walk once she got her certification. Drop-ins could then take advantage of it, and if no one showed up some days, she'd just continue with her regular duties.

I should talk to Will about it, she realized suddenly. Surely talking it over with him would be the logical first step in deciding what to do, now that they were a couple. *I'll bring it up tonight, see what he says.* Logically, she knew he'd encourage her to do it, but it only seemed right to include him in her plans.

He'd spend his free time with Lark, she thought, and then she remembered that Lark would have school on weekdays, so that wouldn't work. It was too bad. She liked Lark, liked her a lot. Once summer holidays arrived, they'd have to invite her to Llangynog to spend time in the country when one or the other of them, or both, had some time off work. It'd be a holiday for them all, exploring local castles and hiking the hills of Snowdonia. Lark loved Bronwyn's old pony Hobbs and Daisy, too, so she wouldn't lack for things to keep her busy while she visited. Lark loved everything, and so she was easy to love back. Bronwyn had the idea that Will would like to take Lark full-time, but from what he'd mentioned from time to time, it seemed his mother disapproved of Will's job and didn't think him capable of being a parent. *She's probably right*, Bronwyn told herself. From what she'd seen, Will would make a terrific dad, but his job did require flexibility that would make parenting hard.

And what about her? Was she willing to take Lark on, if she and Will decided to make their relationship permanent? Living with Will, even part-time, still proved a challenge for her sometimes. Not that she didn't look forward to his days with her at the cottage, but she was still adjusting to having his laundry mixed with her own and with planning meals that could be vegetarian for her but with meat for Will. And then there was her secret life. Although the Twlwyth Teg and Pysgotwr were making themselves scarce these days, she lived in fear of the time when Will would discover her interacting with one or the other of them. He wouldn't see them, but as observant as he was, he'd notice her behaving oddly and confront her about it. How could she explain? She really had no idea, and so she just kept her fingers crossed that the day she dreaded would never come.

So…Lark. If it made Will happy, she wouldn't hesitate to take Lark in and let them be a family together, the three of them. Surely what they could offer Lark was better than what she knew Will's parents offered her. They had the money to support their orphaned granddaughter, but didn't seem to want to invest the emotional support children needed. Was taking in a child an ideal way to start a relationship? No, it was not. She and Will were still exploring and developing their relationship, and a child, especially an inquisitive seven-year old, would put a damper on romance at times. But if the chance came up, it was another door opened that must be walked through, she supposed.

It was mid-afternoon and she was deep in organizing notes for the vendors who'd inquired about the St. Melangell's Day celebration. This year they'd decided that, for a small fee, vendors could set up booths in the parking lot outside the church's lych gate. This would pose a problem for parking, but they'd solve it by shutting off the lane during the foot race and letting the people working the celebration park alongside the road or in the centre's small parking lot and then offering a shuttle for those participants who didn't want to walk back up the lane to Llangynog afterwards. Things would be tight, Bronwyn acknowledged, but anything that brought in more participants would bring welcome funds to the church.

When her desk phone rang, she answered it almost absently, but then sat up when she recognized Will's voice on the other end.

"I'm headed back your way," he said without preamble. "There's been a murder in the area, and it's been assigned to me. And Notley," he amended.

Bronwyn's heart quickened. "Who is it?"

"We don't know yet. A woman is all we've been told. They're saying possible domestic violence, but until we see the scene and talk to her partner, we won't know for sure."

"I hope it's not someone I know." She hadn't seen a Cyn Annwn, the phantom wolf-like creature who portended a death.

"I don't think so. The parents are in Corwen so I don't think she's been there long. I get the impression it's further out away from the village. A farm somewhere," Will told her helpfully. "I wanted to let you know I may be staying the night, if the case looks complicated."

"Here?" she blurted, wishing immediately she could take it back.

He sounded amused. "Yes, at *our* cottage. So, you'd better tell whoever else was planning to stay tonight to keep his distance. "

She blushed, glad he wasn't there to see. "Will!"

He laughed, a sound incongruous with the task at hand. "I've got to go, sweetheart. Notley is waiting. I'll let you know what's happening."

She couldn't help a thrill of happiness, despite that someone had died to create it. "I hope…I…"

"I know," he said. "Me, too."

She sat back as he rang off. What had she hoped? It would be appalling to hope the murder was complicated so that Will could stay on, wouldn't it? To think that, maybe, someone else would be in danger, or that the parents would wait in agony while they sorted out who'd killed their daughter? And then there was the matter of Notley. Will hated working with him, and for sure he wouldn't want the case to drag on and on. Yet, he'd echoed her words.

No matter what, there were things to be done. She scurried out of her office, shutting Daisy inside, and knocked on Janice's open door, poking her head inside. "Janice? I just heard from Will. He says there's been a murder in the area."

Janice stared at her. "Should we lock the doors? It's only…" Janice would be remembering the murder a year earlier that had happened in the churchyard and the near-murder afterward of Bronwyn herself.

"It's probably not a bad idea, at least until we know more what's going on. This is a place of sanctuary, after all. The killer could come here, expecting to hide."

"How about the church? Should we call Reverend Wyclyff?" Janice glanced at her clock. "He said he'd stop in this afternoon. He'll probably be here soon."

"I think we should lock it all up until he gets here." Bronwyn looked over her shoulder toward the door. "I'll take Daisy with me and get the church. You watch my back."

Janice nodded.

Bronwyn watched the door as she strolled toward the main office, tugging the door to her office open on her way to let Daisy out. The dog frolicked beside her happily, looking toward the door longingly, but staying at her side. Bronwyn took the church key from the hook and bent down to pat Daisy on the head. "We're going out, but not for a walk, silly girl. Stay close, right?"

She left Daisy's leash off and opened the door, peeking out before stepping out. "There's a car in the car park," she told Janice, who was standing behind her.

"Probably tourists," Janice murmured. "What kind of car?"

"I can't really see it from here," Bronwyn said. She stuck her head out further. "It's white. I think there's someone in it."

"Stay here, then," Janice suggested. "You're safe here. We can watch for Reverend Wyclyff and intercept him when he gets here." She went silent for a minute. "It's not his car, is it?"

"No, his is blue." Bronwyn squinted at the car. "Maybe this guy is just waiting for someone who's gone inside."

"Why wouldn't he go in, too?"

"I don't know." Bronwyn watched the lych gate. "Maybe he wasn't interested and whoever he's with, was."

"Just come back in and lock the door before he sees you," Janice urged her.

Bronwyn tugged on Daisy's collar and turned back, but just then something caught her eye. "Wait, Janice." She peered toward the car. "Someone's coming out from the church. She's handing him her mobile, I think." She watched the man climb reluctantly out of the car. "I'm going over to talk to them, and then I'll lock up."

Janice peered out the door from behind Bronwyn's shoulder. "I'd feel better if you didn't."

28

"It looks perfectly safe," Bronwyn pointed out. "Just tourists." She gave Janice a grin and snapped Daisy's leash on. "Come on, let's see what's what."

She watched the two strangers as she walked the short distance between the buildings. The woman posed beside the lych gate while the man snapped a photo, and then she beckoned him inside. Bronwyn let out the breath she'd been holding. The churchyard was beautiful in its own way, a nice souvenir snapshot to take home and remember.

When she reached the gate, she called out to them, not wanting to startle them. "Hello! Welcome to Pennant Melangell."

They both turned to look at her. The woman was middle-aged, chubby in her jeans and a peach colored sweater that did nothing to enhance her pale skin and blonde curls. The man looked older, with a white beard and short-cropped graying hair. He clutched the phone in his hand and blinked at her. "Sorry. We thought the church was open to visitors."

"It is," Bronwyn assured them. "I was just coming to lock it up, though. Did you get a good look around?"

"I did," the woman said with a sidelong glance at the man. "I'd read about it and wanted to see it. You're quite a long way from anything out here, aren't you?"

"It's a bit of a drive, but worth the trouble. Are you staying locally?" She didn't want to sound as if she were badgering them, but who knew if they were involved with Will's case or not?

"We're in Llangollen at the moment," the woman said.

"There are some lovely hikes in this area if you're interested." Daisy stared at the couple, inching to the end of her leash. "Or I could give you a short tour of the church. There are lots of interesting features that you don't notice unless someone's there to show you."

"That'd be wonderful," the woman said, "if you have the time? Do you live here?"

Bronwyn nodded. "I actually live in the village, but I work here at the centre." She gestured toward the centre, noting that Janice was still watching from the entryway. "I have time to show you the church if you have time to see it." Maybe having activity there would discourage anyone unsavory from dropping by. It couldn't hurt.

Bronwyn spent twenty minutes showing the couple, who turned out to be Canadians touring the back country in a rental car, the highlights of the old Norman church. By the time they'd finished, made a few purchases in the tiny gift shop, and followed her out through the churchyard, Reverend Wyclyff had arrived and Bronwyn felt safe.

"I hear you have a request to make of the board," he said, once he'd locked the church doors and seated himself in his office.

Janice gave her an encouraging smile. "We think it would enhance what we offer here at the centre."

Bronwyn glanced at her. "I called to check it out, and it seems the only training session they plan to offer is that first week of May, which is just a couple of weeks before St. Melangell's Day." She half-hoped he would tell her no, that it wasn't a good time to be gone.

He disappointed her. "I think it's a great opportunity. Janice is right. We could advertise during the festival when lots of people are here. We'll have to sit down and decide on pricing, meanwhile, and how often to offer sessions. You're thinking both group sessions and individuals, if the opportunity arises?"

Bronwyn bit down her fear. "I hadn't really thought it through. What I've been doing is trying it out on small groups, and then when someone comes in for help and Janice isn't here, I sometimes do it with them to try to settle them."

Daisy, lying by Bronwyn's feet, raised her head and stared at the office door.

"The time off for the class shouldn't be a problem." The reverend reached for a pen and scribbled a note on a piece of paper. "As Janice pointed out, you are so organized, it shouldn't matter even if our festival is right on its heels. I'll talk to the board about paying the tuition. Can I let you know by the end of the week?"

Daisy growled and stood up, and then Bronwyn heard knocking on the outside door. She looked at Janice, who looked back sharply. Reverend Wyclyff stood up. "Considering the information you had earlier, Bronwyn, I think I had better answer that knock and see who it is. You two stay here." He hesitated. "If you see it's trouble, lock yourselves in and call 999."

They watched from his office door as he walked up to the main door. Whoever was there was now pounding on the door harder.

"I'm coming," they heard him mutter as he opened the door a crack and looked out. They heard him speaking, but couldn't see to whom. He looked back over his shoulder. "It's safe enough, I think. It's your brother Maddock, Bronwyn."

A surge of surprise shocked Bronwyn into motion. "What are you doing here?" she called out as she passed Reverend Wyclyff on his way back to his office.

"I came for you," Maddock told her, a grin on his face. "Get your stuff and I'll drive you home."

"What's happened?" This was suspicious. Maddock never came to give her a ride home.

"Get your stuff. You're done for the day, right?"

"I could be," she conceded. It had been a day of interruptions, so she'd might as well give it up and plan on catching up the next day. She handed Daisy's leash to Maddock. "Get her in your truck and I'll be right out."

"Will do," Maddock said obediently, reaching down to snap the leash onto Daisy's collar. He straightened and waved a hand at Janice and the reverend. "Nice to see you two." At their answering wave, he pushed the door open and disappeared with Daisy.

"You'll let us know if you hear anything?" Janice asked as Bronwyn grabbed her bag from her own office.

"If there's any big news, you'll know it anyway," Bronwyn pointed out. "Everyone in the village will know the details and have a suspect all but convicted by dinnertime, I'm sure."

The reverend waved her out the door. "We don't have inside information like you do," he reminded her, and then he smiled. "I'll let you know what the board says about the training course."

"Okay," she agreed, and then she was out the door and heading for Maddock's pickup.

She opened the truck door and slid inside. "Why did you come get me?"

Maddock backed out of the parking space. "Will called me and asked me to come get you. He figured you'd walked to work today, and he didn't want you out wandering around by yourself with a possible murderer on the loose."

"It's a murder, then?"

"Definitely. She was shot, and she didn't do it herself."

That was bad news. "They suspect her partner?"

"That's what I've heard."

"Do we know them?"

Maddock shrugged. "No one seems to know who it is yet."

The truck bumped over a rut, and Bronwyn let the day's frustrations emerge. "I wish Will wouldn't call you to come get me. I can take care of myself." She thought of the Twlwyth Teg. They had come to her rescue before when she'd been in danger. Would they again?

"He just wants to make sure you're safe. There's nothing wrong with that."

"I am safe, and I'm an adult, but for some reason, the men in my life can't treat me as one. Dad hardly let me out of his sight after Glynnis died, you involve yourself in my love life, and now it's Will keeping an eye on me even when he's not here. I felt smothered before, and I feel more smothered now."

"Someone's been murdered, Bron. You can't be out walking the back lanes with a murderer on the loose."

"This is Llangynog," she protested. "We know everyone, Madd. Everyone! No one is going to hurt me, and if someone did threaten me, there are farmers along the way who'd come to my rescue."

"Like they did when Rhonda Morris attacked you?"

She bit back a retort. "That was a unique situation. She wasn't from here."

"Maybe this bloke isn't either. Not everyone who lives here has been here for generations."

She didn't want to admit it, but didn't see a way around it. "Okay, maybe you're right. This time."

32

Maddock glanced over at her. "You should count your blessings. Most girls would give anything to have someone who's enough of a gentleman to care about their safety. Will has nice manners. He's been taught to look out for the fairer sex. That's not a bad thing."

She slumped in the seat. She wasn't really mad at Will; it was just that he'd had to leave her again that morning, and then the subject of the workshop had come up to interfere with yet another of their days off together. Even though they were technically living together, they really weren't. If it wasn't his job keeping them apart, it was hers.

Maddock looked over at her again as he slowed to allow a flock of pheasant chicks to run ahead of him down the lane. "What's going on? Is Will not treating you right? Because if he isn't, Dad and I will be all over him, no matter that you don't want us watching out for you."

Bronwyn shook her head. "Will's wonderful. He's patient and thoughtful, and he's always really good to me. It's just that we don't get to be together as much as we'd like." She told him about the certification. "I know I need to do it, but it'll take me away again when he has time off."

"If he doesn't have a case keeping him busy anyway." Maddock went silent for a minute while he took the turn in the village. "Listen, Bron, I think he's really trying to make this work. Anyone can see when he looks at you, he likes what he sees."

"But why? I know he grew up differently from us. He's used to a city, to excitement, to going out for nice meals and dancing and…I don't know what, but it's not what's here. This is the most remote place he could have found." She didn't mention that he was reluctant to introduce her to his parents. That, if nothing else, told her that she wasn't the sort of girl someone like Will took home to the family. A tear rolled down her cheek and she turned away so that Maddock wouldn't see it.

He let her stew in silence while he drove up the road and turned onto her driveway, and then he shifted the truck into park and turned to her. "Think about this, then, Bron. Will's job has him dealing with all sorts of bad people. He has to see the bodies, he has to track down really awful people, he has to risk his life to bring them in, and that's the world he lives in day to day. It's no wonder he's protective of you, is it?"

She shook her head, mute.

"So, at the end of the day, when he has time off, what could be better than coming here to you? You're the most peaceful person I know, and that has to be really attractive to someone like Will. I doubt he even realizes it, but I'd bet my share of the farm that when he's with you, he's feeling happy and relaxed and in tune with the world, and that's a way of life that he's never known before. We grew up that way; he didn't. You've shown him that life, Bron, and it's part of why he loves you." He reached out and brushed the tear off her cheek. "I really don't see him going anywhere. I think he's more smitten than he cares to admit even to himself."

She smiled.

"And besides, you're knock-down gorgeous. It's a good thing no one stays in Llangynog long, or you'd have already been spoken for long before Will Cooper came into town."

She reached out to punch his arm. "Okay, now you're getting beyond yourself," she said, "but you did make me feel better." She turned to open the truck door. "Thank you, Madd. I do love you, you know."

"I know," he said softly as he watched her open the back door to let Daisy out. He sat in his truck and waited until she was inside the cottage before he turned the truck around and drove back down the driveway.

Chapter Three

Will slowed to cruise through Bala at the posted speed limit and made the turn onto the B4391 toward Llangynog. He didn't know exactly where the crime scene was and it was unlikely that sat nav would get him there accurately, but he figured that if he was on the right road and got near enough, he'd see police activity that would point him in the right direction.

In the nearly three years since his transfer from Cardiff, he'd become a lot more familiar with the small villages that dotted North Wales. True, he still had to ask more frequently than he liked where a place was, but now at least the answer would include names familiar enough that he'd know the general direction of the crime. "Fourteen miles past Bala" would have meant nothing to him a year ago; now he knew almost exactly where that would be.

Once through the village, he eased his foot down on the accelerator. Ordinarily, he'd like to buzz along the narrow roads at speed, but he kept Notley in mind, following him in one of the department's Volvo sedans, a car that couldn't manage the roads as easily as his little MGF could. Bowers wouldn't thank him for leaving Notley in the dust, and he was trying to behave.

He rounded a curve a few miles further on, and a cluster of panda cars came into sight where a left turn marked what was almost certainly the driveway into the farm where the woman had been found. He slowed and then stopped facing the yellow crime scene tape that fluttered between the fence posts it had been stapled to, its bright color competing with bluebells that flourished just beneath it. Notley slowed behind him. A constable frowned and walked toward the car.

He fumbled in his pocket and held up his warrant card. "DCI Cooper," he mumbled by way of introduction. "That's DCI Notley behind me." He wagged his chin toward the rear of his car.

"Your budget must be better than ours," commented the constable, "if you can afford to drive separately."

Will shook his head. "Special circumstances." He didn't explain. "Can we drive up to the house?"

"Sure, let me just move the tape for you," the man said. He strolled toward one of the fence posts and tore the tape from its staples, backing across the driveway to allow them to pass by. "Best be prepared," he called out as Will drove past. "This one's pretty ugly."

The driveway wound east through a rocky pasture. Sheep grazed on both sides so Will kept his speed to a crawl, grimacing as the car bounced across ruts filled with mud and sheep muck. He had the top up on the car and the windows up, too, but he could still smell the sheep. He tried to take shallow breaths. He passed by a small hillock and then the road straightened, and he could see a house ahead of him, surrounded by panda cars, an ambulance, and a couple of other vehicles that probably belonged to the medical examiner and scene of crime people. A rusting older model pickup truck and a small Ford Fiesta had been left parked next to the stone farmhouse, and Will assumed they belonged to the couple who'd lived there.

He pulled to a stop and eyed the house. Built of local slate, it looked to be at least a hundred years old, and he doubted it had been updated much in that time except for the addition of a bathroom or two and perhaps a more modern kitchen. Windows were intact, but filmed with dirt, and even at a distance he could see missing shingles on the roof. The front door was ajar, another constable guarding it. To its left was a large old barn, with smaller outbuildings scattered nearby. It did not look as prosperous as Bronwyn's parents' farm, nor as welcoming.

He got out and stood by his car, waiting for Notley to join him. "The constable on guard at the turn said it was pretty bad," he commented, frowning at Notley's cane. The man looked a fool waving it around, but he insisted on carrying it, and the department was willing to overlook what Will saw as a foolish quirk. Notley was obsessed with Sherlock Holmes, and the cane was one manifestation of that obsession.

"The more bizarre a thing is, the less mysterious it turns out to be," Notley quoted, and Will turned away and rolled his eyes.

They were stopped at the door and told to put on protective suits, booties for their feet, and gloves for their hands, giving Will his usual feeling of being a spaceman or a tech in a biohazard lab. Once dressed, they were escorted through a low-ceilinged sitting room filled to the brim with furniture, past a slate staircase, and into a small kitchen, where a woman's body sprawled on the stone floor in a large pool of sticky, nearly dry blood. The metallic, iron smell of the blood make Will's stomach churn, and he was suddenly aware of the buzzing of flies on the windows. A woman took photos as Francis Ruark, the medical examiner, crouched next to the woman, examining her closely.

"Beat you here this time," commented Ruark with a glance at them.

Will walked over to stand beside him, but he couldn't make himself bend down closer. "What do we have?"

"A young woman in her early twenties, a bit undernourished, but otherwise healthy from first glance." He indicated her head where a blackened hole had leaked blood that matted the darker roots of her blonde hair. "A gunshot wound to her right temple almost certainly killed her."

"It didn't happen today, though, did it?" The nearly dried blood told him that.

Ruark shook his head. "It's hard to say accurately, but my guess is this happened at least two days ago, maybe longer. The flies have been at her, and decomp is well underway."

"She didn't do it herself?"

"No powder residue on her hand," Ruark pointed out. "Whoever did for her held a gun to her temple and pulled the trigger. He might have wanted it to look like a suicide, but I don't think so. The gun isn't here, either."

"We have an ID on her?

"Missing woman's name is Catherine Baines, and she matches the description given us."

"Defensive wounds?"

"I haven't gotten that far yet." He picked up the nearer hand and turned it gently side to side. "Nothing apparent here, but that doesn't mean much. Just because she didn't scratch him or punch him doesn't mean she wasn't restrained and trying to wriggle free." He set her hand down again and frowned, leaning away from her for a wider view. "See the way she fell, how her right arm fell a little behind her? I'm guessing he held her arms behind her with one hand while he held the gun with the other."

"It'd be someone strong then," Will observed, "and definitely a man to be able to hold a struggling woman with one hand and to manage a gun with the other.

"If I'm right about her being restrained, then yes, probably a man. I should be able to tell more once I get her to the lab. If he pulled her arms back tight or she was struggling, she might have some muscle strain in her shoulders."

Notley had been standing near the woman's feet. "You're saying there wasn't a fight, that he just walked in and grabbed her and then shot her?" His dubious look conveyed more than his words did.

Ruark frowned up at him. "I'm not saying anything for sure."

"Seems odd," Notley persisted.

"Maybe they'd had a squabble earlier, something verbal but not physical, and he decided he wanted to be rid of her. He left, got the gun from wherever he had it, and came back to do the job," Will suggested.

"It's all theories at this stage," Ruark agreed, his voice calm. He turned the woman's head a little. "She's had a healing bruise here, just under her eye."

Will squatted down to look. The smell and the buzzing of the flies had him gagging. "It sounded like the parents weren't being allowed to talk to her." He thought of them calling to ask for a welfare check. "Domestic abuse comes to mind."

"They just notified us in the past few days," Notley pointed out. "She'd have already been dead."

"If it *was* just in the past few days," Will argued, despite his resolve not to antagonize Notley. "It could have been going on longer, for all we know. That's probably why the parents were worried. We'll find out."

"Look here," Ruark said, "there's a fresher bruise on the back of her head, like she was pushed back onto a hard surface." All of their eyes wandered to the stone walls of the room. "She may have been pushed hard against the wall and then yanked back out for the shot."

"Maybe that bruise happened earlier when they had their squabble," Notley speculated.

"But why hold her arms behind her back to shoot her?" Will said. "Why not just walk in and do it?"

Ruark looked up. "I'm not sure that's how it happened yet. The arm position just looked odd to me. He may have done just what Sean said, walked in and shot her as she stood here."

"Who is he? Do we have a name?"

"If we do, I haven't heard it yet."

They watched as Ruark continued his preliminary examination. The woman had been dressed in faded jeans and a plaid flannel shirt, now splattered with dark blood. Trainers on her feet were also speckled with blood, the right one more than the left. Her eyes were closed, and Will wondered if Ruark had found her that way or closed them himself to make the exam less unnerving. Her mouth hung open slightly, showing even, white teeth.

After a bit, Will tired of watching and wandered around the kitchen in his booties. A wooden table and four chairs crowded the only free corner, and where cupboards didn't fill the walls, art did. Small and – Will guessed – inexpensive bits of watercolor or acrylic paintings fought for space with a cow clock and two painted Venetian masks. He swung open a cupboard door to find real china stacked neatly on the shelves. He picked up a piece and turned it over. Staffordshire. That was interesting. It seemed an incongruous fit with the cheap art.

"Sir?" One of the forensics people near the back door gestured him over. "Look at this."

He walked over. On the floor, nearly invisible on the slate, was a scatter of hair. He bent down and picked it up with his gloved fingers, peering at it. "It looks human."

"It's too long to be dog hair," the tech agreed.

Will waved Notley over. "Look at this. I think she was grabbed by the hair first and dragged over to where she was shot."

Notley leaned in for a close look. "It's too much to have fallen out naturally, unless she was having cancer treatments."

"Bag it, please," Will told the tech. A picture was beginning to emerge, and not a pretty one.

A thought occurred to him. "Did she have a mobile? A purse with ID?"

"Not lying here," the tech said, "but maybe in the bedroom or the sitting room."

Once Ruark had finished his initial exam and the body had been loaded into the waiting ambulance, Will and Notley took some time to wander through the house. The interior of the house, in contrast to the exterior, was fairly clean and well-organized, even if crowded with too many possessions for its size.

In the sitting room, a 72-inch flatscreen television filled one wall, with an array of cords connecting gaming devices, a blu ray player, a satellite box, and a sound system to it. Theatre-style chairs lined the opposite wall, while off in another corner waited a collection of musical instruments, most prominently a guitar on a metal stand. In another corner a makeshift bar had been set up, the top of a dresser lined with crystal glasses and decanters filled with liquid. Will took the stopper out of one and smelled. "Scots whiskey," he commented. "I can smell the peat."

Notley looked closely at it. "Can't fault him on his taste."

"Or hers," Will speculated.

Upstairs, they found a king-sized bed stuffed into a bedroom far too small for it. The couple would have had to edge around the bed to get in and out of it, and Will shook his head in some amusement. The things people did. Across from the bed another flatscreen television filled the wall. Notley found a collection of DVDs in a drawer. "Movies, most of them, but there's a little soft porn here, too."

Will nodded and went into the bathroom. In a cabinet over the sink, he found bottles. He opened one and shook out a white pill. "What do you think of this?" he asked Notley.

Notley peered at it. "Looks prescription, but there's nothing on the bottle."

"Probably illegal, then," Will surmised.

"Forensics will let us know once they've gotten them to the lab," Notley pointed out.

"And we'll see if there was anything in her system," Will noted. "Wonder how they afforded all this stuff?"

Notley waved a hand toward the window. "I bet either he inherited this place or the rent was low, and if he was any kind of farmer at all, he'd make enough to buy himself some toys and recreational substances."

"Yeah, I guess you can invest in a few nice things if you aren't worried about keeping a place up," Will agreed. "My gut feeling is that he was leasing it. If he owned it, he'd have at least some stake in making sure the house wasn't crumbling into ruin."

"We haven't seen anything too blatantly expensive," Notley muttered. "Lots of blokes would spend money on stuff like this if they could. The vehicles were old. It's just this stuff inside that he'd have spent money on."

Will nodded, thinking of the jumble of cheap art. "Money wasted, for the most part."

Back in the bedroom, they shuffled quickly through a wardrobe that served as a closet for the couples' clothing, finding nothing that looked out of place. The woman's clothing ranged from more blue jeans and tee shirts or flannels to flimsy little dresses she must have worn when they went out. Will pulled one out and held it up, a little sequined number in silver. He raised his eyebrows, grinning at Notley. "Not your typical farm attire, is it?"

Notley ignored him. "It looks like he never wore anything but jeans and tee shirts." He glanced at the dress. "I wonder how he dressed when she went to the club with him wearing that?" He shook his head. "She was trying harder than he was in that relationship."

Will nodded. "I wonder if she worked? Otherwise, he'd be the money, and that would give him the upper hand."

"We'll find out."

They dodged forensics techs as they checked out the second bedroom, a bare room with only a single, unmade bed and a small dresser for furnishings.

"Not a room they used much," Notley observed.

Will pulled out a drawer. "Empty."

"Why bother having it then?"

Will shrugged. "Who knows? Maybe they thought they'd have a guest from time to time."

"This doesn't look like a place anyone would want to visit."

Will couldn't disagree. The room had the air of having been abandoned for a long time.

They found neither a purse nor a phone. Either she hadn't owned either, or they'd been taken away when her partner fled, if he was responsible for what happened.

The sun was beginning to sink behind a cloud bank in the west by the time they'd finished, the silvery edge bright against the charcoal darkness of the clouds. As they pulled out of the farm lane, Will noticed a few spectators had gathered, drawn by the flashing lights of the emergency vehicles. They stood in a group about twenty feet from the turn, well away from the crime scene tape, but near enough to watch the action. He stopped as he approached them and rolled down the window. "Do you know the people who are living here?"

"That'd be Billy Davies," one of the men answered. He took a few steps forward. "He's leasing it."

"He's been here about two years," volunteered another. He reached up and lifted the brim of the sports cap on his head, rubbing at his forehead with his other hand. "There's a woman living there, too. I don't know her name, but I don't think they were married." He looked around at his friends, who nodded their agreement.

"Can you tell us anything?" The first man spoke again, a hopeful look in his eyes.

It'd be obvious to them that someone was dead, with all the activity. "We have a suspicious death," he told them, telling himself firmly that they had no need to know who it was at this point. "I really can't say more at this time." He glanced in the rear-view mirror. Notley would be fuming behind him, worried about missing out on whatever information Will was gathering.

It would be dinner time soon, and Will felt positive about his chances of being allowed to stay in the area, at least for the one night. He thanked the men and drove on, just to the next lay-by, where he stopped and got out of the car. He watched as Notley did the same.

"Should we call Bowers and see what he wants us to do?" he ventured as Notley got nearer.

Notley snorted. "Everyone knows what's on your mind, Cooper. I don't know how you talked Bowers into switching the cases after all you've done wrong in the past year."

"I didn't ask for the cases to be switched," Will grumbled, trying to maintain his patience. "That was all Bowers' idea. He's got the budget to think about, and he likes that I have connections in this part of the district. It's helpful, that, when we get a case here."

"Next thing we know, you'll be here full-time."

Notley didn't know how close he was to the truth. "Then you wouldn't have to work with me, would you?" He couldn't keep the sarcasm from his voice.

Notley snorted. He tapped his cane on the ground. "She won't stay with you, Cooper. They never do."

"She'll stay," he said firmly.

"You're deluding yourself," Notley sneered.

"Just because you can't keep a relationship going, it doesn't mean I can't." Will tried to suppress the anger surging to the brink of control.

"Guess I never thought it worth the cost, dating a suspect."

Will fought for control. "Leave it, Notley. I'm not going to discuss this with you." He waited a few seconds, hoping for an excuse to punch Notley in the eye, but Notley turned away, gazing out over a pasture.

"What did you find out from the neighbors?" Notley said after a long silence.

"I got a name. Billy Davies. He leases the farm, has been there for about two years."

"It's a start." Notley turned back to Will.

"Let's call Bowers, see what he says," Will said again.

Notley grunted, and Will found Bowers' name on his contact list and pushed the green button. He waited for it to start ringing and then put it on speaker.

"Tell me you've got the suspect arrested and are on your way back," Bowers greeted them.

"We're on speaker, sir," Will told him. "We just finished here at the site. It looks like a domestic, probably a fight that got out of control. He'd have grabbed her with his left hand and held her by an arm or her hair, and then he shot her on the right side of the head. Ruark says she's been dead a couple of days."

"Any sign of her partner?"

"He's long gone, sir." Will remembered the two vehicles parked near the house. "We have a tentative name of Billy Davies from the neighbors. Can you get Quigley to find out what vehicles are registered to him, get a BOLO out? There's an older model pickup and a Ford Fiesta at the house, so it'd be something different."

"We'll need a more accurate ID," Bowers reminded him, and Will felt a fool. "The farm is owned by a Nathan Thomas, but my understanding is that the occupants were letting it from him."

"We'll get on that as soon as we're finished here," Notley said. "How about the girl's parents? Should we do the notification?"

"We'll need DNA or a visual ID," Bowers told them, "just to make sure we have the right girl."

"DNA, sir," Will suggested. "She'd been lying there for two days. You don't want the parents seeing that."

"No," Bowers agreed. "You can pay them a visit tonight, though, give them a preliminary report. She matches the description?"

"Yes, sir," Will said.

"Then you can tell them we have a body that might be their daughter and get something to compare DNA with."

44

"So, tonight you want us to see them and to visit the owner of the farm. Is that right?" Notley wanted to know.

"If you can get those two things done, it'll be a good start. Tomorrow you'll need to talk to the parents again, if DNA confirms the ID, and talk to the neighbors, employers, and everyone else. You know the drill."

"Yes, sir. Do you want us back, or should we stay?" Will couldn't keep hope from his voice.

There was a moment of silence, and then Bowers said, "Sean, you get back here with the DNA sample after you do the notification. Will, you talk to the farm's owner, and then you can stay in your house there. Sean will meet you in Llangynog in the morning."

"Thanks, sir," Will blurted, with an embarrassed glance at Notley, who was scowling. He punched end call and turned to Notley. "Follow me back to Bala, and we'll go to Corwin from there. Then you can drop me back at my car and by then, I'll know where the owner is and head that way."

Notley nodded, and Will slid gratefully into the little MGF, thankful to be alone so that he could call Bronwyn and tell her the good news.

She'd been happy to hear he was on his way back, and he tried to keep the joy in her voice in the back of his mind as he and Notley walked up to the neat bungalow on a back street in Corwin. Making death notifications was the part of his job he dreaded most, and anything that helped push his own emotions to the back of his mind helped.

He stood back as Notley knocked on the door. Notley wasn't the most tactful of men, but if he was willing to take this on, Will was willing to let him.

A dog barked inside, and they could hear a man's voice commanding it to be quiet, to go to the corner, and then the door swung open and the man's mouth opened in silent shock as he took them in.

Notley showed his warrant card and introduced the two of them. "Can we come in, sir?"

The man swayed a little, and Will stepped forward and grabbed onto his arm, steadying him. "Please, sir, let's go inside and sit down."

The man looked at him, his eyes blank, but then he nodded and stepped back, stumbling a little but regaining his balance before he went down. "Let me just get my wife," he managed, his voice harsh with fear.

Will released his arm, but stayed close in case. Behind them, Notley closed the door.

The dog, who had gone silent for a moment, now decided to assert himself again, barking sharply from a corner of the sitting room as they entered it. "Who is it, Walter?" a woman's voice came from somewhere in the back of the house, and he answered her, "Police."

It was best to get things over quickly. As soon as they had the couple seated on a sofa, the dog on the woman's lap, Notley glanced at Will and started to talk. "I believe you called for a welfare check on your daughter this morning?"

The man nodded warily. No help there.

"The constables who went to the farm found a woman's body there. We believe it is your daughter, but until we have some DNA confirmation, we can't be sure."

The woman gasped, and her husband turned to her and collapsed against her as the dog squirmed away and leapt off the couch with a foul look at Will. Will swallowed, trying to think of Bronwyn and not this shattered couple in front of him. He looked away from them, seeing family photographs on the wall to the right of him. He waited a moment and then risked a look back at the couple. The man had straightened again and sat with his arm crushing his wife against his side. She seemed almost to disappear as she melted into him.

Notley ignored their distress. "If you have something of your daughter's, a hairbrush or toothbrush maybe, that we could borrow, we could do a comparison and give you something more definite."

"It…it happened on the farm?" the woman managed.

Notley nodded.

"Then it's her," she said, and tears filled her eyes. She seemed unaware of them.

"We'll have questions for you, but they can wait until we know for sure," Notley informed them.

"When?" the man mumbled.

"Tomorrow sometime," Notley said. "We'll hand deliver the comparison DNA tonight, and tomorrow we'll know, one way or the other."

"It was him," the woman broke in. "We knew it was a bad situation, but she wouldn't listen. How did she die?"

Will spoke up quickly before Notley could inflict more pain on them. "We can't tell you that right now, sir, not until the medical examiner is done." It was as good an excuse as any. "What was her boyfriend's name?" If they could get his name out, his car registration, too, maybe they could pick him up quickly.

"Billy Davies," the woman spat, confirming the tentative ID they'd had from the farmers. "We knew he was trouble from the first. We knew he wasn't right for her. Catherine was struggling, but we couldn't talk her into leaving him." Her voice trailed off.

"That can all wait for tomorrow," Will told her again. "Can we call someone to stay here with you tonight?"

The man shook his head and seemed to come to himself again. "We'll be okay on our own." He pulled his wife close. "We always have been."

He glanced at his wife and then got up and left the room, the dog trailing behind him. They sat in silence, not wanting to stir up more emotion, for his return. After what seemed a long wait, the man came back into the room with a hairbrush in his hand. "This'll do?"

Notley pulled on gloves and took it from him. He gathered strands of hair, which he shoved into an evidence bag that Will held for him. "It'll do fine," he said, handing the brush back to the man.

"We'll let you know either way tomorrow, as soon as we know," Will promised as they opened the door to let themselves out. The man was standing in the sitting room, seemingly unaware of them again. It had been a tough notification, this one.

Once Will was back in his own car and Notley off to Caernarfon, he called Quigley.

"Nathan Thomas lives in London," Quigley informed him, seemingly comfortable with the now-late hour. "I could call him and get back to you, or you could give him a call yourself, whichever you want."

"I'll call him," Will said, relieved that Thomas lived too far away for yet another obligation that evening. He was tired, and he longed for his leather recliner, his glass of Famous Grouse, and Bronwyn. He asked Quigley to text him the number and pulled to the verge on the edge of the road.

"Hello, I'm calling for a Nathan Thomas," Will said when a man answered.

"Then you've called the right number," Thomas said, his voice the most cheerful one Will had heard all night. "What can I help you with?"

"I hope I'm not calling too late," Will apologized. He watched headlamps approaching from behind and hoped he'd pulled far enough off the road. "This is DCI Will Cooper. I'm calling for information about a farm near Llangynog in North Wales."

"My dad's place," Thomas said. "But it's let out already, if you're wanting that."

"No, that's not what I'm after." The car passed with a whoosh of air. "I'm afraid there's been a death there, and we need some information about the people who are living there now."

"A death? That's unexpected," Thomas sounded bewildered. "A farm accident?"

"No, sir. This one doesn't appear to be an accident. That's why we're involved. If you could just tell me who leased it from you, that would be a huge help."

"Okay, let me just look here. I have the papers in the file cabinet. It's been some time ago that he leased it, so I want to be sure of the name." Will could hear the snap of a cabinet opening, rustling of paper. "Here it is. William Davies is his name. He said he wanted to try his hand at farming, and I wished him luck. I had my fill growing up there, always having one crisis or another with the animals or the weather. We tried to sell it outright for a few months, but no one bit so finally we offered it to let, and this bloke snatched it right up."

"He's had it for two years or so?"

"The date we signed papers was May 16, so it'll be two years coming up next month."

"He paid on time?"

"It's a farm, inspector. Things happen, and then the money comes in late or not at all. It was feast or famine. We were patient. Anything we got was better than selling it at that point and paying the taxes on the sale. He got behind some months, and other months he paid extra to make it up. Was it him who was killed?"

"No, it was a woman who lived there with him," Will said, knowing he shouldn't, but suspecting the information was already out to the press. "He's our suspect, I'm afraid."

"I could see that," Thomas said. "Kind of rough, that one. No one I'd want my daughter to take up with."

Bronwyn let Daisy out to greet Will as he parked in the driveway in front of the little garage where they stored the lawn mower. She stood nearby watching him emerge from the car, the yellow blouse she was wearing bright in the light spilling out from the open door.

"You've got to be exhausted," she called out while he stooped to ruffle Daisy's ears.

He walked over to her. "You have no idea," he said, pulling her close for a rough embrace. "I need a shower, a big glass of whisky, and a cuddle with someone who's alive and breathing and cheerful."

She laughed. "As bad as that?"

He sobered. "It was a bad day, all told."

"Did you have dinner?"

He shook his head. "No time. We were at the site until half-seven, and then we had to drive to Corwin for a notification." He looked down at her. "It was a hard one."

"I heard it was a young girl."

He shook his head. "Let's go inside. I'll tell you about it after I've settled in."

"I'll make you something to eat while you shower," she offered. "You can eat while you drink your whisky."

"That'd be perfect." He felt he'd come home, at last, perhaps for the first time in his life, and it was a good feeling.

Later, he ate local cheeses, crusty brown bread, and sliced apples while he sipped at his whisky. They sat in the conservatory, small as it was, at the tiny table Bronwyn had set up for informal meals. He told her about Catherine Baines, trying to push the image of her parents to the far back corner of his mind. Bronwyn didn't need to know about that.

"I don't suppose you've heard of her?" he asked.

She shook her head. "If she moved here recently, then no. I'd have only known her if she'd been at school with me or involved with the village somehow. I don't know Billy Davies, either, but I remember old Davyyd Thomas, and Nathan, too. He went to London, I think, maybe an accountant or something like that. He was good with numbers." She thought for a minute. "I wasn't surprised when he didn't keep the farm. Davyyd wasn't very healthy in his older years. I think it was pretty run-down by the time he passed."

"It was. But inside, Catherine kept it clean."

"So, they weren't bad renters."

"According to Nathan, they didn't always pay him on time."

"It's hard, being a farmer. Probably Billy Davies hadn't realized how hard it might be when he took it on. Had he grown up on a farm, do you know?"

Will shook his head. "We haven't even gotten started on him yet. That'll be tomorrow's task."

"Will you be able to stay here for a few days, then?"

Will sipped his whisky. "We'll see. It depends how the case goes, whether we find Billy quickly or have to look for him." Then he set the glass down and reached out to take her hand. "But I have other news." He told her about Bowers' wanting him to be available for cases on the east side of the district. "He made it sound almost as if I could be based here, with occasional trips to Caernarfon for paperwork or meetings, like that."

"But that would be wonderful!" She looked astonished.

"Yeah, well, don't count on it until it happens." Will tried not to get her hopes too high. "There's always a lot of office work to be done on a case, and I'd have to be available to meet with my partners, go to autopsies, attend court, and so on. It sounds better than it'll probably be."

"Still, Bowers seems to be on our side."

"He does. He actually told me he hopes it works out between us."

She smiled, and his heart felt full to bursting. If only all his difficult days could end like this, life would be good.

"I have news, too, Will, and it's not as nice as yours." She told him about the certification course. "It'll mean three days in the Brecon Beacons, on our usual days together."

"That's a couple of weeks away. If this case is done by then and I don't have another keeping me busy, maybe I could come along. While you're doing the course, I could explore the area or maybe even dash down to Cardiff to see Edward. Then in the evenings we could hike. There are tons of trails, really pretty places I think you'd like. It'll be our first holiday together." He'd wanted to show her off to Edward, his old partner, and he'd thought of meeting him in the Beacons, where Bronwyn would be surrounded by trees and flowers and rolling hills and babbling brooks. Maybe if he could manage that, Edward would see what he saw when he looked at her.

"Would you?" That smile…it made him want to do anything to make her happy.

He didn't like to promise. "That's only if I can get away."

She turned serious. "I'll try to get some clues for you."

"Only if they turn up," he told her. "I've always said you don't have to help me; we can solve our cases on our own if you don't come up with something."

"I have a personal stake in this one now, too."

"Yes, you do," he said, and he leaned across the small table to kiss her. "Let's go to bed. It's late, and I don't plan to fall immediately to sleep." He eyed her, and she laughed.

"It's an early morning for me, but I suppose you get to be lazy until Notley gets here."

"That's nothing more than I deserve, after a day like today."

Chapter Four

Will was sitting in the conservatory enjoying a second cup of coffee and thinking about life in general when his mobile rang with the news that Notley had arrived in Llangynog. *So much for a lazy morning*, he thought. Notley wouldn't have wanted to gift him time to enjoy being with Bronwyn, so he'd probably dragged himself out early to make the drive. *The joke's on him,* Will thought sourly. Bronwyn had already left for work a half hour earlier.

He gave Notley instructions for finding the cottage and then got ready for what would probably be another long day's work. *But maybe with a solve at the end of it,* he reminded himself. He wasn't sure if he wanted it to happen that quickly or not. It had been a pleasant evening, coming home to Bronwyn, and more of the same would help maintain the contented mood he felt at the moment. He thought he could even tolerate Notley without complaint if he could come home to Bronwyn every night.

He met Notley outside the cottage, not offering a cup of coffee or tea. They could have sat in the conservatory and planned strategy for the day, but he didn't want Notley intruding on his personal life, and the cottage was just that, so he waited on the front porch and strode out to meet the car as soon as it turned into the drive, to-go cup of coffee in his hand, and climbed into the passenger seat. "What's on for today?" he asked as he snapped his seat belt on. "Results on the DNA?"

Notley backed up, turned the car around, and then he drove to the end of the driveway and let the car idle. "I asked for a rush, but I haven't heard anything yet. Did you get an ID on our suspect?"

"Billy Davies, or William, I guess, if we want to be formal. That's who rented the farm, so chances are good that he's our man. Quigley sent a photo from his passport." He scrolled on his phone and held it over so Notley could look. "I asked him to find out what vehicles are registered to either Davies or the farm, to cover all the bases. He hasn't gotten back to me yet on that."

"We'll find him fast once we have a registration number for whatever he's driving. You can't escape in this country with the cameras everywhere."

"If we interview the neighbors, we may get a tip about where he might have gone."

"Or they may have seen something that leads us in a different direction. It doesn't have to have been a domestic issue."

"It sure does look like one."

"One should always look for a possible alternative, and provide against it. It is the first rule of criminal investigation," Notley reminded him. It sounded like another of his Sherlock Holmes quotes, but Will wasn't sure. Maybe it was just Notley, being unusually thorough.

They drove back through Llangynog and turned onto the B9341 toward Bala and the crime scene. Will relaxed back in the seat and flipped open the lid on his coffee container. He didn't like working with Notley, but they'd settle into the routine now that the initial findings were done, a suspect identified, and the investigation in progress. Usually things proceeded in a predictable fashion once they'd determined what had happened and who was probably responsible, and Notley was as thorough as any other partner, even if he did annoy Will with his Holmes quotes, walking stick, and calabash pipe.

A stop at the crime scene seemed a good place to start on the day's efforts. Two scene of crime vans still occupied the parking area beside the house, and Will and Notley found four technicians still at work when they poked their heads inside the front door and announced themselves.

"We've got a couple of people outside, too," the techs informed them, "going through the outbuildings and looking around the property."

Will's mobile rang as they followed one of the techs through the sitting room and up the stairs. He put it to his ear, stumbling on a stair, and then gestured to Notley. "We'll be along in a minute," he told the tech. "Important call."

The tech nodded. "I'll be in the main bedroom."

Will put the phone on speaker. "What do you have, Quig?"

"Quite a bit, gov. Our Billy Davies had just one vehicle registered to him, a 2020 Ford Kuga, black, with registration number CW 7263."

Will blinked in surprise. "That's an expensive vehicle."

"Yes, sir," Quigley agreed. "But as it's his only registered vehicle and he owns no houses or other valuable property, he could probably have afforded it with two years' savings on that farm, if he was careful."

"He'd have needed something more powerful than that old truck outside if he had to pull a trailer full of sheep," Notley pointed out.

"Okay," Will conceded, although he felt uneasy about the expensive vehicle. It seemed out of character with what they knew so far about Davies. "Any sightings?"

"CCTV cameras have him in Oswestry on Saturday at 10:52 a.m. and then in Wrexham about two hours later."

"Nothing since then?"

"Nothing. He was pulling a livestock trailer in both locations so maybe he turned off onto secondary roads to make a delivery."

Will scowled. "Odd, that. Why would a man kill his wife and then take time to load sheep and deliver them on his way out of the area?"

"Maybe he needed the cash," Notley suggested. "You can't run without money, and credit cards are a wonderful tracking device, so he'd need some cash in hand."

"We'll have to get an appeal out to the local farming community, see if anyone bought the sheep off him." Will liked it when a case took on a rhythm, when they didn't have to wrack their brains trying to figure out how to proceed.

"He had an account at the HSBC bank in Bala, but there wasn't a lot in it," Quigley interrupted his thoughts. They heard the click of fingers on a keyboard. "£697 and some change. As far as I've been able to find out, he didn't have a lot more in assets. No property deeded to him, no investments, like that."

"Do you think he left the Kuga somewhere after Wrexham, maybe traded it for another vehicle?"

"That's be my guess," Quigley said. "Or he holed up somewhere there and is waiting for the pressure to lessen so he can move on."

Will took a deep breath. "Okay, thanks. We'll alert the locals in the area to be on the lookout for that vehicle."

"Already done, sir," Quigley said.

"Good job, as always," Will told him. "We wouldn't get half done without you." He hit the end call button and looked at Notley. "Looks like he might have stayed nearby. Maybe there's something he needs to come back for."

"We'll ask for someone to watch the place, in case," Notley agreed.

The tech leaned out the bedroom door. "If he had something of value here, it's already gone missing."

They followed him into the bedroom and squatted down with him to look under the bed. He aimed a torch toward the front right corner, back a couple of feet from the edge of the bed. "See how the dust has been disturbed there? I'd say there was a box, about a foot square and eight inches high, in that space until very recently."

"A hide hole for his cash?" Notley speculated.

"No way to know," the tech said, "but you can see the box was dragged out. See the marks on the floor?" He directed the torchlight beneath the bed. "The rest of the house was kept pretty clean, but who dusts under the bed?"

Will stood up, and the others did the same. "I guess he didn't spend it all on the truck," he commented.

"That's about all we've found of interest so far," the tech told them, "unless someone outside has something for you. You know about the pills, right?"

"We saw them, but we don't know what they were. Any word on that?"

"Not yet. Looked like Oxy to me, but until they check them out, we won't be able to say for sure."

"Drugs, money…this guy had it all going," Will commented as he and Notley left the house.

"Should we report it to Bowers?" Notley asked. "It sounds like what he said at the meeting, someone unexpectedly having a nicer vehicle than he should be able to afford."

Will thought about it. It made him uneasy, too. "For all we know, that Kuga was financed to the hilt. We can find that out. Even if he bought it cash, he'd be a small-time dealer, just a link in the chain, not the guys in charge that we really need to look out for. And the quantities were small here, personal use."

"We'll include it when we give him our next report, then," Notley decided.

Outside again, they were shown into the barn by another man, a technician who'd been going through it bit by bit.

"You can see there," he pointed, "where the stock trailer was kept. I have no idea why he kept it inside, but maybe he left it hooked to his truck and used one of the other vehicles for other purposes. He'd have wanted to keep that vehicle nice." This man obviously knew about the Ford.

"Nothing suspicious in that, though, is there?" Will wanted to be sure.

The man shrugged. "It looks like a regular barn to me." He gestured. "A stack of hay over there, not much, but it's spring so the supply would be depleted. It looks like he mainly used this building as a garage, and the animals were left to their own devices outside. Cuts down on work, that, if you don't worry over them that way."

The barn did smell cleaner than the one Bronwyn's dad worked in, and he supposed a renter wouldn't want to be bothered with mucking it out. "I'd like some background on this man. Did he have any farming experience? Where did he even come from?"

"Call Quigley and ask him to look into it for us," Notley suggested.

Will nodded. "Yeah, then we'll know a little more about him, at least."

When they'd finished, they drove to the next farm over. They could see a house from the main road, a little bungalow that looked as if it had been added to over the years so that it sprawled over the hillock on which it stood. A man met them in the yard and watched them park. He wore faded denims and a flannel shirt, the uniform of farmers everywhere.

"Inspectors Will Cooper and Sean Notley," Will told him, holding out his warrant card for the man's inspection.

"Lew Glynn," he said. His weathered face looked a little weary, although his gaze was sharp. "You'll be here about what happened next door?"

"We are," Will told him. "How much do you know?"

Glynn eyed them. "I know a woman was murdered, shot to death, from the local gossip. I know you're looking for Billy Davies for it."

"Did you know Mr. Davies?"

Glynn took his time. "I knew him, but not well, just to wave to when we ran into each other out and about."

"You never talked to him?"

"Just to pass the time," Glynn said. "He wasn't the kind of neighbor you'd invite over for a meal or meet at the pub for a drink at the end of the day."

"What do you mean by that?" Notley broke in. He was taking notes on a little pad of paper.

Glynn thought. His answers were slow in coming, but Will thought he just wanted to be careful with what he said. "He was a newcomer, that's all, didn't really fit in with the rest of us."

"Did you know his girlfriend, Catherine Baines?"

"I saw her around once in a while, mostly driving in the little car on the way to do some shopping or whatnot or getting the post. I don't think I ever spoke to her."

"Do you know if there were any problems between them?" Will pushed him.

Glynn nibbled at his bottom lip and then slowly nodded. "My wife said she'd have a black eye now and then, or bruises on her arms if she wasn't wearing long sleeves. She worried over her, but there wasn't anything we could do to help her if she didn't want it. Davies was a bit of a rough one. Anyone could see it."

"What do you mean?"

"Ah, you know, the language he used, couldn't get a sentence out without a curse word in it. That's a sign, isn't it?"

"Sometimes." Without more, it didn't really mean anything.

"Do you know if he was selling some sheep this weekend?"

"He was always hauling them around," Glynn said, "moving them from one pasture to another, and sometimes he'd load them up and come back with them the same day, or at least his trailer would be full, but it might have been a different lot he was bringing back. There was some traffic into his place on Saturday early, and then I saw him going out with a load, passed him on the road, and he looked like he was in a hurry."

"What time was that?"

Glynn thought again. "Must have been around 9:00. Early in the day, anyway. I didn't see him come back that day."

"And you haven't seen him since?"

"Not a peep. Is that when he did for her?"

"We can't say for sure yet. We're waiting on the autopsy." Notley dashed his hopes for more gossip.

"What did you mean when you said there was traffic into his place?" The man's words had triggered his interest.

"It must have been around seven, maybe a bit before. I heard a vehicle coming down the lane, but I didn't really pay attention to it. I thought I heard it turn into his place, but I won't swear to it. It might have gone on past."

"Any idea what type of vehicle it was?"

Glynn shook his head. "I was heading to the barn, my mind on my work."

A disappointment, that. "Can you ask around, see if anyone bought that load of sheep from him on Saturday?"

Glynn nodded, his movements as slow as his speech. "I'll make some calls, let you know."

They handed him one each of their cards and left.

The next two farmers were even more reticent than Glynn had been. Yes, they'd seen Davies passing by now and then, but no one seemed to have talked to him beyond a few pleasantries. Neither of them seemed to have much regard for his farming abilities, but neither offered any specifics to support their opinions.

"They won't tell us if they bought those sheep," worried Notley.

"Yes, they will," Will argued. "They didn't like him. They probably will keep their mouths shut if they didn't, but they'd tell us if they bought them. They won't protect him if he did shoot Catherine Baines, and it's looking more and more like he did." The possibility of Davies trading the Ford for a second vehicle worried him, though.

"We'll find him," Notley said again, and Will hoped he was right.

They'd stopped for lunch at the New Inn in Llangynog when Notley's phone buzzed. He answered it and turned it on speaker.

"DNA results are in," Francis Ruark informed them, "and it's definitely Catherine Baines I've got here on the slab."

There'd been little doubt, really. Will wasn't surprised, yet he dreaded another visit to her parents' house.

"Cause of death was the shot to her head. Death would have been immediate; she didn't suffer."

"Except for the minutes preceding the shot," Will mumbled.

"Time of death is sometime late Friday night or early Saturday morning. It's hard to be precise, but my best guess is about 6:00 a.m. on Saturday. She had some healing bruises, a pulled muscle in her right arm that shows me it was wrenched back behind her, and the hair loss from being grabbed and pulled by the hair. I'm still waiting on toxicology reports."

"Thanks, Francis," Notley said. He ended the call and turned to Will. "The time of death is interesting if other vehicles were at that farm that morning."

"Glynn said around seven, or just before." Will thought it over. "Either Billy killed her just before they got there, or they were involved. Which is it?"

"My guess?" Notley reached up to scratch at his balding head. "He killed her and then met them outside. There'd be no reason anyone else would want her dead."

"It'd take a cold character to kill a woman and then head outside to conduct business."

"Depends on the business," Notley insisted. "If drugs are involved, Davies could probably pull it off one way or another. It wouldn't be like he'd invite them in for coffee."

"Okay." Will let that roll through his thoughts. "Let's head to Corwin next and talk to the parents, and maybe by then Quigley will have some contact information for Davies' family and we can pay them a visit later."

They took time finishing their lunch, avoiding topics of conversation that would lead to conflict. Obviously Notley was in no more hurry than Will to see the Baines again, this time to give them definite news that would only dash any hope they still held. He didn't mention Bronwyn or quote Sherlock Holmes, and Will was grateful.

When they finally parked on the street in front of the Baines' bungalow, Notley held back before opening his car door. "Your turn this time," he informed Will, and so this time it was Will who stepped up, took a deep breath, and knocked on the solid wood door.

It was opened immediately. Mr. Baines looked as if he'd stayed up the whole night, waiting for them to return with the news he dreaded. His wife stood behind him, her face already crumpling into tears. Both looked like they'd aged twenty years overnight.

They were invited in, and they sat on striped overstuffed chairs in a neatly-kept sitting room. The Baines sat on a floral couch across from them. Will hadn't noticed the décor the night before; now he thought it homely and cozy. A few children's toys filled a basket in the corner, and books lay on the table that stood between their chairs. The dog barked from the back garden.

"You've come to tell us it's her," Mr. Baines said with an obvious effort to keep his voice steady. "You've gotten the DNA results."

"Yes," said Will, "to both statements."

Baines' eyes filled with tears and his wife reached over for him, her own face convulsing with uncontrolled but silent sobs.

60

"As you know, we found your daughter Catherine yesterday after you called for a welfare check. She'd been shot, and death would have been almost instantaneous." It was brutal, telling them, but it always went down best if he just said it and got it over, and sometimes the details helped them accept what had happened. "She'd been shot at close range in the right side of her head with a pistol. We've placed time of death on Saturday morning about 6:00 a.m."

"I hope he shot himself, too," Baines managed, allowing anger to overcome his grief for the moment.

"No, he did not, not that we know of, anyway," Will told him. "Billy Davies has disappeared. We are trying very hard to find him. Anything you can tell us about him, about them, might help us do that."

Baines took a deep, shuddering breath. "I don't know what we can tell you that'd lead you to finding him."

"How long were he and your daughter together?" Will asked, keeping his voice soft. It was all he could offer them in the way of comfort. Notley had remained silent, letting Will control the situation thus far.

"She started seeing him about two years ago," Mrs. Baines spoke up now, her voice unsteady. "We didn't approve of him, told her so, but she wouldn't listen to us."

"Why didn't you like him?" Will tried to keep his voice reasonable, non-judgmental.

"He couldn't say a sentence without a curse word in it, and he was mean, always saying terrible things to her and her brothers, belittling them."

"You have other children?"

"Yes," Mrs. Baines nodded, "Catherine has two brothers. She was the oldest by six years. We didn't want them to be around him, to have that influence…to maybe turn out like he was, so we asked her to visit without him."

"And did she?" Notley sat forward now.

Mrs. Baines looked at him. She swayed a little. "At first, she'd come once in a while. She asked if he could come for this last Christmas, for dinner, and we said no. She turned up with him anyway, and that was the end of her visits. We wouldn't let them in the door, so she stopped coming by." She swallowed hard. "We tried to keep in touch, paid for a phone so we could call, but she didn't seem to want to talk."

"She never initiated the calls?" Notley held his pen poised over his notepad.

"No, we usually called her, and sometimes she'd talk a little if he was out, but if he was there, she'd hang up."

"How did you know that he was there when that happened?"

"She wouldn't have done it otherwise." Mrs. Baines looked defiant. "She wanted to see us, to be with our family. We were always close. She loved her brothers. She'd never have turned her back on us unless he made her do it."

"Well, we'll take it as a working hypothesis for want of a better," Notley spewed out a quote, rudely, Will thought.

He decided it was time he took over again. "If you're paying for the phone, you can authorize access to the phone records. That might help us find Billy, if he used the phone, too."

"Of course," Mr. Baines also took charge again. He patted his wife's hand protectively. "We'll sign whatever you need to get that done."

"Thanks." Will hesitated, thinking. "They'd been on the farm for two years?"

Baines shook his head. "It's only been about eight months that Catherine," he stumbled a little over her name, "lived there with him. They'd met in Bala, in a pub, of course. We didn't like Catherine going, but she said she was eighteen so we couldn't stop her having fun with her friends." He nodded to himself. "There's not much on in the small villages, so we didn't argue as much as we would have if we'd known what it'd lead to."

"Did she ever talk about Billy abusing her?" Will hated the sound of the word, but it had to be used.

"She never said, but we knew. You can just tell, can't you, when she's one of your own?"

"Bruises? Broken bones?" Notley pushed them.

Will glanced at him, disgusted. "Of course you know when she's your own child, don't you? You can tell if something's off, even if there's no physical evidence to support it."

62

"Yes, it's just that feeling. He wouldn't let her see us, and after a bit he wouldn't let her go out without him."

"She didn't work?"

"No, I don't think he'd have let her."

No joy there. "Sir, would you have any idea whether Billy had family and where they might be? Or do you remember any names of friends he'd talk about?"

He shook his head and looked to his wife, who also shook her head. "We never had much to do with Billy. He was older than Catherine, maybe mid-thirties, and on his own for a long time, I gathered." Will was older than Bronwyn, too, not quite so much, but near to it. "I think he had a mother in Cardiff, maybe. I'm not sure."

"Can you think of any place he'd go if he were running away?" Will was desperate to get something from the interview.

Baines thought again for a long moment, and then his lips turned down in regret. "Catherine might have gone to her friend Gwen's, or here home, but we wouldn't have an idea where Billy would go. I'm sorry. I wish we could help."

"It's okay," Will reassured him, "we'll be able to get information about his family and maybe the phone will show us some friends he might run off to. We'll get him."

"Justice, at least, for Catherine," Mrs. Baines murmured, her eyes shining with tears.

"Yes," Will said. "We'll see it done for you."

Back in the Volvo, they sat and thought about what to do next. Notley tapped his knuckles on the steering wheel, irritating Will, but he suppressed the urge to mention it, fearing that if the man's hands weren't busy, he'd pull out his pipe.

"Call it an early day?" Will wondered.

"You'd like that, wouldn't you?" Notley sneered. He gripped the steering wheel suddenly and turned to glare at Will. "Why'd you shut me out of the questioning?"

"You were being rude."

"I was asking questions that needed answers."

"They were grieving, shattered. You didn't need to push them so hard. There are nicer ways to go about it."

"You think you're my role model now, Cooper? Be gentle? Caring? Coax the information out by coddling the suspects?"

"The Baines aren't suspects," Will snapped.

"But your girlfriend was," Notley persisted. He reached into his pocket for his pipe and tapped it on the edge of his open window, emptying the bowl, and then he pulled a bag of tobacco from the centre console and started to fill it. "I know how you went about getting information from her."

Will tried to suppress his anger. "Let's call Quigley and see if he has anything on Billy's family situation."

Notley's lip curled. He thought he'd won that argument, Will guessed. "You call while I have my smoke."

When Will pulled out his phone, he saw he'd missed a call from the very man. He called back and put the phone on speaker.

"Hey, inspectors, thanks for calling back. I have lots of information for you." Quigley's voice was excited.

"Hit us," Will said. "We need something. We're at a standstill here."

"Okay, first off, I have a registration for the stock trailer, CW 899-2. It's a standard 18-foot stock trailer with rails on the sides but no top. The Kuga was seen in Wrexham, still pulling the trailer, but it hasn't been spotted since. The cameras caught three more black Kugas heading northeast near Chester, but that's the A483 and it's pretty congested with traffic through there so it wouldn't be unheard of for several of them to pass by."

"Were they new, like Davies' was?" Notley watched Will from his own seat, puffing on his pipe.

"It's hard to tell. We captured registration numbers and we're tracking them down. I'll let you know if any are stolen numbers." Quigley was quiet for a minute, probably checking notes, Will thought. "I checked, and the Kuga is owned outright by Billy Davies. No loan on it. The stock trailer belongs to Nathan Thomas. I called him and he said the vehicles that were on the farm were included when he let it out."

"That'd be the older truck and the Ford," Will guessed.

"Exactly," Quigley said. "I also checked into Billy Davies. He has a mother, Sharon Davies, in Liverpool and a brother, Robert Davies, in Carlisle. The father listed on his birth records appeared to be out of the picture, having died when Billy would have been just a child. By the way, we have an age for Billy of 37. He has form for everything from petty theft to armed robbery, with convictions for drug possession and dealing thrown in. He's been in and out of gaol most of his adult life. He is five feet ten inches tall and his listed weight is 180 pounds. Brown hair and brown eyes, no scars, a tattoo of a marijuana leaf on his left shoulder. You saw the picture."

"Tell me about the dealing." Will glanced at Notley, who was listening intently, his lips pursed around the stem of the pipe.

"Not-big time stuff, just supplying the locals with enough to keep a good little business going."

"How many customers?"

"I don't know." Fingers tapped on a keyboard. "He had enough stuff on him when he was arrested to be dealing, more than for personal use. Pills, mostly, but marijuana, too. No heroin or cocaine, anything like that."

"Do we need to call Bowers with this?"

"No, when I couldn't reach you, I filled him in on what I had, in case he had other stuff he wanted me to look for."

"Did he?"

"No, he said he'd talk to you later. I guess that'd be now."

Will glanced at Notley and nodded to himself. "Okay, thanks. Keep looking for that Kuga and the trailer. We'll talk to Davies' mother and brother."

When Quigley finished the call, Will scrolled to Bowers' number and hit the call button.

"Bowers here," his voice boomed inside the car, sounding louder than Quigley's.

Will filled him in on what they'd accomplished that day. "The Baines are shattered, sir. They'll help any way they can."

"Can you take a picture of their authorization for the phone records and then text it to me? I'll have Quigley get started on that this afternoon."

"Of course. What do you want us to do here?" Liverpool was a long drive away, and Carlisle not much closer.

"It's a fair distance to Carlisle." Bowers must have been reading his mind. "I'm a bit short on constables at the moment. They're all up on Anglesey. Why don't you two drive the back roads around Wrexham for a bit? That's the last place the Kuga was sighted, so if Davies sold the sheep, it might have been near there. I know it's spinning our wheels, but it's better than just sitting on your thumbs. Check the local farms. Ask around. Maybe he sold the trailer with the sheep."

"Not many farmers keep that much cash on hand," Will pointed out.

"There'd be banks nearby, I'm sure, but not one we can ask about large withdrawals without more to go on. I'm asking you to get me more."

"We can cover more ground separately," Will suggested, hoping he wasn't being too transparent.

"It'll be on your way back to Llangynog." Bowers was not to be pushed. "I'd like you to spend a couple of hours looking, and then you can call it a night. Sean, you'll need to book into the B&B at the pub. That way the two of you can get an early start to Carlisle and Liverpool tomorrow, unless something more turns up in the meantime."

Chastened, Will watched Notley tap out his pipe and lay it carefully on the console between them. He pulled a map up on his phone and then directed Notley to a route that would get them to Wrexham as quickly as possible. From there, they'd explore some of the B roads that ran past most of the farms in the area.

"I guess Bowers doesn't always enable your bad behaviors," Notley commented as he signaled and turned onto the motorway.

"Leave it, Sean," Will told him, staring out the passenger-side window at the passing countryside. Hedgerows blocked his view of most of the pastureland, but breaks in the foliage gave him glimpses of what lay beyond.

To his relief, Notley fell into an awkward silence that stretched the miles to Wrexham. Will watched the countryside pass and thought of Bronwyn. He wished she wouldn't push the issue with his parents. He knew he'd have to introduce them, but he wanted it on his own terms. If they went to Gloucester on a Sunday, his mother would expect them for a meal. Sunday roast, he supposed, which wasn't so bad, but it would require conversation among them, which could be awkward. His father would eat in silence while his mother asked about Bronwyn. He could almost hear her. *You grew up on a sheep farm, I understand? Have you ever been to the ballet? We hoped to take you over Christmas, but William had to work.* He'd endure it, and he'd hope Bronwyn would survive it. She was very different from other girls he'd known, and he thought that might be what drew him to her the most. He wanted anything but his parents' life.

Near Wrexham, Notley signaled and turned off onto a small lane.

"Slow down," Will told him, trying to see past the hedgerows. "I think we need to stretch our legs a little when we come to the farm tracks so we can see what lies beyond our view here."

"You want to hike?" Notley's raised eyebrows showed what he thought of that idea.

"It makes sense. If Davies' car or trailer are here, they're not going to be parked right alongside the road. He'd have to know we're looking for them. Even if he isn't the smartest man in the country, he'd figure that out."

Notley grunted in response, but he pulled to the verge when the first tiny lane appeared to their left. "Go for it," he told Will.

Will got out and slammed the door. "I won't be long. You'd better be here when I get back."

Notley laughed.

If only he knew, Will thought, *that I love hiking now that I've learned to get out and about.* Of course, it was a lot more fun with Bronwyn, but still…the spring day was bright and the wildflowers along the edge of the lane gave the air a sweet scent and anything other than sitting in a car with Notley was a boost to his morale. *And I get to spend another night at home with Bronwyn,* he told himself, and an unexpected contentment made him smile as he trudged away down the lane.

Chapter Five

Bronwyn hummed to herself as she typed more names into her spreadsheet for the St. Melangell's Day pilgrim's walk. She couldn't help it. The sun, partially shaded with puffy white clouds, shone outside, she could hear birdsong through her opened window, Daisy lay snoring at her feet, and Will had come home to her the night before, unexpectedly, on an evening she'd normally have spent alone, missing him.

It had been bliss having him there. Their days off together were nice, but they always felt more like a holiday or at least a weekend away, rather than like a normal everyday life. Last night had felt like a real relationship, both of them coming home from work to the cottage they shared. She'd loved relaxing with him, watching him sip his whisky and listening to the details of the case that had brought him home.

She hadn't been familiar with Catherine Baines, nor Billy Davies, either. She supposed they had come occasionally to one of the two pubs in the village, the Tanat or the New Inn, but she didn't know everyone who came for a meal or a drink at the end of a day, and she'd have had no reason to interact with either of them unless they sought out counselling at the centre or even wandered in as pilgrims. Will had shown her a picture of each of the two on his phone, and she hadn't recognized them.

Once they knew the identities of the victim and her probable killer, Bronwyn had called her dad and quizzed him about them. He'd known old Davyyd Thomas, and he'd heard things about the farm after it had been let, local gossip being disapproving of the way the new tenant was doing things. "He called it 'modern farming methods, organic farming,'" her dad informed her, "but what it really meant was lazy farming. He ran the sheep from one pasture to another every week or so, and sometimes he'd be gone all day and come back with the same sheep. I hear he didn't bother inoculating them, wasn't 'natural,' he said, and if they went over a fence onto the roadway, well, you'd just better look out for them because he wouldn't be bothered putting them back in and mending the fence."

She'd passed the information on to Will, and he'd filed it away in his notes. "That squares with what Davies' neighbors told us. The rent on the place must have been low if he managed to save up enough to buy that Kuga when he so obviously didn't know the first thing about farming."

"Did you look to see if he was growing anything illegal?"

"We did," Will had told her, "and we didn't find anything suspicious. Still, it leaves me wondering why he'd choose farming when he had no past experience with it. Nathan Thomas, old Davyyd's son, says he was late with the rent more often than not."

Yet there was the Kuga, an expensive vehicle. "Could he have inherited the car?"

"We'll find out," Will had said. "Quigley's onto finding family for him and, if they're anywhere local, we'll sit down and have a good talk with them. Maybe we'll find him hiding out with them. That'd make things a lot easier, if we did."

And now Will was off to the farm and then probably back to Corwin with Notley, and Bronwyn was sitting in her office, humming. She knew Will dreaded seeing the Baines again, but once that visit was over, maybe things would start to fall into place.

Daisy stirred and looked up at her, her expressive eyes suggesting a walk.

"Just a few more minutes and I'll have this done," she told the Labrador, ruffling her ears. She'd already settled the group who'd booked in for a conference and, once she finished entering the registrants' information into her computer for the walk, she could take a break with Daisy until lunchtime, when she'd have to cart the sandwiches, crisps, fruit, and tea to the conference room for their meal. After, she'd clean up and then have a go at a schematic for the vendors who'd shown an interest in setting up booths in the car park during the St. Melangell's Day celebration.

Her office phone rang, and she answered it, scheduling in another group for a Wednesday in mid-June. Maybe by then she'd have her certification and could offer them a bonus during their noon break – forest bathing. She didn't mention it, not being sure of how things would go.

She rolled the term around in her mind. *Forest bathing.* Whoever had named it had it all wrong, in her mind. She supposed they were thinking that a bath required immersion, and this type of natural meditation also required immersion, but it was very different. Surely, they could have named it something better, perhaps forest experience, or, her preferred term, nature meditation. And it didn't require a forest, either, she thought. What she did, and what she understood them doing, could be done in any type of natural environment, be it forest or meadow or sea scape or jungle or even a park. What mattered wasn't that a person must be in a forest, but simply in nature. It was getting away from the clutter of modern life that mattered.

She finished the final registration and pushed back her chair. It was time to get outside. She'd asked Will whether they needed to keep the buildings locked again, and he'd thought it over and then said no. He felt pretty certain that Billy Davies had fled the area, and with a group using the conference room, she'd be surrounded by enough people to be safe, anyway. He asked her not to walk to work, and she hadn't wanted to anyway, lingering over breakfast with him as long as she could before both of them set out for the day's endeavors.

She wandered with Daisy out through the little car park, past the van the guests had arrived in, and toward the churchyard. Daisy would run around the area, stretching her legs, while Bronwyn sat on the bench inside the lych gate and watched her. She'd been lucky with Daisy. She was a very reliable dog, one that she could let loose to take care of business without having to keep her leashed or monitor her every move.

70

She loved everyone. She'd be a good therapy dog someday and, meanwhile, she was a great companion.

She smiled as Daisy flushed a pheasant from beneath a gorse bush just where the walking path left the lane. Daisy leapt into the air, woofing softly, and then she stood and watched the bird flutter down the path as fast as it could scramble. She looked at Bronwyn, knowing her limits, and then ambled over to her, laying her head on Bronwyn's knee.

Bronwyn scratched her ears, mumbling endearments, then she sat back on the bench and closed her eyes. She could hear Daisy's soft breath beside her, and then a thump as the dog lay down at her feet. She could feel Daisy's heavy head on her shoe, a comforting weight. A whisper of breeze stirred the yews surrounding the churchyard, a portent of rain to come, maybe as early as that evening. She took a breath. She could smell the mud of puddles not dried up from the last rain, and the scent of freshly mown lawn. Someone had been trimming in the churchyard around the tumbling gravestones earlier. She let her mind wander.

Will had sounded excited about her certification, eager to make it a holiday for the two of them if he could get an extra day or two free. She'd dreaded telling him about it, but now she felt excited. Her role as St. Melangell's heir seemed to develop of its own accord, without her having to think it out as much as she'd thought she'd have to. Perhaps Pysgotwr had a hand in that, directing fate so that opportunities came to her rather than her having to seek them out. For whatever reason, she was grateful not to have to worry over it.

Her thoughts drifted back to Will's case, and she wondered how quickly they'd find Billy Davies and close it up. Maybe if he had to work through a week or more without a break, he'd be allowed to take a Saturday soon so they could go and see Lark. She knew he missed her. If he came to Llangynog on a Friday night, they could drive down on Saturday, see her that day and on Sunday, and then come home on the Monday. Gloucester was a bit of a long drive, but if an extra day came available, it'd be worth it.

With her luck, she'd have to work the Saturday. She often did, weekends being popular times for groups to book in so that they didn't interrupt their regular work week. If that happened, then Will would go by himself to see Lark, and she'd miss out on yet another chance to finally meet his parents.

How often did she tell people to live in the moment and not worry about the future? Yet here she was, not only fretting about her future with Will, but even about the little things, like seeing Lark and wondering if he'd ever feel ready to introduce her to his parents. She didn't understand his obvious reluctance in that regard, but she couldn't stop it intruding on her thoughts more and more often these days. Firmly, she pushed the thoughts out of her mind. The day was too nice to spend time worrying over things she couldn't control.

She opened her eyes and glanced down at Daisy lying on her foot. The dog noticed her movement and looked up at her, her brown eyes adoring and her mouth curved in a slight smile. When Bronwyn didn't respond, she stood up and looked at Bronwyn inquiringly, her ears cocked up.

"Okay, let's go in. It must be nearly time for their lunch." Bronwyn stood up, stretched, and reached down to pat Daisy on the head, and then a movement caught her eye.

A tiny fairy fluttered its wings near the entrance to the lych gate. She blinked, wondering if she was seeing a hummingbird, but the fairy's features were clear: a tiny body dressed in pale lavender flowers, a buttercup hat covering its pale, shimmering silver hair, wings transparent as stained glass in vivid tones of blue, turquoise, and green. It hovered, watching her.

She peeked past it quickly and then back, reassuring herself that it was alone, at least for the moment. Maybe the others would follow. She stood shock still, not wanting to scare it away.

It treaded air like a human would tread water, floating in place as its wings beat rapidly. Its tiny face, a peeked nose, pinpoint eyes, and pursed lips, turned side to side as it watched her. It seemed neither male nor female, but something between, neither beautiful nor ugly.

She waited, listening intently for a message. From the corner of her eye, she could see Daisy looking up at it now, watching it but, like Bronwyn, not moving. She felt reassured that the dog saw it, too. Sometimes she thought she imagined them.

"Tell me," she whispered when she couldn't stand to remain silent any longer. "Where are the others?" Usually they surrounded her, circling her as they revealed the words they meant to give her. There'd be three messages, sometimes more, given in medieval phrases that she'd have to remember long enough to look them up to determine their meaning. Then they'd count to three – once, twice, thrice – and disappear, leaving a circle of mushrooms in their wake.

This one, though, remained silent for another long moment, and then it whisked away toward the church, disappearing against the green of the yews. As it flitted away, she thought she heard a word in the fluttering of the wings. *Simple*, it had trilled at her as it flew. Twice, it had said it: *simple*. Or had she just imagined the word in the sound of the humming wings?

Bronwyn shook her head, pondering what had just happened. Was she meant to follow it as it zipped out of sight? She wouldn't have been able to keep up. Why, then, did it come to her?

She stared toward the yews for another minute, and then she walked across the churchyard, Daisy following at her heels. On the other side, she peered cautiously through the yews, seeing nothing. She looked upward, again seeing nothing but the green of the trees. From the peak of the church roof, a rook cawed out into the silence, its rasping voice breaking the spell she thought she felt after the fairy's visit.

She sighed. If they had a message for her this time, they'd have to be more forthcoming with it.

In the mid-afternoon, as Bronwyn was wondering what else she could do in the office, her office phone rang. It was her father.

"I wanted to let you know that we've organized to take charge of the sheep on the old Thomas place. They let us onto the property around one this afternoon, and we've been busy since marking them. We thought to leave them on their home pastures, but with the fences being somewhat neglected, now we are going to divide them up and take them to our fields until other arrangements can be made. I suppose Nathan will have to take charge of them?"

"I don't know, Dad. Unless Billy Davies turns out to be innocent, I guess Nathan will be left to sort it out."

"You'll let Will know?"

"Yes, of course. He'll be back tonight, it seems. Unless things change, he has to go to Carlisle and Liverpool tomorrow, and they're much closer from here."

"I'm glad of it." Her father's voice was soft, almost shy. "With a killer on the loose, we feel better knowing he's there with you."

"It feels more like home with him here," Bronwyn confessed.

She could hear her father's sigh, almost repressed. "He's a good man, love. It's nice to see you settled."

Not really settled, she thought. They'd like to see her married. "I'm happy, dad."

The group in the conference room, members of a flower society in Llangollen, stayed late, unfortunately. Often groups did, taking advantage of the fact that no one would actually boot them out, and the ones who ended early were a rare bonus. When they finally finished inside, they wandered out into the sensory garden, where they spent a long half hour making suggestions as to how to improve it. Bronwyn tried not to let her impatience show. When the last woman thanked her and got into her car, she locked the door and hurried to her own car, letting Daisy stop to empty her bladder and then opening the back door to let her in. The wind had picked up, and dark clouds scurried in from the west, threatening rain for the evening.

Will beat her home, opening the door with an open bottle of wine in his hand and beckoning her inside. "How was your day?"

"It was good." She smiled at him. She couldn't mention the fairy, of course, but she'd kept the morning's feeling of contentment through the entire day. When Will had called her mid-afternoon to say he'd be spending another night at "home," she'd even ventured in to tell Janice her good fortune, wanting to share her happiness with someone.

He bent to kiss her and glanced beyond at the sky. "It's working up to a good rain, isn't it?"

"I think so. I felt it coming earlier in the day. I think we'll get a thunderstorm."

"I'm grilling for dinner, so I'm afraid there'll be no relaxing with a pre-dinner drink, if we want to beat the weather."

"You're cooking?"

"It's not a lot, but I made a salad and dashed into a shop for salmon and steak when we passed through Bala this afternoon. There's a fresh baguette, as well."

He was excited about it, she could tell. The grill had been one of his indulgences when they'd furnished the cottage, along with his leather chair. "What a treat, Will. I didn't expect you to make dinner."

"I wanted to. We had a rather lazy, slow day, and I thought you'd have been busy."

"My group stayed late. Otherwise, I'd have been here a half hour ago." She'd made no plan for dinner. Will's unexpected extra days left the larder empty. She had the habit of eating simple meals from whatever was leftover or dropping in at her parents' house on the days Will was in Caernarfon, leaving the shopping until the day before she expected him. Maybe that wasn't such a great idea if he was going to turn up unexpectedly.

Inside, she shrugged off the cardigan she'd worn for work and went into the bedroom to change her trousers for jeans and the blouse for a sweatshirt. Comfortable then, she walked out onto the tiny patio where Will was busy scraping the grill to clean off the dregs of whatever they'd grilled last. Halibut, she thought. It had been a real treat, much more expensive than the ubiquitous salmon, which always readily available. But salmon was her favorite, in the end, so this was a treat, too.

"Grab the meat from the counter, will you?" Will called over his shoulder. "I think we're ready to go."

She turned back and grabbed the plate, then sat down on one of the mismatched lawn chairs they'd found in a thrift shop. Will plopped the steak on the grill, carefully set the salmon beside it on its foil base, and then, satisfied, closed the lid on the grill and sat down beside her.

He reached for the bottle of wine and poured two glasses. "I hope you didn't have big plans for the evening."

She took her glass. "I didn't have a clue what we'd eat for dinner."

"So, this is okay?"

"I can't think of anything better." She looked up at the sky. "I was hoping for a walk after dinner since I didn't manage to get out today at all, but it looks like that's not going to happen."

"You wanted to go to the pool of water, to see if you could get me some clues," he guessed.

What would he think if he knew the truth, that most of the clues she got him came from the Twlwyth Teg and not the pool of water? "No, I just thought Daisy needed to run a bit." They had to keep her close at the cottage, with neighbors right beside them. "And I wanted to get outside, too."

"I had some walks this afternoon," Will said, and she felt a stab of jealousy. But once she was certified, being outdoors in nature would be part of her job. She suddenly felt a bit of gratitude for the opportunity rather than resentful at the time away it would require.

She told him about the farmers caring for the abandoned sheep. "No one's mentioned buying any sheep from him, though."

"It's nice, that. His neighbors rallying to help out with the livestock."

"Farmers do that all over the world, Will. They help each other if there's a need. It isn't just here."

He looked at her quizzically, his head turned to one side. "That's so different from the way I grew up. In the city, it's every man for himself."

She didn't know what to say. "Are you glad to be here, then?"

He laughed a little, as if he saw a private joke. "Here with you? Or here, in a tiny village? Or here, in North Wales?"

"All of the above, I guess." She knew he was happy being there with her, didn't she?

"Then, yes, to all of it," he said firmly.

"Even though we don't have theatres, and fancy restaurants, and art galleries, and lots of fancy shops?"

"I've found I don't need any of those," he told her. "I'd rather go hiking with you than go to the theatre, and I'd rather grill dinner for the two of us than dress up to go out. I have your art to look at when I get a craving for that, and we found enough furniture in the second-hand shops to keep us comfortable. That's all I need."

Thunder rumbled in the mountains to the west, and Will looked up at the blackening clouds. "I think we'd better pull this stuff off the grill and get inside, done or not."

"Let's take our dinner into the conservatory and watch the storm while we eat."

"That sounds perfect.." He put the meat on a plate while she gathered up the wine bottle and glasses.

The storm crashed down onto the Tanat valley in a torrent of rain, wind, and booming thunder. Flashes of lightning lit the little cottage like a strobe light. She could hear the rain dripping from the eaves by the window and smell the ozone in the air. Birch and maple seeds flung themselves against the windows, hitting like hail. They'd turned on the overhead lights to dispel the darkness of the storm, but within a few minutes they blinked out with a sigh. They'd lost power.

They sat at the little table, eating slowly so as to savor the adventure. Daisy, nervous from the storm, hid at their feet and refused to eat her own dinner, but Bronwyn thought she'd never enjoyed a meal more, the salmon flaky and melting in her mouth, the salad crisp, and the bread crusty on the outside and soft in the middle. She lit a candle as it grew darker, and she and Will talked and joked about their days as the meal disappeared.

They'd finished and were drinking the last of the wine when she made a decision. Will had said he was happy in Llangynog, with her, and she hadn't needed much convincing. He took every opportunity to stay as long as he could, and he'd taken a huge step when he rented the cottage, knowing that he'd be paying the majority of the cost. The wine had mellowed her to the point where she felt she could tackle one of the big issues that remained between them, and so she gathered her courage. She only hoped not to dispel the magic of the evening by bringing it up. "I really want to meet your parents, Will."

He looked at her, sighed, and stood up. "Let's go inside to the sitting room where it's quieter if we're going to have this discussion."

She nodded and followed him through the doorway. He stopped in the kitchen to pour a measure of Famous Grouse, but she didn't think it had anything to do with her request. He nearly always drank a small glass of whisky in the evenings, and the half bottle of wine he'd already drunk wouldn't satisfy that craving.

He sat beside her on the sofa, turning to the side to face her and setting his glass on the end table. The room was dark, the gloom of the storm not dispelled as much there as it had been when the lightning flashed through the multiple windows in the conservatory. "I know you want to meet them," he said calmly. "You've asked, and you've been nice enough not to push the issue."

"It's been a year, Will." She hesitated. "Well," she amended, "a year since we first met. A year since I met Lark. A year since you met my parents. I know at first you weren't serious about seeing me," she hated to admit that, "but we've been together pretty much for the past six or seven months. I just think it's time."

He took a deep breath, not meeting her eyes. "It's past time," he admitted, "and, for the record," he glanced at her, amusement tugging at the corners of his mouth, "I was always serious about you. I just didn't want to admit it to myself for a while."

She swallowed, silent. *Why hadn't he wanted to admit it?* She didn't dare ask, fearing the answer. "My parents like you a lot. Maddock probably likes you even more."

"I know. But it's different with my family, sweetheart." His voice was soft. "I've tried to tell you. They aren't like your family."

"Tell me about them," she said, really hoping for details this time. "I want to understand, Will. Is it me? Are you reluctant because I'm not as sophisticated as they are? Is it because I live in a tiny village, and I didn't go to university, and..." She couldn't say 'because I see visions in pools of water "....and because I prefer to tramp about in the fields rather than going to the theatre? Are you embarrassed by me?"

Will blinked at the torrent of words that had surprised her as much as him. "God, no, sweetheart. I could never be embarrassed by you. You're brilliant, and all those things are the reasons why I love you."

He'd said it. He loved her. He'd said it before, but he'd never gone beyond the short phrase.

"Then why, Will? Why do you find excuses every time we have a chance to go to Gloucester together? We haven't even seen Lark since before Christmas."

He breathed out, long and slow. "I promise you, it's them I'm embarrassed by, not you, love." He turned a little and reached for his glass, taking a slow sip of the whisky, and then he lowered the glass and held it in both hands in his lap, looking down at it. "My father is a solicitor, a very successful one. He's successful because he works all the time, always building up the firm's reputation because he's a partner; he owns half of it. He makes loads of money so they have a huge old house with a garden, and his dream was to have one of his sons study law so that the firm could be passed down from one generation to the next." He paused. "My brother George went off to Canada after Lark's mother Julia died. He sells real estate there. I know that Father was counting on him, but when it didn't work out, he turned to me as a poor substitute. I was already working for the police force, and I wanted none of the life he was offering. It would have required a return to university, and the thought of working day and night and then spending evenings and weekends entertaining or going out to fancy events didn't appeal to me. When I joined the force, especially when he found out I was working undercover most of the time, my father pretty much disowned me. He barely speaks to me now. I'm sure I'm a great disappointment to him."

"You couldn't be a disappointment to anyone, Will," she murmured, trying to ease the obvious distress caused by the confession that she hadn't expected when she'd asked to hear about his family.

"You don't know," he responded with bitterness. "You've never lived with a family like mine."

She bit at her lip, not knowing what to say.

After a moment, he went on. "My mother does talk to me, sometimes too much. Nothing I do pleases her, and she isn't shy about letting me know it. She uses Lark as a weapon, denying me opportunities to see her or talk to her if something I've done has made her mad. But she needs me, or at least she makes me think so. Lark was a surprise to them. They hadn't expected to have a young granddaughter join the household in their old age. Mother was used to having free time, time that she spent going to social functions, parties, and shopping. Lark put a damper on that. Now Mother has to be home in the evenings and on weekends, unless she can arrange a playdate for Lark or unless I take her off her hands. I'm sure Lark will be sent to boarding school next fall. She'll be just eight, but that was the age the rest of us were sent off. I'm sure that Mother will hope that I can take Lark on holidays so that she can have her old life back again." He paused again, thinking. "She is angry with me when I make plans with Lark and then have a case come up so I have to cancel. I've tried to think how I could take Lark full-time, but I can't see a way that would work."

"Now that we're together…" Bronwyn started.

"No, I'm not asking that of you. We need time to ourselves, too."

She agreed, but didn't like to say so. "School holidays, then?" She'd like that, and so would Lark.

"I don't know." Will took another long drink. The glass was emptying fast. "Mother knows about you, and she's asked to meet you. She wanted me to bring you for Christmas, but thank God I had to work." She could see him smile in the dim light. "I know it seems like I'm putting it off, and I am. I know Mother won't approve because she doesn't approve of any of my choices." He went silent again for a long minute. "I've been thinking that what I want in life is very different from how I grew up. I don't want a girl who dresses in the latest fashions and wears perfect makeup and has her hair styled every other week. I don't want to go to the theatre or concerts or fancy restaurants or dancing. Or to parties. I dread them."

She reached for his hand, encouraging him. He'd never opened up like this before.

"I want to live in a tiny cottage in a little village where people know each other and help out when it's needed. I want to have a dog, at least one, that I can talk to and go walking with when I feel the urge. I want to go hiking in my free time, to be outside where there's no city and no congestion, where it's peaceful. I want to solve crimes, to feel like I make a difference in this world." He reached out and took her hand with his. "And I want to be with you, my beautiful, fey Bronwyn."

Fey. She hated the word, but when he said it, it almost sounded like an endearment. "I'm sorry I pushed you about this, Will. I didn't know…"

He squeezed her hand. "You couldn't have known, sweetheart. And I made it sound worse than it is." Even in the growing dark, she could see that he now looked abashed, a little embarrassed. "There are lots of kids who grow up in far worse circumstances, even in tiny villages like this one. I know that's true. We were well-cared for: there were always au pairs when we were young and someone home when we were older, even if they didn't want to be. We traveled some, to the south of France and the Spanish coast. It wasn't until I was away at school and going home with my friends for holidays that I felt the difference. Their homes were popping with dogs and ponies and mothers who stood ready with a burger or a pizza when we were hungry. I'll admit it, once I saw your family in action, I knew it'd be hard to introduce you to mine. But I know you need to meet them, and I'll get it done, I promise."

Did she dare suggest it? "If you get some days free when I go to the certification in the Beacons, maybe we could go on the Sunday and drive all the way to Gloucester. I could meet them and we could see Lark, and then we could leave early on Monday morning to get me there in time for my class."

He nodded, barely perceptible in the dark. "What time does the class start?"

"I think nine in the morning."

"We'll find Billy Davies in a day or two, and I'm banned from the big drugs investigation up in Anglesey, so unless something else comes along, I might be able to take a few days off. I'll talk to Bowers when I get back to Caernarfon." He released her hand. "I've been dreading having you meet them, but it'll be good to have it over and done with."

She smiled. "It's getting dark, Will. I wonder when the power will come back on?"

"The storm's letting up," he said. "Let's take Daisy out in the garden for a few minutes, and then call it a night."

"You always know the perfect thing to do," she told him echoing his words from earlier, and she smiled at his answering chuckle. It had been a difficult conversation, but she felt more relieved than he could ever know.

Chapter Six

The shrilling of Will's mobile woke him from a deep sleep. He bumbled for it on the nightstand, and pushed the green talk button, mumbling a raspy hello.

"Good morning, guv." Quigley's cheerful voice came loud into the quiet room.

Will glanced over at Bronwyn's side of the bed, but it was empty. *Good, the phone didn't wake her, then.* "What's up?"

"I've been through phone records on Catherine Baines' phone. Good job, that, sir, getting permission to access them."

"You found something helpful?"

"There wasn't a lot there so it was a quick job. Most of the calls were from her parents, one every few days or so, sometimes less often. They called her more than she did them, and sometimes she answered, but other times she didn't. They left messages when she didn't."

"You listened to them?"

"Yep. It was mostly just 'we love you, call us' and like that. The last ones were a bit more insistent, when she didn't answer, but nothing you wouldn't expect. There's nothing out of the ordinary there."

Will propped himself on one elbow and squinted at the clock. 7:10. Light beamed through the window and lit the far wall, where Bronwyn had hung one of her little sketches. It looked highlighted in the sunlight, as if lit by a spotlight. "Any other calls?"

"There were a few to someone called Gwen Roberts, a friend I'm guessing. Those conversations were long, sometimes an hour or more."

"Email, texts, twitter?"

"Texts from her phone to Gwen, mostly things like asking if she was okay and like that. Nothing detailed. I didn't find any social media accounts for her, which is odd given her age. She was on Facebook and Instagram when she was younger, but that all seemed to end about eight months ago."

"That's when she moved in with Billy Davies." It sounded like Davies wanted to socially isolate her, augmenting the physical abuse they suspected.

"Here's the interesting thing, though, guv. There are two calls going out to a pre-paid phone, one four days ago, so before the murder, and the second on the morning of the murder."

"A burner," Will said. Why would Catherine be calling someone who was using a burner phone?

"Yes, and the second call was made at 9:06 a.m."

Will sat up. "So those calls were Billy's."

"I'm guessing they were," Quigley said. "The first call lasted four minutes, twenty-two seconds, and the second call, the one on the morning of the murder, lasted two minutes, forty-four seconds."

"Any idea where that burner phone was when it was called?"

"I was able to track it to just outside of Liverpool, to a place called Wirral. It looks like an upscale community, connected by train to Liverpool, with farmland and big old houses. The call was made three days ago, so just a day before the murder."

"Can you give me a specific address?"

"No, but I can get you pretty close. I'll text you the details."

"We'll check it out today. We're headed to Liverpool to talk to Davies' mother." Will thought for a moment. "Could you track Catherine's phone at all?"

"It's dead, sir. It went dead right after that last call, and there's been nothing since. Either it's been turned off, even the tracking on it, or more likely it's been destroyed."

"Okay, thanks, Quigley. Text me that information, would you? I'll call if I think of anything else you can do for us."

"Always at your service, guv," Quigley quipped as the call ended.

Will hesitated, and then he scrolled to Notley's number and called it. They were already days behind Billy now, but perhaps he was still in the area. They probably needed to get to Liverpool, or Wirral, at least, as quickly as they could.

Will pushed out of the bed and pulled on nylon pants and a tee shirt. He wandered into the kitchen, where he found Bronwyn busy frying bacon and toasting bread.

He walked up behind her, pushed her hair aside, and kissed the back of her neck. "You don't have to make me breakfast, love. I'm used to grabbing something easy."

"I wanted to, after the dinner you make me last night."

"Bacon," he observed. "I didn't think you'd have that in the house. Are you sharing with me?"

"I'll have an egg," she said, flipping the bacon onto a plate. "I had the bacon in the freezer, in case you wanted a real fry up one morning." She cracked eggs into the pan. "I'm making you a couple of eggs, too."

"I won't need lunch," he observed. "Has Daisy been out for her walk yet?"

"I let her out for a few minutes and watched her from the door. I'll take her out after we eat." She tossed him a smile. "The sun's out again."

"I see. Big plans for the day?"

"I have another group coming in, but just for a half-day. I hoped to go to Llangollen, if I can get away for a bit later. There's a garden shop there I want to check out. The group yesterday gave me some ideas to make our little sensory garden better." She pushed eggs off onto plates. "Janice is off today, so I usually stay in case of pilgrims who need help, but I've had an idea in the night that once I get my certification, I'd like to develop the sensory garden more so as to give us more to experience when we do a session. If I can't go today, there's always tomorrow."

"Maybe wait until after the classes to see what's needed," Will suggested. He liked seeing her excited about the new project. "Can you keep that warm for a few minutes? I need to get in the shower and get ready. Notley'll be here in a few minutes. We're off in a rush to Liverpool."

She looked a query at him.

"Davies made a call to a place near there. He's already a few days ahead of us, but it's a lead we need to get to as fast as we can."

Will showered quickly, and then they took their plates to the conservatory, where sunlight steamed windows still damp from the night's rain. "You'll be in Liverpool before noon," she observed.

He nodded. "After Liverpool, we'll have Carlisle, too. We're in search of Davies' mother and brother, and now we've that phone location to track down, as well. I'll be gone all day, love."

Her lips twerked in a half-smile.

Daisy raised her head and barked, a quick short woof. Will looked out the window. "Looks like Notley's here already," he moaned. He looked down at his nearly-full plate. "I think I'll make him wait while we finish here."

"That'd be awkward," Bronwyn smiled. "There's no extra for him."

"Well, it's not exactly the type of meal you can pack up and take along," Will pointed out. He pushed away from the table. "I'll just tell him he'll have to sit in the car and let me finish."

"At least invite him in."

Will shrugged. He wanted Notley as far from his personal life as possible. He forked a mouthful of bacon and egg into his mouth and stood up. "Back in a minute, love."

He met Notley at the door. He couldn't summon up enough selflessness to invite him inside, so he told him he'd be out in a few minutes. "Look Wirral up on Google maps while you're waiting," he suggested, closing the door almost in Notley's face.

He stopped by the bedroom to add a tie to his wardrobe for the day and then he took a minute to stand by the table and finish his breakfast, trying not to stuff it down in a hurry. "Don't walk to the centre today," he told Bronwyn between bites. "It's still not safe, not until Davies is behind bars."

"I'll need my car if I'm to drive to Llangollen, so I'd be taking it in any case," she told him. "I'll be safe, Will."

He nodded, and then stood and picked up his plate. He bent to kiss her. "Stay there and finish your breakfast. I'll just drop this in the kitchen on my way out." He touched her cheek with his free hand. "With luck, I'll be back here again tonight."

Notley was leaning against the Volvo's driver's door when he emerged from the house. "Lazy morning, Cooper?" He didn't seem put out by Will's closing the door on him.

Will ignored him. "Let's get going. Billy's a few days ahead of us, but we still might find him if we get there fast enough." He slid into the passenger seat and fastened his seat belt. "Turn right out of here and go through the village. I'll get the sat nav programmed."

As they pulled out onto the lane that ran past the cottage, Will told Notley more of what Quigley had said. "I've got the location in Wirral," he said. "It may be a dead end, but maybe not."

"Liverpool first, then," Notley decided. "It's often the mother who takes them in when they're in the wind so I say we find her first, and then look for where the call went." He signaled and turned left toward the village.

"But he called whoever this was right after the murder," Will argued. It made sense to him, Davies calling someone to ask for shelter after the crime. "He won't be at his mum's. He'll have gone to wherever the call went to."

"It'll be faster to find the mother. We have an exact address." Notley shot him a glare. "This case is taking more of our time than it should. It's just a simple domestic, not a big, complex case. Things must be done decently and in order." The Sherlock Holmes quote must have reminded him of his pipe because he reached into his pocket and pulled it out, tapping it against the steering wheel.

"Yeah, well, we won't know for sure it's a simple case until we find Billy Davies, will we?" Will fumed.

Notley frowned, but he fell silent. After a moment, he tapped the button to lower his window and shook the tobacco dregs out of his pipe into the wind, then replaced it in his pocket. When it became apparent that he didn't intend to smoke while driving, Will relaxed to let the miles go by without conversation. It was probably safer to let Notley have his way most of the time, in order to keep the peace between them. Of course, Will would share in the blame if it was a mistake to go to the mother's first, if they missed Billy by a hair. But what was the likelihood of that, with so much time passed since his call? With a lot of luck, they'd find hm hiding out at his mother's or at his brother's, he'd confess, and they'd put an end to the case. That would mean a return to Caernarfon and his lonely studio flat. Despite Bowers' implication that he'd be able to work from Llangynog from time to time, he knew it wasn't something he'd be doing full-time.

He watched the countryside go by. At first there was the big climb out of the Tanat Valley, with high bluffs on the one side and sweeping views on the other. He watched the clouds creating shadows that moved over the far hillside, patches of light one moment and deep shadow the next. The shadows seemed almost alive, like giant birds soaring over the landscape. Once they reached the top, the land flattened out but remained barren, miles of grassy pastureland stretching as far as he could see. Llangynog was truly remote, he thought. Why couldn't Bronwyn be from Bala or Ffestiniog or Conwy?

He regretted much of what he'd told her the night before. His family wasn't so bad when you considered the things he saw every day on the job. What did it matter if they weren't as warm and welcoming as Bronwyn's family were? They'd provided well for him, giving him security, a good education, even some holidays abroad. He shouldn't complain. He only hoped they wouldn't make Bronwyn feel inadequate when they met. That was his real fear. He thought her brilliant, and he couldn't stand them being critical because she came from a different background from theirs.

They arrived in Liverpool before 10 a.m. Notley navigated the busy motorway while Will watched the sat nav and gave him instructions. Billy Davies' mother lived in an older neighborhood in the central part of the city, but she worked at a restaurant on the docks, and they felt they had a better chance of catching her there than at home.

Will watched a colorful yellow bus pass by while Notley cruised for a parking spot. "Magical Mystery Tours," he read aloud from the side of the bus. "You ever go on one of those tours?"

Notley signaled and pulled into a space. "No interest in that," he said.

Probably not, Will thought. "You were a Sherlock Holmes fan from the start, then?"

"I liked the books," Notley said shortly. "I read them as a teenager, and they just stuck with me through the years. I still re-read them from time to time."

"And that's why you became a detective," Will concluded, ducking his head and smiling to himself.

Notley didn't bother denying it.

They got out and locked the car, looking around. "Which way?" Notley wondered.

Will consulted the sat nav. "I have no idea. It's here somewhere, so I guess we just walk around until we stumble on it."

"Hmmph," Notley snorted. "Some navigator you are, Cooper." But he didn't offer to look at the map. Instead, he followed Will as he chose to walk to the left around what appeared to be a big square full of shops, restaurants, pubs, and tourist stops.

Café at the Pier was halfway around the big square of buildings. Seagulls cawed and dove for crumbs, children dressed as pirates ran alongside the water, and a big cargo ship blasted a warning as it approached the docks. It was a busy place, even on a weekday, Will thought. He wondered if it was something Lark would enjoy.

They went into the café and approached a hostess, who offered to seat them. Will flipped out his warrant card. "Police," he said.

The woman looked closely at the card. "Major crimes? What's going on?"

"Nothing you need worry about," Will assured her. "We're looking for a Sharon Davies. I believe she works here."

The woman blinked and backed up a step, obviously apprehensive. "I'll just get her for you."

They watched her walk up to one of the waitresses, talk to her quietly, and then return with the woman following. Sharon Davies looked to be in her late fifties, with neat black hair pulled back into a ponytail and a wiry look that would come from physical exercise. She looked at them with concern in her eyes. "What can I do for you, inspectors?"

"Is there someplace we can talk privately?"

Mrs. Davies eyed them a moment longer and then tossed her head to one side. "That corner is about as private as it gets." They followed her gesture to an area behind the hostess' table. It wasn't exactly private, but if they kept their voices down, it'd probably suffice.

They stood in a small, awkward group, Mrs. Davies facing the restaurant and the two detectives with their back to it. Will suspected the hostess was straining her ears to hear the conversation, but as he couldn't see her behind his back, all he could do was to keep his voice as low as he could.

Unfortunately, Notley wasn't as careful of Mrs. Davies' privacy as Will was. "We're here looking for your son," he boomed.

Her eyes went from Notley to Will and back. "I haven't seen him in several months." The dismissal in her voice didn't match the concern on her face. "What's he supposed to have done?"

"This time it's big trouble," Notley told her, his voice still louder than Will would have liked. He tapped his cane on the floor for emphasis. "His girlfriend's been found dead on the farm near Llangynog he was letting. He's a suspect in her murder."

Her face paled. "Billy's been hard to deal with since he was a teenager, but murder is beyond what he'd do, Inspector." Her voice was steady. "You're sure it was murder, not a natural death?"

"She was shot in the head," Notley barked. "No weapon at the scene. There's no doubt it was a murder."

She considered that for a minute in silence, shrinking further back into the corner as if to hide. "He's been doing better lately," she said very quietly. "He stays on that farm now, and he's made it profitable. He got a new SUV last fall, and he paid cash for it. It's just possible she shot herself, and he found her dead, grabbed the gun, and ran, thinking you'd blame him for something he didn't do, considering his past."

"It wasn't suicide. She was murdered by someone," Notley insisted, "shot in the head and no weapon nearby or residue on her hand. If Billy didn't do it, he's made himself look guilty by running."

She stared at him. "Billy wouldn't," she murmured, but it was obvious her mind was running through the possibility and coming up with suspicion.

Will decided to risk Notley's wrath and take over. "Are you sure you haven't seen him?" He kept his voice low and reasonable. "He headed this direction when he left the farm two days ago, and home is a good place to run when you're in trouble."

"Billy would know I couldn't hide him. He wouldn't come here." But they could hear the doubt in her voice.

Will glanced around at the hostess, who was ignoring a growing line of customers. He lowered his voice even more. "Could we get inside your house, ma'am? If we could look around, we'd be sure and we'd leave you alone."

She looked past them at the hostess. "Let me see if someone can cover my shift for a bit, and I'll take you there." She focused on Will. "I have nothing to hide. If he's there, he's arrived since I've been here on the job today."

Will nodded. "Thank you. We'd appreciate your help here."

"You've driven up from Llangynog? That's a bit out of your territory, isn't it?"

"We're actually based in Caernarfon, so yes, this is far from our home turf. But sometimes you have to go where the clues lead."

They followed her from the restaurant and she gave them an address to enter into the sat nav. "I'm just parked over here," she waved toward a nearby car park, "so I'll be there before you."

Will hoped she didn't plan to warn Billy off, should he be there. They'd need to hurry to the car and get there fast. "We'll be there as quickly as we can, ma'am."

Notley had the same idea. They jog-walked back to the Volvo and pulled out as quickly as they could. Traffic was light that time of day, and in no time, they took two turns and found themselves in an older neighborhood of row houses, nicely kept, but aging. The sat nav stopped them in front of a trim little house connected to the neighboring houses on both sides. "Two up, two down," Notley observed, and Will thought it wouldn't take long to search.

He was right. Mrs. Davies had waited for them on the front stoop. She unlocked the door and waved them inside. "Look around," she invited them, "but be quick, please. I'm missing out on work to do this, and I need to get back as quick as I can."

She didn't sound worried, Will thought as he walked into a crowded but pleasant sitting room. Two inexpensive wing chairs faced off across from a beige sofa with an electric fireplace fixing the focal point between them. Bookshelves held a mix of novels and children's books interspersed with figurines, small vases, and other knickknacks. The room looked lived in, but devoid of anything suggesting a house guest had been there recently.

They went on into a small but bright kitchen, clean and neat. No used plates or glasses lay in the sink, no spills marred the surface of a wooden table. Chairs were neatly pushed in and pillows plumped on the banquet that served as seating on the window side of the table. "You live here alone?" Will asked Mrs. Davies, glancing aside at her.

"Since my husband passed," she said, "fourteen years ago, and since the boys left home, of course."

Will nodded. He followed Notley up the narrow staircase to the second story. Three doors stood open to the hallway, and they went to the first and looked in.

This one seemed to be Mrs. Davies' bedroom. A flowered duvet covered a double bed, with multiple decorative pillows plumped on top. To one side, a nightstand held a clock and a framed photo of a family: mother, father, two small boys. A dresser facing the bed showed off a small jewelry box in the center, and a book lay to its side, obviously abandoned when it had been read, but not yet filed away on a shelf. There was nothing there, and they didn't need to intrude further on the woman's personal space.

A door across the way led to a bathroom. A claw-foot tub with a shower lined the far wall, and a vanity with a mirror sat across from the toilet. Will wanted to open the medicine cabinet, but he thought he'd find nothing of interest so he quelled the impulse. Again, the room was clean with no sign of a stray razor or extra, used towels. A single toothbrush occupied the jar on the vanity.

With little hope, they looked into the remaining bedroom. There, they found a daybed with a window seat opposite, and on the daybed sat a doll, looking absurdly cheerful with blonde hair and blue eyes and a frilly dress that, upon closer inspection, featured a reindeer in bold red and green.

"My granddaughter likes to stay with me for holidays," Mrs. Davies said from behind Will's back, and he thought of Lark, with her own bedroom at the cottage that she had yet to furnish to her personal taste. They made a hasty exit, allowing Mrs. Davies to get back to her job.

"I really haven't heard from Billy in a while," she said upon parting. "I have your card, and I will call if he shows up."

They climbed back into the Volvo, Notley's straight posture conveying a desire not to be criticized for making Mrs. Davies' house a priority over Wirral. Will indulged him. It had been five days since Billy disappeared. The chances that he was at either place were slim to none.

Wirral was about a half-hour's drive away, through traffic. Will programed the coordinates Quigley had sent into the sat nav, and once they left the city behind, it directed them onto an A road through a pleasant countryside dotted with horses and occasional large old houses. Will found himself wondering what Billy's connection would be to this obviously upscale area.

Eventually, though, the road wound past the nicer homes and further into the countryside. Now sheep and cattle appeared, and the homes, although some were still substantial, were less modernized and interspersed with clusters of smaller homes obviously designed for more budget-minded buyers.

The navigation ended with them alongside a pasture dotted with black and white cows. Notley looked at Will, his eyebrows raised.

"Maybe the guy was driving when he got the call," Will suggested. He looked away across the field, where a big gray stone house loomed and gave a nod toward it. "Let's try that."

Notley pulled forward to the next driveway a quarter mile down the road and turned around. "You're sure it's not this one?" he asked, gesturing toward a white two-story house.

"No, it's definitely behind us," Will told him.

They drove onto the driveway and up to the house, where a man of about forty was busy working on the front porch with a hammer and a can of nails. The man straightened and watched them drive up, and then he walked over to the car.

"Can I help you?" he asked. He wore denims and a checked shirt, with a Liverpool United cap containing brown hair just a little too long.

Notley reached for his warrant card in his shirt pocket. "Police," he said.

The man blinked and backed up a step. He stared at them. "William Bruce," he introduced himself slowly. "What's going on?"

Will got out of the passenger side and leaned over the Volvo's front fender. "We're looking for a man called Billy Davies," he said. "We tracked a phone call he made to here."

"Here?" Bruce looked bewildered. "I don't know anyone with that name."

"May we look at your phone?" Will asked, stepping around the front of the car.

"Sure, follow me," the man said, and Will followed him to the house, where he grabbed a mobile phone from off a bench on the front stoop. "I keep it close in case someone calls." He handed it to Will.

Notley had followed them. "Do you ever use pre-paid phones?"

Bruce turned to look at him. "I don't even know how they work," he said.

Will had been scrolling on the man's mobile. He looked over at Notley and shook his head. "Are you sure you've never used a pre-paid phone? What they sometimes call a burner phone?"

Bruce shook his head. "I only use this one."

"Your wife, then?" Notley pushed him.

"She has her own phone, and the kids don't have their own yet. They play on ours sometimes, mainly my wife's. Would that mean anything to you?"

Will handed him back the phone. "No, this was definitely a pre-paid phone, not a mobile like you have that uses a monthly plan."

The man studied them for a moment, thinking, and then he said, "Maybe it's Peter's."

They both looked at him. "Who's Peter?" Will asked.

Bruce shrugged. "Peter O'Connell. He rents an old cottage from me up behind the house a bit. It was the original farmhouse here, but they abandoned it and built this one in the early 1920s. It was pretty run-down, but he offered me a hundred quid a month for it, and you can't say no to easy money, can you?"

"Where is it exactly?" Will felt a thrill of anticipation run through him. This was it, what they'd been looking for, he was sure of it.

Bruce waved toward the back of the house. "You can follow that track behind the house. It winds along about a half-mile, and then you'll see it just ahead. There are a few outbuildings that we don't use and the old house. He's fixed it up a bit, that was part of the deal, but you'll see it's still barely habitable."

"Have you seen a black Ford Kuga come past in the last few days, maybe pulling a stock trailer?"

"Not that I've noticed, but I have a job so I'm gone most days. It could have been by while I was out." He squinted at them. "What's he supposed to have done?"

"We really can't say at this point," Will told him. "We're looking for Billy Davies in connection with a case we're working, and he made a call to a phone in this general area. It sounds like it may have been your renter."

Bruce nodded, to himself. "That Kuga has been here before, a couple of months ago. I hope Peter isn't involved in anything criminal."

"We hope not, too, sir," Will responded automatically, but truthfully, it'd help get the case solved quickly if he was.

They thanked William Bruce and got back into the Volvo. The lane was rutted and lined with puddles and weeds, but they could see that enough vehicles had been down it recently to keep it passable.

"It'd be a trick pulling that trailer down this road," Notley echoed Will's thoughts. He grabbed at the steering wheel as it jerked through a ditch.

"But not impossible. I wonder what this Peter O'Connell was doing with the sheep? He doesn't own the farm so he probably wouldn't be in the market for them."

"The plot thickens," Notley observed, and Will cringed in response.

They found the little cottage nestled beside an old lilac bush that was just coming into bloom. Despite its cheerful lavender color, the lilac did little to dispel the gloom of the cottage itself, with its discolored old stone, a pitted and scratched wooden door, and windows in need of a thorough cleaning. Outbuildings, also built of stone, scattered the area near the house, and an older model Saab sedan sat parked in front of the cottage.

They got out of the car and walked up to the door. Will pounded on it, and they waited. Will pounded on it again and called out, "Police. Please open up." Still, nothing.

Will turned to Notley. "What do you want to do?"

Notley nodded toward a window. "Look inside." He brushed past Will to squint through the dirty window. "I don't see any movement."

"The car's here," Will pointed out. "He's got to be somewhere around." He walked to the corner of the cottage and looked around behind it. Something caught his eye. "Come here, Sean. I think the stock trailer is back here."

Notley followed him as he moved cautiously alongside the cottage, watching the stock trailer emerge into view as he caught sight of more of the area behind the cottage. Suddenly, none of this felt right. It reminded him of his old days, working undercover in drugs, and he wondered if he was being watched. He felt eyes on him, just an instinct, but it had served him well in the past. He drew back. "Something's wrong here, Sean."

95

Notley stared at him and drew back tighter against the cottage. "You think he's here."

Will breathed out for a minute in silence. "If he is, he's got a pistol, and he's desperate. He won't just let us take him." He studied the outbuildings. "There are lots of places he could hide. Behind or inside those buildings. He could be watching us."

"The Kuga isn't here," Notley pointed out, but Will could see he was scared.

Hell, so was he. He knew something was wrong, and he still felt eyes on him. "What do you want to do?"

"I think the cottage is one room. That's all I could see. He's not in there."

Will eyed the open space between the outbuildings. They'd be sitting ducks if they tried to go building to building to search. "Let's call for backup."

Notley couldn't get it out fast enough. "Yes, that's a good idea." His Sherlock Holmes quotes seemed to have deserted him.

Will pulled his mobile from his pocket and called Bowers. "Sir," he said when the call was routed through to his boss, "we have a situation that we think requires some backup help." He explained. "We feel like Billy Davies might still be here. Maybe with Peter O'Connell. The thing is, we know Davies had a gun when he left the farm in Llangynog, and we feel a bit like sitting ducks here, if we try to look in the outbuildings. What do you want us to do?"

Bowers understood. Maybe he heard the fear in Will's voice. He'd tried not to let it show, but he felt it, a panic rising the longer they stood there. He still felt eyes on him.

"I'll call the station in Liverpool. You two stay where you are until they get there to help you out. Don't go back to the car. Don't walk around. Just stay there. If something develops before help arrives, I know you can handle it. Use your best judgement. Stay together."

They waited, leaning against the stone cottage as close as they could get. No one had shot at them so far, so maybe they had cover there. Or maybe when backup started arriving, Davies would panic and the shooting would start. They had no way to know. If he thought they could get away with it, Will would try to get back into the Volvo and drive away, to make it look like they'd found nothing suspicious and were leaving. But he still felt someone watching him, so if that was true, whoever it was would know he'd made a call. He'd know the two of them were staying where they had some protection. He'd know the gig was up.

The outbuildings, there were three of them, littered the area behind the house, about ten to twenty yards from the cottage. One was small, no more than a shed for storing a lawnmower or garden tools, not that anyone had used such implements there in a long time. The other two were larger, and Will thought they'd formerly served as small barns. A man could hide in one of those and peek through the cracks, and they'd never know it. He wondered if the buildings had back exits, a window or broken boards where Davies could get out and run up the hillside behind it. They'd not see it if he did unless he made noise.

Will tried to listen, but all he heard were rooks cawing in the trees. After what felt like hours, but his phone told him was eighteen minutes, a caravan of black SUVs with flashing blue and red lights came trundling up the lane. When they stopped in front of the old bungalow, men poured from them, dressed in protective gear and carrying weapons.

Will and Notley gathered their courage and emerged from the corner of the cottage, hands in the air. A tall man with a black mustache and clipped black hair beckoned them over, and they ran across to him, ducking behind the closest vehicle.

"Rees Montgomery," he introduced himself. "I've been filled in. You stay here, and we'll clear the site."

Will nodded, and he stood with Notley behind the vehicle while six men ran toward the cottage. One of them kicked the door in, and two of them disappeared inside. The others edged along the wall toward the back of the cottage, guns held ready.

"Very proficient," Notley mumbled. He looked relieved.

"Yes, this is their job," Will said. "They'll have it sorted soon enough." He hoped they'd find something, He really didn't want to look the fool, calling in the calvary for nothing.

The small building was closest. Again, they kicked the door in and peered inside, apparently seeing nothing because they quickly moved on to the nearer barn-like building. Now they paused, seeming confused, or stalled. "Big lock here," one of them called back to Rees Montgomery.

He gestured at them to wait. He looked at Will. "I don't suppose you got a key?"

Will shook his head.

Montgomery grinned. "We can cut through it." He waved at one of the men who remained by the vehicles, and he ran across with a tool, a bolt-cutter, Will assumed.

They watched as the man cut through the lock. It took him a long minute or two, but finally the lock fell apart and one of the men pulled it from the hasp it had secured and opened the door. He stepped back almost immediately. "Got a body here, sir."

"Check the last one, and then we'll have a look," Montgomery called to him, and some of the men moved on. The last building was unlocked like the first. It took only seconds for the men to clear it, and then Montgomery glanced at Will and Notley. "It looks like we're clear to go in. Let's see what they've found."

His fear dispelled, Will walked on steadier legs toward the barn. He could smell it now, decaying flesh. He wondered if Billy had done for himself, or if his friend Peter O'Connell had taken matters into his own hands and shot Billy.

Neither was right. The body in the outbuilding, lying in a pool of dried blood on the dirt floor, was not Billy Davies. Will supposed it must be Peter O'Connell. They'd get an identification fast from William Bruce, and Billy would now be on the hook for two murders.

But Billy was gone, fled again into the camouflage of civilization, gone who knew where?

Chapter Seven

Bronwyn was disappointed.

Will had been kept in Liverpool overnight. First, they'd had to examine the crime scene in Wirral thoroughly with the team of crime technicians, followed by a more formal interview with the owner of the property. Once all that was completed, he'd had to be interviewed himself back at the station in Liverpool with the local police force, afterward filling out reams of paperwork to make sure every detail was documented and supported by Notley's own portrayal of the facts. He hadn't finished until well after midnight, so other than a short call from the crime scene to tell her he'd be tied up, she hadn't heard from him until morning.

He'd called at eight as she was finishing her toast and jam. They'd already been to notify Peter O'Connell's parents of his death, and he'd been on his way to the autopsy lab for detailed information about how O'Connell had died when he called. "The coroner's saying he was killed around Saturday noon," Will had told her. "It looks like Billy was in a rage about something."

"Maybe Peter and Catherine were having an affair?" Bronwyn suggested.

"If that was the case, they should have hidden it better," Will said. "I'm not convinced, though. I've been trying to tell Notley that this doesn't prove Billy's guilty, to get him to consider other alternatives, but he isn't having it. Once he gets his mind set on something, there's no changing it."

"I wish you'd found him hiding out behind one of the buildings. That'd make me feel better about it." He'd told her about the feeling of being watched, that it persisted after they'd found the body. "You'll be careful, Will?"

"Don't worry, love," he'd reassured her, "I got lots of experience at being invisible when I was working drugs and alcohol down in Cardiff. I'm safe enough."

"Will you be home tonight?" she ventured, crossing the fingers on her left hand.

"No, sorry, not tonight." Will dashed her hopes. Once they finished in the autopsy lab that morning, he and Notley were instructed to head back to Caernarfon, where more paperwork awaited them. "With no leads on Billy Davies, there's no excuse for us to stay in the area," he explained. "But I should be able to come back on Saturday night unless there's a development in the case that prevents it. If we don't find Billy or more bodies, there'll be nothing to keep me in Caernarfon, and Bowers would probably like me closer here anyway, just in case Billy shows up at the farm or the local pub."

With that promise to keep her going, she'd ended the call and gone off to work. That Friday called for her to be at the centre until late hours, with two groups booked back-to-back in the conference room. The second group had booked in for the Saturday, as well, staying over at the New Inn's B&B, and every indication was that they would use every minute of the second day, since they'd originally wanted the entire day Friday and Saturday, but had settled for less after some fast talking by Bronwyn. It was probably just as well that Will wouldn't be back until late Saturday night. She'd have had no time to spend with him anyway.

She drove to work, trying to relax into the drive. The little lane remained muddy, dotted with ruts and puddles with weeds flourishing in the center between them, but tiny bluebells bloomed in the tangle of the hedgerows lining the roadway, and that cheered her. The sky overhead threatened more rain, but she thought it would hold off until afternoon.

That thought led to the St. Melangell's Day celebration. Please God it would be dry on that day for them. No one wanted to do a road race or set up an outdoor market in the rain.

She startled as a flock of young pheasants burst from nearly beneath her front tyres and scurried up the road in front of her car. She slowed until the hedgerows broke and allowed them to flop off into a pasture dotted with sheep. She shook her head. The hoard of pheasants always made her smile, silly things. When they found themselves trapped on the road in front of a vehicle, they never seemed to realize they could fly.

Just after noon, Will's little MGF zipped into the car park beside the centre, and he got out. She saw him from the window of the conference room and hurried into the little kitchen to deposit an armful of dirty dishes left from the morning group. The afternoon group hadn't yet arrived, but she had to rush to clean up the morning mess before they turned up. "You go." She turned to see Janice over her shoulder. "I'll finish this up for you."

Thankful, Bronwyn called to Daisy, pulled on a cardigan she'd left on a hook by the door, and emerged from the building just as Will reached for the door knob. He grinned and held up a bag. "I've brought lunch."

"Do you have the time?"

"Notley dropped me by to get my car. He's on his way back to Caernarfon, but I drive faster than he does and I know the shortcuts, so I figure I can spend a half hour with you and still be back near to when he gets there."

She smiled back. "Are you okay with a picnic?"

He glanced up at the threatening sky. "Sure, that'd be better than squeezing into that tiny office of yours."

"Then let's go into the sensory garden," she suggested. "That way I can keep an eye out for the next group while we eat. If it starts to rain, we'll have to duck into the church."

"Wherever you are, I am happy to be with you." He seemed cheerful, but she sensed it was a bit forced. It couldn't be easy finding two bodies in the same number of days, and she hoped he was as disappointed as she was that he'd been called back to Caernarfon for the next two days.

They walked into the little garden and settled on a cement bench that was only slightly damp beneath their trousers. "I should have brought a rug," she lamented. "I can go get one."

He reached out and touched her hand. "No, it'll be okay. I can't stay that long, and it's not really that wet. Don't waste the time." He shuffled his feet a little, though, and she could see the mud along the edges of his brogues. He opened the carrier bag and pulled out a wrapped sandwich, peering at it. "I think this is yours. Roasted vegetables with cream cheese, it is."

"Yum."

"And for me, a ham griller with fig jam and cheese."

"That sounds good, too," she admitted.

"You ever think about giving it up?" He handed her a packet of crisps.

"Being a vegetarian?" She pondered the thought as she unwrapped her sandwich. She'd been eating vegetarian for a year now, with the exception of fish when it was available and sounded good. She supposed that made her a pescatarian. She still ate dairy and eggs, things like that, but she just didn't like the idea that an animal had to die for her daily meal. It didn't seem right, and if St. Melangell had protected the creatures as well as women, then she felt she was meant to follow in her footsteps as much as her conscience would allow her to. "No, I think I'm pretty committed." Someday she'd explain it to him, but she wasn't secure enough yet in their relationship to tell him that she was trying to continue the role of an ancient holy saint in the modern world.

A patter of rain hit the top of her head as she bit into her sandwich. She looked over at Will, who was shaking his head. "Couldn't it hold off for a few more minutes?"

"We'd might as well go inside," she said. The dark clouds swirling overhead portended wind, as well as a soaking rain. It would turn into a squall any minute.

They gathered up their lunch quickly, but as they approached the lych gate, the skies let loose in a torrent. Rain pounded the ground around them, mixing with hail and drenching them in an instant.

They ran for the lych gate. "It's sheltered here," Bronwyn huffed with a shy grin, "and we can enjoy the storm and watch for my group to arrive. It might be better than trying to dash through the rain to better shelter."

"I'm game if you are," Will told her, and he took off his light jacket and spread it on one of the benches that faced each other under the shelter of the stone arch.

They ate their impromptu picnic happily then, Daisy sitting in front of them begging for bites and the rain pounding down around them. A smell of wet grass, stone, and mud attracted even Will's notice, and the humidity brought a fresh dampness to their faces. Neither complained of the cold, although the rain had brought a chill to the spring air. *This will be a memory,* Bronwyn thought. *Something to cherish.*

Will told her about finding Peter O'Connell's body and then, hesitatingly, about their interview with Catherine Baines' parents, a topic he'd avoided the previous evening, obviously wanting to put it to the back of his mind when the discomfort it brought was so fresh.

"I wish I had something to tell you," she said when he'd expelled everything that was on his mind.

"It's not important," he said, dampening her spirits a little. She liked to think herself helpful with the clues she gave him, after all. He saw her downtrodden look. "Well," he amended, "it is important because usually it's what solves a case for us. But I've told you, if you come up empty sometimes, it's okay. Not all our cases can be that easily figured out. Sometimes, I have to work harder at it."

The rain had lessened to a light drizzle by the time they finished eating, with the promise of a rainbow in a sun-lit spot between the clouds. They gathered up the remnants of their picnic, and she walked with him to his car. "I stayed rather longer than I meant to," he told her, leaning down for a kiss. "I'll call you tonight."

The rest of the day flew by in a blur. The group of school psychologists who'd booked for that afternoon and the next morning proved to be a needy group, with lots of requests for extra pens and paper and, at one point, for a re-set of the computer system which the rain had somehow knocked offline. Bronwyn was kept running in and out of her office, and by the time they left at five o'clock, she was exhausted and looking forward to a quiet evening by herself.

But that was not to be. Her mother called just as she was locking her office, inviting her to an impromptu dinner. "You never make the Monday night dinners anymore," she scolded Bronwyn, "so I decided a Friday night would be just as good."

"Isn't Mai working?" Bronwyn's sister-in-law was a part-time server at the Tanat Inn, and weekend nights were their busy times.

"She's got a cold, as it happens, so Cecil told her to take the night off. They'll manage without her, and he doesn't want her giving her germs to all his paying customers."

"So…just to us," Bronwyn mentioned.

"I'll seat her at the far end of the table," her mother countered. "You'll come? You and Daisy? Or is Will here, too?"

"Just Daisy and I," Bronwyn said, and she smiled to herself. Despite her exhaustion, and she had to admit that extra nights with Will at the cottage were as much as cause of that as the busy day had been, she looked forward to her mother's homey cooking and a visit with her family, who might tease or push her for information about her relationship with Will, but who did it because they loved her, and she knew it.

She stopped at the cottage long enough to change into her jeans and a tee shirt, threw a jersey over her shoulders, and loaded Daisy back into the Land Rover. Daisy had watched her with some anxiety, not wanting to be left behind, so she grinned as she leapt into the back seat and hung her head out the opened window. Daisy didn't care where they were going, just that an adventure of some sort waited at the end of it.

Bronwyn let herself into the house through the back door, emerging into the kitchen and finding her mother busy at the Aga, basting a tray of roasting vegetables with olive oil. "Yum, smells good," Bronwyn said, tossing her jersey over a chair back. "Can I help?"

"I'm roasting a salmon filet," her mother said. "You can get it ready to go in after the vegetables are ready to come out. Maddock and the family will be here any minute, and your dad's on his way in from the barn."

She heard her dad's steps at the back entry. She opened the wrapped salmon and put it into a glass dish, then microwaved butter to season and pour over the top. When she'd finished, her mother took the dish from her and her dad came in, boots and work jacket removed.

"How are the sheep?" she asked him, throwing him a smile.

"Doing well," he answered, peeking at the vegetables over her mother's shoulder. "We're getting more cattle this year, as well. Maddock says we have to diversify if we're going to prosper."

"Well, it's important to prosper," she said. She exchanged a look with him, and grinned.

They heard the front door opening, and a patter of footsteps announced the younger generation's arrival. Bronwyn's nephew Griffyn and niece Maegan ran into the kitchen, chasing each other. "Can we play with Daisy?" they wanted to know.

"Say hello to everyone first," their mother Mai reminded them, and they dutifully repeated her greeting.

"I hear Will's been spending extra nights with you here," Maddock observed when they were all seated and had loaded plates with food.

Bronwyn glanced at her dad, who was studiously examining the vegetable bowl. She still wasn't sure how her parents felt about her living with Will in the cottage, but on the surface, they seemed to have accepted her right as an adult to choose. "Are you keeping an eye on me?"

"It's a small village, Bron. Everybody knows what goes on here."

She wanted to ignore him, but couldn't see how. "As long as Catherine Baines' case stays local, Bowers likes that Will has a place to stay in the area. It saves money when the department doesn't have to pay for lodging." She looked over at Maddock. "It actually looks like it might happen more often. Bowers is saying he'd like Will to be available to take cases that come up when he's on this side of the district. It'd make a faster response that way. If that happens, he'll be more or less based here while he works the local cases. He'll have to go back to Caernarfon for paperwork and so on, but he'd have more time here than he does now." She treated herself to a bite of sweet potato from the roasted vegetables.

"It sounds like things are working out for you two," her mother said, giving her a small smile.

"We're happy," Bronwyn told her, a little defensively. It was time to change the subject. She turned to her dad. "Did you get Billy Davies' sheep all rounded up?"

"I think so," he answered, with a little shake of his head. "I'm hearing on the grapevine that stray, unmarked sheep are showing up all the way between here and Wrexham, and we're wondering if those might be his, as well. Do you know if he had pasture leased further in that direction?"

"I don't know, but I'll ask Will. They look like his?"

"Same kind of sheep, and most of us mark ours for identification, so it's a good guess they're his."

Maddock broke into the conversation then. "I have news, Bron, that you don't know yet. It's something you'd never guess. I'm going to university starting this summer."

She stared at him. "What are you talking about? Isn't the farm giving you a good enough income?"

"It's fine. No worries. But I've been thinking about it for a while, and I want to give organic farming a try, not that we're not already basically organic, for the most part. But if I get a degree, we'd be able to advertise as such, and the fancier restaurants in the area would carry our meats, at least, and maybe some vegetables, as well. Mum and Mai are willing to take on a bigger garden, and if it's successful, they may quit their other jobs sometime down the road. What do you think? Good idea?"

"I think it's brilliant." She did. It'd catapult them right into the modern world.

That night she tossed and turned as a flood of thoughts tumbled through her mind. She had nights like this, nights where, for no apparent reason, her brain wouldn't shut down. Maddock's news was at the forefront. She loved the ideas he had, and it was a good bet that none of it would have happened had he not taken on much of the work as their father aged. She was proud of him.

Will also occupied her mind. She missed him when he wasn't at the cottage with her, and she'd have liked a more thorough update on his case. He'd sounded as tired as she was when he'd called, having spent much of the day in Liverpool, and then making the long drive back to Caernarfon, only to have more paperwork and a meeting awaiting him. No matter what Bowers suggested, he would always be officially based in Caernarfon, and he'd have to spend time in the office there even if most of his assigned cases were on her side of the district. He might get tired of the commute after a year or two, and then what?

She banished that worry and turned her thoughts to the Twlwyth Teg. She wondered if she'd get a clue to help him along this time. She didn't see as much of the Twlwyth Teg these days, and she didn't know if it was because of Will or because of her moving to the cottage or because the world, their world, was changing despite her efforts to keep Pennant Melangell as natural and spiritual a place as it had always been. She thought about it sometimes, but in the end, she couldn't change what was. There was no profit to worrying over it.

Her Saturday proved as exhausting as the Friday had been. She'd been able to anticipate some of the group's needs, but they still kept her dashing back and forth with requests. Whoever had planned this conference hadn't done much of a job, in her opinion. Between times, she entered information from registrations for the pilgrim's walk and the mountain bike ride into her computer, made a list of jobs for the volunteers, and she escaped for a few minutes here and there to brave the rain with Daisy, umbrella in her hands.

The rain had poured down all day long, but the sky looked lighter as she locked the centre and left right behind the van carrying the group of school psychologists home to Welshpool. She hadn't offered them a session of nature meditation, and she felt a little guilty about it. Surely, in their careers, they'd have occasion to employ her techniques with children who needed a way to engage their senses in something other than trouble at home or school. In the end, she made a makeshift flyer,

"Coming soon! Forest bathing!" on her computer, printed out a copy, and handed it to the leader as they left. "Maybe this'll be something you'd like to try in the future with your group," she'd told him. He'd just looked at her and stuffed it into his bag.

She'd gotten up early and cleaned the cottage for Will's hoped-for arrival that evening, and once she'd left the centre she turned away from her lane and headed for Llanfyllin to do some shopping before she went home. She liked to stock up on the evenings he was expected so she'd have something to prepare for their meals, as well as other things they were short on like toilet paper and dish soap. She spent some time choosing lettuce, cucumber, tomato, apples, and strawberries, and then two steaks, bacon, sausages, and a pork chop, as well as scampi and salmon for herself. She stopped by an off-license afterwards to get another bottle of Famous Grouse, and picked up two bottles of red wine, one an Australian shiraz and the other a Malbec from Argentina. She'd developed a fondness for the Malbec and tried to have at least one bottle on hand.

It was dusk by the time she arrived back at Llangynog, near to seven-thirty. She expected Will between seven and seven-thirty most nights when he came back from Caernarfon, but he'd called to say he'd been held up at the office at the last minute and then again from the road to say there'd been a lorry accident that had the road blocked, so it would be late when he got to her this time. She'd have to make him another cheese and bread supper or a sandwich that he could eat while they relaxed with a drink; it would be too late to make a real meal.

She got out of the Land Rover and opened the back door to let Daisy out. Her carrier bags occupied the other half of the back seat, so she walked around to that side and opened the door. She looped the two bags of groceries over her arm, hung her purse there, too, and grabbed the bottle of Famous Grouse. She'd have to come back for the wine.

She unlocked the cottage door and went through to the kitchen, flicking on the light and putting the carrier bags on the counter. Then she turned to go back for the wine and froze.

A man stood between her and the door in the dark room, watching her with curious eyes. He smiled at her, an easy smile that didn't dispel her panic. "You must be the young lady who keeps Will here in the north."

She couldn't think how to answer that, so she said nothing. She watched the man, wishing with all her heart that Will would arrive early, but knowing he wouldn't be there soon enough.

The man stayed by the door, a distance away from her but blocking any thought of exit. Behind him, Daisy peeked through the still-open door and then sat on the porch, watching them.

Some watch dog, Bronwyn thought.

"Can we close the door?" the man asked then. She could see him in the light from the kitchen. He was nearly as tall as Will, but wiry and rough looking with long, disarranged and curly light hair, an earring in his left ear, and a prominent tattoo of a bird, maybe a hawk, on his forearm. He wore faded jeans and a flannel shirt with the sleeves rolled up, and his trainers were mud-splattered and tattered on one edge. She could smell him from across the room, a feral scent that alarmed her more than his appearance.

"Who are you?" she managed. She wanted to ask him more, what he wanted and why he knew Will's name, but she couldn't seem to get the words out. She was terrified, frozen with terror, she thought incongruously, and smothered a nervous giggle. She didn't want him to close the door, shutting her inside.

"I'm Edward," he said. "Will's old partner, Edward Smythe." He turned back, called to Daisy, patting his knee and urging her inside, and then quietly shut the door and fixed the lock.

She stood where she was, still frozen with fear. Will had talked about Edward sometimes. The name was familiar, at least.

"Who might you be?" Edward asked, his eyes amused, but wary.

"I'm Bronwyn."

"You live here with Will?"

"I…" she didn't know what to say. What if he wasn't who he said he was? What if he was dangerous to Will, or to her?

After a long moment, he glanced around. "Listen, I need you to go into the kitchen and put your groceries away. It's important that things look normal here, in case I was followed." He glanced at the lamp on the table. "I'm going to keep that off, and when you finish, if you could turn the light in the kitchen off, as well?"

She nodded. Keeping an eye on him from the corner of her vision, she went back into the kitchen and put things away. Meat in the fridge, vegetables in the crisper drawer, fruit divided between a bowl on the counter and the fridge. She left the Famous Grouse on the counter.

The back door was just a few feet away. Could she get it unlocked and opened fast enough to escape out the back and run? She glanced toward the sitting room. He was sitting on the sofa, petting Daisy who was lounging in front of him, looking up into his face. If she could get out, what would she do? The Land Rover was out of the question. It'd take too long to get inside, and her keys were in her bag on the hook near the front door. Graeme and Maeve might be home. If she screamed, would they hear and come to help? A fence separated their cottage from hers, and the other side was blocked by a thorny hedgerow. Behind the cottage and past the small garden area, the slope descended to a ditch with brackish water this time of year, and on the other side an open pasture would be difficult to run across. But she had to do something.

She edged closer to the door and then flashed over to it, grappling with the lock as her heart hammered in her chest.

"You don't want to do that, love." His hand closer over hers, pulling it away from the door knob. He'd come fast into the kitchen on silent feet.

She jerked away from him quickly, and he didn't stop her. They stared at each other in silence.

"Let's go into the sitting room...Bronwyn, is it?" He spread his arms wide, hands open. "I'm no danger to you, I promise. I just need to talk to Will."

She nodded and made herself brush past him to go into the sitting room. She sat on the sofa and patted the cushion beside her, inviting Daisy to fill the empty space. The last thing she wanted was him sitting that close to her. She could still smell him from where he'd sat earlier.

He'd switched off the main light in the kitchen, but turned on the pale light on the stove, so the room wasn't entirely dark. Now he gave her a wry grin and pulled the chair across from her closer to face her. "Look, I know you don't know who I am," he said, "and I don't blame you for being scared of me." He looked down at himself. "I mean, face it, I'm obviously an unsavory character. Will was, too, at one time. It's the nature of the job." He studied her, assessing her with eyes that she thought missed nothing. "This isn't the way I wanted it to go, meeting you."

She watched him. "Are you really Edward?"

He grinned again, and now she could see a bit of charm in it. "I'm really Edward, Will's old partner and probably his best mate still." And then his eyes lit up. "You're the one Will got suspended for last year!"

She could feel a blush crawling up her cheeks, but in the dim light, she hoped he wouldn't notice. "That was all a misunderstanding. He solved the case."

"I know, with your help, from what I heard." He was quiet for a moment. "Things are starting to make more sense now."

"Can I call Will?" She was beginning to accept that he was who he said he was, but she wasn't ready to welcome him with open arms, not yet. If she could ask Will about him, she'd feel a lot better.

But he frowned, considering her request. "Would you usually call him this time of day?"

"Sometimes," she hedged.

"He's on his way here?"

She swallowed. "Yes."

"Then let's just wait. I don't want to set off any alarms with a phone call." He glanced toward the windows, taking a long moment to look through each one from where he sat. "This is your place, then," he surmised. "I thought Will was still living in Caernarfon, so when he came here, I thought he was working undercover again, maybe."

"Will and I share this cottage. He commutes to Caernarfon when he has to be in the office or when he's on a case there or in court, but he stays here when he can. How did you find it?" She'd offered more information than she'd intended, but she was curious. Not even most of Will's colleagues knew about this cottage, as far as she knew, and his official residence was still the flat in Caernarfon.

"I followed him a few days ago, after they found Catherine Baines. He was in another vehicle, with his partner, I assumed, and then he was dropped by here. His car was here, and he went inside without knocking, like he lived here."

"Why didn't you talk to him then?"

"I thought he'd be working that case as a murder, maybe a domestic since Billy was missing, but after I saw him again in Wirral, I thought he must be onto the drug operation."

She thought about it while he studied her in silence. "Are you working undercover?"

"Yes."

So that's why he was nervous about being seen. "On the murder case Will's working? Billy Davies?"

Now it was his turn to hedge. "That's the common thread, but the case I'm working is different."

"Then why come to Will?"

Edward took a quick breath. "I'm in trouble, and I need his help. I really can't say more than that. I don't know who the enemy is. The only person I trust is Will."

"Don't you have another partner?"

"I do. I did, anyway. But she's disappeared, and I don't know where she is."

Bronwyn thought about that. "Don't your superiors know where she is?"

Edward clamped his mouth shut. He glanced again at the windows. "When do you expect Will?"

If his superiors didn't know where his partner was, what did that mean? "I think he'll be here soon. He was delayed at the office and then again by an accident on the motorway." It had grown quite dark by that time, and Bronwyn guessed that it was well after eight, maybe close to nine. "You made plans with Will for New Year's Eve, didn't you?" She remembered now that Will had mentioned it. Had her surprising him in Caernarfon interrupted his plans with this man?

"I mentioned that he should come to Cardiff, celebrate with his old friends from the squad there, but he said he had other plans, and I assumed that meant a girl. He didn't deny it. I'm guessing, then, that he was here with you?"

"We were together in Caernarfon. We didn't have this cottage yet."

A swirl of headlamps announced Will's imminent arrival. Edward looked up, taking charge. "Meet him at the door. You can tell him I'm here, but be subtle. Don't shout it out. Just act like you usually do until you get him inside."

She nodded. Something had him on edge, that was for sure. She stood up and walked to the door, her legs steadier than they'd been earlier. She still felt uneasy, though. If this wasn't really Edward, if it was someone else, then Will might be walking into a dangerous situation. It might be better if she went out as the man instructed and then yelled a warning to Will. Unless he had a gun, they could probably escape to the road, at least, and maybe find someplace to hide. They knew the neighborhood better than he did, and if they could make it to the trailhead, Bronwyn knew several places they could conceal themselves until he'd given up finding them. On the other hand, though, he'd trusted her enough to let her go out and meet Will. If she took a few moments to retrieve the wine still waiting in the back seat of the Land Rover, she could give Will a better idea of the situation and let him decide what to do.

She turned back to him. "I left some wine in the Land Rover. Is it okay if I get it when I go out?"

"Yes, but get moving. Will's going to be inside the door before you get out."

She opened the door and stepped out, letting Daisy out. The dog ran to Will, running circles around him happily, and he stopped to greet her, setting his kit bag on the ground and squatting down to ruffle her ears. Then he caught sight of Bronwyn and smiled. "Why's the house dark? I thought you weren't home yet."

She reached out for him and raised her face for a kiss. "Someone's here, Will," she whispered into his mouth. "He says he's your friend Edward, but I'm not sure."

He hugged her close and then kissed her again, longer and more insistently. "What's this strange man look like?" he murmured into her lips.

She looked up into his face and saw the worry in his eyes. "He's about your height, thin, with curly light hair that's all over the place."

Will's shoulders relaxed. "That sounds right." He kissed her again, quickly, and then stooped to pick up his bag. "Let's go inside and find out what's going on."

Chapter Eight

Will pushed Bronwyn behind to follow him into the cottage, just in case. The man she'd described, however briefly, sounded like Edward, but he'd learned in his previous life with drugs and alcohol in Cardiff never to take something as a sure thing until it was proven to be. If this man wasn't Edward, then that meant trouble. Walking into a dark cottage to meet him was a stupid thing to do, but he supposed he'd done stupider.

"Edward?" he called out softly as he edged his way in, squinting to see in the dark. If it truly was Edward and he'd made Bronwyn sit with him in the dark, then Edward was wary of bringing danger to himself and, by default, them. Will would not want to call attention to their uninvited guest until he knew what was going on.

"It's me," the voice came from the sitting area, and Will turned his head to see a familiar shape in the dark.

"What are you doing here, in the dark?" He strode across the room and embraced Edward, who'd stood up to meet him. Relief flooded him, making his legs feel weak. "If you wanted a visit, you could have called ahead."

Edward laughed quietly. "Not this time, I couldn't." He turned serious then. "I'm in trouble, Will, and I think poor Bronwyn here thought I had come to murder her, or you, or torture you for information or something." He tossed her a glance, squinting in the dark. "I'm really

115

sorry about that, love. I'm sorry about sitting in the dark, but I'm never sure when they'll catch up with me."

Will saw the glance and understood it. Whatever it was that had Edward spooked, he wasn't sure it could be shared with Bronwyn. *It's my own fault,* he told himself. *If I'd made a point of introducing them before, or even if I'd talked to Edward more about her, this would be going down differently.* For one thing, he wouldn't have scared her half to death when he'd shown up. "I'll just pour us a small dram and then we'll talk," he suggested. Pouring the whisky would give him a minute to think, not so much about what Edward's problem might be, but whether he wanted Bronwyn involved. "Okay if I turn on the hallway light so it's not quite so dark in here?"

Edward nodded and sat back down in the chair.

A couple of minutes later, he handed Edward his drink and sat down beside Bronwyn on the sofa. Whatever had Edward worried, Bronwyn might come up with something to help, especially if it turned out to be complicated. He shouldn't be involved, himself, after having been not only transferred away from Cardiff, but also warned off the current drugs operation. But if Edward needed him, he knew he'd risk it all to help if it was as serious as Edward was making it out to be. "Tell me what's going on."

Edward took a sip of his whisky. "You always had good taste," he commented. Then he took a breath. "It's to do with the massive number of drugs coming in right now. Fentanyl, opioids, meth…they're flooding in and no one seems able to stop them. I'm involved over my head, I think, and I don't know what to do, whether to try to figure out what's going on or whether to just try to run and wait it out somewhere."

"I can't be a part of any drugs operation," Will warned him. "I've been warned off as recently as a week ago."

Edward gazed at him. "It's too late. You're already involved. I thought you knew."

Davies' Ford Kuga. He'd told Bowers they needed to look for inconsistencies, and the price of that SUV had nagged at him, but he'd pushed the thought away, wanting to think it a simple domestic, like Notley did. Then there was Peter O'Connell. Sure, they could explain it away as an affair gone badly wrong, with Billy killing the two of them

116

over it. But he knew better than to settle on the easy explanation, even if that was the one Notley was pushing. If he added it all up – the deaths, the obvious easy money, Davies' lack of farming expertise – it spelled drugs. "Billy Davies," he muttered finally.

Edward had been watching him think it through. "You really didn't have any suspicions?" His eyes flicked to Bronwyn again and back quickly.

Will caught it. "Bronwyn's not going anywhere," he said, taking her hand and squeezing it. "If you're going to tell me about it, you can tell her. We have no secrets."

"I've heard she helps you with cases, but I didn't know things were this serious." He grinned at them. "Just when were you going to tell me about this?"

Will ignored him. "Not now, Edward. It looks like we have more important things to talk about"

The grin left Edward's face. "How much do you know?"

Will thought. "We were called here because Catherine Baines had been shot and Billy Davies was in the wind. He'd leased that farm for a couple of years, but now that I think about it, the neighbors thought his farming methods a little suspect. Still, it wasn't unreasonable to think he'd managed to save a bit if the rent was low enough on the place."

"You tracked the Kuga?"

"Yeah, it wasn't hard to find on the cameras, pulling a stock trailer, but we lost track of it after Wrexham. By that time, we'd been given permission to access Catherine Baines' phone records, and there were two calls we thought Billy had made to a pre-paid mobile. We tracked the mobile to Wirral, and that's where we found Peter O'Connell."

"That's not bad police work, but you were a little late."

"We didn't find Catherine until Tuesday, three days after she was murdered. We were way behind Billy at that point, but we gave it a shot, thought he might be hiding out there with his mum or a friend."

"Scared you, finding the place deserted, didn't it?"

Will frowned. "That was you? I felt someone watching us. I thought it was Billy. And we knew he had a gun."

"Billy's gone, probably dead by now. They loaded the stuff from the stock trailer into a couple of SUVs, including that Kuga, and Billy had a companion in the car when they left Wirral. Once they delivered it to wherever it was going, someplace near Liverpool I'm guessing, Billy would have been excess baggage. He couldn't go back to the farm, and there were warrants out for his arrest. He was a dead man walking when he left there."

"Why not shoot him with Peter?"

"I'm guessing it was because you were looking for him, thinking he'd done for both Catherine and Peter. You'd have figured it out if they left him dead there, too, so they used him as bait to keep you thinking it was a domestic. What'd you find out about O'Connell?"

Will felt a bit of a fool. "We don't have much yet." They'd called Quigley to do some research, but he hadn't come up with a lot. "He seems to have grown up in the area, went to school in Liverpool, but didn't bother to distinguish himself much. The parents still live in the area. We'll try them for more information later."

"They were shattered, then? Not expecting Peter to get himself in that much trouble?"

"According to them, he was a pretty normal kid. He got in a bit of trouble here and there, tried a little weed and got caught, but not charged, and otherwise had a good childhood. Both parents were present, still married, and Peter'd had a younger brother and an older sister. They said he'd tried various jobs and ended up serving up drinks in a pub because the tips paid more than other jobs he'd had."

Edward shook his head. "He either met Billy at the pub or they were school mates. It doesn't sound like their paths would cross otherwise."

Will sipped his whisky. "So, when are you going to tell me the whole story?"

"Give me a refill first." Edward held out his empty glass. "It's a long story."

Will stood up and took the glasses into the kitchen, filling Edward's in the dim light from the stove. "Want anything?" he called to Bronwyn.

"The wine's still in my car," she said.

"Want me to go get it?"

"No, it's fine. I'm good." What she meant was that she didn't want Will out there in the dark if there was danger lurking.

He knew it and loved her for it. "I'll just slip out for a minute. It'd be a good excuse for having a little look around."

He handed Edward his drink, and then he called to Daisy and opened the door. 'If I'm not back in three minutes, don't come looking for me," he joked weakly.

He tried not to look nervous as he walked to her Land Rover. Unlike the SUV Billy Davies owned, Bronwyn's was rather tattered, for want of a better term. She had bought it as a used vehicle in the fall, and it was dependable, if not beautiful. Sometimes he'd taken it when he went to Caernarfon, if the roads were icy or snowy, and it had always gotten him there and back.

He opened the door and grabbed the wine bottles, and then he stood there and watched Daisy dashing around the garden. Surely, she would sound an alarm if a stranger were lurking nearby? It made him feel safer when she didn't.

Inside again, with the door safely locked, he opened the Malbec and poured Bronwyn a glass and then another for himself. He'd had his one whisky; that was his allotment for an evening. He opened the fridge and found fresh cheeses, so he cut off some slices and arranged them on a plate around a half baguette. Juggling all this in his hands, he went back into the sitting room and settled next to Bronwyn on the sofa again, setting the plate on the end table nearest to Edward. "Thought you'd be hungry if you're on the run."

"Cheers," Edward said. He pulled off a piece of the baguette and helped himself to several chunks of the cheese, chewing in silence for a long minute while they waited.

Will suspected he was gathering his thoughts, wondering how much he could share with them, especially with Bronwyn there. He reached for the bread and tore off a piece for himself.

"It started before you left," Edward began. "Think back. Things seemed different. Contacts we'd worked with disappeared or just didn't have any information for us, leads we were following led us in the wrong directions, things just seemed out of synch. We were killing ourselves to get arrests, and we got some, but they didn't stop the flood of drugs. It seemed like we were spinning our wheels and losing ground. Then you were transferred, and it got worse. I thought it was because you were

119

gone, that it was just the change of partners, that I'd have to find a new rhythm with her and then things would straighten out in time. It felt like we were on the losing side of the battle, though. Nothing we did made any difference, and the problem was growing bigger, not smaller."

Will found himself leaning forward, listening intently, trying to read between the lines. "Who's your new partner? Anyone I know?"

Edward shook his head. "They brought her over from Dover. I thought she'd be good, having worked there where things are busy. Her name's Jill, Jill Osbourne." He looked a question at Will.

"Not familiar," Will said.

"No, nor to me. She'd only been there a year, but still, I thought she'd be okay."

"So sometimes we go through slumps like that," Will pointed out. "Maybe it's not as big a deal as you think."

Edward shot him a look. "This is different. After a while, things started to add up. Like I said, we were making busts like always, but at the same time, cities were being flooded with drugs. The bigger loads were getting past us. I started to think that there was a new player in the game, someone with enough power to block our efforts, but at the same time ensure that the old dealers were being taken off the streets. Whoever it was, they were set on eliminating the competition. When I looked at the bigger picture, it seemed obvious that someone in the department was bent, and whoever it was, it wasn't just a peon. This person had the power to know what was going on in all our investigations, not just one or two, and he had the information to recruit our contacts to his side. A lot of people are in his pay, and you never know who else might be joining the opposing team, day to day. This person can manipulate all of us, one way or another."

"But that's crazy."

"I thought so, too. But it makes sense. I think it's someone who directs where and how our investigations are carried out, Will. He, or she, would be able to divert personnel and resources away from things like ports and storage areas, like that. My idea is that big loads of product are coming in from the mainland. They're bypassing the English ports now after the big Dover bust, so whoever this is, he's someone in Cardiff. We were involved with Dover." He glanced at Will. "We were ordered over to help them for nine days, and during that time I'm sure another shipment came into Wales, as big or bigger. Whoever it is, though, doesn't want suspicion to fall back on him, so he can't have the loads coming into Cardiff. He has to have the stuff come in further north. He's got customs inspectors in his pay who looks the other way at a lorry full of appliances or car parts or whatever's supposedly being sent over, so he's able to get a lorry aboard a ferry without his load being checked. That'd require someone at both ends of the ferry line, right?"

Will nodded. That wasn't unusual. Customs officials were watched closely by their superiors just to avoid this sort of thing. He didn't point that out, however. If this was as big an operation as Edward thought, who knew how far up the chain the corruption went? "You think someone in the department is heading this up? A chief inspector or someone like that?"

Edward nodded fervently. "I do. Maybe even a chief super. But I don't know who it is, and it may be several working together, so I don't know who to trust, if anyone. I'm kind of alone here."

"Your partner?"

"Who's to say she wasn't leading me off on wild goose chases on instructions from someone higher up? She may have been brought in just because she was in their pay and could block my efforts. If more than one of my bosses is in on it, it may be a network that functions all over the country. We're powerless against them because they can track us in an instant if they suspect that we suspect." He looked at Will intently. "I'm telling you, this is big."

He sounded paranoid, and Will wondered if it was a matter of the job getting to him. "You're accusing law enforcement of running a drugs operation?"

"A big one, maybe the biggest in history. That's why it's so hard to stop. I don't know who to trust, so I can't go to anyone, and I can't solve the whole case on my own." He paused, agitated.

Will shook his head. It was a crazy idea. If, on the off-chance it was true and not just a product of Edward's paranoia, how could the two of them alone have any impact at all?

Edward saw his hesitation. "About six weeks ago, I went off the grid. I broke away from my partner, I stopped checking in, I dumped my phone. I knew I couldn't use department resources if they were being monitored, so I did my searching the old-fashioned way, with legwork and luck. I got onto Billy by chance, asking around. He'd been selling a bit here and there, mostly in Wrexham but sometimes as far north as Chester. As far as I could tell, what he was selling was part of a bigger shipment, so I started following him, hoping he'd lead me back to the source."

"If it's the department coordinating this, you'd have to follow it all the way back."

"Exactly. If we can track the shipment back, then we get to someone who knows who's in charge. I think the shipment came in from France through Fishguard."

"Not Holyhead? We had information last week that a big shipment was coming in there."

Edward sat straighter. "That's just what I'm talking about. Diverting resources and personnel. I bet a bunch of people were sent to Holyhead, told to check lorries, maybe even set up checkpoints, right?"

Will nodded.

"And the real shipment will come through Fishguard while everyone's busy up north. See why I think it's a chief inspector or the chief super? They're the ones with the power to do that. And they can do a lot more."

Will watched him, his mind racing. Beside him, Bronwyn was watching him, too, her face rapt.

"Listen, three weeks ago, someone tried to run me of the road when I was following Billy. I was driving my own car, that old clunker Saab we used to run around in. The Swedes build them solid. It survived the first hit, and I slammed on the brakes to avoid the second one. They backed up into my bonnet hard, but I got out and high-tailed it for the field across the way. About that time another vehicle came by, just by sheer luck. The guy stopped, and I begged a ride. The Saab was done for. When I got to Bala, I called and had it towed, and then I turned it in to insurance. I got a check five days later, and I took it out in cash. I know I was followed from the bank, but I dodged into shops and alleys, and after a bit I lost them. Then I laid low for four days, sleeping rough."

"Weren't you afraid someone would turn you in for tip money? I mean, if they were really looking for you…"

"Not in a town. I slept in an old, tumbled down cottage in an empty field. No fire, no anything to draw attention. I ate what I had in my backpack, and I had water. When I figured enough time had gone by, I bought a motorbike from an ad in a newspaper, and I paid cash and scribbled a name on the paperwork. I figure the Saab had been tracked, so I didn't want anything in my name again. Even using police resources, I figured they'd have a hard time finding me if I didn't have a vehicle or a mobile to track."

Will nodded. He was starting to believe Edward. It was mind-boggling, though, to think of corruption at the highest levels of the police force.

Edward tossed down the last of his whisky and went on. "I got a tip week before last from Dylan Meyrick. Remember him? He was always a reliable contact, even if half the time he didn't know diddly. It led me back to Billy, which made me suspicious because I figured Billy was what put them onto me in the first place. I decided to be a no-show, but I was there. I watched most of it from across the field in a ditch. They were watching for me, I'm sure of it."

"Who?"

"Some thugs in farmer's clothes. There were four of them, and they grabbed Billy right away and went inside. I could hear the girlfriend screaming, and then she went quiet. After a few minutes, they came back out and that's when I figured they were waiting for me to show up. They stood around and shuffled their feet and, finally, they grumbled a bit and went back inside and got the show started. I'd have been as dead as Catherine Baines and Peter O'Connell are if I hadn't been suspicious. I heard the shot, and I knew someone was dead. Only one shot. In a few minutes they came out of the house and left, and Billy scrambled around loading that stock trailer and the Kuga with boxes and more boxes. He looked to be in a real hurry, and I figured then they'd shot the girlfriend and told Billy he had one last chance."

"Or they blackmailed him," Will said. "Maybe they made Billy shoot her. If we ever get the gun, we can find out. We thought Billy took it when he left. That's why we were so careful in Wirral; we thought he was armed."

"After that, I followed Billy. At first, he stuck to the main motorways north. Just about at the English border, he turned off onto an A road, and then eventually he ended up in Wirral. I saw him turn onto that farm lane, so I ditched the bike and walked the long way around to watch from a grove of trees behind the cottage and outbuildings. The thugs had already turned up by the time I was set there, but I heard the shot and thought Billy was dead. One shot, but it turned out to be his friend."

"Why did they leave Billy alive the whole time? Why kill Peter?"

"I've thought and thought, and this is what I've come up with. Billy had to know when he left the farm that he was a dead man walking. I think he decided to go for broke. He called this friend he'd had dealings with before and thought he could deliver that big shipment to him and then make a run for it. He must have thought, if he could get off the motorways and away from the cameras, he might make it. It was his only chance."

"So, you watched the place in Wirral and saw me there," Will surmised.

"I'd seen you here, too, but at that point I didn't think you knew about the drugs operation going on. Major crimes stick to murders, most of the time, and they refer the drugs cases to us. I hear you live here now, part time."

"We do," Will said, "but my official residence is still Caernarfon."

"Who knows you have this place?"

A few days ago, Will would have said only Jay Mehta, his sometime partner. But now, he knew that department gossip had probably informed most of the people he worked with. "Most of my colleagues in Caernarfon probably know," he admitted. "Only two of my partners have been here, but that's enough to get the grapevine going."

"That's why I'm being careful. They know we were close. They might figure I'd come to you for help."

Will glanced at Bronwyn, settled beside him on the sofa. He didn't like the thought of putting her in danger. He'd need to get Edward well-away if he could, before anyone knew they'd communicated.

"I tried to find Dylan, but he was gone. He was in my pay, but obviously he was in the pay of someone else, too, and for all I know, in the pay of a dozen people who are more powerful than I am."

"They sent you to Billy's, though. Why take the chance?"

"The tip had to be close enough to the truth to lead me to a real person who was involved in the business. I'm not stupid. They knew I was already onto Billy. By that time, as far as the department knew, I'd disappeared for a bit. Mathews, my chief super, kept trying to contact me, and they sent Jill to set up a meet before Catherine and Peter were killed, but by that time I wasn't trusting anyone, not even her, so I guess you could say I went rogue. Dylan found me in a bar in Bala. I'd worked with him before and thought I could use him, but obviously that wasn't a great idea." He glanced at Bronwyn. "I figured they brought the drugs in on a big lorry, and then they met somewhere, a warehouse or something where a truck wouldn't be out of the ordinary, and then they divided the load into smaller bits. People like Billy would load up a van or a stock trailer and store the stuff in a barn or big garage for a while. Once enough time had passed that it wouldn't raise suspicions, they'd give Billy a call and have him bring it in small loads nearer to wherever they were distributing it to local dealers."

"Not a particularly original set-up," Will observed.

"No, but with all the inside information they get, they were able to take out a lot of the competition, weren't they? They could put us on the other guys' shipments, all the while keeping us out of the way for theirs."

"It's brilliant, really." Will stirred. Involuntarily, he glanced toward the windows. "What's your plan, then?"

"I want to keep following the trail backwards, if I can. If I can expose people as I find them, sooner or later one or more of the ones at the top would have to step up. That's my thinking, anyway. They'll run out of underlings to do the job."

"And you're going to do that on your own, without backup?"

"I can cause a lot of havoc if I need to."

"They'll know it's you."

"I know, but I have no choice. I don't know who's running the show, how many of them are involved."

"And what if you're wrong?"

"Then my career is over, isn't it?" He ran his hands across the stubble on his cheeks. "I'm not wrong, Will. I know my suspicions are right."

Will took a deep breath and nodded, trying to decide how far he was willing to go to help. Even if Edward was right and people high up in command were involved, Will would lose his job over a breach like this one. He'd been specifically told to stay away from the drugs case. But if he were to convince Bowers that this was going on? "I can't help you without talking to my chief superintendent."

"I don't want you to help me. I came to warn you off, to keep you from looking further into Billy Davies and Peter O'Connell until I can get more information on my own. I'm not asking you to join me. This's my case. It'll mean the end of my career, but if I can pull it off, I'll retire knowing I took some of them with me, and that'll be people who have a lot more to lose than I do."

"But I could use my resources to get information for you. I'd make it look like I was chasing after Billy. We've got a guy, Quigley, in the station who can find anything using technology. I'd use him to track Billy's Kuga, to find Billy's contacts, to track phones."

"Weren't you listening to me?" Edward's voice rose to a frantic pitch. "Everyone's a suspect. Everyone! You can't trust anyone, not without risking your life, and I mean that. There've already been two attempts on mine. I'm on my own on this one. Completely on my own."

"Then, what are you doing here? You obviously want my help."

"I'm here because I trust you." Edward made a visible effort to get his emotions under control. "The best thing would be if you could convince everyone that Billy Davies is your suspect, that you are after him for the two murders, and then you keep the investigation going in that direction while keeping an eye out for something, anything, that would help my case along. No one has to know you're doing it, would they? You could keep your partner in the dark?"

Will thought it over, trying to see through the situation. It wouldn't be hard to steer Notley toward Billy Davies; he already thought Billy guilty of the two murders. Maybe he could muddle things up a bit so that Notley would go off on this or that tangent, keep him out of the way.

"I can probably keep my partner out of the way, but I think you need more help than that."

Edward sat back and grinned. "I *knew* you'd be with me on this. But it won't be easy, mate."

"Like you said, create mischief where we can, expose the underlings so that the guys in charge have to step up, and then swoop in for the kill."

"That's it. We'll lead them a merry little dance." Edward relaxed into the chair. "I feel better now."

"If only you smelled better," Will told him. "You need a shower, mate. I'll get you a change of clothes and a towel."

"Then a good night's sleep in a real bed?"

"I think we can provide that," Will assured him, "although it will be my niece's room you'll be in, so it's a daybed and your feet will hang off the edge."

"It's got to be better than wrapped in burlap in a tumbled cottage," Edward said. Then he looked seriously at Will. "You're okay with this? You're sure?"

"I don't know what else to do," he admitted. And he didn't. It was too late for Edward to back out now; he'd already dug himself in too deep. Not helping would condemn Edward to an untimely death, he knew that as a certainty. But involving himself might condemn them both. How committed was he to his old career, to stopping huge shipments of dangerous drugs into the country, enabling addiction, homelessness, and death to thousands? In good conscience, he couldn't say no to Edward, even though it almost certainly meant the end of his career, too. *Maybe that's not a bad thing,* he mused. He tried to picture himself farming, and failed. *Maybe I could find something to do nearer to Llangynog, though, and to Bronwyn. If I survive it.*

An hour later he sent Bronwyn to bed. "I'll be in after I take Daisy out," he told her, but really, he doubted he'd be able to fall asleep with all that was now on his mind so he was stalling as best he could, not wanting to toss around and keep her awake.

Edward had already disappeared into the spare bedroom, where Bronwyn had made up the daybed with sheets and a blanket. He'd looked much improved after the shower, and he smelled better, too.

He opened the door and let Daisy out, then followed her. He leaned against the wall beside the door and watched as she scurried around the garden, checking the smells. He still thought that Daisy would sound an alarm if someone were watching the cottage.

The door slid open and Edward came out to join him. "Couldn't sleep, huh?"

"You told quite a story," Will admitted. "I have a lot to think about. I'm trying to figure out what I can do to help you track the drugs back to the source."

"It's good to have another mind running that thought around. The best place to start would be to try to follow the Ford Kuga around on CCTV cameras. What's the most direct route to Fishguard?"

Will shrugged. "I don't know. I'll have to put it in my Google maps and see."

"You've been out of this a while. You can't do that on your phone. If they're monitoring it, they'll know you're onto them."

"An old-fashioned map, then." He'd have to be on his game or there'd be trouble. "I can do that. I'll make up some excuse for Notley." Poor Notley. He'd be beyond furious once he found out what Will was doing. And he was still uncomfortable with leaving Bowers out of the loop. He wondered if he dared talk to him, behind Edward's back, of course.

"So, Bronwyn…" Edward gave him a sidelong glance.

He'd made it a statement, but Will understood the implied question. He didn't really want to discuss Bronwyn with anyone, despite that Edward was probably his best friend, whatever that meant. At one time they'd been as close as he imagined brothers might be, if they'd grown up in circumstances different to his own. But he had yet to figure out his intentions toward Bronwyn. He certainly couldn't explain them to Edward. Still, he had to say something. "Yes, Bronwyn," he finally managed after the silence had stretched out too long.

"It's serious?"

Will took a breath, taking the time to steady himself as he'd seen Bronwyn do from time to time. "Yes, I think it is," he admitted after a moment.

Edward considered this, his gaze direct. "She's very different from Lesley, and this," he gestured to take in the cottage and the tiny lane and Daisy still snuffling around the garden, "it's totally opposite of what I thought you were after."

"I know. It's not what I imagined for myself."

"Then why? Does *this* make you happy?" Will didn't think he imagined the note of criticism in Edward's voice.

"It does." *How much should he say?* "When I was in Cardiff," he started slowly, trying to think it through, "I thought I was happy. I liked working with you in drugs and alcohol, and Lesley was a bonus. We had fun, but it was all...I don't know if I can explain it. It was living on the edge, I guess. Not a real life, just pretending to be people we weren't, pretending to hang out with rough people so we could catch them, pretending to be all sophisticated in our free time, going to concerts and wine tastings and dancing. But now... I just don't think that's me, that's all."

Edward responded to his hesitation. "So, Bronwyn's why you broke it off with Lesley?"

Will shook his head quickly. "I hadn't started dating Bronwyn yet when I decided not to see Lesley anymore."

Edward watched him quizzically, letting the silence lengthen.

"Look, I never pictured myself living this life," Will blurted. "But I was investigating a murder here in the village, and I'd met Bronwyn, and the attraction was there, I'll admit it." He stopped his headlong admission, thinking fast. He hadn't been aware of it then, the attraction of a small, quiet village and a pretty girl with old-fashioned values. If he could admit it to himself now, that attraction included a picture of himself with a family like hers, a family who made it clear they loved each other through thick and thin. Part of that was rebellion against his parents; part was something else he couldn't define. "Then I went to see Lesley, and everything she said was wrong. I just knew, all of a sudden, that I wanted something different."

"And you really are happy?" Edward persisted. "I mean, what on earth do you do here?"

"Believe it or not, I've turned into a hiker. This is a brilliant place for walking, and it turns out I like being out in nature more than I like being in a city. Sometimes we go to historic sites, and there are local events we go to. If I have my niece Lark here…Julia's daughter," he looked a question at Edward. He didn't remember if he'd ever told him about Lark. "If Lark's here, she does those things with us."

"You've turned into a family man." Edward's flat tones implied disdain. "I never would have thought it."

Will didn't bother replying.

Edward shrugged. "You like your job here?"

"I like working major crimes. It challenges me, and there's a thrill with a solve. I don't always like working with the partners I get. Policy here is a rotation, and when Notley comes up on my rota, it's a lot harder to get through the day. But some of them are okay, and a lot of the time I break away on my own."

"Your guv is okay with that?"

Will nodded. "He's not happy with everything I do, but he tends to overlook the little things."

"Like you living here in the middle of nowhere."

Will smiled. "I have a flat in Caernarfon for when I'm needed there. I come here on my days off. And sometimes it works out that there's a crime nearby that we're investigating, so I can get away with staying here rather than in a hotel room. That's something that's actually being encouraged at the moment. It looks like I might be assigned the majority of the cases in this part of the district."

Edward sighed. "Well, she's pretty in an unconventional way, I guess, if you like the village lass sort."

Will laughed. "My parents would have preferred Lesley. She represented everything they considered desirable; she was sophisticated, ambitious, worldly. They won't approve of Bronwyn, which is probably what first attracted me to her." He twisted a wry face. "You asked me if it was serious. Well, Bronwyn isn't the sort of girl you casually date. Her brother has made that very clear to me."

"Yet, there you are, living in sin with her."

How did he get away with that? Her dad had been decidedly cooler to him since they'd moved in together, that was for sure. "I have some decisions to make," he admitted finally. But perhaps he'd already made them when he'd rented the house for them to share.

Chapter Nine

They all slept late the next morning. Clouds scudded across the sky, threatening rain, but it had not yet begun to fall when Bronwyn let Daisy out to do her morning duty. She looked out the door, scanning the front garden, and saw nothing amiss. Nor did Daisy run to bark at – or greet- a stranger hiding out in the hedge. Everything seemed normal.

Except it wasn't. Will had tossed and turned in the night, obviously worried about how to handle the situation. She knew what he'd do, or at least what his intentions would be. He'd told Maddock he was an honorable man, and she didn't think that only applied to her. If there was corruption at the highest levels of the Welsh police force, he'd fight to expose it. She'd wondered why they couldn't just report their suspicions to the anti-corruption agency in the force, which she knew from Will existed for situations like this. But perhaps they feared the corruption extended even to the people in charge there, she thought. Edward hadn't known who was involved, and it had been obvious he was very scared, despite his efforts to hide his fear.

Bronwyn was in the middle of a proper fry-up when Edward wandered into the kitchen to join her. "That smells better than anything I've had in recent memory," he told her, with what she'd come to think of as his trademark grin. He'd showered again that morning, and his wet hair was tousled in untidy curls, and when he grinned at her, she was charmed, despite herself.

"Well, you didn't get much of a proper supper last night, so I thought this a good idea to make up for it."

He sat down on a stool they'd put in the one corner of the room. There hadn't been room for a proper table and chairs. "Will seems at home here," he said, his voice cautious. "How long have you had this place?"

"It's been about four months."

"And before that?"

She turned to look at him. "What do you mean?"

"Did you stay with him in Caernarfon?"

She turned back to the stove, feeling a blush color her cheeks. "No, I was here, and he was there. We only saw each other on our free days, and usually we met halfway between somewhere."

He digested that. "You work here locally?"

"I'm the coordinator at the counselling centre at St. Melangell's, just up the lane a couple of miles. I organize the calendar, book groups in for meetings, schedule counselling sessions for our psychologist, things like that."

"And you grew up here?"

She bobbed her head, her back still turned. "Yes, my family has a farm just the other side of the village. I was still living at home when Will and I met."

He was quiet for a minute.

She flipped the sausages and bacon onto two plates and then broke eggs into the pan. Will was showering and should be ready in a minute. She checked the oven for the scones. Nearly done.

"How did you and Will meet?"

She turned to him. "I thought you knew that story. Everyone else seems to."

He nodded. "I know you were a suspect in a case, but that's about all."

"She solved that case." Will strode into the room. "I ended up in hospital, while she caught the killer red-handed." He kissed Bronwyn by the stove and went to pour himself a cup of coffee. "Want some?" he offered Edward.

Edward nodded, so Will poured two cups, handing one to him. "I want to hear the whole story."

Bronwyn slid the eggs off onto three plates and set tomato halves into the pan. They'd be ready now in a minute; it didn't take long. She took the pan of scones from the oven and put them on a plate, then spooned the tomatoes off onto the other plates. Will couldn't tell him the whole story; even he didn't know the truth about how she'd figured it out...or how she'd escaped the killer's attack after Will had been knocked unconscious.

They took their plates into the conservatory, filling the small table with their clutter. Edward pulled an extra chair up to the table, glancing through the windows as he did so.

"I think Daisy would let us know if a stranger were hanging around," Will told him. "This would be a hard place for surveillance. The village is tiny; a stranger would be noted, especially if he were to drive up the lane to find the place."

Edward nodded, then picked up his fork and put a mouthful of egg and sausage in his mouth. He closed his eyes and chewed dreamily. "I see why you like it here."

Will grinned at Bronwyn. "The food is a bonus, but it's not the major draw."

Edward opened his eyes. "Yeah, I can imagine what else keeps you here." He tossed a smile Bronwyn's way. "It must be quite a commute."

"I come here when I have free days. It's usually three in a row, if I don't have an active case keeping me in Caernarfon. Other people have long commutes, too, sometimes. It's worth the drive."

Bronwyn ignored the blush she knew was coloring her cheeks. She knew Edward was studying her, trying to figure out what drew Will to her. She'd dressed carefully that morning, wanting to make Will proud. Blue jeans, of course, but she'd worn a newer shirt she'd bought in the fall and put earrings on.

"We've got to make a plan." Edward changed the subject abruptly. "You said personnel were being diverted to Anglesey?"

"For two weeks, and that was a week ago. We're going to have to get busy if you think the request was designed to keep interest away from Fishguard until the shipment is in."

"If I get it right, we'll have two days now before anyone expects you back in Caernarfon, right?"

"Yes, that's right, unless…unless it's useful for me to go back for a bit, check things out. Notley and I are working a murder case, so it wouldn't draw too much notice if I were to try to track Billy's vehicle back toward Fishguard on the cameras. If he has a credit card, he may have used it, as well. We'd be looking for somewhere Billy would run to as far as anyone else is concerned, at least until we find a body." He shot Bronwyn a look. "Or Billy alive. I guess it's possible. He may be more useful to them than we think."

"It's best if we don't find him," Edward noted. "If Billy turns up, that'd put paid to you pretending to work the case while we try to track him back to his source."

"Yeah, Billy has to stay in the wind. I'd probably get another case if this one ends. If I get some leads in the office that hint at some connections for Billy in the south, I can try to arrange for Notley to check out what's toward Liverpool, and maybe I can head there."

"That's not a bad plan. No one would be suspicious? Your chief super?"

"I don't think so. He knows I hate working with Notley, so if I can make it sound logical for us to split up, I think it'll be okay. I think he'd guess that I'd rather work independently than to cause more conflict. Notley already hates me."

"And going in on what should be a free day wouldn't be unusual?"

Bronwyn watched Will turn it over in his head. Bowers knew that Will would snatch at any opportunity to spend time in Llangynog. He'd wonder, at the least, why Will was so focused on finding Billy Davies that he was willing to sacrifice free time that had been granted him.

Finally, Will looked at her. He took her hand and stroked it where the thumb met the hand. "He wouldn't think it odd if I let it be known that Bronwyn and I had a messy split, that we aren't together anymore. If that happened, I'd have no choice but to get back to Caernarfon. It's the only other home I have."

She jerked her hand away, her heart pattering. *He doesn't mean it.*

Will nodded to himself, a decisive movement that said he was not to be argued with. "Listen, sweetheart, I can't let you be involved in this case. To say this one's going to be dangerous is understating the danger. It may well end my career, but this is big enough, if Edward's right, that it's going to cost more lives, and mine will be at risk along with lots of others. I can't let yours be one of them."

"But…"

He shook his head, interrupting her. "You'll be helping us out most if you just go along with it. Let them think we're done, that the relationship is over. That's the only way I can get back into the office and get information without it raising flags. You could even move back in with your parents for a bit, make it look like we've abandoned the cottage and the whole idea of living together. You'd be safer there, and I'll function better if I'm not worried about you."

"I'll have to tell them what's going on."

"No." Edward said it without thought, but his voice made it a command.

"They'll know," Bronwyn argued. She looked to Will. "You know they will. I can't keep secrets from them. They'd see right through it."

Will rubbed his face with his hand. "She's right. They'd know. And if they didn't, then her brother'd be here in a flash to give me what for." He looked at Bronwyn. "I can't lie to them. I want to stay in their good graces. They tolerate me fairly well right now, but if I lie to them, or worse, have their daughter lying to them, it'd be hard to fix something like that. And I know Maddock wouldn't just let it go, either way. If I can admit to it," he smiled ruefully, "I'm a little scared of him."

"You won't be here," Edward pointed out.

"He'd search the country until he found me," Will retorted. "You don't know her family, Edward. They won't say anything. I'm serious about not lying to them. It'd be a lot bigger problem not telling them the truth than letting them in on the plot."

"Then how about this? She tells them you're working a case that'll keep you away for a bit. Top secret. They can't say anything or it'll compromise the case."

"It probably wouldn't hurt if she told them we have to pretend to be split up, in order for me to be free to work the case without putting her in danger."

"I guess that'll have to do." Edward swept a hand through his unruly hair.

She didn't know how to ask without Edward wondering what it meant. "What if I see something out of place?" she blurted, interrupting whatever he was going to say. "What if I hear something that'll help?"

Edward's eyes drifted toward her with interest. Now they narrowed a bit as he chewed on that question.

"We'll figure out a system." Will looked over at Edward. "She lives here, mate. Of course, she's going to see and hear things once in a while that helps solve a local case. And Billy is local, in case you've forgotten."

"How about this, then?" Edward said. "If she gets ahold of something she thinks is useful, she can call you and pretend that she wants to make up, wants a second chance. Or she could text you. That might even be better. It'll be a record of the fact that you did, in fact, break it off with her and she's desperate to get you back. You could say, 'Okay, I'll meet you somewhere', and then you could get together for a drink or something, and she passes you the information. What do you think?"

It sounded like a good idea, she thought, like it would work.

Will looked at her, catching her eyes and holding the look. "I don't think so. That's putting her in danger again, and I won't be here in the area, most likely, if the action is happening in Fishguard. It'd be awkward for us to meet."

"Then she calls you using a throwaway phone, and she can leave a message if you can't answer it. We'll have to use them, too. Yours would be traced otherwise."

Will gave her a stern look. "You'll only call if it's something really important, right?"

"I thought you tracked Peter O'Connell's pre-paid," Bronwyn reminded him.

"We did, but only because Billy called it, and Billy used Catherine's phone so we had access to her records. You can't call me on my phone.

Both of them will have to be burners. I'll get some in Bala when we go through."

"How will I get the phone from you? Am I going to Bala, too?"

"No, you aren't going anywhere near this." He looked at Edward. "You head to Bala and I'll follow in about ten minutes. We can watch for anyone following us that way. You buy the phones. It'd look more suspicious if I did it." He paused as a thought occurred to him. "How'd you get here? You didn't ride your motorbike."

"I left it in the car park in the village and walked. I didn't want to draw attention to myself, riding it on a back lane where people'd notice."

Will nodded. "Okay, find a shop with no cameras, if you can. I'm guessing you'll need some money." Edward nodded, and he went on, "You get the phones and just brush past me when you come out, hand-to-hand. Then you, love, I'll get yours to you somehow or other. You won't need it right away, and if no other opportunity comes up, I'll mail it off to you, put it in a big box like I'm cleaning your stuff out of my flat."

"Okay," she managed, worrying that she'd forgotten something. She'd miss Will's nightly calls, but it seemed they had no choice.

He looked at her and sighed. "Look, why don't you get out and take Daisy for a walk before the rain hits. Maybe behind your parents' house, you know, where you'll be safe enough?"

He wanted her to check for visions in the pool of water. It was their secret, and she loved that he'd found a way to connect with her that didn't allow Edward to edge in. She nodded, giving him a smile. "You'll still be here when I get back?"

"Edward has yet to tell me what he's going to be doing while I'm back in the office tracing Billy's whereabouts, so I'd say yeah, we'll still be here."

She gathered up the dishes and dropped them in the sink, and then she snatched up her mac and her boots, struggling into both while standing at the door. As she grabbed Daisy's leash from the hook, she heard Edward and Will murmuring with lowered voices.

"I saw that look between you," Edward said. "What's the secret?"

She could hear Will's soft laugh. "Leave it, mate. That's just how you look at a girl you regret leaving behind."

She opened the back door of the Land Rover and let Daisy jump in, and then she slid into the front seat, started the car, and pulled out onto the lane toward the village. Her parents' house, the family farm, was just beyond the village on the opposite end from the cottage. Since the village consisted of just a dozen or so houses, two pubs, and a church, it didn't take long to drive the length of it. The streets were quiet on this Sunday morning, but music drifted from the church at the crossroads and a lone collie trotted ahead of her car as she passed through. She wondered who it belonged to.

Their own sheepdogs greeted her car as she drove up to the old stone house. Built of local slate, it had always felt solid and welcoming to her, but then, she'd lived there all her life. The cottage seemed flimsy and plain by comparison, but it had been all that was available so it'd have to suit them well enough for now.

She opened the door and called out, but no one was at home to answer. They'd probably be at church services so she'd have to wait until after her walk to sit down with them for a cup of tea and an explanation of the whole affair. She wondered how they'd react. *They'll probably just be happy I'm well out of it*, she told herself.

She called to Daisy and set out across the pasture, stopping to pat her old pony Hobbs who ambled slowly over for a treat. She'd forgotten again, and she felt bad. She resolved to rob the fridge of an apple after her walk for him.

As she ambled across the pasture, she thought about Will's words about her family, glad that he cared what they thought of him and amused that he'd hinted that Maddock worried him. Will knew, of course, that Maddock wouldn't really come after him if they ended their relationship. But Maddock liked to tease him, to threaten him even, and she thought both of them enjoyed the friendship that had developed between them.

She climbed over the stile on the far side of the pasture, stepping up and down carefully as the boards had deteriorated through the years since she'd leapt over them in childhood. Then she was in the forest, surrounded by oak, rowan, beech, and hawthorn, all of them a riot of greens in their spring glory, and she tried to turn her thoughts to nature, to the meditations that might, she hoped, bring her something to tell Will about before he left.

Birch tassels glowed golden against the stormy sky, and oak worms carpeted the path, oozing into the mud that sucked at her boots. She paused to close her eyes. The wind was cool on one side of her face, with the other side warmed by a stray ray of sunshine that had broken through the clouds. She took in a deep breath, smelling the mud, but also a sweet scent of flowering shrubs, bluebells, and sweet woodruff that tumbled between the trees in a joyful white carpet. She opened her eyes to see Daisy racing after a squirrel that ran along an overhead branch, only a few feet above her head.

The pool of water was restless in the breeze, ripples traveling the length of it to lap at the rocks that edged it. Bronwyn settled herself on the flat rock, patted her side to urge Daisy to join her, and then placed her hand on Daisy's head to keep her quiet. She quietened her breath, slowly breathing in and out deeply and regularly. She closed her eyes for another minute, listening to a rook call from a nearby tree and something small scuttling below her in the tangle of shrubbery. She could hear the ripples lapping at the rocks and tried to match her breathing to the rhythm it created. Slowly, she let her mind go empty, and then she opened her eyes.

The pool of dark water drew her eyes downward. She tried to ignore the eddies of unsettled water and looked toward the deeper edges, the more protected spots that provided a better mirror for the vision she hoped for. Directly beneath the rock she sat on was the ideal place, and it was the place she most often saw something, if anything appeared at all.

She watched, trying to force a vision. The dark water stirred, marring the smoothness of the pool. She stared past the ripple, forcing her eyes to bore into the depths of the water. She saw reflections there, the trees above dimly moving in the watery mirror. An oak worm blew onto the surface from the tree that overhung the pool, followed by several of its mates, marring the smoothness of the water. Bronwyn sighed. There'd be no vision today.

Discouraged, she lumbered down off the rock and set out for the farmhouse, keeping an eye out for movement that might indicate a visit from the Twlwyth Teg. Most of the clues she gave Will came from them, after all. The visions were rarer. But Daisy dashed to and fro ahead of her on the trail, and nothing appeared to alter her joyful bounding. She felt empty.

*Simple*s, she realized suddenly. The little hummingbird fairy hadn't said, "Simple," she'd said, "Simples." Wasn't that a medieval word for medical remedies back long ago? They'd made potions from plants, if she remembered right, and used them for everything from treating illness to attracting a lover to poisoning someone clandestinely. Simples were back then what drugs were now. The fairy had given her a clue for Will, after all; she just hadn't understood it, and now it was too late for that one.

Her parents hadn't arrived back yet when she got to the house, so she climbed back into the Land Rover and drove back through the village. She knew Will and Edward were anxious to be off on their mission. She could visit her parents later; she'd have plenty of lonely hours to fill with no work to occupy her and no Will to spend time with. She wondered where Will and Edward would stay while they were undercover. Edward had said he'd slept rough, and Will would surely be longing for the comfort of their own cottage. How long would their efforts take? She didn't imagine that Will would be back to accompany her to the Brecon Beacons when she went for her training. It panicked her a little, thinking of driving all that way by herself, but she couldn't be selfish when Will was risking everything – his career and even his life – to catch whoever was selfish enough to use his position to enrich his own pockets while ignoring the damage done to other lives.

Will and Edward were still sitting in the conservatory when she returned. They were laughing at some old story, oblivious to the seriousness of what they were undertaking. She gave Will a subtle shake of her head to tell him she'd nothing to give him, and he frowned a little in response, obviously disappointed.

Turning her back on them, she went into the kitchen and started cleaning up the breakfast dishes. She couldn't help rattling them around a bit. *Face it, I'm in a mood*, she told herself. It didn't happen often. She'd been gone a good hour; the least they could have done was to wash up. Instead, there they were, laughing it up about old cases they'd worked together and probably getting pretty excited about the one to come. Who wouldn't want to take down their bosses, right? One or two of them had been responsible for Will's unwilling transfer to major crimes, so that gave him an even bigger motive. They were probably thrilled to be working together again.

Is this how my life is going to be? She'd tried to be tolerant of Will's job, to be supportive and encourage him. She knew he had no choice when a case took time away from the two of them, and she knew he had to put his life on the line sometimes. Could she live with that, day to day? For years?

She went back into the conservatory and stood watching them as they talked, serious now, heads bent together. What was really bothering her? If she was honest, it was the fact of Will leaving when he'd been there extra days and it'd almost felt like they were a real couple. It was the fact that he couldn't call her in the evenings like he usually did when they were separated, and she knew she'd worry about him, not just miss him. It was even a bit of jealousy, knowing he looked forward to working with Edward despite the danger this case posed, looked forward to spending time with *him* rather than her.

Will looked up, and saw her in the entryway. "All right, love?"

He must have seen something in her face, and now tears filled her eyes, unbidden and unexpected. She'd never cried in his presence before except when old Nan died, and she didn't want to now. She nodded quickly and then turned away, hurrying through the sitting room and down the hallway to the bedroom, where she looked around blindly, rubbing at her eyes with wet fingers. Taking a deep breath, she walked across to the window and looked out. The rain, threatening earlier, had now begun, pattering on the rooftop and splattering the window. The ditch beyond the garden was obscured; it looked like an abstract painting. She slid the window open an inch, just to hear the rain better, and the scent of it flooded in. She could feel the coolness on her face, standing by the opening.

Daisy nudged her hand, and absently she reached down to pat her head. She didn't look at her, but she knew Daisy would be anxious at her distress, sitting at her feet and wanting to comfort her.

She heard Will's footsteps as he came into the room. He came up behind her and reached around to hug her from behind, nuzzling at the back of her neck. "Let's talk, love," he whispered, and he turned her and looked down at her face, smiling a little. He reached out to brush at her cheek. "It's going to be okay."

He led her to the bed, where he sat down beside her. He put his arm around her and pulled her tight against his side. "I know this all sounds like too much a risk," he said. "You could see as well as I could that Edward is running scared. I might not have believed him, but there are the attempts on his life to consider. That means he's in serious trouble. I don't know if he's right in thinking his chief super is running the operation, or even a chief inspector in the department, but if people that high up are involved, it has to be stopped." He hesitated, reaching out again to brush a tear from her cheek. "I've never talked to you about my time in drugs and alcohol. We saw things…bad things. People got bad drugs and died horrible deaths. People overdosed and died. People got addicted, and their lives went to shame. They were homeless, sick, hungry. They committed crimes just to satisfy their need for a fix. Their children raised themselves and then followed right behind them when they were old enough."

"You saw it with Lark's mum, didn't you?"

He went silent for a long moment. "Julia died of an overdose, but I didn't know she was addicted until later, after she'd died. She was always different from other kids, and I was already away at school when she was born. To my shame, I just didn't bother with her." He pondered that admission for a minute. "Poor Lark lived with her in a run-down flat that was filthy from neglect, but at least it was a roof over their heads. Julia would have qualified for the flat because she had Lark, and that's the only thing that kept her from living on the streets. How Lark grew up to be the way she is, I'll never know. It was nothing Julia did for her. I gathered she spent all her time watching a little telly while her mother slept or partied."

That explained his devotion to Lark. He'd be trying to make up for not having a relationship with her mother. She didn't say it, though.

"That's not important. My point is that I've seen what drugs do to people. It'd be against everything I believe in to ignore this, if what Edward says is true."

She nuzzled into his shoulder, wiping her wet eyes on his shirt. "I know you have to do this; it's just that I wish you didn't."

"Don't worry, okay? I'm going to be fine. Edward is the one in danger, but I'll make it look like I'm looking for Billy, and no one will be the wiser."

"Bowers?"

He went silent again. "I still don't know what to do about Bowers. It might save my butt afterwards if Bowers knows what I'm doing. I think I trust him, but what Edward says makes good sense, to trust no one until we know. I'm still thinking about that, love. I have the drive from here to Caernarfon before I have to make a decision."

She tried to corral her thoughts. "What'll happen after, Will? I mean, you'll have gone against your orders to stay away from the drugs operations, and you'll have gone off on your own. You'll have gone after your superiors. And what about Notley?"

"Let me worry about all that, love. Tell you what. After we're done, and that'll be within a week if we're meant to catch this shipment, we'll take a holiday." He put his finger on her lips, quelling her objection. "I know, you have the certification coming up and then the St. Melangell's Day celebration. I'm still going to go with you to the Beacons, like I said, and I'll take you to meet my parents then, too. Maybe after all that's over we'll get some real time off? We'll go somewhere quiet and just be together, the two of us."

"And Daisy."

He grinned at her. "And Daisy, if you must have her."

She swallowed, feeling the tears had abated for the time being. She'd have a good cry after Will left, when she was alone and no one there to see. "You need to go, don't you?"

"I do." He bent down and kissed her softly. "I'll be in touch, love. Whenever I see a chance, I'll find you or at least call you."

"Only if it's safe," she murmured.

"For us both," he responded. He patted her knee and stood up, watching her.

She forced a smile. "Just come back to me. Promise me."

"I promise," he said, and then he walked out the door. She heard him pause to gather up a bag he'd obviously put together while she'd been out walking earlier, and then the front door snapped shut. She scurried into the living room to watch him out the window as he ran through the rain and unlocked the door to his little MGF. He looked up at her then, one last look, and she waved as he put the car in gear and backed out onto the lane.

Chapter Ten

Will wished he felt as confident as he'd tried to make Bronwyn feel he was. Truth be told, he was terrified. No matter how things turned out, this would be very bad for him. There was no way around it. If it hadn't been Edward asking, he'd have probably looked the other way, let the drug smuggling continue to enrich the pockets of whoever was running the show and ignore the consequences to the humanity he'd sworn to protect when he'd joined the North Wales police force.

Maybe he'd be looking for another job in a week or two. His father would be pleased if he showed interest now in following in his footsteps, in someday taking over the law firm. Hell, he'd probably pay for Will's schooling and happily if he saw an opportunity to snare him into that career. It'd make Lark happy, too, because then he'd be forced to live in Gloucester, and he could see her every day, if he wanted to. Will gritted his teeth. That wasn't the answer for him.

Will took the B4391 toward Bala after passing by the village church, St. Cynog's. He'd driven that little B road so many times now that he could almost drive it on mental cruise control, unless a stray sheep lurked around a curve. Edward would be a few minutes ahead of him, and when he arrived in Bala, he'd park and watch traffic to see if anyone had driven the road between the time he and Will had. It didn't get much traffic, so anyone they did spot could easily be followed until they were sure there was no threat. Once Will arrived, Edward could do his shopping and then they'd part ways for a few days. It felt good working with Edward again. They'd always been in synch with each other, working almost as a single unit and trusting each other wholly.

Will let his mind drift as he settled into the drive. He had to think things out, to prepare for the consequences that he knew would be waiting at the end of the case so he could make some decisions. Was it a case? Yes, he had to think of it that way. He was working a drugs case, flagrantly ignoring every instruction he'd been given since his transfer away from the drugs unit. The bigger question in his mind, though, was if it was a drugs case he was working, was there anyone else he could trust to help them along? Specifically, Bowers. And maybe Quigley.

If he tried to keep everyone in the dark, he could still pretend to be working the Catherine Baines and Peter O'Connell murders. Billy Davies had family up north; that's why they'd focused their attention there. That didn't mean, however, that Billy wasn't smart enough to use his family connections to divert attention away from his real intentions. Perhaps he was smart enough to let his vehicle be seen on cameras heading north, and then, when no one suspected, he'd turned to the B roads in the opposite direction, misleading the pursuit. *No*, he shook his head with a grimace of self-recrimination, *Edward saw him in Wirral.* That meant he'd gone at least that far north, giving Will no real reason to look for him in the other direction. Unless he withheld the information he'd gotten from Edward, which he could easily do at least until the SOCOs found evidence to place Billy at the scene of O'Connell's murder. That would be the first step, then, to present a theory that Billy had misled them and suggest that he and Notley split up, with Notley continuing to look for him in northwest England and him going south toward Fishguard. He'd have to make something up, some sort of possible connection for Billy in that area. Or would a gut feeling be explanation enough for why he wanted to look for Billy to the south rather than where his family was?

He could enlist Quigley's help to try to track the Ford Kuga, and with luck, that vehicle had been driven toward Fishguard on the main roads where cameras would have been in use. If Edward's guesses were right, then it made sense that it'd head that way, with Billy or without him. If they could find email or social media accounts for Billy, that would also be a huge leap forward, but it might be information he'd have to hide from Notley. He, or Quigley, could scan them for connections to people that might just lead them to the next rung up the ladder. He suspected there were many Billys in that chain, many farmers with barns to store product in on its way to markets, where it could be released in controlled quantities as demand indicated. At least a few of them would talk, he was sure, bragging to friends about their new lucrative business ventures. Most people couldn't keep a secret from everyone they knew. They had to talk. Above Billy would be someone who owned a bigger facility, a place where the product would first arrive in the country and be split up into smaller units for transport. That was the person Will would like to find. He would probably have names he could supply, if pushed hard, and someone would probably be there when the truck arrived with the product who directed the distribution of it.

The research he'd like to do could be accomplished without anyone being the wiser, he thought. It was afterward that he worried about. He thought he could give legitimate reasons for trying to track Billy to Fishguard, or near there, but if someone in leadership was truly involved in getting the drugs into the country, then that person could have access to Will's whereabouts if he suspected Will of investigating not just the murders, but the underlying drugs operation that had led to them. He would almost certainly be aware of Will's previous partnership with Edward, and with Edward having disappeared from their radar and his being assigned to the case so close to the drugs operation, they'd be stupid not to monitor his actions. Bowers would hardly see a reason to keep it secret that Will was looking for Billy. Whoever it was in charge, he might go so far as to ask that Will be taken off the case involving Billy Davies. He could probably come up with some reason why. Bowers might wonder about it, but he'd probably go along with it. That'd be the end of his investigation, unless he wanted to go rogue, like Edward. And that would end his career and put him in the crosshairs, along with Edward, for sure.

His other choice was to talk to Bowers. Edward would object if he knew, but he didn't have to know. If Bowers was brought in on it, he could enable a lot of what Will needed to do. He could allow him to go undercover and send backup if he and Edward uncovered other people on the chain or – the best of all worlds – who was running the show. He could cover for Will and help him keep Notley at arm's length. Most importantly, in the end, Will could claim that he was only following orders, and Bowers would take the fall if things went badly wrong. He'd also be able to protect Will's job if it went right, for the same reasons. That all sounded good. But how far could he trust Bowers? If he was a part of the conspiracy, that would mean Will's death, he was sure. No one in the position of leading such a large criminal enterprise could ignore Will's being a thorn in his side. It was an impossible decision to make, yet it had to be made quickly. If Bowers was to be in on it, it had to happen before Will started his investigation. He had to be part of it from the start. He just didn't know what to do.

He arrived in Bala without having made a decision. He drove slowly through the village, looking for a take-out food place that'd look like a natural stopping place on his trip back to Caernarfon. He saw Edward's motorbike in a car park behind the village church and kept driving. A bakery drew his eye, and he drove on until he found a parking space a few shops beyond it. He parked and went inside, keeping an eye out for anything out of the ordinary.

Inside, he ordered a black coffee to go, along with three croissants that he reasoned would keep until later, since he was anything but hungry after the huge fry-up Bronwyn had made that morning.

"Having a Sunday drive?" the young woman behind the counter asked, bagging his croissants. "Only, I saw the cute little car when you drove past." She smiled at him, and he wondered if she was flirting or if it was his imagination. Whatever, it wouldn't hurt to have something on the camera he saw in the corner overlooking the counter and cash register.

"Had a big fight with my girlfriend," he confessed, trying for an air of frustration. "I'm off to Caernarfon, giving her a few days to think it over."

"You want her back?" The woman handed him the bag and turned to pour the coffee into a paper to-go cup. "Bet you could find someone else pretty quick."

"Yeah," he smiled back at her, "a few days away will give me time to think what I want to do. It's not just all about her, after all. I have a voice in the matter. I have to decide what I want."

"You do," she told him. "Come back soon, will you?" She handed him the coffee.

He paid her with his card, hoping it would lead someone to watch the camera footage if they tried to track him. "I will."

Back outside, he strolled casually back to the car. He'd left the top down and, sure enough, a small package had been tossed casually onto the floor on the passenger side. He grinned and started the car up. He wouldn't see Edward in Bala, but he could keep track of him easily enough from now on.

Will still hadn't made a decision about Bowers by the time he drove back through the opening in the city walls of Caernarfon in early afternoon. He stopped at his flat to put his things away and change his clothes, and then he drove to the station, knowing that his colleagues would wonder about him showing up on his Sunday off. Bowers would be off today, as well, being high enough on the hierarchy to have his weekends free unless something huge was brewing. That gave Will one day's grace before he had to make a decision, and he intended to make a good start on his research before he committed.

As he'd expected, his colleagues' eyes followed him as he walked to his desk in the big common room they all shared. The other DCIs were in attendance, having obviously finished with the case up in Anglesey, and his sometime partner Beth Holway gave him an openly curious look and rolled her chair over to his desk the minute he sat down.

"Is your case so important it has you working on the Sunday?" she asked. "Only, we heard your suspect was in the wind and you had no leads toward finding him right away, so you were taking the usual days off."

Time to get the rumor mill started. "It happens that I've had a falling out with Bronwyn," he told her, having practiced in the mirror what the look on his face should be when he admitted that: something partway between sad and angry, with a little bitterness thrown in. "I'm back and need something to take my mind off things, so I thought I'd come in and do some work. Anything wrong with that?" He narrowed his eyes and tried to look challenging.

She sat back in her chair, but didn't roll away. "I'm sorry, Will." But she didn't look sorry. He'd always thought she had an interest in being his partner in more ways than policework.

"Your case done, then?" He thought it best to change the subject before she got suspicious. In their line of work, they learned to read body language, and they could almost always tell if someone was lying to them.

"It looks like a simple fall from a cliff," she told him. "We spent a couple of days up there, but nothing pointed toward a crime."

"What did forensics say?"

"They thought a couple of his bruises looked suspicious, but he landed in the rocks just off-shore, so it's hard to tell. We're heading back up there after the SOCOs finish up, if they find anything more."

"They're still looking at the scene?" Will found it hard to believe.

"They thought they were done, and then a hiker found some broken bracken up the trail just a bit that might show a scuffle took place there, so they're taking another look."

Anything to keep major crimes far away from Fishguard, Will guessed, thinking the incident was rather convenient if you wanted to keep North Wales law enforcement far away from the real action. It strengthened Edward's case. "That's not a bad place to spend a spring day," Will told her.

"How's your case going?"

Time to be careful again. "We've two bodies and one suspect who's fled into oblivion," he told her, at least somewhat truthfully. "I've had an idea that I want to pursue further."

She looked at him, arching an eyebrow.

"It looks like a domestic. You know, the two victims having an affair, and him finding out and going off his head. He's got hold of a gun somehow, and he shot her and then drove north and shot her boyfriend, too. We're assuming he's hiding out up there because that's where his family is, Liverpool and Carlisle, but I'm thinking if he's smart, he'll get well away from there. I'd like to see if he tracked back down through Wales."

"Mobile phone?" she wanted to know.

"He seems to use pre-paid. Maybe he couldn't afford a plan, I don't know. I want to check his internet accounts, see if he has friends somewhere else he might be holed up with. I'd also like to look at cameras, see if I can catch his vehicle anywhere."

"Sounds tedious. I wish you luck." She smiled and rolled her chair back to her own desk.

He thought he'd managed that encounter brilliantly.

He started up his computer and got busy. Google searches turned up Billy Davies' name several times, mostly in connection with his previous arrests. He went to Facebook, Instagram, and Twitter, finding accounts on the latter two, but when he tried them, he found limited access and even more limited use. Billy didn't seem to utilize his social media accounts much, and Will wondered why he'd bothered to create them at all.

He tried Catherine Baines and had more success there, finding pictures of her with Billy and occasional remarks on Twitter that showed strong opinions about everything from what she considered rude behavior from strangers to her own life choices. About Billy, she'd had nothing but complimentary things to say, portraying him as a reliable mate who knocked himself out to provide her with life's luxuries. He studied her face. She'd been an average-looking young woman, with a thin oval face, hair too blonde to be natural, and eyes exaggerated to the point of looking like some of Lark's dolls and beanies, the ones with eyes too large for their faces. In fact, if he had to describe her look, he'd say she looked rather like a Barbie doll, teeth too white in a fixed smile that looked faked and eyebrows shaped in an artful curve over eyes with lashes so long they had to be artificial. Various poses made him wonder if she fancied being a fashion model, the fake smile turning into an artful pout at times and other times to what she must have thought a sexy come-on look. He had a glimpse of the future, and he promised himself to encourage Lark's interest in horses rather than glamour dolls.

None of this gave him any ideas how to track Billy's movements in the days preceding the murders, however, and he had no idea how to access email accounts or traffic cameras. It was time to enlist Quigley's help.

Quigley seemed never to take a day off work, and Will was glad of it. He grabbed one of the fold-up chairs kept alongside the outer wall of the office and pulled it up to Quigley's desk. "I need some help," he told the tech whiz.

Quigley listened as Will detailed his efforts, ending with a plea for how else to track Billy. "We've got notices out already for any sightings of Billy's Ford Kuga," he told Will, "and you'd need a warrant to get access to his personal email account, if he has one. That's protected information unless you have a valid reason for getting into it."

"Would him being a suspect in a double murder be reason enough?"

"I'd think so. Want me to see what I can do?"

"Thanks, that would be great." Will thought for a minute. "Can I get into Catherine's? Billy used her mobile, so maybe he used her email, too."

"That's easier. You just need permission from her next-of-kin – the parents, right?"

Will nodded. "Verbal permission okay?"

Quigley frowned. "Written is better. It'll hold up better in court."

"Okay." Maybe he could get someone from the constabulary up there to visit them and get a signed document that could be faxed to him. That shouldn't be too hard. "How do I go about looking at camera footage from before the murders? Only, I think Billy's ditched the Kuga, but if I could place him with friends somewhere earlier, it might give us someone else we could question about his whereabouts."

"That's easy enough. I just have to enter the information into the database with a time frame, say two weeks prior to the murders? Or you want to go back further?"

"Two weeks is a good start. If we don't come up with anything, we can always go back further, right?"

"Yeah, we can expand it anytime we want to, but it'll take some time if you don't have a particular area or time to narrow it to. CCTV cameras are everywhere these days."

"We've already searched north into England," he improvised, "so let's go south this time. Say...toward Fishguard, like that area."

Quigley studied him. "You have a lead down that way?"

"Just a rumor I heard. Made me wonder if he was thinking of fleeing to Ireland and then on to Europe."

"Okay, we'll start with the A483. That'd be the most logical route down from Wirral."

"Is there anything else you can suggest? Any other way of trying to find him?"

"You might look at his old files, from his prior arrests. Sometimes there's a mention of an associate in them that gives you a lead. Or check about his time in gaol. Maybe he made friends there."

"That's a good idea. The files are online now, I suppose? Not paper files any longer?"

"Some of each. It depends how old the cases are. I'll request them for you, shall I?"

"Thanks." He'd might as well go for broke. "Can you get files for Peter O"Connell, too? He's our other victim, but you never know. Something in his past may lead us to Billy."

Quigley tapped keys. "Looks like Billy spent most of his prison time at Berwyn."

"Berwyn? That's Wrexham?"

"Yeah. You could call and talk to the warden about him, but a personal visit would probably give you a better feel for him. I know it's a drive across to there, but maybe worth the time."

Time that might be better spent than sitting in the office, waiting for files to arrive. If Billy Davies' farm was a depot for a cache of drugs, he might have been recruited in prison or maybe upon his release. It made sense. "When do you think his files will get here?"

"I'll have them by the time you're ready to call it a day."

"Peter's too?"

Keys tapped again. "It doesn't look like O'Connell had much in the way of form. He was pretty clean."

"Maybe I'll take Billy's files home with me tonight, then." He wondered about O'Connell, though. He couldn't be totally clean if he was involved with Billy's circle of friends.

154

"You can't access the computer files from home. They'll be restricted."

"Then I'll have to make do with whatever paper files I get today and finish up with them tomorrow morning before I go to Wrexham." He wished there was a way to check for lorries that had entered Ireland from the mainland and then left again from Rosslaire, but he'd have no excuse for that type of research. Even better would be a record of travel information for Llewellyn Mathews, the chief superintendent in charge of drugs and alcohol, or even the commander, Areon Williams. He'd never met the commander, but he'd worked under Mathews who'd kept him on a tighter leash than he'd have liked and who'd requested that he be transferred away from the department after his sister Julia's death of a drug overdose. It had seemed excessive to him at the time, and now he wondered if it was just a convenient way of getting rid of an officer who came just a little too close to the truth.

At the end of the day, he'd found little trace of Billy either before or after the two murders, and he wondered how someone could disappear so completely without a trace. How hard would it be to erase camera footage that showed Billy's movements? He didn't suppose Mathews or Williams had the expertise themselves, but someone like Quigley, if he was in their pay, could probably manage it. He'd watched Quigley from his own desk, wondering if he would make a call about Will's requests or even send someone an email. Quigley could hide his digital efforts, of that Will had no illusions. He thought Quigley was trustworthy, but Edward's paranoia was rubbing off on him and suddenly, he wasn't sure of anyone.

His colleague Jay Mehta stopped by his desk as he was gathering up a few notes and a slim box of files on Billy's earliest arrests to pursue from home. He wanted to make sure he'd left nothing incriminating on his desk, which was in a common area and open to a casual search, if anyone was interested.

"Want to get something to eat later?" Jay wanted to know.

Will considered the offer. He liked Jay, and he didn't mind having company for a meal when he was alone in Caernarfon, but he didn't want to involve Jay in any way in what he was planning, and nor did he want to discuss Bronwyn with him. That, and the fact that Jay's degree in psychology gave him insight others didn't have, made him wary of spending time with him.

Jay was impatient. "Hey, it's an easy question. Do you, or don't you?"

He shouldn't have hesitated. "I've got stuff on my mind tonight, Jay. I wouldn't be good company, I'm afraid. Rain check?"

"You'd be better off not sitting home alone brooding about her," Jay persisted. The rumor had already made the rounds of the office then. That was good news.

"Who says I'm brooding?"

"I've seldom seen you so involved in a case. You were really focused on your computer, and that on a day off work for you. I can only think you want a distraction."

"Not tonight, okay? I want some time to think."

"Tomorrow, then?"

"We'll see," Will hedged. "That'll depend on whether you get a case and whether mine sends me out and about." He could see the disappointment in Jay's face. The kid had made it obvious he idolized Will a bit.

But Jay rallied. "Okay, then, but I'm holding you to it."

At home that evening, Will microwaved a curry he had in the freezer. He ate it, and then he poured a glass of Famous Grouse and sat in his chair, looking across at Bronwyn's sketch. He missed her already. It had been a long while since he hadn't at least heard her voice in the evening, but he didn't dare make a call, in case someone was listening in. He hoped she'd see something to help them along, and that seemed a strange thought. Not long ago, he'd struggled with the thought of her going into that trance and seeing visions, but now it seemed natural and expected. He'd come a long way, he supposed.

He opened the box of paperwork on Billy and set it on his lap, lifting a page at a time from it. Billy's career had begun when he was young. His first arrest, for shoplifting, occurred when he was only fourteen, with a second offense for underage drinking only a few weeks later. There followed a few months' grace, probably because he'd been monitored for a while. Just before his sixteenth birthday he was arrested for his first dealing offense when several baggies of marijuana had been found in his school backpack by a headmaster who'd been tipped off by one of Billy's classmates. That one had earned him counselling time rather than detention, but again it was followed quickly by a second incident in which another boy, a Randall Evans, was beaten up in a fight on his way home from school.

Will thought that over. Almost certainly Randall Evans had been the tipster, and Billy had gotten his revenge, adding detention time to the counselling at that point. He hoped the education system in juvenile detention facilities were good because Billy spent enough time in them that his potential for future employable skills would be dismal if not. He wondered if it would be worth the effort to track down whoever had been the warden at the facility Billy had been sent to. All of it had been years in the past. It seemed to him that if Billy had been recruited for a drugs operation, it would have happened much later. The chances that anyone he'd met in juvenile detention had led him to his current situation were slim.

The last case file in the box was the longest. At age twenty-one, Billy had been arrested after a pawn shop had been robbed of several thousand pounds and some items of value, including several guns. The robbers, wearing Halloween masks, had brandished what looked like pistols, but had later been proven to be air guns. Nevertheless, with the stolen guns unrecovered after the arrest, both men were sentenced to twelve years in prison. Billy had been released on time and his partner in crime, a man called Morys Howell, got out after seven for good behavior. Will assumed Billy hadn't mended his ways, but his other adventures would be detailed digitally and Will couldn't look at them until the next day when he was in the office.

He made a note of Morys Howell's name, careful of the Welsh spelling, and then he set the box aside. He wondered if he could do a search for Morys Howell on Google without it being a problem. He could probably still pass it off as part of the investigation into Billy Davies' whereabouts, but he didn't want to do anything that might attract attention. Still, maybe it was better to do that sort of research from home. It was more likely his department computer was bugged than his mobile. Who knew? Edward said to trust no one.

He opened a search bar on his phone and typed in the name. The arrest for the robbery showed up, it having been newsworthy at the time. He read the accompanying news story, gleaning the fact that Morys Howell had originally come from a place called Llandrindod Wells. He clicked on maps and typed the name, finding it in central Wales. That was interesting. He'd have to try to do some research on Morys Howell. What if he also had a farm there? Or an unused warehouse or garage? The idea was that the drugs were brought in on a lorry and then distributed to smaller storage areas for a time before arriving at their ultimate destinations. It couldn't be that easy, could it?

He decided a call to Edward was in order. Glancing around his flat, he considered his options and decided it was better to be safe than sorry. He took one of the pre-paid mobiles out of its box and put in the number that had been scribbled on the cardboard box before it had been dropped into his car, then stepped outside and walked down the stairs to the street before hitting the call button.

"Got something?" Edward was brusque.

"Maybe," Will hedged. "I might have a name for you." He explained about Morys Howell.

Edward caught the idea immediately. "You think Howell was another of the couriers, that either he brought Billy into the organization or the other way around."

"It'd be pretty convenient if that were the case, wouldn't it? Can you get to Llandrindod Wells and snoop around a bit tomorrow?"

"No way to tell if Howell owns property there?"

"I can probably find out tomorrow morning. I don't think it'd draw undue attention to follow that line of inquiry. If he owns a farm or unused buildings, Billy could be hiding out there, so it makes sense to check."

"If you get close to people involved in this organization, they'll know. They don't want you going anywhere near them. The Billy Davies debacle is bad enough; if they see you tracking another of their couriers, they'll have to stop you, officially or otherwise. Be careful, Will. Check your car for tracking devices, will you? Or bombs?"

Will laughed for Edward's sake, but he knew it wasn't a joking matter. "I know the drill, mate. Remember, we used to do this sort of thing all the time. We are invincible when we put our heads together. Speaking of which, what have you accomplished since this morning?"

"Nothing as exciting as you've done. I do think Morys Howell is worth checking into. He won't be anyone in charge, but we need to create some mayhem in order to draw those guys out." Edward's voice faded for a moment. "Sorry, I'm in a pub in Aberystwyth, trying to make a new friend or two. I've not made much progress, but I did ride the back roads today on my bike, looking for likely storage places."

"Any success?"

"I've noted one or two possibilities. I want to check them out further tonight."

He meant in the dark, when he'd be sneaking around peering in windows and looking for big locks on the doors. "What are they, barns?"

"No barns. It'd look funny for a lorry to pull up to a barn, right? There's an old industrial area on the western edge of town, plenty of abandoned buildings, but some still in use, so a lorry driving up wouldn't look too out of place. The problem is that an SUV pulling a stock trailer full of sheep *would* look out of place."

"It can't hurt to look, though."

"Any way you can check out that drugs bust in Dover? Maybe track down whoever went down for that one and see who they think is blocking them?"

"Now you're getting to things that would be harder to explain away."

"Only if they're monitoring your computer."

"Which is probably happening." Maybe he should take Quigley into his confidence. Quigley could probably tell if Will's computer was compromised and maybe even know a way around it.

"I'm trying to make some new contacts here. There have to be guys who were suppliers in the past, and I'd think they'd be pretty unhappy at the turn things have taken in the business. They might know something that'd give us a lead."

"And if they can be talked into helping us out, we'd have more feet on the ground than just ours." It wasn't ethical in any way to use a cartel as a partner, but they were already in over their heads, so what did it matter?

Edward's voice turned softer. "Hey, mate, I don't want you getting all melancholy now that you can't see Bronwyn and do something stupid to speed things along."

"Get away with you," Will retorted, but his heart wasn't in it. He did miss her.

"I think I like her, Will."

"I'm glad you finally got to meet. I fancy her, too, quite a lot, actually."

"Just don't forget you have to schedule the wedding for when I can be best man. You can't make the biggest commitment of your life without me at your side."

"You're talking crazy stuff now, mate. I'm nowhere near that idea yet. Scares me silly, that."

"Then you aren't a lost cause. There's still hope," Edward teased him, ending the call.

Afterward, he slipped the phone into his pocket and set out to walk the streets. Noise from pubs and all-night off-licenses accompanied him as he wandered toward the harbour where the castle loomed, lit at night as it never would have been in its heyday. He kept an eye out for threats, seeing nothing to disturb his solitude. A misty fog was rolling in from the sea, dampening his hair and chilling him despite his jacket. He liked it, though. It gave the city an air of mystery. Wales was a country of imagination and magic, after all. A land of chivalry. Was what he and Edward were doing chivalrous? He liked the thought, turning it around in his mind.

At the harbour, he found a bench and sat looking out to sea and thinking about the case. It would be a busy day tomorrow, perusing files in the office early and then heading off to Wrexham after to talk with the warden. He made a mental note to have someone call ahead for an appointment, and he'd forgotten to call about getting permission to access Catherine Baines' email account. Quigley could do that for him. He wished there was time to go to Dover to search out the suspects in that arrest, and then he wondered if there'd been other drugs busts lately that were more local. If so, he could try to talk to someone involved, see if they'd open up to him about their opposition. Surely, they'd suspect someone had insider information, and they must have some idea of who it was.

His phone chimed, but it was just a text from Jay. "All right?"

He texted back, "I'm good," and let it go at that.

He still didn't know what to do about Bowers. He'd be in the office in the morning, so that was his deadline. Should he confide in him, or not? That could be the detail that made or broke the case, in the end. It could be the decision that meant life or death for him and Edward, as well. He might have to tell him what was going on just so Notley wouldn't figure it out or resist working the case separately. He thought he could trust Bowers, who had always been fair to him. But now? He wasn't sure if he should take the risk.

At the moment, he didn't want to think about it, so he put it to the back of his mind, closed his eyes, and listened to the water lapping against the wharf.

Chapter Eleven

Will woke to the voice of a pigeon cooing from the rooftop of the building opposite, its voice melodious against the tapping of heels on the sidewalk below, the hum of traffic on the street, subdued voices, and somewhere, the ringing of a mobile.

He checked. It wasn't his. That is, it wasn't any of his since he now owned his own, plus four pre-paid ones. He rolled over in relief. He'd like a few more minutes to drowse in bed, to get his day planned in his mind before he slipped into the shower and ate whatever he could find for breakfast.

The little fridge in the flat was nearly empty, with just a limp head of lettuce, an apple, some deli meat probably gone bad, and a carton of quickly souring milk on its shelves. He had food in the freezer, but he didn't want to take the time to defrost it, plus most of that consisted of quick dinners for his bachelor nights alone. He filled the kettle and set it on to boil, then spooned instant coffee into his to-go mug. He'd drink that while he checked his phone for messages, and then he'd pick up something more appetizing on his way to the office.

He checked in at seven-thirty, much to the surprise of his colleagues who'd grown used to him arriving late to work. They gawped at him from behind computers and files, and he heard the words, 'maybe now his mind will be on work rather than romance,' before sending a glare toward the offending person, one of the detective sergeants whose name he couldn't recall.

A sticky note graced the front of his computer. "Files available – you'll see the link" in Quigley's scrawl. Good. He glanced over and saw that the tech guy wasn't at his desk, so maybe Quigley did actually take days off – or he was occupied in snitching on Will's activities. He didn't like to think like that. He liked Quigley, but at the same time he knew everyone could be bought if the price was high enough. He had no illusions about that.

He rolled his chair closer to his computer, took a bite of the bacon roll he'd bought, and started to scroll through the files.

Billy'd had three arrests since he'd been released after the armed-robbery gig. The first was for dealing again, and again the amount was indicative of a small-time street dealer, but pills this time rather than marijuana. The other two arrests were for petty theft: shoplifting in a Safeway and in an off-license. He'd been given six months in gaol for the drugs and time served for the shoplifting convictions. The most recent crime had occurred two years previously, about the time Billy had leased the farm from Nathan Thomas, which was interesting. Will's instinct told him that Billy had already been recruited at that point and instructed to find a place for let that would allow him to receive shipments of drugs, store them, and then redistribute them to a place nearer to the market for them. It seemed reasonable to assume that someone he'd met during his time in detention, most likely during the six months' time for the dealing, had seen his potential as a link in the chain and talked him into joining the organization. If he'd been recruited during the longer sentence, they hadn't bothered to use him right away and he hadn't bothered to stay out of trouble.

"What are you doing here on the Monday?" A voice interrupted his reading.

Will's heart raced. At least he hadn't had the file on Morys Howell open when Bowers was wandering through the common room, checking that everyone was busy working. "I had a bit of a personal setback, sir, so I thought I'd come in on my days off and see if I could get any leads on Billy Davis."

"We've got a warrant out for him," Bowers said, "and it's only a matter of time before someone comes across him. You don't think he's likely to commit more murders meanwhile, do you? I thought you'd decided it was a domestic."

"We did, sir, but since I didn't have a lot else on my plate, I thought I'd do a little searching into his past, maybe find a friend who'd let him hide out for a bit."

Bowers was studying him. "And?"

Will had the feeling that Bowers had seen right through his lie. "I've got a couple of interesting tidbits, sir. Can I fill you in a bit later, after I've fleshed them out a bit?"

Bowers studied him for another long minute. "I'll be in my office when you're ready." He hesitated. "I'm sorry about you and Miss Bagley."

"Yes, sir, I'm afraid it was too much, too soon, moving in together." He'd thought out his cover story the day before. "She says she needs space."

"Women can be like that." Bowers lips twisted in what passed in him for a smile, and he walked on.

Quigley had sent files on Morys Howell and sent him emails about Peter O'Connell and William Bruce. He read the emails first, them being the easiest task.

As Quigley had told him, Peter O'Connell had seemed to stay out of trouble. If he'd had a juvenile arrest for possession, it didn't show up in his records. Quigley had taken time to research him further and included pertinent data. Peter O'Connell had been thirty-seven years old, about the same age as Billy Davies, which might mean they'd been school mates in Liverpool years earlier. Will wrote himself a note to check what schools they'd attended. He'd seemed to stay near to the area: the employment history Quigley had assembled listed unskilled jobs, mostly consisting of construction labor, retail sales, and restaurant work. He'd spent the last two years bartending at a pub in Liverpool. Will made another note to check when O'Connell had moved into the cottage on William Bruce's property. Logically, that would give him a timeline for

Billy's involvement with drug smuggling. O'Connell had social media accounts, and Quigley had left a note asking if Will wanted him to track down a few women who appeared in photos with him. Will set that idea aside for the time being since it would require a long drive and he didn't think Peter O'Connell would lead him to where the drugs were coming in, but he made another note to ask Quigley to get names and contact information, at least, in case things stalled and he was desperate.

William Bruce also appeared to be a solid citizen from what Quigley could find. He was forty-two years old, married, with two children in their teens. The farm had been in his family for at least two generations, and he'd taken it over when his father died four years previously. He raised cattle and some sheep, but a horse boarding facility he'd built up brought in more money than the other enterprises combined. It seemed Wirral was upscale enough to cater to people who wanted horses to ride, but wanted someone else to have the responsibility of caring for them. Bruce had built a new home near the stables, leaving the old buildings empty until O'Connell had moved in. Will made a note to ask when that had happened, and how it had happened.

Morys Howell provided a more interesting subject, in part because whoever had investigated the armed robbery had dug deep into the two suspects. It may have been overkill at the time, but now it gave Will a lot of information that might become useful. Howell had been born in Shrewsbury, but raised in Llandrindod Wells until his teens, when his parents split up and he moved with his father to Cardiff. The father had been interviewed at length. He'd said his son had been troubled by the divorce and had started using drugs when the two parents were fighting prior to the split. He'd hoped the move to Cardiff would give him a fresh start, but it had been a downhill struggle from there on. Howell had done poorly in school and dropped out at age sixteen, becoming involved with a gang that led to drug abuse. He'd been in and out of rehab until he turned eighteen, when he left home and started living on the streets. He'd been just nineteen when he'd been arrested for the armed robbery which, interestingly, hadn't been in Cardiff but in Shrewsbury.

Since his release from prison, Howell had apparently stayed clean, at least on paper. Will wondered if a visit to his father might provide an update on what Howell had been doing with his life in recent years.

165

There would be a probation officer he'd have checked in with for a while who might also have information. Will made a note. He had too many notes and too short a time. He'd have to go through the list and decide what might be the most informative in the long run.

A message popped up on his computer screen. Quigley. 'I have info when you have time.'

He wandered over to where the young tech guy was watching out for him from behind his computer, trying not to look too intrigued. "What's up?"

"I've been looking into Morys Howell, just from curiosity more than anything. When I did a Google search on him, his name came up as a suspect in a double murder down in Cardiff."

"Before or after the armed robbery?" *Why hadn't there been any information about that in his file? It should have warranted a mention, at least.*

"After. It'd be just about four months after his release for the robbery. When I tried to follow up on it, it was big news for a couple of days, and then it just died away. The last reference I found said charges had been dropped."

"Can you get me that file?"

Quigley looked up at him. "That's the strange thing. There isn't one, at least not that I can find."

Will frowned and leaned closer. "What does that mean?"

Quigley glanced around and lowered his voice. "I don't know. Usually there'd be something, even if it didn't go to trial."

"So, you're telling me two people were killed, and there's no record of any investigation into it?"

Quigley looked distinctly uncomfortable. "I can keep looking. Would it be possible it was assigned to a different jurisdiction?"

"It'd probably be South Wales major crimes, but we'd still have access to the records," Will said.

"I meant, like Scotland Yard or something?"

"You tell me. You're the expert."

Quigley shook his head. "We'd still have the initial investigation on file even if it was eventually assigned to someone else."

Will thought that over. *Interesting*. The drugs unit was based in Cardiff, and Edward thought they were intentionally diverting shipments elsewhere to avoid drawing attention to his immediate boss, who seemed to be his chief suspect. Could a chief inspector make a file disappear if it contained information he didn't want out? Could a chief superintendent? A commander? "I'm going out for a day or two to try to trace Billy Davies. Can you call me if you turn up anything else about this?"

"I don't know how it would relate to your murder case. Charges being dropped against Morys Howell wouldn't lead you to finding Billy Davies, I wouldn't think. I was just looking for his current whereabouts when I stumbled on that."

"You never know what might be helpful," Will insisted. He tapped his fingers on the desk. "I've got to get going. Let me know, right?"

He spent a few minutes gathering up his notes and then made a quick 'to do' list. He thought it worth a trip to Wrexham to talk to the warden at the prison and, if he could get a name, he'd like to talk to the probation officer assigned to Billy and, hopefully, Morys Howell, as well. Quigley's discovery had him intrigued, and he thought one of the two of them might have information that was apparently unavailable elsewhere about the double homicide. He only hoped his inquiries about Howell didn't attract undue attention. Once that was finished, he'd probably head south to meet up with Edward and rely on Notley's efforts to turn up additional information that might help. He sat for a minute, running through the lists in his head. He'd probably forgotten something important he needed to do, but he couldn't think what.

Which brought up the subject Will would rather avoid thinking about. It was decision time. He'd have to talk to Bowers, to tell him he was splitting up with Notley for a time, at least, and to give him an update on the case. Beyond that? How far did he trust him? Confiding in Bowers would do one of two things: either it would destroy their investigation and condemn both him and Edward, or it would give him a small hope of saving his career when all was said and done. It all depended on whether Bowers had succumbed to the seduction of easy power and money or whether he remained an ethical man dedicated to his life's work. There was no way to know for sure.

He walked through the common room, trying to look like it was just another working day, and then took a deep breath and knocked on Bowers' door.

"Come in." If he'd hoped that Bowers was out of his office, that he'd get a reprieve, his hopes had just been dashed. He knew, though, that he'd feel better as soon as it was done, either way.

He opened the door and stepped inside. "Sir, I'd like to update you on our case now, if you have the time."

Bowers looked up and nodded. "Are you done here for the day, then?"

"Yes, sir," Will tried to keep his voice calm. He was quaking inside. "I'm planning to go to Wrexham, to talk to the warden at the prison about Billy Davies."

Bowers considered that, studying Will intently. "I'm really sorry about Miss Bagley. I know you had great hopes there."

"Yes, I did." *Less, said, the better.*

"You have a board for me to look at?"

"We do, but I haven't added much to it since you saw it last." He took a breath. "Sir, I know it's highly unusual and probably against some rule or another, but would you consider going across the street and having a sandwich with me while I fill you in? It's just…I hadn't planned on being here these past two days, and my cupboard is as bare as old Mother Hubbard's. I'm famished, and I think I'd do a lot better job telling you about this case if I had a bite to eat." If he was going to confide in Bowers, and he thought he would, he wanted to be well away from the station in case someone had planted bugs. It wouldn't do to set off alarms. Logically, though, what he'd usually do was to just eat something first and then come back and talk to Bowers. It was a flimsy suggestion, and Bowers would probably see right through it, as would anyone else listening.

Bowers' eyebrows arched, but he answered calmly enough. "I've felt something of a pariah since I've been chief inspector here. You all seem to be fine with grabbing a drink or a bite to eat with each other, but I seem to be untouchable." He smiled again, this time more visibly.

"Should we meet in, what, twenty minutes, but not across the street. Do you know Llewellyn's Grotto?"

Will nodded, mute. He'd committed now.

"Okay, I'll see you there."

Will's knees were shaking as he walked back to his desk. He avoided catching anyone's eye as he gathered up the papers he wanted to take with him, but he could feel them watching from behind his back. He didn't want to leave anything behind that might reveal his motives. He reached for his mobile, and then he headed for the door, trying to appear as relaxed as possible. They'd all know about his breakup with Bronwyn. Some would be sympathetic, some probably gloating, and at least one hopeful. He grunted and shook his head. If they knew what was really going on, their reactions would probably be the same, except more intense.

He decided to walk to Llewellyn's Grotto, making a quick stop to put the papers in the car and grabbing a light jacket in case the sky opened up while he was away. A brisk breeze blew at his back as he strode down the sidewalk, propelling him toward a meeting he dreaded. One way or another, it would all be over in the next hour or so. He'd either be on his way to Wrexham for information or he'd be on suspension and fleeing south to find Edward. As far as he was concerned, Bowers would have to put him in gaol to stop him at this point, and he didn't think he'd do that.

He arrived at the pub before Bowers did and chose a table in a secluded corner. He shook his head at the barmaid's offer of a drink and studied the food menu while he waited.

Bowers walked in the door just minutes after Will had. He saw Will at his corner table, ambled over, and sat across from him. "This is about more than the Billy Davies case, isn't it?"

Will nodded. "Are you recording this, sir?"

"Do you want me to?"

"I'd prefer it if you didn't." Will twitched nervously at his napkin, and then he took it and set it firmly in his lap.

"I'm listening, then, if you want to tell me what's going on." Bowers caught sight of the approaching waitress from the corner of his eye and snapped at her, "Mineral water, please."

She looked at Will. "Ginger ale," he managed, thinking it would settle his queasy stomach.

"Will you be wanting to order food?"

"Maybe later," Bowers told her, waving her off. He waited until she was across the room before he looked at Will and raised his eyebrows. "This sounds serious."

"It is." Will swallowed and thought for a minute. *How to begin?* "I want you to know that I was following orders, sir. We were chasing the Billy Davies case, and that's all it was, at the start anyway."

Bowers watched him, waiting.

"You know that Catherine Baines had been shot in the head. Her parents had reported suspected abuse, and we figured he'd snapped and shot her. Billy and the gun were both missing, so we tried to track where he might go." As he got into the rhythm of his story, his nerves settled. "The parents gave us access to her mobile, and there were two calls that had gone to a pre-paid phone, one after her death. We tracked that phone's location, figuring that Billy was headed there to hide out and was giving whoever it was a head's up. We knew he was heading north because his Kuga was seen on cameras, not all the way to Wirral, but we knew he was going north."

"Yes, so you followed the phone to its location and found Peter O'Connell, also dead of a gunshot wound. That much I know." Bowers voice betrayed some impatience.

Will fought for control. He had to tell it right, or Bowers would think he'd gone mental. "That's right. You know all of this, sir. We talked about it late on Saturday when we had the conference call with you to decide how to proceed."

"You thought the two victims were probably having an affair, and Billy had found out."

"Yes, so we didn't think he presented much further danger at that point. As there was a warrant out for his arrest, you agreed that we should just back off for a couple of days and see if he was found. No one can stay hidden long."

"I remember. I told you to take your free days and then, if Billy still hadn't appeared, we'd look at it again on Tuesday. But then you came in on Sunday."

"I have more to tell you, sir." Will felt his nerves ramping up again, his heart racing in his chest. "When I got home on Saturday night, my old partner from the drugs unit was there waiting for me."

The waitress interrupted them with their drinks. She set them down, asked if they wanted anything else, and then scurried off when Bowers waved her away impatiently. "Go on."

"I should have seen it before then, sir. I told you myself to look for inconsistencies, and there it was, that Kuga, which Billy Davies should never have been able to afford. His landlord said he was late with the rent more times than not; that should have been our clue. But I let it go, going along with Notley and taking the easy way in the investigation."

"Your old partner...what was his name?"

"Edward, sir. Edward Smythe."

"Yes, I'm guessing he had more information about the case? That drugs were involved?"

"In a big way, sir. Edward works undercover, but for the past couple of months, he's been totally off the grid. He's been suspecting for some time that something was off." He glanced at Bowers, seeing the man's rapt attention focused on him now. "Something off in the police force, sir. They were getting arrests, but the drug problem was growing, not decreasing. Resources were being concentrated on activity that Edward had come to realize diverted attention away from the real shipments of drugs coming into the country."

"Us sending personnel up to Anglesey is an example?"

"Yes, sir. Edward is sure there's a big shipment coming in through Fishguard. He's been tracking people back to the source, but he's not there yet. Billy Davies was one of them. Edward thinks the product is coming over on the ferry, with customs officials bribed to look the other way. It's then taken to a warehouse or a barn or somewhere where it can be divided up into several smaller loads. These are then taken to other storage facilities, spreading the product out in various directions. Billy Davies would have provided one of those storage facilities. He'd load up some sheep in the stock trailer, and then he'd go pick up a shipment of drugs and carry them back in the trailer, with or without the sheep, to the farm he was leasing. They'd be in his barn for a week or two, and then he'd take them to a metropolitan area, in his case probably Liverpool, for the dealers to pick up."

Will could see Bowers turning this over in his head. "Where does Peter O'Connell come in?"

"We think that Billy was stealing some of the product and giving it to O'Connell, and then O'Connell would send it out to dealers he'd recruited and share the profits with Billy. Whoever was in charge must have found out. We think they killed Catherine Baines to scare Billy into compliance, but then Billy panicked. He took everything he could of value and pretended to drive toward Liverpool, but his actual destination was Wirral, intending to have one last big score with O'Connell, and then they'd both take the money and run."

"But whoever's overseeing Billy figured out he was running, so they followed him and killed O'Connell, too. Why not kill Billy?"

"We think they were afraid we'd get onto them if they killed Billy. They wanted us to think it was a domestic issue, which we did, and then we'd be trying to find Billy instead of getting onto their operation."

Bowers thought for a long moment. "Why does Edward think someone in the force is involved?"

"Not just involved, sir, but running the whole operation. Think of it: a chief superintendent or even a commander would have the resources to stop their competitors and eliminate the competition almost entirely. They would have the power to track their enemies, for one thing. They'd have inside knowledge so they could arrange to blackmail or bribe the people they needed to enable their shipments to get to their destinations. They'd have ways to threaten them if they don't comply. They'd be able to divert attention away from possible confrontations. Best of all, they'd know if someone was onto them, someone like Edward. There were two attempts on his life, sir, just in the past two weeks. They know he suspects them, and they think they need to stop him."

Bowers was nodding now. "Does he have a specific suspect in mind?"

"He just doesn't know, sir. He doesn't trust anyone at this point. All our informers, the people we used to pay for information, are in their pay now, or at least it looks that way. Every way he turns, someone is there watching him or, worse, trying to kill him. In fact," he glanced at Bowers, "he insisted that I not tell you. There may be more than one individual involved, maybe more than one chief superintendent."

"So why did he confide all this in you? He wanted your help?"

Will shook his head. "No, he wanted to warn me away from the case. He was sure I'd see the drugs connection, if I hadn't already. I'm embarrassed to say that I hadn't until he pointed it out. He wanted me well away from his investigation so we wouldn't interfere with what he was doing."

Bowers leaned forward, resting his arms on the table. "And now you want to be a part of it, despite my specific orders to stay away from any drugs cases. What if I tell you to leave it? Will you still follow orders?"

Will let out a deep, quavering breath and brushed a hand through his unruly hair. "I don't think I can, sir. To give credit where it's due, Edward really didn't want me involved. He just came to warn me away from it. But he can't do it alone. I spent the past day and a half using police resources to look for connections, to try to find leads for him to follow." He didn't want to go into detail, in case Bowers was one of the enemy. If whoever opposed them didn't know he'd given Edward Morys Howell's name, maybe that'd be the break he'd need to figure out who was running things, even if Will were to be taken out of the game.

"You found some?" Bowers hadn't taken his eyes off Will's.

"I'd rather not say, sir," Will stammered. "I know that's being insubordinate, but the fewer people who know what we're doing, the more chance we have of getting to the bottom of this. No disrespect, sir."

Bowers shook his head. "I understand your wariness, Cooper. I'm a little insulted, but I get that you don't trust anyone right now, including me."

"I trusted you enough to share all of this with you," Will pointed out, defensively.

"Yes, you did. Now what do I do with the information?"

Will waited in silence. He'd opened the floodgates and shared as much as he thought he dared; now the ball was in Bowers' court.

"You thought my office might be bugged?"

Will nodded. "I'm sure if it is, they saw through my little ploy, but at least they don't know what I know…yet." He hoped Bowers wouldn't notice the hesitation.

If he did, he ignored it. "You're going out into the field to help Edward? Working undercover again?"

Stated baldly like that, Will could see how much trouble he was in. He'd been transferred from drugs and alcohol just to keep him from working drug cases undercover, and then he'd been specifically told not to be involved in the latest efforts in the north. "Yes, sir, that's my plan. We thought the two of us could disrupt their network enough to cause them problems and hopefully draw out the leadership."

"And then what? The two of you can't take them on alone."

Will hadn't thought it through that far. "I don't know, sir. If we can find out who it is, maybe we can go above their heads at that point."

Bowers hesitated, took a sip of his water. "How can I help?"

Will blinked in surprise. "I hadn't meant to draw you in, sir. I just wanted you to know what I intended to do."

"What are you going to do about the Davies case? What about Sean?"

Will took a breath. "Sean *can't* know what I'm doing, sir. You know how he feels about me. I hate to say it, but I don't trust him not to talk, and I can't risk someone hearing what we're doing. We're in a lot of danger as it is, but if Sean's involved, he could point his finger right at us."

"You don't think he'll figure it out when you suddenly drop the case?"

"I hadn't thought to drop the case. I hoped that we could split up, that Sean could keep trying to track Davies' whereabouts up around Liverpool and Carlisle, while I tell him I've a lead toward the south. That way people would think we're still chasing Billy and that their ploy is working."

"And when Sean finds him? Because he will, sooner or later."

Will thought fast. "We'll have to cross that bridge when we come to it, sir. Billy's almost certainly dead. What use would he be to them now? His farm is compromised, and Billy knows too much. Even if he doesn't know who's running the operations, he knows where to go to pick up and drop off his loads. They wouldn't risk it. They've killed him already, and we'll probably never find his body."

"So, you want me to lie to Sean, to send him off to track down someone he'll never find?"

That would be obstruction of justice, at the least. "No, sir, I wouldn't ask you to lie. I just want you to agree with me when I suggest it. You can't look like you're involved. I would never ask you to give up your career to enable us in this situation." Although he'd like Bowers help, if it were to be offered.

"And how about Sean's career?" Bowers sounded a little angry now, although his voice was still low enough not to be overheard. "You do know what this'll do to him? To know he'd been lied to and to suspect I've been complicit in that lie? To know I didn't trust him with the truth? To know he's been sent off on a fool's errand when he thinks he's working a serious case?"

"Please, sir, you can't tell him what's going on. You just can't." Will was pleading now, desperate to direct the conversation away from Notley, to what he realized would probably mean the end of his partner's career. "I know Sean won't like it, but he can blame me for it all. Face it, I won't be here anyway after this. I'll have disobeyed a direct order and gone rogue on my own. How can you keep me on after that?"

"Then why tell me what you're doing?"

That was the crux of the matter. Bowers wasn't stupid. He'd know why Will wanted to tell him. "I hoped to have your blessing, sir," he admitted. "I hoped that, if Edward and I are successful, that people would know that you helped catch some really bad people, people in our own organization that needed to be brought down. That you used me because you knew with my past history, I'd have a chance at figuring it all out. That you directed me to go undercover and find them, if I could."

"That I could save your career by sacrificing my own."

Will lowered his eyes, brushing his hand through his hair again where it flopped onto his forehead. "I couldn't ask that, sir, but if there's a chance of saving both of our careers, I hope you'd try for my sake."

Bowers studied him in silence for a long moment. "I need to think this over," he said finally. "I don't like the idea of using Sean as a pawn, of sacrificing him even if it is for a noble cause. You and I both know it would be the end of his career. He's too proud a man to stand being lied to by his superiors, to know he wasn't trusted with the truth."

Will nodded.

"Where are you off to this afternoon?"

"Wrexham, to talk to the prison warden."

"And then?"

"It depends what I find out. I'd like to go undercover after that, to head south toward Fishguard and help Edward. I think I've found out all I can here for the time being."

"Can you check in with us in the morning? I'd like to meet with you and Notley so we can plan your approach to the case. I'll talk to you alone first so you know what my decision is."

"That sounds fair, sir." That'd be the moment of greatest risk. If Bowers was involved with the running of the drugs operations, Will would be arrested that next day on some charge or another to keep him out of the way. He knew that's what he would do if the situation were reversed.

Bowers gave him a little nod. "You and Bronwyn haven't really broken it off, have you?"

"No, sir. Time is short if we want to stop this next shipment, and I needed an excuse to be in the office on my free days. It seemed the easiest explanation."

"And you want her well away from this case," Bowers concluded. He picked a tenner from his wallet and laid it on the table. "It's a dangerous tightrope you'll be walking, Cooper. I hope you come out of it alive." He studied Will's face, his own stern. "I'll see you in the morning."

Will walked back to his car, got in, and headed through the opening in the town walls toward the A55, the fastest route to Wrexham. The rain that threatened still hadn't begun to fall, but the sky swirled with the looming clouds. He'd make this trip and then return to Caernarfon for the night. If traffic stayed light and the interview went quickly, maybe he could detour through Llangynog and see Bronwyn for a few minutes on the return trip. If someone was tracking his car, they'd see the detour and that would conflict with the rumors he'd spread about their breakup, but who was to say that he couldn't stop in and try to talk her into reconciling? He'd talk to her outside in the garden in case the cottage had been bugged. He shook his head. Edward's paranoia was really rubbing off on him. Then again, Edward had been twice lucky, and Will might not be as alert as Edward had been. He needed to be on top of his game.

He was passing by Conwy when his phone jerked him out of his reverie. He grabbed it from where it lay by the gear shift and looked at the screen. His mother. What did she want now?

He'd might as well get it over with. He hit the green button. "Hello, Mother."

"William! I wasn't sure I'd catch you." She sounded friendlier than normal, and Will was instantly suspicious.

"I'm actually working a case, but you caught me in the car so I can talk for a few minutes. What's up?"

He heard her take a breath and wondered if his speech had been too casual for her taste. "Lark is missing you, and I wondered if we could schedule a visit for you here soon. The weekend after next she has the Friday off school, so I thought that might be a good time. It would be a nice, long weekend."

"I usually work on Friday and Saturday, but if this case wraps up, I might have the Sunday free. I may be able to arrange a few extra days off." That was the weekend following Bronwyn's conference and it would be ideal if they could drive down to Gloucester from the Beacons on the Thursday and bring Lark back to Llangynog for a long weekend. She could finally decorate her new bedroom in the cottage, that's if Will still had a job and money to spend, and she could ride Hobbs, Bronwyn's pony. He'd probably be on suspension by then at the least, which would leave him broke but with plenty of free time. Edward seemed to think the shipment was coming in by the coming weekend, so whatever was going to happen, it would probably be all over by the time Bronwyn went to her conference.

"I know you can't make plans that far ahead, but do try, William. It's very important." She sounded unusually urgent.

177

Will wondered what was really going on. There was something she wasn't saying. "Do you have plans yourself for that weekend? I mean…I can't promise anything at this point."

"I know that, William. It's been the same story for years now, hasn't it? We don't plan to be out socially that weekend so if you can't come, we'll just tell her you'll come another time."

"I'll let you know as soon as I can," he promised her as he hit the red 'end call' button. *That was strange*, he thought. *Not her typical call. She almost sounded understanding.*

High razor-wire topped fences surrounded the concrete building complex at HMP Berwyn outside of Wrexham. It looked like a communist block of 1960s flats, Will thought, except probably better kept and without the strings of laundry hanging from balconies. Inside, concrete floors contrasted with bright green railings that lined staircases leading from one floor to another. He went through security, having nothing to surrender other than his mobile, and was escorted to the governor's office.

Inside, he shook the man's hand and introduced himself. He briefly explained that he was looking for a fugitive, Billy Davies, who was wanted for two homicides, the first in North Wales and the second in England, near Liverpool.

"I'm not sure how I can help," the governor, Harold Perkins, told him. He was tall and stocky, with closely-trimmed but thinning gray hair and a clean-shaven face. His posture was straight despite his age, and he looked almost military in his uniform.

"We're interested in people Billy might have had contact with here," Will explained. "We think he's hiding out somewhere, and any leads we can get will help us in our search."

Perkins sat down and tapped at his computer for a minute. "I remember Billy, but only vaguely," he told Will. "After you called and scheduled this meeting, I talked with some of my men to get their impressions of him."

"I appreciate the effort, sir."

Perkins gave him a smile. "As we recall him, Billy Davies was a man to take the easy way out whenever he could. There was always a scheme whereby he could get an easier deal, whether it be on cigarettes or yard time or lighter duty. He didn't want to work very hard to earn the rewards he thought he deserved."

That fit with someone who might rob a shop or help transport drugs to a destination. "Did he have a temper, sir?"

Perkins considered that. "Not so you'd notice, but he did like to bully the men who were less mainstream, if you know what I mean. The physically weaker ones, mostly."

"Did Billy have friends?"

"He always had a cellmate, and I can give you a list if you like before you leave."

"Can you tell me anything about the man who was arrested with him for the armed robbery?"

Now Perkins nodded firmly. "Morys Howell I remember well. That one was more of a leader, if you can call stirring up trouble leading. He was an organizer of men, directing who sat where in the cafeteria, who was on which team in the yard when a football game was organized, like that. I always thought he'd have been the mastermind behind that robbery, and Billy was the grunt worker."

"Do you know what happened to Howell after he was released?"

"I know he was arrested for a double homicide somewhere in Wales, but somehow evidence was lost and he was released before a trial could take place. Other than that, he's stayed quiet, as far as I know."

Lost evidence. If a chief superintendent saw potential in Morys Howell, could he make evidence disappear in order to recruit him? Could he make sure nothing else appeared on Howell's record after that? Could he protect him in order to use him? If so, how important was Morys Howell to this organization? Could he be a major player, the organizer of a network of drug smugglers? Will took a breath, excited but not wanting to get ahead of himself. He'd have to be extraordinarily lucky to stumble onto the right suspect so early in the investigation.

He thanked Harold Perkins and checked out of the prison, glad to leave the concrete walls behind. It was a newer prison, but depressing nonetheless.

He stopped in Wrexham at a deli to buy a sandwich for the road and turned the car toward Llangynog. With luck, he'd be there by half seven and have an hour or two with Bronwyn before he had to make the drive to Caernarfon. *Too much time in the car*, he mused as he drove. It was a good thing he had a car he enjoyed driving as much as he did the little MGF.

He pulled into the driveway at the cottage at seven-twenty, just as dusk was fading to night. He hadn't been able to call ahead, fearful of his phone being bugged, but lights on inside assured him she was home rather than staying with her parents, as he had suggested. He didn't know whether to be angry with her or happy that she'd ignored his suggestion.

Happy won out when Daisy barked at the door and then Bronwyn appeared, looking out the front window and then opening the door and running out to meet him. He hugged her fiercely, holding her tight to his chest with both arms. "Everything's okay, then?"

"All fine here," she said, "except I'm lonely all by myself in our little cottage." She smiled up at him, and he wanted badly to tell her it was all over, that he was staying for good.

"I'm going to put my car in the garage." He handed her a box. "Here's your phone. Just use it for really important things, okay?

She nodded. "If I hear or see something."

"That's it." He hesitated. " Do you want to go for a little walk up the lane? I was in Wrexham and I couldn't be this close without stopping to see you, but I have to get back to Caernarfon tonight, and then I'll be out of touch unless you call on the pre-paid." He didn't want to risk someone seeing his car in her driveway. As far as he knew, even the people at the station who'd heard he was staying in Llangynog didn't know the actual place, and he didn't want that to change. If they knew, they could threaten Bronwyn to get at him.

"You can't drive to Caernarfon in the morning?"

He loved the disappointment in her voice. "Not this time. I've a meeting early, and then I have to get to Edward. I can't take a chance on roadworks or an accident delaying me."

She nodded and went inside for a jumper to wear against the night's chill while he put the car inside. If someone had followed him up the lane to the cottage, he'd have noticed. There was something to be said for living on the outskirts of a tiny village where every vehicle would easily be seen and remembered, especially if it weren't familiar.

Once the car was safely stowed, he took her hand and they walked toward the farmland where the lane dead-ended after a mile or so, Daisy frolicking ahead. There was no traffic to worry about. As they walked, he told her about Morys Howell, the missing information about the double homicide, and about his talk with Bowers.

"You trust him, then?"

"I think so. I didn't feel like he was hearing information he already knew. He's reluctant to lie to Notley, though. That seems to be his major concern."

"If he goes along with it, will he help you?"

"I don't know. If our roles were reversed, I don't think I would. He has a lot to lose. It'd be better for him, once it's over, if people believed that I did this on my own and he didn't know what I was doing. There's no proof I talked to him, so he could still deny everything."

She was quiet for a few paces. "Is there anything I can do to help you? I mean, beyond getting clues that probably won't come this time. I don't usually see things that aren't affecting this area."

"You can help by doing what I asked: stay at your parents' until this is over. I'm going to be overwhelmed these next few days, and I can't add worrying about you to all the things in my head. If they figure out I'm onto them, they'll come at me every way they can to stop me exposing them. I don't think they know about you unless Bowers is involved, but we can't take that chance."

"I hadn't thought of it like that," she murmured. "I'll go, Will. I'll be careful."

Rain began to patter on them, softly at first, but threatening to increase quickly. "Let's go back. I can stay about an hour, and if we keep the lights off, it should be safe enough."

"I'd like that," she said, and then she called out to Daisy, and they turned for home.

Chapter Twelve

After Will had left on Saturday night, Bronwyn had let her emotions loose. All evening she'd sat and listened to them talking, calmly for the most part, about taking down a huge drugs operation that, if they were right, was being run by the most powerful people of all – those in charge of law enforcement in the entire country. The fact that Edward had only suspicions and didn't know who all was involved complicated what was undeniably a dangerous mission. She'd kept herself under tight control through the evening, but once Will had driven out the driveway and onto the lane, she'd let go. She'd sobbed for nearly an hour, pacing through the cottage with Daisy following anxiously on her heels, and then she'd sat by the window and thought through the night, sending all the positive energy she could muster his way. She didn't think it was enough.

Her Sunday had passed slowly as she wondered what Will was doing and tried not to imagine him confronting the people running such an operation. She could imagine how profitable it would be for whoever it was, but she could also imagine how secure they'd feel, being able to monitor police endeavors and manipulate operations. Unfortunately, she could also imagine what they would do if they felt threatened – and it was not a pretty picture. She didn't often watch crime shows on the telly, but she'd seen enough to know the world of illegal drugs was terrifying dangerous. And Will and Edward were alone.

When her thoughts had threatened to overwhelm her, she'd put on her boots and hiked the whole footpath to Pennant Melangell with Daisy, trying unsuccessfully to focus on the verdant greenery that had arrived with spring rather than her worries. Once there, she'd sat for a while in the churchyard trying to recall which flowers she'd seen in bloom and which birds had called from the treetops, and she'd realized she hadn't noticed anything that she could remember. She just couldn't concentrate. As soon as she'd felt rested, she hiked the whole footpath back, thinking she would exhaust herself into a night's sleep that evening. It didn't work. If only she could hear from him, she thought, it would comfort her at least a little. But he hadn't called.

Monday had brought more of the same. Bronwyn had washed her face and put ice packs on her eyes, and then she'd gone to dinner at her parents' house that evening. She'd tried hard to pretend that everything was fine, and if they'd noticed that she'd looked upset, they'd decided not to mention it. In the end, she'd told them as they finished up the meal that Will had an undercover assignment so he'd be out of touch for a week or two. She hadn't told them what the assignment involved, but she had mentioned that he wanted to pretend they'd broken off their relationship as part of the subterfuge. She hadn't missed the concerned look that passed between her parents at that announcement, but she'd chosen to ignore it. They worried too much about her, and she wasn't about to encourage them in that regard. She hadn't had the heart to stay long after they'd finished eating, wanting to be alone with her fears, so she'd left shortly after giving them the story she'd thought up.

Thankfully, she'd gotten home before Will stopped by. If she'd been gone, would he have come looking for her? She hoped so, but now that he was trying to stay out of sight, maybe that would have exposed him too much, not that anyone in Llangynog would be looking. Still…at this point, only Notley and Jay Mehta knew exactly where the cottage was, and if he'd successfully convinced his co-workers that they'd broken off their relationship, maybe no one would come looking for him there. At least she'd be safe.

She was overjoyed to know that Will had detoured through Llangynog, adding at least an hour to his journey, just to spend a few minutes with her. She couldn't help throwing her arms around him and pushing her face into her chest to smother the tears that came with his arrival. They'd walked hand-in-hand and she'd listened while he told her everything he'd discovered during his research in the office. She'd asked questions and they'd talked over his answers, as she knew he'd like to do. She'd told him she liked Edward, not an actual lie because he was charismatic and hard not to like, but she'd kept to herself that feeling of jealousy she'd had when she'd watched them planning their investigation together.

After the walk, they'd sat in the darkened cottage and had a glass of wine, and she was glad of the dark because it disguised her still-swollen eyes. Will told her then that his mother had called and asked if Lark might come the weekend following her workshop. "It'll all depend on what happens with this case," he cautioned her, "but if I can get there in time, we'll go and you can meet my parents."

A flutter of nerves erupted in her chest at that announcement. She wanted desperately to meet them, to take that step with Will that she felt was crucial to their moving forward, but at the same time, it scared her silly now that Will had described them as so – what could she call it – cold? Unwelcoming? Uninvolved? Surely, they couldn't be as bad as he'd made them out to be.

Despite that they kept the lights off inside, it had almost felt like a normal evening together until he stood up abruptly and told her it was time he left, already later than he'd planned. She'd swallowed her disappointment, wanting him to kiss her and tell her he'd changed his mind, that he'd stay the night, but she couldn't miss the set look to his face that told her that wasn't going to happen.

He asked then to switch vehicles with her, explaining that his little MGF could be tracked. "If you could leave it in the garage, out of sight, that'd be best." She could tell he didn't want to ask that. It meant she'd have to walk to work and everywhere else until her car was back so that the more-visible little convertible wouldn't be caught on CCTV camera or, worse, spotted by someone who shouldn't know she had it. It also meant she'd have to take the MGF to the Brecon Beacons when the time came, driving an unfamiliar car on unfamiliar roads.

Will had stopped and looked down at her in the dark before getting into the Land Rover. "Edward thinks the shipment is coming over this weekend sometime, but if not, we'll be working on tracking it down through the next week, or until it does arrive. In some ways, it'd be better for us if it's later because then we'd have more time to figure out what we're going to do." He'd taken her hand and squeezed it. "I'm hoping it works so I can take you to meet my parents and see Lark, but if not, you'd be fine on your own?"

She wanted to say no, she wouldn't be fine going off to a place she'd never been before all alone, that she wanted all the undercover stuff to be over, with him safe and all the secrecy behind them, that she'd never be able to concentrate on the workshop with her mind focused on him, but she kept it all inside. Will didn't need more to worry about and she didn't want to chase him away with neediness now that their relationship had moved to a place where it didn't feel like he would abandon her at a whim. She hugged him instead, whispering into his chest that he should stay safe, please, and then she'd raised her face for his kiss and watched him drive away.

By Tuesday, she was exhausted. She'd tossed and turned after Will left, driving Daisy off the bed and onto the floor before the night was an hour old. She'd been three nights with little or no sleep, and she was running on empty. *At least it won't be hard to convince people Will and I are over*, she told herself as she looked in the mirror. They'd agreed that the subterfuge should include anyone she'd come into contact with, just in case someone came looking, and her pale skin and swollen eyes should back up anything she said.

Janice noticed immediately that things were wrong. "What's up, love?" she asked, her eyes full of concern. "It's not Will, is it?"

How can I explain? "Will and I are going through a rough patch right now," she managed. "He left on Saturday night, and I don't know when, or if, I'll see him again." *At least, that's the truth, even if not all the truth.* "I'm so worried about him."

"I'm sure he'll come to his senses," Janice comforted her. "Do you want to talk about it?"

She shook her head adamantly. "No, I'm better if I concentrate on work just now and try not to think about him." *That's the truth, for sure.* "I've got the workshop this next week, and I have a lot to do if I'm not to fall behind while I'm gone."

"What's on while you're away?"

"There's a group coming on Tuesday and another on Thursday. They've called Daryn Reese in to help out while I'm gone, and she'll take care of them. For a change we've nothing happening on Friday, so I'll be coming back for the next group we have booked on Saturday." She wished she could have the Saturday off, as well, if Lark was coming for the weekend, but she could hardly ask for another day after having the week off. Besides, having Lark for the weekend was a long shot. Chances were even or better that Will would be tied up and not able to go fetch her.

"I'll help Daryn if she has questions," Janice offered. She smiled. "It sounds like you need a few days free to enjoy yourself and learn something new to keep your mind occupied."

"That's it," Bronwyn agreed with a tired smile. "I need to get away." But she doubted she'd be able to concentrate on the workshop, and she wondered if the certification would be a waste of time and effort. She wished she hadn't signed up for it.

She left her office door open in case of unexpected pilgrims and checked her schedule. She'd have to have things prepared for her absence, which meant a detailed plan for Daryn to follow each day. Daryn could settle the groups and take care of their needs, while Janice would have to take on the walk-in pilgrims in addition to her scheduled counselling sessions. That would leave a gap that Bronwyn usually filled, but needs must. There was no other way to handle things when one or another of them had to be gone for a few days.

She woke her computer and brought up an empty document, checking the schedule to remind herself who was expected and what they'd need. The centre was closed on Mondays so the first group on

Tuesday was a board of directors for a church in Shrewsbury. She'd have liked to have been there for that group, to give them a tour of St. Melangell's and to show them its features. She made a note for Daryn to do that, and she knew that Daryn would do her best, but Bronwyn was more familiar with certain interesting historical curiosities she'd have loved to describe, giving life to the little Normal church. She typed her notes, detailing how many were expected, what to serve for lunch and when to serve it, what equipment they might need.

Simples. The word came into her head as she worked, and her mind kept returning to it like a song whose lyrics stuck in her head. She'd thought the fairy had said 'simple,' but now with the information Edward had shared, she knew the creature had tried to tell her what else was involved in Will's case besides a murder.

She glanced around. Daisy would let her know if someone was coming into her office. She brought up Google and searched the word, 'simples.' She scanned past ads and the reduction of the word to the singular and found several articles on medieval 'drugs,' or 'simples.' She read through each definition carefully. In medieval days, healers made potions from plants that they called 'simples.' Unlike the drugs of today, these potions involved only the simple distillation of flowers, leaves, bark, and the like, rather than being distilled into compounds or using artificial materials. They were used to treat everything from sore throats to unrequited love. They were very different from today's drugs, Bronwyn knew, but for the Twlwyth Teg, it was the only word they'd know to communicate a concept to her.

If she'd realized it sooner? She considered the ramifications. If Will had suspected that Billy was part of a drugs operation, he could not have ditched Notley as easily as had to be done. It was likely that Edward would still have sought him out, though, so perhaps things would have been more difficult had he been aware of the drug connection earlier. She didn't think she'd hurt anything by withholding information she hadn't realized she had. She resolved to be more diligent in the future, to explore everything she saw or heard thoroughly, just in case.

She got off the internet and went back to her work. At lunchtime she'd go outdoors and try to connect with nature, to free her mind of the worry that now threatened to overwhelm her. Was this what married life, and perhaps later, motherhood, would feel like? She didn't like to think of it.

Time passed by slowly, but by noon Bronwyn had sketched out plans for Deryn to follow the next week and had sorted through the mail. After lunch she'd have to enter registrations for the pilgrims' walk into her database and make phone calls. Before she left for the Brecon Beacons, she'd lay out the items Deryn would need during her absence. She wondered what sort of thank you gift she could leave for her? Some special tea, perhaps? A basket of homemade scones?

This done, she glanced down at Daisy. "Ready for your noon walk?"

The Lab jumped to her feet, tail wagging happily. She frolicked around Bronwyn as she put on her jumper and walked to the main doors, then raced away in circles when they stepped outside.

The sun had come out to illuminate a glorious spring day. The yews cast a shadow over the churchyard, but the grass wore its brilliant spring green, the blades growing almost before her eyes, and as she had this thought, a man came from the shed beside the centre, pushing a lawn mower. She waved at him, and he waved back.

She sat on the bench in the sensory garden and unwrapped her lunch: a small baguette, slices of cheeses, some very early strawberries. Daisy explored the little garden while Bronwyn ate, sniffling at a shrub here and sticking her nose into the dirt there, searching out a buried acorn or a bulb or even, perhaps, the burrow of some small rodent who was lying in wait to devour bits and pieces of her carefully-planted oasis. The spring perennials, lilies and peonies, were growing well with stout sprouts pushing up through the ground in clusters. Bright purple and yellow crocus already colored the flower beds, and daffodils would be in bloom within a week, with tulips not far behind. That was it for the spring bulbs, but she had also encouraged daisies, foxglove, and lupin to flourish in the narrow beds. She closed her eyes. A rook scolded Daisy from the branches of one of the yews, and she could hear Daisy's feet pattering across the small bit of lawn in the middle of the garden. It smelled fresh, with an underlying dampness from the rain that had pestered them off and on for the past week.

After a bit, she opened her eyes, feeling rested and more in control of herself. She eyed the garden critically. Would the board spring for a few pounds so that she could add more plants this year? One of the villagers had suggested a plant called a rock Daphne, known for its pervading sweet scent early in the spring, and she thought that might be a good addition. She wished they could have a fountain for the noise of the water as it splashed down, but considering that there was no electricity to run it in the garden and that the battery-powered one she'd tried quit after just a few days, the current birdbath would have to suffice.

Janice emerged from the centre and headed her way. "Hi, can I join you?"

Bronwyn nodded and scooted over on the bench. "I was just enjoying the sunshine."

Janice sat down. "It is a lovely day to be out." She opened her lunch box and pulled out a salad container. "I don't want to bring up a sore subject, but you look a lot more relaxed than you did this morning."

"I am." She hesitated. "Janice, I have a confession, but you have to promise not to tell anyone, okay?"

Janice eyed her. "You're not pregnant, are you?"

Bronwyn laughed. "Thank God, no." Janice was too good a friend not to know at least part of the truth. "It's Will, though. We didn't really have a break-up. It's just what we're telling people for a few weeks."

"But why?"

"Will has a difficult, dangerous case right now he's working, and he worried that it would put me in danger if people knew about me. He thinks someone might use me to manipulate him. It's better if people think we're done with each other."

Janice smiled and reached out to touch her arm. "Thank you for telling me."

"You're probably the best friend I have, other than my family and Will."

"Why were you so upset when you came in this morning?"

"I can't totally explain it because I can't give you details, but whenever I think of what he's trying to do, I panic. I'm so afraid something will go wrong and he'll be killed. I just can't shake it off. It's really very dangerous work." Edward had talked of two attempts on his life, and now Will would be a target, too. "I haven't really slept for three nights, but just sitting here right now in the sunshine and sharing my fear with you, I'm feeling better, at least for the moment." She gave Janice a faint smile. "But you can't tell anyone any of this, and if someone wants to know where the cottage is or anything about us, you have to pretend to know nothing. Even if it's someone we know, or another policeman, or anyone. No one can know about me right now."

"What he's doing must be really dangerous."

"It is." She glanced around, locating Daisy lying in a patch of sun next to the emerging tulips. "It'll probably be good for me to go to the workshop next week and get my mind off him for a few days, but he was going to come with me because I'd never been there before, and now I doubt that's going to work out so I'll probably have to go alone. I know it's not good to obsess," she gave Janice an embarrassed look, "but I wanted so much to meet someone who'd be my partner, and now that I have, I don't want anything to change."

"Things are serious between you, then?"

"Well, there's the cottage and us living together, at least half the time. His boss thinks he'd like him here more so that someone is on this side of the district when a suspicious death comes up. So, yes, I think we're pretty serious at this stage." She ducked her head, her cheeks blushing hot. "We haven't talked about marriage or anything that permanent yet. I don't think either of us is ready for that. I know I'm not. The thought of it overwhelms me."

"Why?"

"It's such a huge commitment, and I'm not sure yet how that would fit into my life plan. I know I want to stay here and to continue as best I can St. Melangell's mission of making this a sanctuary, but if I marry Will, then I'll have to consider his situation, too. I'm not sure he's cut out to live in a little village like Llangynog. He grew up in a city, with all the amenities that offers. He went to boarding school, and he had an upper-class upbringing. He didn't live on a sheep farm in a hundreds-year-old house with a brother and parents who overprotect me at every turn."

"I suspect that Will is having the same conversation with himself," Janice smiled, "but he's chosen to rent the cottage here because he knows you're committed to staying near to your family and your job, and he obviously wants to be with you more than he wants to live in a city. He and Maddock get on fine, don't they?"

"When Madd isn't threatening him."

"And your parents like him, too. I think you need to take your own advice, Bronwyn. Get out into nature and do your meditation. Let nature sooth your worries into the background. No matter what Will is up against right now, you worrying won't help."

"I know that intellectually, but emotionally is another story. I guess now I'll have more empathy for the women who come in here overwhelmed by something they can't get off their minds."

"That's a good way to look at it." Janice began to gather up her lunch things and put them back in the bag. "I've got another client coming in a few minutes. You stay out here and enjoy the sunshine."

"Thanks, I will." Bronwyn brushed crumbs from her lap. "And thank you, Janice. I needed to tell someone my secret. Secrets," she amended. "Even my family doesn't know all the reasons I wonder about Will's and my future."

"I really don't think you need to worry," Janice reassured her as she walked away.

Bronwyn sat in the sunshine as long as she thought she could get away with it. No one monitored the length of her lunch break, as long as she got her job done. Daisy wandered over and sat in front of her, laying her head on Bronwyn's knee and looking at her with concerned brown eyes. Bronwyn bent lower and rubbed her ears. "Silly dog. You know I'm not my usual self, don't you?"

Movement caught her eye, and she caught her breath. They approached silently, as always, darting across the lawn or alighting from the sky and making a circle around her as she watched, repelled, yet fascinated. Grotesque and exquisite, delicate and sturdy, extravagant and simple, the Twlwyth Teg in all their variety surrounded her as she sat there, slowly circling and leaving mushrooms in their path. She felt dizzy with watching them, and she held Daisy with firm hands, not wanting to frighten them away.

"Two strings to the bow," whispered one miniscule creature, her lavender wings so translucent as to be almost invisible. "Twice failed."

"Corpse on the galley," announced another voice, this one belonging to an even-tinier being that fluttered waist-high rather than walking in the line surrounding Bronwyn. A shimmer in the air echoed the beating of its wings, silvery in the still air.

"Waiting at Hoylake's herberge," uttered a third one, a mesmerizing creature several inches tall that wore an elegant dress made of violet petals, layered from top to bottom on her lithe body. A tiny cap of spiderdown caressed her silvery curls, and she watched Bronwyn with pale grey eyes.

"Thank you," Bronwyn breathed. The Twlwyth Teg usually only communicated when something happened in the immediate area, and Bronwyn wasn't sure that Billy Davies' flight from the farm qualified. Maybe they knew she was upset and wanted to help.

"Once, twice, thrice," they chanted in unison then, and they were gone in a flash, leaving only the circle of mushrooms to show they'd been there moments before.

Bronwyn sat for a moment, putting their words into her memory and allowing herself a minute of gratitude for their visit. Then, taking a deep breath, she gathered up her things, called Daisy to heel, and went back into her office, thrilled to have an excuse to call Will with information. Just to hear his voice would be a treat, and if the information helped, she'd feel encouraged to know that she was a part of what he was doing, that she was helping. Sure, he and Edward would be working side-by-side, but she wouldn't be left out entirely.

She accessed the now-familiar website for medieval words and phrases and typed in 'two strings to the bow.' A definition came up immediately: to hedge one's bets. She frowned in concentration, turning it over in her mind but coming to no conclusion about the meaning. She thought it meant that a person would have a backup plan, that if his first effort didn't succeed, he'd have something else to fall back on. In the case of Billy Davies, maybe it referred to his stealing some of the product he was meant to deliver and selling it himself so that he'd end up with some money, no matter what happened with the drugs operation in the long haul. Satisfied with the thought, she decided to move on before she forgot the rest.

'Corpse on the galley' seemed easy enough to understand, but she double-checked with the dictionary anyway. Coming up with nothing different after her search, she settled on the obvious. A corpse was on a boat, or a ship. She imagined that was Billy, murdered and dumped into a body of water so that his body would not be found.

Hoylake was not in the dictionary, so she Googled it, finding that it was a small coastal village south of Liverpool. That accomplished, she typed in the final word, 'herberge.' A definition of 'harbour' made perfect sense. If the corpse was Billy Davies, his body was on a boat in the harbour at Hoylake.

She'd call Will, of course, if not immediately then later that evening. If Billy was dead and his body dumped at sea, it probably wouldn't affect his case at all to know about it. But they'd said the galley was *waiting* at the harbour. Perhaps whoever was in charge hadn't managed to get rid of it yet. Time might be of the essence, after all. She knew that Will was counting on Billy not being found so that Notley would be kept busy looking for him. Or maybe it wasn't Billy at all. Now she thought about it, it might be possible that the corpse was someone else entirely. Whoever it was, she shouldn't wait to get the information to Will. He might make more of it than she could.

She dug into her bag and found the pre-paid burner phone he'd left for her, and then she called to Daisy, changed into her wellies, and walked out of her office. She called out to Janice, telling her she'd be back in a few minutes, and then she hurried to the lane and started walking. There was no mobile service at Pennant Melangell, but it wasn't far to where she could get a signal.

She kept an eye out for the Twlwyth Teg or Pysgotwr as she walked, but she saw nothing. No vehicles trundled up the lane as she walked. All she could hear was the squelching of mud on her wellies. Five minutes later, the phone showed a signal. She stopped then, hesitating over the number pad. How would Will explain the information to

Edward? She didn't think she wanted him to know about her visions, but Edward would surely wonder why Will was suddenly aware of what had happened to Billy, or whoever it was in the boat at Hoylake.

Taking a deep breath for courage, she decided to leave it to Will to explain and hit the numbers for one of Will's pre-paid mobiles.

"Bronwyn!" He sounded happy she'd called.

"Are you okay? Only, I've been worried."

"That's why you're calling?"

"No, I saw something that might be useful, I think."

"That's brilliant. What did you see?" No hesitation. He obviously wasn't worried about how to share the information with Edward.

"It's just…I'd rather Edward not know that I see things in the pool of water, Will."

"No worries. I'll figure out a way to tell him that doesn't give away your secret, love. What was it?"

"I think Billy is dead and his body is in a boat at a village called Hoylake. I looked it up. It's just south of Liverpool."

There was a moment of silence as Will considered what she'd said. "We thought Billy was probably dead. It makes sense that they'd get rid of his body in a way that he wouldn't be found so that we'd keep wasting time searching for him. Wonder why they haven't dumped him at sea?"

"Maybe they haven't had time or the tides are wrong or something." She didn't think she needed to share the first part of the message with him, mainly because she couldn't think of how she'd have seen it in a vision. They already knew that Billy was stealing from his stockpile and that he and Peter O'Connell were selling the stolen drugs on their own. The Twlwyth Teg had said his efforts to hedge his bets were a failure. Surely, being followed to O'Connell's house and both of them murdered meant a failure on their part?

"Thanks for this, love. I'm not sure we'd have wasted time chasing after Billy at this point, but it's useful to know where he is so that I can send Notley in a different direction. It's better for us if he isn't found. How are you holding up? Did you miss me on the weekend?"

"You know I did," she said. "I've been worrying over you, but at least everyone here believes we've broken it off because I look a wreck."

"That doesn't sound like you. What happened to living in the moment? To connecting with nature and finding peace in it?" He sounded concerned. "I don't want you to worry about me. I'm going to be fine. I did this sort of thing all the time before. Edward and I know how to stay safe."

"I know you do, but I can't seem to help myself." *I love you*, she wanted to say, but she didn't.

"I can't say anything on the phone about what I'm doing or where I am, but everything's going okay here. I'm glad I talked to Bowers. I think I can trust him, and it's good to know he has my back, if I need it."

"I miss you."

"I miss you, too. You'll have the conference in a few days. That'll take your mind off things." There was a pause, and she could hear him talking to someone else, but couldn't get the words. "I've got to go now. Hey, next time, can you tell me when to expect the shipment on the ferry, or where it's going to be split up, or maybe who's running the whole operation?"

"I'll try." Her heart sank a bit. The information she'd given him hadn't really been very helpful, but maybe it was all the Twlwyth Teg knew. They lived here, in the Tanat Valley, not in Fishguard or Ireland or on the west coast. Maybe they didn't have a network that extended that far away.

"I love you, sweetheart. Remember that, no matter what happens." He said it softly, and she knew he was admitting that he didn't know whether he'd come home or not in the end.

"I love you, too. Please be careful."

"I will," he promised, and then the phone went dead in her hand.

Perhaps because they knew Bronwyn would be missing Will, her parents had invited her for dinner again that night. She stopped by the cottage to change into her jeans and a tee shirt, and then she dutifully walked to the farm just on the other side of the village, finding that Maddock and his family were there, as well.

"What's this thing that Will's involved in?" Maddock wanted to know, almost before they'd sat down.

"I can't talk about it," Bronwyn said, tired of explaining to people that she couldn't tell them about Will's cases.

"But it grew out of the Billy Davies case?"

She didn't think it'd hurt to give them that much. "Yes, when they were tracking Billy, things got more complicated. You know about the other murder? Peter O'Connell?"

"We heard," her dad put in. "They're not treating it as a domestic violence case then?"

Bronwyn took a breath. "It looks like Peter and Catherine might have been having an affair, and Billy took matters into his own hands." It was a complete lie, but she didn't know how else to get them off the topic.

But Maddock was persistent, if nothing else. "So why do you have to pretend you split up, if that's all it is?"

She tried to keep from exploding at him. "I don't know, okay? I don't have all the answers you want." She set her fork down with a clatter. "Even if I did, I couldn't talk about it."

Her parents exchanged a look, as she suspected they would, but they said nothing.

Maddock was watching her, his fork halfway to his mouth. "So, I'm guessing that case turned into something really big, and Will's told you to keep mum about it."

She looked at her plate, seeing nothing, saying nothing.

After an uncomfortable moment, Maddock shrugged and went back to eating. "Whatever he's up to, he'd better not be putting you in danger."

"He's not," she shot back. "That's why we're telling people we're not together any longer. It's to protect me. I thought you'd figure that out on your own."

"He's always been good to our Bronwyn," Mai interjected, obviously trying to smooth things over. "Leave her alone, Maddock."

He turned to glare at his wife, a look that quickly dissolved into a smile, and that was it. The conversation diverted to ideas for the organic farm, and before long even Bronwyn's mind was diverted, her worry for Will pushed to the darkest corner of her mind.

"The garden is going to be huge," her mother said, "and both Mai and I will be quitting our other jobs so we can manage it."

"Beans, squash, peas, carrots, pumpkins, turnips, potatoes…" Mai's list was long.

"And berries," her mother added, "of all kinds."

"And an orchard," Mai was not to be outdone, "with apples, peaches, apricots, and pears. Of course, that will take a few years to establish, but the rest can be done quickly."

"Your dad already has the garden plot ready for us, and we've planted the early crops," Mai put in with a smile. "Maegan and Griffin helped us plant the seeds."

"It's our garden, too," Maegan said proudly.

After dinner had been eaten and the dishes washed, Bronwyn wandered out to the pasture with an apple for Hobbs. She was standing beside him, petting his shaggy mane out of his eyes, when Maddock joined her.

"I've something I need to talk to you about," he said, and his voice was serious. He reached out to pat the pony on the neck. "I didn't know how to bring it up and I've tried to ignore it, but I don't think we can put it off much longer before it gets to be a bigger problem."

Her heart sank. *Why does Maddock always find some reason Will and I can't make it work between us?* She pushed Hobbs away and turned to him. "What's going on?"

Maddock eyed her nervously, fidgeting with Hobb's mane, flipping it back and forth over his neck. "Do you still see fairies?" he blurted finally.

Startled, she backed away a step. "Madd?"

"It's only, Maegan says she is seeing them now, just like you used to when you were her age. We're worried about her." He hesitated. "We don't know how to handle it."

"I'm sure Mum and Dad didn't know how to handle it either."

"No, well, none of us did. I tried to protect you from the bullies, but I wasn't always successful, was I? I don't want her bullied."

"Or sent for counselling, either, I don't imagine."

"No, not that either, if we can avoid it."

She took a deep breath, considering how she could answer him. Thank goodness it wasn't about Will this time, but this subject was maybe even harder to handle. Should she admit that she still saw them, that they talked to her and gave her clues to help Will solve crimes? How about Pysgotwr? Should she mention him? She plucked up her courage. Maddock would love her anyway. "I do still see them, Madd, and they talk to me sometimes, as well. I used to think I imagined them, but what they tell me is true, and it sometimes helps Will to solve his crimes. So now I do believe they're real, but that only some people can see them, people who are more sensitive to the spirit world, maybe. Maegan must be like me." She looked up at him earnestly. "It's a special ability, Madd, a gift, and you should treat it like one."

"I just can't...I can't believe they're real, that they exist."

"Why not? There are lots of things we don't understand about our world. This is just one of them."

"They actually talk to you?"

"That's just something recent," she admitted. She couldn't tell him about being the guardian for Pennant Melangell, which is why she thought they communicated with her. "Remember, Pennant Melangell is a special place, a thin place, where lines between worlds can be crossed. It has always been. Maegan obviously is one of those few who are in tune with the other world. She may grow out of it, but I don't think she will. I never did."

"Does Will know? I mean, if you have information for him that comes from them, then he must wonder how you get it."

"He thinks I have visions, that I see things in pools of water. Which I do," she told him, "so I let him think that's all it is. He saw me once, so I had to tell him. I'd die before I told him that I see fairies and they talk to me, though." She glared at him. "Don't you dare ever tell him about that."

"I won't," he promised, "but Maegan might give it away when she starts shouting about the fairies in the trees or something."

"He'll just think she's playing, pretending to see them. She's only three, after all."

"She won't be three forever," he warned her. "So, we just go along with it?"

"I think you do, at least at home. Believe her. That's important." She had an inspiration. "But teach her it's private. She is old enough to understand that some things must be kept to herself. Tell her that she's special, but in ways that people outside the family shouldn't know about. It'd be her secret with you. If you can convince her to do that, then she'll have an easier time than I did. I only learned later that I should keep some things to myself."

"And you do a good job of it," Maddock complimented her. "I wasn't sure you'd even tell me now."

"Well, it's Maegan, after all. I want to help, if I can."

"Will you talk to her about it sometime?"

She didn't want to. She wanted to keep a distance, to keep her secrets far away from Will. "Sure, of course, I will."

They walked back to the house, and she went inside long enough to say goodbye, then called Daisy and headed for home. She walked into the growing dusk, which she knew Will would disapprove of considering the danger posed by his case, but she couldn't help it. The sun had been shining earlier, the birds had been singing, and the scents of spring drew her outside. It was hard to say no to dinner with her family, and she didn't dare take the little convertible out of the garage in case someone took note of it. Anyway, walking gave her time to think. Would Maegan give her away to Will? If Maegan started babbling about seeing fairies, and worse, hearing them, would he put two and two together and uncover what she was desperate to keep secret? If he did, what would he think of her then?

As if she needed more to worry about.

Chapter Thirteen

Will drove southwest, toward the center of the country, his mind too busy to notice the green countryside as it passed by. At the last minute he'd thought to trade Bronwyn cars, so he was driving her old Land Rover. That way if someone suspected he was onto them and tried to track him, it'd be harder for them. It wouldn't fool them for long, but he only needed a few days and then the whole thing would end, one way or another.

The morning briefing had gone well. He'd arrived early at the station and walked across the street to a coffee shop where he'd found Bowers, making it look like an accidental meeting. Will had gotten a grudging promise from Bowers to keep quiet about Will's activities and to support a separate investigation, with Notley going toward Liverpool and him going southwest toward Fishguard. Not that Notley would know where Will was headed other than a general direction, but if he could be convinced that they had two separate possible destinations for Billy Davies, it would seem reasonable to him to pursue them separately. Will had hoped that Notley had already heard about his and Bronwyn's breakup; otherwise, he'd wonder why he was headed north and Will the opposite direction. If worse came to worse and he'd questioned it, Will would have had to feed him more lies.

Will had taken time to check his computer for messages before Notley arrived, finding an email from the warden at HMP Berwyn detailing a list of Billy Davies' visitors during his time inside and a short note from Davies' parole officer, expressing willingness to meet with Will but offering no information otherwise. Will had thought of shuffling that one off to give to Notley, but decided to wait on it. If Notley did do it and he came up with anything, he'd share it with Will anyway, but maybe someone on the warden's list would catch Will's eye and need to be checked out, too. He'd given the list of Davies' visitors to Quigley to check on. He wouldn't get any information Quigley had until he checked into the station on Thursday, but it was the best he could do.

Notley had arrived on time, and the two of them sat down around a table in a conference room with Bowers to review the case and decide on a plan of action. Will had tried to maintain an air of innocence as they'd discussed the known facts and what evidence they had, and he'd encouraged Notley's belief that the case was a domestic violence incident gone terribly wrong and supported his assertion that they needed to locate Davies as soon as they could, to get him off the streets before he could do more damage.

There were a few tense moments. When Will had mentioned Morys Howell and suggested that they split up so as to cover more area, Notley had objected strenuously. "You've had a tip," he'd accused Will, "and you want to go off on your own so I don't get credit for the solve. What is it? Another pretty young suspect?"

He'd shot a look at Bowers, who'd met his eyes. "This makes sense, Sean. Howell might be a lead you two should follow together, but you can't neglect the Liverpool area, either. It's just for a day or two, and on Thursday you can share notes and work together again, if it makes sense from there."

Notley had narrowed his eyes, suspicious at Bowers' support, but he'd agreed in the end to go back to Carlisle and Liverpool to talk again to Davies' mother and brother, to re-interview William Bruce, and to talk to Peter O'Connell's family, who'd by now had time to digest the fact of his murder and might have additional information they could use. He'd also agreed to request that the forensics team look more closely at the stock trailer that had been abandoned after O'Connell's death. Lastly, he would attend Catherine Baines' memorial service, on his own unless Will was free to join him. He'd insisted that Thursday was the best day

201

to meet and to report their progress, and Will could think of no reasonable excuse to disagree. *At least he'll be busy for a few days*, Will had mused as they'd wrapped it up. He'd felt no guilt but only relief at how easy it had been to steer Notley away from the real case and onto a wild goose chase.

Will had talked at length about Morys Howell, but had left out the part about him being charged with a double homicide, charges that had been subsequently dropped along with the case. He'd had no luck thus far in finding out whose names were on that case as investigating officers, that information having also been deleted from the files. Bowers had scratched his graying head over that interesting tidbit, and Will felt that it gave him more credibility as far as Edward's suspicions went. Who else, other than someone high up in the force, could not only make charges against someone disappear, but also officers' names and supporting evidence? He was left feeling that Morys Howell provided a major lead for him and Edward to follow, perhaps the very lead they'd need to flush out the major offenders in the case.

If they could find him.

There were still alerts out for Billy Davies and his Ford Kuga, neither of which had been seen for nearly ten days. Davies could hide or be hidden, if he were dead, but the vehicle posed a bigger problem, literally. Unless it was permanently parked in a garage or barn, they'd eventually come upon it and it could be examined for evidence that might point to the real perpetrators. He'd left Bowers with one of his pre-paid phones and a request to call him if the vehicle turned up or if Notley reported in with information they could use.

Bowers had agreed, shaking his head. "Do you really think my phone is bugged?"

"I've learned working undercover to assume the worst, sir. It may well be monitored," he'd answered, earning a querulous shake of the head from Bowers. His chief superintendent had devoted his life to stopping crime; he wasn't eager to believe that one of his counterparts was committing it right in front of his eyes.

Will's attention was drawn back to the road as a spring squall hit, splattering a vicious rain shower on his windscreen and obscuring his vision. He slowed, gripping the steering wheel against the pull of wind and the dangers of a drenched roadway. He'd arranged to meet Edward in Aberystwyth, reasoning that it was the first major stop on the motorway north from Fishguard and an ideal first destination for a load of drugs destined to be divided up and sent in various directions toward major cities. Morys Howell and Llandrindod Wells would have to wait. Although Llandrindod Wells wasn't far from Aberystwyth, it was inland and not on a major motorway. Will and Edward had debated it for nearly an hour and finally decided that a coastal town was a more logical first destination for the truckload of drugs and so the logical start to their investigation. Aberystwyth was where Edward had already been concentrating his efforts.

The storm eased as he exited toward Aberstwyth. He was unfamiliar with the town, but he'd pre-programed the name of the pub where he and Edward had agreed to meet into his sat nav, so he found it easily. He drove by it slowly, and then he took the next turn and drove another block before parking.

The dimly-lit pub provided perfect dark corners for secret assignations. Squinting in the gloom, Will spotted Edward seated at the far side of the room near the washrooms, a pint on the table in front of him.

Will looked around, examining the other patrons, most of whom seemed to be elderly men stopping by their local for a noon refresher. Two of them had dogs lying by their feet, a collie with his chin resting on a table leg and a husky Labrador that reminded Will of Daisy, except in black. No one seemed a threat.

He stopped by the bar and ordered a pint of their local specialty, then took it back to where Edward waited, his own stout nearly gone. "Want lunch?" he offered.

"You'll have to buy," Edward informed him. "I'm down to my last pennies, and I can't risk using an ATM at the moment. I hope you brought plenty of cash."

"Yeah, well, I didn't spend all those years working undercover with you without learning a few tricks. I'm surprised you got caught short."

"I've been hiding out for six weeks," Edward reminded him, "and this time the people chasing me have access to my personal banking information."

Maybe a sandwich would put him in a better mood. "I'll just go order us something, shall I?"

"They have pasties here," Edward hinted.

"I'll be right back." He walked back up to the bar, asked the barman what he recommended, and put in an order for four pasties: steak and mushroom, cheese and onion, ham and cheese, and steak and potato. Edward could have three of them, and he figured he'd eat one. Edward had probably been hungry since he'd left the cottage. Neither Will nor Bronwyn had thought to send him with a supply of food.

He sank into a chair across from Edward. "Tell me what you've discovered."

Edward leaned forward, glancing around cautiously. "I'm still watching that abandoned warehouse," he said. "It's just on the edge of town. It was originally a textile factory, but then they found out that those jobs could be done more cheaply overseas. It was sold to a distributor who cleared out the inside and made it into a big warehouse for storing furniture and office equipment. By the time that business went under, the building was outdated and crumbling so no one wanted it. The property was put up for sale with the thought that someone could demolish the building, but the expense of doing that evidently put buyers off."

"Wouldn't someone notice trucks pulling up to it?"

"I don't think so. It's part of an old industrial park. From what I've gathered, it's sometimes rented out as a temporary storage building for various things, most often as a place where people can put a caravan or a boat when it's winter and they want a place that's enclosed. Vehicles come and go periodically, and no one takes notice."

Will rubbed a hand across the stubble on his face. He'd let his beard grow for a week or so now, rather than keep it shorter as Bronwyn liked it. "That sounds like a promising start."

"I think so. I've been watching it, but I haven't gone inside yet. I waited for you." He grinned.

The barman walked over and set plates on the table. Steam rose from the fragrant pasties and from the big basket of chips that accompanied them. Will took a chip and popped it into his mouth. "Not bad."

"The food's cheap here and good, another good reason for this to be our base."

Will nodded. He reached for a pasty and broke it open. Steak and potato. His stomach rumbled in anticipation.

"Tell me what you found out," Edward said through a mouthful of his own pasty. "I know you didn't just waste those two days."

"No, I didn't waste them." He told Edward about Morys Howell, about the double homicide charge that had just vanished into nothingness without a trial or much of a written record beyond a listing as unsolved.

"There were no investigating detectives listed?" Edward looked incredulous. 'How could they get away with that? Someone would notice."

"Apparently no one did, or if they did, someone paid them off."

"If this is as big as I think it is, they'd have plenty of money to pay lots of people off."

"The only thing is, I don't know where Morys Howell is. He has an address listed in Llandrindod Wells, but my bet is he doesn't actually live there, not if he's as involved as I think he might be. He'd be stupid to make himself that easy to find."

"Sometimes the best thing is to hide in plain sight," Edward pointed out. "That way he doesn't look like he's up to something."

"Maybe," Will hedged. "We can check it out. Llandrindod Wells is only a few miles away, and I have a car." He chewed another bite of his pasty.

Edward picked up his glass and took a long swallow. "It'd probably be better to check out Llandrindod Wells than to bet everything on this warehouse. I'm only guessing with it. Now that you're here with a car, we should check out some other places, too, and see if anything else pops."

"I traded Bronwyn cars, so I have her Land Rover. It's a long shot that someone would figure out I'm working this case, connect me with her, and then track her car."

"Smart, that," Edward complimented him. He took another bite of his pasty and chewed thoughtfully. "She seems nice, Will. Not what I pictured for you at all, but I'm warming up to the idea of you and her. Lesley will be broken-hearted."

"No, she's moved on. It's been over a year."

"She dates, but no one lasts long with her. I think she's still carrying a torch for you."

"Why don't you try it with her?"

"I'm not her type. She knows we can't last long working undercover, and she knew your background. She had high hopes that she could snag a future barrister in you, mate. Wherever I ended up, it wouldn't have given her the life she craved. Besides, I wouldn't want to be second choice. I'd always know it."

"I don't want to follow in my father's footsteps. That was one of the issues between us," Will told him. "She mentioned it, and all I could think was that I wanted something different for myself."

"That's because you grew up well-off," Edward observed. "If you hadn't had money for top schools and nannies and trips abroad, you might have a different outlook on it all. Some of us would like the chance to stop worrying about whether the paycheck will stretch far enough from month to month."

Will didn't have an answer for that. He'd enjoyed dating Lesley, but after he'd met Bronwyn, even before they'd started dating, he'd known deep down that Lesley wasn't the right partner for him. Actually, now that he thought of it, breaking it off with Lesley had been the first step toward admitting the attraction Bronwyn held for him. He hadn't seen it, but it was true. He shook himself out of his reverie. "What do you want to do?"

"We've still got half of a day today. Let's go south toward Fishguard and check things out along the way, see if we find anything else that could serve as a storage place for a load of illegal drugs."

"You don't have any contacts in the area that might help?"

"No one I'd trust now, not with how things went the last time I used an informant. That's not to say we couldn't put the word out that we have a barn that could be used and that we are eager to be a part of things."

"Your idea is to find the most logical place for warehousing the load, and then to hang out and watch it?" Will didn't see how that was going to help them catch whoever was in charge.

"It's a start," Edward said defensively. "If anyone comes and goes from there, we can follow them and see where they lead us."

"Put a tracker on their car? That'd be more efficient."

"If it looks like the place, maybe we could stage a break-in or a fire? Something that would force them to look for a new location?"

"Or if there's activity there, we could plant something on them and call in an anonymous tip, get them arrested. They're already short one guy, with Davies compromised. If we could take out another one or two, they'd have to scramble."

"Then maybe they'd be open to hiring a couple of guys off the street?"

"You mean the two of us?" Will thought it over. "They'd check us out first, for sure, and we're both well-known to everyone in the drugs squad. We'd never pass muster."

Edward looked downtrodden. "No, I guess not. We'll have to go at it a different way."

"You have an idea?"

"Not unless you know for sure when that load is coming in and who's meeting it and where its first destination is."

"So, we just need a little information…"

"Yeah, knowing what vehicle it's on would help, too."

Will laughed. "You never said it would be easy."

Will threw money onto the table. One of the phones sang out as they approached the door, and he waved to Edward to wait while he answered it.

Happily, it was Bronwyn's voice on the other side. She must have seen something that would help. *Thank God for Bronwyn.* He ducked to a space beside the door, turning his back on Edward while he listened to her story.

The information wasn't as helpful as he'd hoped. They'd assumed Billy Davies was dead, but they didn't want his body found. Now he'd have to decide whether it was worth a day's drive up to Hoylake to hide it, or whether to take a chance on someone coming across it before it was dumped. It was at least a four-hour drive, which would make it eight hours round trip, plus the time to do whatever he had to with the body. He almost wished she hadn't called.

Another rain squall had begun, so they hugged the buildings to stay as dry as possible while they hurried to the Land Rover. Will unlocked the doors and they slid inside.

"Are you going to tell me about the call?" Edward slung him a look that wasn't happy.

"I didn't see any need to stand in the rain while I explained," Will tried to placate him. Lying to Edward wasn't going to be an option. "Bronwyn heard something."

"Okay. Are you going to make me drag it out of you?"

"No. She heard that Billy Davies' body is on a boat at a small harbour in a village called Hoylake, just south of Liverpool. That's all." He glanced at Edward, saw his face lightening as he considered the information. "I don't want to spend – what? – ten hours driving up there and back, so I don't know how that helps us out. What do we do? Take a day and go hide the body or cross our fingers and hope no one finds it in the next few days?"

"What if they do find it? You know they'll make it look like a suicide. The logical conclusion would be that Billy killed the other two and then killed himself in remorse."

"I'd have to go investigate with Notley," Will pointed out. "I wouldn't have an excuse for searching down here once Billy is found."

"How about this, then? You go up there for a day, determine a cause of death of suicide, and then tell your boss you want a couple of days off after?"

"There'd be mounds of paperwork to do."

"Shove it off on your partner."

"That might work. That's only if someone finds him." He thought it over. "I don't see another option. I guess we'll have to let it go and hope things turn out our way." He felt uncomfortable with it and knew it would nag at him.

"Now, mate, tell me how your lovely Bronwyn happened to hear this crucial piece of information."

Will's heart beat a tattoo in his chest. "It's a small community. Gossip is rampant in those places."

"But if you follow the chain of information back to its source, wouldn't that give us the murderers?"

"She only hears bits and pieces. I wouldn't want her trying to figure out the source of the information. It'd put her in danger."

Edward studied him. "I don't think that's the whole story, but okay, I'll give you this one, but only because I can see how she shouldn't get too close to this whole deal. But later, you're going to explain."

"Give me directions," Will told Edward, happy to avoid taking the issue further, and he eased out of the tight space.

"Back to the main street and then we'll have to take the back roads. There are six or seven villages between here and Fishguard, and we'll want to check out the countryside, so we can't just take the A487. It'll take us all day and probably tomorrow, but if we take our time and look for buildings that seem abandoned and then spend our evenings chatting up some of the locals, we might find what we're looking for."

And, so, it began. Will drove slowly from one to another of Welsh coastal villages with unpronounceable names: Llanrhystud, Aberaeron, New Quay, Synod Inn, and Aberporth. He took turn after turn, traveling through the villages past colorful waterfronts and then beyond, to rural areas littered with cottages, sheep, and occasional large homes. Discouragingly, most of the waterfront areas offered storage warehouses, too many to explore thoroughly. Most of the farms looked occupied, but that didn't mean some ambitious farmer wouldn't agree to let them use his barn or machine shed if he were compensated well.

At seven in the evening, they turned back and took the A487 back to Aberystwyth, reasoning that it was a bigger town and might offer the chance to strike up a conversation that would point them in the right direction. Once there, they abandoned the Land Rover for a corner pub. Purposefully, they chose the pub that looked busiest, both for its potential for decent food and drink and for its patrons, whose tongues might be loosened as they relaxed after a day's work. They'd played this game before. They snugged up to the bar and ordered two of the local brews.

Twenty minutes later they'd struck up conversations with the bartender and the men sitting either side of them. Keeping it casual, they remarked on the area, how remote yet beautiful it was with its colorful fleet of boats and brightly-painted buildings. Questions about how the local economy was faring elicited information about warehouses being turned into waterfront restaurants and even, in one case, high-end condos. None of their companions mentioned empty buildings that might be used by outsiders. None complained about lorry traffic coming and going at all hours or vans and trailers appearing for no apparent reason on a back street.

"Well, that's Aberystwyth," Edward commented later as they dug into steak and mushroom pies and chips at a table near a window. "One of the smaller villages might be telling a different story."

"Your warehouse here is starting to look better to me," Will admitted, blowing on his spoonful of meat, gravy, and potato. "We don't want to make too much a nuisance of ourselves or word'll get back to our targets that we're in the area. We don't want to scare them off."

"No, it's a fine line between tracking them down and pushing them to make a new plan." Edward reached for a chip. "Should we check out the warehouse tonight?"

"Go out there after dark and break in, have a look around?"

"If we can do it without them knowing," Edward hedged. "We could make it look like kids breaking in, leave a mess of broken windows and graffiti."

"It won't hurt to at least have a walk around it, even if we can't get inside. Do you think it'll be guarded?"

"Wouldn't that draw attention?" Edward looked up, over Will's shoulder. He watched something for a moment, his eyes intent. "I think we've been made."

Will kept eating, his fork moving methodically from plate to mouth. "Tell me what you see."

"There's a guy at the bar. He's been talking to the bartender, and he looked our way. Now he's on his mobile, calling in reinforcements, I'd guess."

"Well, that didn't take long," Will commented. It was a bit of luck, really, that someone had taken notice of them. The chances of stumbling on someone involved with the drugs operation were low, but if this resulted in some sort of conflict, it might indicate that Edward was right about Aberystwyth being the initial destination for the load. Of course, this might be something entirely different. Maybe the guy just didn't like strangers.

"What do you want to do?"

Will considered. If they finished their meals and then walked outside, chances were good they'd find more thugs than they wanted to face waiting for them, if it were true they'd drawn suspicion. On the other hand, the steak and mushroom pie was good, and he was reluctant to abandon a well-earned meal. "How many can we take?"

"Two for sure; maybe four if we're really good."

"We might be better off if we find a way to slip out the back and then follow that guy to see where he goes."

"He'll stay inside to keep a watch on us until his friends get here," Edward warned.

"Then we'll split up," Will decided. "He's only one guy, right?"

Edward nodded. "He seems to be alone."

"You stay here, and I'll go out. He'll have to either watch you or follow me."

"You're assuming his friends aren't here yet."

Will laughed. "If no one's waiting, I'll meet you at the off-license down the street toward where the car is parked." He shot back his chair and stood up, raising his voice. "See you tomorrow, mate."

Edward nodded and raised his glass. "Cheers!"

Will ambled toward the door, trying to keep an eye on their watcher from the corner of his eye. The man had his mobile to his ear again, and he stood up, looking uncertain. Edward had been right: the man was onto them. He might not know for sure they were trouble, but he definitely had suspicions.

Will let the door bang shut behind him and looked around the street. An old man wandered past, touching his hat as he walked by, and behind him a young couple held hands, seeming in a hurry to get to their destination. In the other direction, he saw two men in trousers and

211

jackets, looking like nothing more than two friends heading for a drink after work hours.

He walked slowly toward the shop. Edward would follow in about five minutes, giving him time to elude any followers or, if he encountered trouble, in time to come to the rescue. They'd used this scheme before, with success.

He saw the man before the man saw him, so he ducked into a convenience shop and watched from inside. The man, unfortunately, must have seen him at the last moment, though, because he stopped beside a light pole outside the shop and lit a cigarette, facing the door Will had gone through.

Will evaluated him from behind the window. He was as tall as Will and heavier, his hair trimmed so short that his scalp showed through and his face free of beard or shadow. A lump in the back of his jeans spoke of some sort of weapon, but Will doubted he'd bring a gun to a street fight. Maybe a knife or some sort of club.

He saw Edward come out of the pub. When the man turned his head to look at Edward, Will seized the moment. He slammed out the door and into the man, bowling him over as if he'd stumbled onto him hard.

"Sorry, sorry, mate," he said as he rolled to his feet and extended a hand to help the man up. "I tripped on the door mat. Didn't mean to knock you over. You okay?"

The man took his hand and pulled him to the ground as he lunged to his feet. He followed up with a punch toward Will's stomach, which he'd been expecting. He rolled away fast and to his feet. "Woah, man, I said I was sorry." He backed away, holding his hands out in supplication.

The man growled and swung at him, catching him a clip on the side of his cheek. Will whirled around just in time to see Edward club the man over the back of his head with two clasped fists. The man went down, but the man from the bar was just behind Edward. He grabbed at him and swung, pummeling him hard as both fell to the ground.

It was Will's turn to come to the rescue. He hauled at the man to get him off Edward and then tried to sit on him, but the man heaved himself upward, throwing Will off. Will rolled upward and caught sight of Edward, who grabbed the man by one arm. Will grabbed the other and lowered his face toward the man's. "Why'd you attack us?"

"You went after my friend."

"You were watching us in the pub. Why?"

"We don't need people here snooping into things that're none of your business," the man growled.

"What things?" Will lifted the man by the collar and slapped his head back onto the pavement. He was aware of a growing crowd, so he tried to be subtle with it. He and Edward would have to be gone quickly if they were going to avoid police attention. "We were just looking for a little easy work, if you know what I mean." He pulled the man's head up again and held it there.

"They don't take people who come looking," the man snapped. "They find those they want in other ways."

"How?"

"Will," Edward interrupted. "Time to go."

Will snorted in frustration, but he let his grip on the man's collar relax and got to his feet. He reached in his pocket for his mobile and snapped a photo of the man's face, quickly.

"Hey, what the…"

Will spun and clicked another photo of the second man. That one would be out of focus, but maybe good enough for an identification.

Edward was nodding to the gathering crowd, smiling reassuringly. "Just a misunderstanding," he called out. "My friend tripped and knocked him down. We'll be off now. No damage done."

Will joined him and they pushed their way through the onlookers and walked away from where the Land Rover was parked. They walked fast, but they didn't look back.

Twenty minutes later they had circled the block and were back in the car and pulling out onto the roadway.

"You haven't lost your touch," Edward complimented Will as they took turn after turn, pulling over occasionally, to make sure they weren't followed. "I thought now, with your main task being interviewing people, you might have lost a little muscle mass. You weren't even breathing hard."

Will hmphed. "I can't remember the last time I was in a fight, but I've taken up hiking now. It keeps me in shape." He reached up to touch his cheek. He'd be sporting a big bruise there in another day or so.

"Ah, the professional man's workout," Edward teased. "I suppose that's down to your new romance?"

"Bronwyn loves to hike, has done it all her life. If I was going to win her over, I had to learn to like it, too." He paused, and then added, "I couldn't even keep up with her at first, but I've gotten better with practice. I used to have to stop and pretend to enjoy the view, just to catch my breath."

"So…is she like that in all aspects of your life? What else is it you have to practice in order to please her?"

"God, Edward, you're hopeless," Will groaned, but he was pleased at the teasing. At least he had a girl in his life. "How about you? When are you going to find someone to please?"

Edward shook his head. "It's hard, living the life I do." Then he turned serious. "Maybe after this, when I have to find another line of work, I'll find the time for a love life."

"You'd like that?"

"Yeah, I'll admit I'm a bit jealous of you there. Maybe this is a good thing. It'll push me into something safer and less demanding. I think I'm ready for that."

"You couldn't work undercover forever."

"You got out at a good time. I know it wasn't your choice, but in the end, it turned out great for you." He brushed at his hair with a free hand, riffling his curls. "I don't know what my future holds, but I hope I'm as lucky as you were."

They parked on a lay-by on the main road that lead toward the warehouse and walked the mile and a half so as not to raise alerts. It hadn't appeared that anyone had followed them, but they approached cautiously, in case someone was guarding the warehouse. Other buildings offered plenty of shadows they could utilize for that purpose.

"Cameras." Edward pointed as they peered around the neighboring building, another warehouse that appeared to be still in use as a boat factory.

Will looked up. "There are probably cameras on all these buildings."

"But maybe not all monitored by the same people." Edward adjusted the hood of his jacket so that it covered more of his face. "Come on. Let's walk around and have a look."

Will pulled on his own hood, pulling the drawstrings so that only a small bit of his face was visible, and followed Edward toward the building.

The building was part of an old industrial park, with various businesses occupying most of the buildings, but not all of them. Made of old cement, it still seemed solid despite the neglect it had endured. Big sliding doors would allow for a van or a small truck to pull up inside, but a lorry would have to pull up to a loading dock and be unloaded from outside the building. The only exterior doors featured solid locks. They may be able to pick them open, but it wouldn't be easy. The only windows were at least twelve feet high up on the walls, caged over with wire and inaccessible unless they had a ladder.

"As impregnable as a castle," Edward commented.

"At least we can see the lay of the land," Will said. "We can keep watch on the doors from the back, across there." He pointed to an old parking area, littered with crumbling concrete barriers and garbage. "We can snug ourselves in behind one of those barriers and watch what's going on."

"Sounds like fun. Have you ever slept on pavement before?"

"Once or twice, back in the day."

"How many nights are we going to do this?"

"Hey, *you* got *me* into this, not the other way around. Stop complaining."

"There's got to be a better way."

"If we find Morys Howell tomorrow, we can follow him around instead."

"If he's even involved."

Will took a deep breath. "What is our plan, then, mate? I feel like we're just bumbling around here, wasting time. Even if this is where they take the load to distribute it out, how are the two of us alone going to stop them? You know they'll have armed guards. We don't even have firearms. We can't just call 999 and ask for the local constables to come out, and you know as well as I do that this area is remote enough that no bigger force would get here in time. The best we can hope for is to watch until they bring the load in and then hope they wait a day or two before they distribute it. That way we can at least get the drugs off the street. But I don't see us exposing whoever's running the show this way."

Edward shook his head. "I thought we'd get some leads, that we could draw out whoever is in charge, maybe film them when they're splitting the load up and take it Scotland Yard or someone higher up than we are."

"That won't stop the drugs getting out there."

"Not this shipment, but it'd put a dent in their ability to carry on."

Will sighed. "Are you sure you don't want to involve my chief super in this? Or at least someone we could bring in when we get close? I don't like this stumbling around without any resources or backup."

"Then go back home. No one knows you've been doing this. You can still get out."

"I don't want to fight with you, mate."

"Who's fighting? I know you won't give me away, and I get that you might not want to risk your life over this, especially since it's not even your job anymore. I never asked you to help me, just to keep away from my investigation when you were searching for Billy Davies."

"I know that. I want to help you. I'm just not sure we're accomplishing anything this way."

"Then how do you want to do it? If you have a better idea, say so."

Will took a deep breath while he gave it a moment's thought. "I don't know. Unless we get a tip saying who's in charge or when the shipment is coming in, I think we're spinning our wheels over nothing here."

"So, we talk to people, get that tip. Tell you what. Tomorrow we'll try to track down Morys Howell. You know he must be involved, if that double homicide just disappeared."

"Those two guys who jumped us…we should follow them, too, if we can. You said we'd disrupt. What if we plant something on them and call in a tip? We'd have to time it right, but if we could do it when the load was already on the ferry and on its way, I bet that'd cause some issues."

"If we find him, we can do the same with Morys Howell. The more of their people we can tie up, the better. If they're really short of personnel at the end, someone high in the organization would be forced to step up."

"That works for me." He grinned in the dark. "And I'm not sleeping here tonight."

"You've turned into a real softy. In the car, then? We really can't risk renting a room somewhere."

"In the car," Will agreed.

Chapter Fourteen

That night, while trying and failing to sleep on the Land Rover's seats, Will and Edward reconsidered finding Billy Davies' body. Will argued that it would be good to do their own investigation as to his cause of death, and then to hide him somewhere else for the foreseeable future. It would mean wasting a whole day that they could spend doing other things, but Will's uncomfortable feeling about knowing where the body was and ignoring it pushed him to argue that there were enough advantages in it to warrant the time they'd have to spend. If Davies' body was found by Notley or someone else, Will would be called to investigate. He'd no longer have an excuse to track Morys Howell or to be anywhere near Fishguard, and he really didn't want to leave Edward on his own. Even if Notley didn't find Davies' body, their opponents could enable its discovery if they thought Will was getting too close, with the same result. Either way, Will wouldn't be able to continue to help Edward, probably not even to track Davies' acquaintances on department computers. He'd be blocked for several days, at least until forensics and the coroner had their work done, and by then, the drugs would have arrived and it'd be too late to catch the perpetrators in the act.

Besides, if he powered up his mobile once they were far enough north, anyone tracking his movements through it would guess he was still trying to find Davies in England. That would also work to their advantage. That argument, in the end, won Edward's approval of the plan.

They still had at least three days until they estimated that the shipment would arrive, time enough to follow the two men who'd attacked them outside the pub and to locate Morys Howell and figure out if he had a role in the operation, even if they took a day to drive to Hoylake. Time was short, but if they were lucky, they could squeeze it all in.

Will called and made an appointment with Davies' parole officer, hoping to get information about Morys Howell as long as they'd be in the area. Edward also pointed out that, if they were lounging around Liverpool, they could probably score some drugs without drawing attention to themselves. They'd need to keep something on hand on the chance that they could plant contraband on their suspects and get them arrested long enough to disrupt the arrival of the shipment. Surely, they had enough experience to figure out how to go about obtaining what they'd need, and it would have been hard to make a buy in the smaller towns on the coast without being noticed and probably arrested themselves. It was, after all, important for the right people to be contained – and they weren't the right people.

Liverpool also offered opportunities for clandestine shopping. They agreed that a couple of cameras would be worth the investment, allowing them to monitor the warehouse and, once they knew where their suspects lived, their homes for activity. They knew they couldn't be physically involved in the bust; they simply did not have enough manpower or weapons to make it work. Cameras might be the only way they could prove who was involved and bring the investigation to a close. True, they could film the actual event using their mobile phones, but remote cameras watching the warehouse and other possible destination sites for the shipment might catch something they wouldn't see for themselves.

Lastly, Will would have to check in at the station on Thursday morning. Notley would be back from his investigations and expecting an update and a new plan to move forward with the investigation. That would definitely be a waste of time, but he had no choice. His challenge would be to find another excuse to keep Notley far away for a few more days. He'd been thinking about that and, so far, had come up empty. With Notley as suspicious as he was, he'd have to have something really good, even with Bowers' backing.

They'd slept late, both having tossed and turned most of the night in the uncomfortable seats of the Land Rover. It felt like trying to sleep on an airplane, trying hard to doze off only to jerk awake again as awareness of their surroundings startled them upright. Both finally drifted off in exhaustion, waking after ten in the morning, cramped and stiff. *I'm getting too old for this stuff,* Will told himself.

They took the A470 northwest from Aberystwyth, a route that would pass Oswestry, which was near to Llangynog. Will thought about trying to meet up with Bronwyn, but in the end, he rejected the idea. He and Edward had been cautious, but just in case someone was monitoring them, he didn't want her connected to him in any way. He also didn't want Edward to know how much he wanted to see her. In his mind, he tried to brush the impulse off as an indulgence, something just to make her happy. He didn't want to look as tied to Bronwyn as he was starting to feel he was. Besides, he needed a shower and more sleep before he was ready to present himself to her.

As he drove, Will kept himself awake by telling Edward stories about his cases, exaggerating when he could and trying to make him laugh. It wasn't hard to create humor from his experiences with Sean Notley, who made himself a spectacle by emulating his hero, Sherlock Holmes, and if that failed, he could always joke about the Welsh place names that still tripped him up as often as not. When he worked his way around to the case that had introduced him to Bronwyn, Edward sat up straighter.

"I never understood what you were thinking, mate. You know you can't date a suspect."

"It wasn't really like that," Will protested. "We weren't actually dating. There was no romance. It was just two people having lunches out, talking about the case and trying to figure it out. I never did think she'd done it."

"But you did it behind your boss's back, right? And your partner's?"

"There were reasons for that. Notley puts people off, and Bronwyn told me she had information, but she'd only talk to me, not to him. What else could I do?"

"Ah, he doth protest too much. You could have gone to her house and interviewed her again. You didn't have to sneak around and take her for what I'd imagine were long drives in your little car and intimate picnics in remote places. I know you too well. You had ulterior motives."

"No, I really didn't." When Edward cast a skeptical look his way, he went on. "I thought she was a nice girl, but I didn't really fancy her, not then, or if I did, it was just a temporary thing. I really thought I was just using her to help solve the case. I never intended for it to go beyond that."

"Who're you trying to convince, me or yourself?"

"It's true. After the case, I didn't call her for months. And then we landed another case in the area, and I thought of her, and I guess that's when it really started. I couldn't stop thinking about her. I told myself I wasn't going to get involved, but despite my best intentions, I did." He shrugged. "I'd tell myself I was taking her out to break it off and that was all, but then I'd end up kissing her and, somehow, before I knew it, I was committed."

"How long have you been living together?"

"Just since late January. It's a bit of a commute, but I don't mind it. Wales is a beautiful country to drive across and I get to work feeling very relaxed."

"I bet." Edward faked a frown. "You never even told me about her."

Will swallowed guilt. He could have confided in Edward, even at the first when it was just trying to wring information from her. He hadn't treated him as the good friend he was. A thought struck him. Was he as reluctant to introduce Bronwyn to Edward as he was to his parents? If so, what did that mean? Whatever, Edward was owed an apology. "I'm sorry. I intended to introduce you, but I wanted it to be in person, not just a casual mention on the phone."

Edward snorted.

"No, I mean it. Bronwyn's got a training session in the Beacons next week, and I'd planned to give you a call to see if you were free. Not that it's easy to get ahold of you when you're undercover. You wouldn't have taken that call, would you?"

Now it was Edward's turn to look abashed. "I couldn't have my mobile with me or they'd have tracked me. Still," he defended himself, "you've known her a year and obviously been pretty serious about her for at least half that time. You could have mentioned her."

"You're right." There was nothing else to say. "I hope now you can get to know her properly."

"Well, I'll probably have some free time on my hands. I'm sure this'll mean an end to my brief career in law enforcement."

With that declaration echoing in their ears, Edward started telling Will about his efforts to uncover what was going on, detailing what he'd done after disappearing from his assignment. He hadn't shared much about that when they'd talked at the cottage, and Will was surprised to learn that he'd managed surveillance on his own chief superintendent and even, for a brief few days, on the commander.

"You were lucky not to have been caught," Will marveled. "Was it worth the risk?"

Edward considered that question long enough that Will was forced to glance over to see if he had fallen asleep. "I didn't get anything specifically incriminating on either of them, but I do think it was worth the time. Mathews made some calls outside his office on what I assumed was a pre-paid mobile so that's definitely suspicious. He might have been using his own mobile, though, and calling his wife or girlfriend. Who knows? It just looked suspicious to me, him going outside to call. He looked around first, too, like he was trying to avoid being seen."

"Where were you?"

"I'd planted myself in the pub across the street, making sure I wasn't so close to the windows as to be seen watching him. I followed him on foot afterward, but he went to his car every time, so that was the end of it. I had no car so I couldn't follow him."

"There was no checking his phone records to see if he'd made a call around that time?"

Edward frowned and shook his head. "Even if I'd had access to that information, you don't think he'd know I was checking him out? I'm not that dumb."

"How are we going to draw him out then? I don't imagine he actually gets his hands dirty. He'll be paying someone else to do all the work. He'd just organize it from afar."

"Unless we can get onto whoever is running it for him, we probably won't get him." Edward stretched and looked out the window. "I have high hopes for Morys Howell. If he looks to be really involved, we can arrange for him to get himself arrested just before the shipment arrives, and that would force Mathews, or whoever is running the operation, out of his office and into the open. I really do think it's Mathews, maybe coordinating with one or two others."

"I don't know how we're going to get all that information, but you're right. That'd do it."

"First, we get onto Morys Howell. We find him, and we follow him. We track his every move and monitor his phone calls, if we can. We plant some drugs in his car or his house. We watch the warehouse or put a camera on it, to see if there's any activity there. Then we head to Fishguard and watch the ferries."

"That's leaving a lot to chance."

"Of course, it is. But it's all we've got right now."

They arrived in Wrexham just after noon, giving them time for a sandwich before Will's appointment with Neil Brown, the parole officer. Will took time to clean up a bit in the pub's washroom after they ate, hoping his appearance was presentable. He'd brought clothes for undercover work, not for meeting someone in a professional capacity. His cleanest jeans and a buttoned shirt would have to suffice. Edward didn't matter. He'd have to stay in the car and wait since his presence with Will would alert his bosses that the two of them were working together.

The parole office was located about a mile from the prison, in a building that also housed welfare offices, housing authorities, and social services offices. Will supposed it made sense to have all the services in the same building so that clients could easily go from one to another, as needed. He gave his name to a secretary who left him sitting in a waiting area for nearly fifteen minutes before a man stuck his head out a door and invited him in.

"Neil Brown," he introduced himself, offering Will a hand to shake. He was shorter than Will and thinner, wearing a black suit with a bright yellow tie. Although he gave Will a bright smile, Will felt something false about him, perhaps a fake camaraderie as he tried to make Will feel that they were co-conspirators in tracking Billy Davies down. He doubted that Neil Brown really cared whether they found Davies or not.

Will took his hand, finding the handshake limp as their fingers brushed. He introduced himself and showed his warrant card. "We're investigating two murders that took place about a week and a half ago," he explained. "As I said on the phone, our main suspect, Billy Davies, is on the run, and we're trying to discover where he might be able to hide out. We thought any information you could provide, whether it be living arrangements he might have had since he's been out or contacts you might know of, would be helpful in our search."

Brown shuffled some papers on his desk. "I've pulled his files, but I don't know how much help they'll be. I only saw Billy once a month, and not at all in the past year and a half."

"Is that typical?"

"Yes, it is. Once we feel they've integrated successfully back into society, we usually release them. It's hard for them to keep up appointments when they're trying to work and keep themselves afloat. Of course, I'd have been alerted if his name came up in a police report, and then I'd have insisted that he come in for a chat."

"But that hasn't happened," Will surmised.

"No, Billy's done well. Last I heard, he'd leased a farm near Oswestry and was raising sheep, keeping himself out of trouble. They often do, you know. Keep out of trouble afterwards, I mean."

Will felt that the man was being evasive, but didn't know how to push him further. "We're also looking at a man called Morys Howell. He did time for the armed robbery that he and Billy were convicted of."

"Howell? Why him?"

"He and Billy got into trouble together in the past. We thought that's who Billy might run to when he found himself in trouble this time, too. You do know Morys Howell?"

"Yes, well, he's one of my clients, too. I haven't seen him in a long time. I think he was released even before Billy was."

"He was arrested for a double homicide a couple of years ago."

Brown shook his head, looking at the papers in his hands. "I don't know anything about that."

"You would have been notified, though, wouldn't you? Maybe you forgot. Can you pull his file and check it out?"

"I can." Brown's obvious reluctance didn't make Will feel better about him. "I do recall that there was an incident, but I don't think it went anywhere." He walked over to a file cabinet and opened a drawer, shuffling through files until he found one and pulled it out. He walked back to his desk and sat down, flipping the file open and scanning it. "Yes, here it is. Charges were dropped for lack of evidence."

"You wouldn't have met with him then?"

"I'd have had no reason to. I only see them if they commit another crime. There was no crime here. No evidence, no crime."

Will wondered if there was a way to check records, to see if Howell had met with Brown anyway. He didn't like the man's evasive answers. If Brown was involved in the organization; he was probably the man who recruited people who were desperate not to return to prison and willing to do anything for promises to overlook their crimes. He eyed the man, hoping for a guilty look, but Brown looked right back at him defiantly, in silence. In the end, he just thanked him and walked out.

Back in the Land Rover, he and Edward sat and talked it over.

"Obviously, there's someone who's in charge of everything, the one who organizes it all and negotiates with the supplier in Eastern Europe or China or wherever to provide as much product as they can sell. That, by itself, would cut into profits made by other importers, who must be furious about the takeover of the market."

Will mused about that for a moment, then dismissed the thought flirting at the edges of his mind. "The man in charge wouldn't want to be anywhere near the actual drugs so he'd have a lieutenant, the man who actually runs the operation. That man would be waiting at the warehouse for the shipment to arrive and oversee the dividing up of it into smaller loads that could then be transported to various bigger cities."

"He's the one we need to find and take out, if we want to draw out the main player, or players. Remember, more than one of our superiors might be involved. If they're losing evidence and altering files, that points to people who have access, and I'm not sure Mathews could do it without cooperation from your chief super, or someone like him."

Guilt ate at Will. He trusted Bowers. Surely, he couldn't be involved. "Beyond that, we have several people who transport the drugs to the cities. That's people like Billy."

"What's left? We probably have at least one customs agent letting the load through."

"And enforcers, guys who provide protection and do things like killing Catherine Baines and Peter O'Connell. They're the ones who make sure their recruits stay committed."

"That's quite a lot of people," Edward commented. "We won't get them all."

"We never do," Will snorted. "The old cartels were huge employers, too. How do you think these guys are recruited then? They're not gangs, like in the inner cities."

"No, they're either offered bribes or they've been accused of crimes that can be erased, like with Morys Howell."

"That leaves us back where we were, looking for someone who can be manipulated to lure whoever's in charge of the whole show out of their cozy, safe offices." Will shook his head. "I don't see how we're going to accomplish that unless we get access to more information."

"We've already got leads on a few people," Edward pointed out. "There was Billy, and maybe your crime scene people will come up with fingerprints or DNA that'll point to others. You'll be able to talk to them tomorrow when you meet with your partner at the station. We know about the two guys who jumped us outside the pub. They're probably enforcers. I've a pretty good idea Howell is involved, too. Everything we hear suggests he is."

"But we have no proof."

"No, not yet. Maybe I should go find him and follow him around."

"It's too late now. We're miles away and already committed to hiding a corpse tonight." Will didn't relish that thought. "What do you want to do until dark?"

"Let's cruise through Hoylake and see what it looks like, and then maybe we can lay low for a few hours somewhere."

"Rent a room and get some rest?" Will asked hopefully.

"Yeah," Edward ran a hand through his tangled curls, "that."

Hoylake was a small coastal village on the Wirral Peninsula. They drove through it slowly, seeing colorful seaside cottages and a long, sandy beach upon which several boats rested, either tethered to anchors in shallow water or dragged up onto the sand. There was no marina, which they thought good, and a few of the boats were scattered far up the beach just to where rocky cliffs began. There weren't a lot of them; it wouldn't take long to check them out, see if any sheltered a dead body. A few local residents dotted the beach, some jogging or walking and a few with children who ran from the waves as they washed to shore or played with sand buckets and toys. A bank of dark clouds hovered on the horizon. Will hoped they'd move in later when they'd need darkness for their clandestine activities.

From there, they drove into Liverpool and used Google maps on Will's personal mobile to locate a large chain hotel near the city centre. Will used his credit card to book a room, reasoning that he could be expected to use the card in pursuit of Billy Davies anyway, and since they were in England and far north of where they expected the drug activity to be centered, no one would alert to his location and worry about it. Indeed, if they were monitoring his movements, it'd probably ease their minds that he was distracted far away from where their shipment would come in. Using the card and the phone seemed a good idea every way he looked at it.

They found their room, pulled the heavy curtains over the windows, and fell on the beds, asleep in minutes. Despite the location near the city centre, the hotel was quiet, and they slept for nearly five hours before Will's phone alarm began singing to wake them up.

"Harry Potter theme?" Edward rolled over in his bed and glared at Will.

"My niece Lark chose that as my alarm tone," Will admitted sheepishly. He'd forgotten about it.

Edward sighed. "You want to shower first, or should I?"

"I'll go. You try to sleep a few more minutes." Will slid to the edge of his bed and stood up, stretching to ease the ache in his shoulders. He wasn't used to street fighting, nor to sleeping in a vehicle. The few hours in a real bed had done him a wealth of good, but it wouldn't last. They'd be out after midnight looking for Billy Davies' body, and then they'd have to hide it somewhere before they could drive back to Caernarfon for his morning meeting with Notley. He'd get no sleep the coming night at all.

A half hour later, with Edward taking his turn in the shower, Will pulled out his mobile and called Bronwyn.

She sounded delighted. "I didn't think you could call."

"I shouldn't, but if we keep it really short, I hope it'll look to anyone checking on me like I called to try to make it up with you and you turned me down flat." He tried to keep his voice light.

"Then I'll say what's important. I love you, Will, and I miss you a lot. Time seems to drag when you can't be here."

"I promise to take some time off after this is over. If I don't make it to the Brecons with you, we'll go somewhere else together after the St. Melangell's Day festivities."

"I'd like that."

He pictured her, tousled and half-asleep, knowing she'd have been snuggled in bed with Daisy when he called. It wasn't late, but she was an early-to-bed, early-to-rise sort of person. "I love you, too, sweetheart. I'd better go. I'll see you soon."

As he touched the end -call button on his mobile, he smiled, glad he'd been able to sneak in at least a short call. If she'd had more information for him, she'd have said. He hadn't expected that she would. He'd just wanted to hear her voice. It gave him courage for what lay ahead.

He and Edward got fish and chips from a takeaway near the harbour and ate them sitting on a bench, watching late-night shipping traffic and the few pedestrians wandering through the area. Afterward, they relaxed, hoping to be approached by someone offering to sell them something illegal. Neither of them was familiar enough with Liverpool to know where dealers likely hung out, but they supposed this tourist mecca could draw out someone interested in making some quick cash as well as any back alley in the city. When no one immediately wandered by, Edward walked to an open off-license and bought containers of beer and a bottle of Famous Grouse, figuring that opening drinking would make them look more derelict, more likely to be interested in an illegal purchase.

The ploy worked, but not exactly the way they imagined. As they opened the beers and took cautious sips, two young women walked by, eying them openly. Both wore short, tight skirts, with sequined tops, one purple and the other pink, and tall heels that threatened to catch on the cobblestones as they walked. Will watched them, frankly returning their gazes, glad that they'd drawn attention, even if the wrong type. At least they were being noticed.

The women walked past, and then one of them turned back, stopping her friend with a hand on her arm. "Are you two interested in a party?" She tossed the words over to them casually, but with a definite come-hither smile.

Will wondered how Edward wanted to play it. He waited.

Edward slid closer to Will. "Not the type of party you're hinting at," he said, taking Will's hand in his own. "We're looking to score some pharmaceuticals, maybe. You know of anywhere we could get something along those lines?"

"We'll give you a finder's fee," Will added as an incentive.

The girls' smiles disappeared, and now Will could see that they looked older than they'd first appeared, street-worn. "How much?"

"Depends on what you find us," Edward hedged. "You bring us someone who can sell us something special, we'll see you well-compensated. Maybe you could go back home and get some sleep, with your pockets full of cash."

The girl in purple shot a look at her partner. "Are you looking for anything specific?"

"No weed," Edward told them. "We've got that. No roofies, either. We're after something more adventurous, and enough to last us a few days. We're on holiday, and we'd like to enjoy it to the max."

"That's not as easy as it used to be." The girl in purple seemed to be the spokeswoman.

"But you must have some contacts." Edward wasn't giving up easily. "A city this big, I know stuff is available. You know where to find it."

The girl studied him, wary. "You aren't cops, are you?"

Edward put his arm around Will's shoulders and pulled him tight against his side. "Do we really look like cops?"

Will pushed Edward away and stood up. He pulled out his pockets, showing them empty except for the pre-paid mobile he'd brought along. "What do you think? I've got no ID, no real mobile, nothing."

"Then where's the money?" Pink girl spoke up, her face twisted with mistrust.

"I've got it." Edward pulled a roll of bills from his shirt pocket, holding it up and waving it for the girls to get a good look. "But it's obvious you aren't the contacts we're looking for. Why don't you go on your way, and let someone else find us?"

Now the girls went quiet. Pink girl nodded toward a darker corner and purple girl followed her. There, they engaged in a quiet chat, glancing from time to time toward Will and Edward, keeping their voices down. After what seemed like a long conversation, purple girl walked back to them, trailed by her friend. "Okay. You wait here, and we'll be back in a few."

"You aren't cops, are you?" Edward asked, startling Will. That thought hadn't occurred to him. If they stumbled onto a sting, that'd put an end to everything: their efforts to discover who was running the operation, the bust they hoped to enable, and their careers, as well. The two women had seemed cautious, but maybe that was just a show to earn their trust.

But those hardened looks would be hard to fake. Purple girl laughed. "You'll have to trust us if you want to make a purchase."

"Okay, we'll be right here," Edward said, committing them to what Will knew was the only path open if they wanted contraband to plant on their suspects.

"It's too open here," pink girl said. She pointed. "Go sit by the docks, by that little building."

Edward and Will looked, seeing a small building deep in shadows. "Okay," Edward agreed.

Will hoped they weren't about to be attacked. That would be worse than being arrested…maybe. "Tell whoever you're going after that we have more money where this came from. If we like what he's selling, we'll be open to buying more before we leave Liverpool. Like you said, it's harder to get stuff now than it used to be, and it's more expensive, too."

"I'll tell him," purple girl promised, and then the two women walked away, their ludicrous shoes clopping on the cobblestones.

Will and Edward watched them disappear into the shadows. "I hope this all works out right," Will said uneasily.

"I've got my ID if not," Edward told him. "We can claim we were after a bust if they turn out to be cops."

"I'm more worried about being jumped," Will confessed. "Street fighting isn't my thing anymore."

"Nor mine," Edward agreed. "We're getting to old for that type of stuff."

The buy went even better than they'd hoped. The girls returned after twenty minutes, accompanied by just one well-dressed man in his late twenties. He wore neat trousers with a jacket that screamed designer, and he looked at them through suspicious eyes. "I hear you're looking to buy some fun."

"We are," Edward agreed easily.

Will kept a sharp lookout around, but he saw no other people lingering in the shadows. The two women had stayed in the open, and Will hoped they just wanted to be able to run away should things go wrong.

The man unzipped his jacket, his movements slow and methodical. He held it open so they could see pockets inside bulging with packets and bottles. He watched them, obviously ready to run if the situation called for a quick escape. It made Will feel safer. If the man was prepared to flee, he wasn't likely to be a cop or to try to steal their cash.

Edward put a restraining hand toward Will and then walked closer to the man. "That looks good," he said. "What all have you got?"

The man looked from one to the other of them, and then he made a decision. He pulled out a bottle, holding it out for their inspection. "I've got prescriptions: opioids, fentanyl, like that. I've got coke and heroin, as well,"

Edward nodded. He glanced at Will. "How much if we take the lot?"

The man blinked. "All of it?"

"If we can afford it."

The man thought it over. He reached up and scratched through his short-cropped hair. "I suppose I'd take three hundred pounds for it all."

"Two hundred," Edward bartered, knowing it would be expected.

"I could give you a little of each for that," the man wheedled, "but not my whole supply."

"Two-fifty for the whole lot," Edward countered.

Will found himself holding his breath. Edward was spending a lot of money that Will had taken from his own account. He doubted he'd ever get it back.

"I'll do it," the man capitulated. He started pulling bottles and packets from the lining of his jacket, setting them on the bench Edward and Will had been sitting on while they'd waited for his arrival. He worked fast, and then he looked at Edward and held out his hand. He looked nervous, as he should. If they were police, this is when he'd be arrested. If they were going to steal from him, this is when they'd attack. He had the girls as backup, but they didn't amount to much of a threat.

Edward handed him the roll of bills, saving out a few for the women.

They could see the relief in his face as it relaxed into a grin. He fanned the bills greedily, and then nodded quickly. "Ta! Enjoy yourselves!" He hurried off toward a building and disappeared behind it.

The two women approached, greedy and eager now that they felt safe. Edward paid them while Will snatched up the bottles and packets and shoved them into his pockets as best he could. They'd gotten quite a lot for their money, enough to frame several people if it came to that. He felt happier now. The evening had started encouragingly, and he felt the worst of it was over. It was a sad world when it was easier to dispose of a dead body than it was to buy a stash of drugs, but that's how it was.

Chapter Fifteen

The beach at Hoylake, so picturesque in daylight, felt spooky in the dense fog that had drifted ashore at dusk. Will and Edward parked the Land Rover as near to the beach as they could get it, and then grabbed torches and went exploring, the light from the torches blunted by the opaque darkness. They'd hidden the drugs in a cache in a rocky area just up the road. In case they were discovered, they didn't want drugs in the vehicle when it was searched. They'd waited until well after midnight to search for Billy Davies' body, a time when no one should be out and watching, unless a guard had been set to watch over Billy's body.

"It'll be one of the boats furthest away from the village," Will suggested, and so they trudged along in the sand, headed toward where the rocky cliffs blocked their ability to walk further along the water's edge.

They used their torches to explore the first two boats they came to. Will had known instantly that they weren't the right ones; despite the smell of rotting fish and seaweed, the scent of rotting flesh would stand out. Still, they aimed their lights around the insides of the boats, satisfying themselves that no bodies were hidden in built-in boxes or lower berths invisible to a casual glance.

When they reached the place where the cliff blocked the beach, they found that they could actually walk around the rocks, it being low tide, if they waded knee-deep in the cold water. They removed their shoes and socks and rolled up the legs on their jeans as best they could, and then they flinched as the icy water splashed against their shins and washed up onto their jeans nearly to their waists at times.

"I hope we get back before the tide comes in," Edward grumbled, "or we'll have to swim."

"That'd be hard to do with Billy Davies' body in tow." Will cringed at the thought.

"No, we'll find a place to hide it up the beach, on that side of the rocks. As long as it's not in the boat, they won't find it right away. They won't want to be obvious when they're searching for it so it'll take them some time."

"I don't want it in Bronwyn's Land Rover if we can help it." They'd already discussed this, but Will wanted it to be clear. They'd brought tarps and gloves, and there shouldn't be any trace of it even if they did have to transport it, but he didn't want to take any chances. "If we can hide it here, that's better."

"We'll hide it here," Edward grunted, leaning away as another wave washed over him. He held his torch higher. "I think we're almost around it."

Will followed him as they edged around the last of the rocky outcropping. The rocks curved inward then, allowing for a small, sandy cove to be protected from the worst of the waves. An ancient boat lay on its side on the sand, faded wooden boards splintered badly and the color no longer discernable. It lay high above the high tide mark, and probably hadn't been used in years.

They waded through deep sand toward it, shining their torches ahead through the fog to light the way.

"This'll be it," Will said, sure he was right. He handed Edward his torch and clambered over the upper edge of the boat, standing on what would have been the leeward side, had the boat been sea-worthy. He nudged his chin toward the bow, where a boxed in area was secured with a newer padlock. "Want the first look?"

"I'll hold the lights. You look." Will could see Edward's wide grin in the backlight from the torches. "It was your tip, after all. You get the honors."

"Thanks," muttered Will. He couldn't smell anything beyond seaweed, salt water, and bird droppings, but the box was pretty tightly sealed. "Wonder who owns it?"

"It's abandoned property. No one will charge you with trespass."

Will snorted. Edward stepped closer and shone the lights on the lock as Will pulled on latex gloves, took it in his hand, and looked it over. "You brought a bolt cutter?"

"I think we can just smash the wood in." Edward pointed the light. "It's pretty much rotted through. That lock isn't meant to keep out people as determined as we are." He laughed.

"Give me a rock to smash it with." Will was anxious to get it over with. "And quit laughing. If I have to look at it, you get to carry it out."

Edward turned the lights away and went looking for a suitable rock to use as a club. Will was left standing on the boat in the dark. He listened intently, hearing the hiss of the waves as they broke onto the shore, but little else.

Edward was back in less than a minute. "Here." He held a sturdy rock about the size of Will's fist in his own gloved hand. "Try this." He turned the light on the door.

Will grasped the rock and took a breath, then swung his arm hard toward the ancient hull. The wood splintered inward as the rock struck, and pain shot up Will's arm. He ignored it and reached for the hole he had made, then yanked on the wood. It gave, sending him backward onto his bum.

Edward was doubled up with laughter. "Nice job, mate," he managed.

Will shot him a dirty look. "Give me my torch." He grabbed it out of Edward's hand and sent the light into the opening, leaning close to peer inside. "There's something there, for sure. I can smell him." He grabbed the wood and ripped more of the boards away.

Edward squatted down beside him and pointed his own light into the hole. "Looks like we have Billy."

Will set down his torch. "Help me rip the rest of this away. We need a bigger opening if we're going to get him out."

They pulled at the boards, managing to rip most of the front of the opening away. Once they judged the opening big enough, they reached through together and pulled on the tarp-covered bundle inside, gagging from the stink. The bundle slowly slid their way, emerging partway out before snagging on the boards that remained.

They tugged more of the boards away and then took hold of the tarps and heaved, inching the bundle further out of the hole. It wasn't so much the weight of it that stymied them as the awkwardness of a long, narrow package. They heaved again, moving it nearly a foot before it snagged again. Frustrated, Will pushed it over a few inches and told Edward to stamp on the snag. He did.

They pulled in earnest now, moving the body more quickly out of its hiding place. Finally, the last of it emerged. Out of breath, Will stopped and picked up his torch. He pointed it at the bundle. "Looks about the size of a man." He fumbled in his pocket and got one of the pre-paid mobiles. Pointing it at the scene, he snapped a picture, then another and another.

Edward used his own torch to examine the wrappings. "Wrapped up like a mummy," he grumbled, picking at duct tape holding the tarp firmly. He peeled a bit off. "Plastic beneath."

"They didn't want the smell drawing attention." Will leaned in to take some closeup snaps. He doubted the photos would do any good, but he felt it important to somehow record what they'd found in situ.

Edward pointed his torch away from the boat, toward the rocks, swinging it in an arc. "We're not going to hide the body here. There's no place for it, and they'd find it in an instant."

The cove was small, with sheer walls rising up from it. Edward was right.

"You always knew we'd be taking it with us," Edward told him. "I know what you said, but it was all but certain we'd have to carry it off further than a few feet away."

"We'd better hurry, then," Will said, disgusted at the thought of the rotting corpse occupying the cargo area of Bronwyn's Land Rover. He'd

237

have to work really hard to get the smell out before he returned it to her. "The tide's rising. I don't swim well enough to tow a body along."

"And we still have to carry it up to the car and find someplace to dump it." Edward looked down at the body. "We'll have to go in the dark. There's no way to carry our torches and him, too."

"God, we're going to get turned around and carried right out to sea," Will groaned. "Can't you put your torch in your mouth?"

"Ha, ha, funny," Edward snorted. He leaned down and picked up the bundle from the edges, fumbling until he got a good grip.

Will put his torch and the phone in his pocket. They'd get wet, but there was no help for it. He bent down and grabbed his end of the bundle. Together, they hefted it up and edged toward where the rocks blocked the beach, trying to find their way in the foggy darkness without tripping over anything. The body was heavier than Will had anticipated, but they could manage it if they worked at it. He only hoped no one would be about to see them load it into the Land Rover.

They waded into the water around the rocks and lowered the body to the water's level on the side toward the sea. To Will's surprise, it floated roughly on the choppy water. He reached into his pocket and pulled out his torch. "If you can steer the body in the right direction, I can support it with one hand and still have another free to hold my torch."

"Thank God for that," Edward grunted.

They made their way around the rocky outcropping, wading nearly waist-deep in the rising water that splashed now up to their faces as the waves washed in. Another few minutes, and they'd have been stranded in the little cove. Will sent a silent 'thank you' to whoever was watching over them and watched nervously as Edward gripped the bundle and guided it forward.

After what seemed like an hour, but was probably five minutes, they rounded the outcropping and were able to wade back onto the sand. They pushed the body away from the water and then sat on the ground to pull socks and shoes onto frigid feet. It was impossible to get all the sand off before the socks went on, but Will figured he could ignore the grit more easily than the cold.

Once dressed again, they lifted the body and began the trek to the Land Rover. Although they had parked near to the beach, the uphill climb had them sweating and breathing heavily by the time they struggled through the deep sand in soaked jeans that clung to the clammy flesh of their legs. They laid the bundle on the tarmac on the side of the road while Will unlocked the doors, laid down the rear seats, and spread more tarps to cover the cargo area.

Edward was watching the area nervously while Will worked. "I don't see anyone, but who can see anything in this fog? Can you hurry?"

"I'm doing the best I can. The fog's worked in our favor so far, but the drive's going to take a while unless the weather improves inland. Sometimes the fog only hangs on the coast."

"Yeah, that's right," Edward murmured. "Where are we going to dump him?"

"I've got a plan," Will told him. He turned and nodded at the bundle. "Let's get him in and get going. It's going to take most of the night, but there's a way back that'll take us on deserted roads past sheep pastures and rocks and not much else for miles and miles, if I can find it. It won't be hard to find someplace to put him, and he'll not be found for quite a while."

"Sounds good," Edward agreed. "Can I sleep while you drive?"

"No, I need you to keep me awake," Will informed him. "You can sleep at my place in the morning while I'm at my meeting."

"That's fair enough." Edward bent down to grasp his end of the bundle, "Come on. Let's get him inside."

Together, they lifted the heavy bundle and edged it into the back end of the Land Rover, pushing and shoving at it until they could get the door closed. Poor Billy. Will didn't even want to think about the indignity of it all.

Edward looked down at his soaked clothes. "Can we take a minute to change our clothes? I don't know about you, but I can't ride all the way back to Caernarfon in soaked jeans."

Will glanced around nervously, but the street near the beach looked deserted. "Yeah, good idea," he agreed, and he opened the back door to grab his kit bag from behind the seat. He sorted through it in the dark, pulling out fresh jeans and a dry shirt from feel, digging deep into the bottom of the bag for dry socks.

He stripped off his wet clothes standing on the beach side of the Land Rover and yanked the dry clothes over skin still wet and cold and resistant to being dressed. Finally, he settled into his seat in the car, throwing his wet clothes on the floor in the back, and they drove slowly through Hoylake, squinting to see even the dim streetlights through the fog.

Will let himself breathe normally again once the village lay behind them. No headlights trailed them in the fog, so he felt sure they hadn't been spotted, nor followed. He'd programmed his sat nav to take them on the backroads, and he had no choice but to trust it to guide them to the deserted hills he remembered from a previous journey. If not, they'd come up with a Plan B.

They stopped to retrieve their stash of drugs from its hidey hole, hoping against hope that they hadn't been seen and followed. As they wound their way inland, the fog lightened and then the moon appeared to light their way toward their goal. It was nearly full, but not quite. Bright enough they'd be able to see to carry Billy Davies' body across a pasture to where it wouldn't be quickly discovered, but also bright enough that, if some farmer with insomnia were to happen upon them, they'd be revealed. He worried about it then. He'd thought he'd be able to relax once they got the body and drove away, but now he realized peace wouldn't come until they'd gotten the body out of the Land Rover and were safely on the road to Caernarfon.

It was after four in the morning and early dawn was beginning to light the distant sky when Will pulled to the side of the road. They hadn't seen a house for forty minutes, and nothing showed in the distance ahead. "We'd better do it here," he said, and Edward nodded.

They opened the back of the Land Rover and surveyed their surroundings. There were no fences here; it was a free-range area. Rocky hills lumped the distance, and a small river wound across the pastureland maybe a mile away. Will glanced at Edward, who sighed and hefted his end of the body.

They stumbled over rocks and tufts of grass as they made their way away from the Land Rover into an area populated only by sheep. The bundle got heavier and heavier as they walked. Will's arms ached from the effort of holding it up, but he wasn't about to complain to Edward who'd only tease him about being weak, so he stumbled on.

Finally, it was Edward who stopped and said, "This is far enough." He continued to hold his end of the bundle as he nodded toward a little rocky hillock. "We'll put him behind that. He won't be visible from the road so unless someone is out herding up the sheep, he'll stay hidden until it doesn't matter anymore."

Will nodded, and they walked the remaining few steps to where they laid the body down between two bigger rocks. It was light enough now to see a few details, and Will was in a hurry to move out of the area, but he took a minute to squat next to the bundle and tear at the tarp and then the plastic beneath it. "I want to make sure it's Billy," he explained, and Edward helped him to open enough of the covering to see part of a face.

"That's him," Edward said. "I followed him for a couple of weeks, and I'd know him."

Will paused to take two photographs, and then he tucked the torn tarp back around Billy's face and stood up. "Let's get out of here."

They drove faster then, detouring north toward the A55. Will was looking forward to a roadway not occupied by random, wandering sheep, and the bonus of more traffic to blend into lured him to speed a bit. When they finally merged onto the busier motorway, he felt he could relax at last, re-living the night's adventure in his mind detail by detail until he convinced himself that they'd been careful enough not to bring trouble onto themselves until it was too late to matter.

Edward had fallen into a doze, but he reached over and shook him with a free hand. "We're not there yet," he informed him. "You don't get to sleep."

Edward blinked himself awake and started talking, entertaining Will with exaggerated stories of near-misses with drug lords and territorial dealers until they drove through the city walls of Caernarfon at six in the morning, exhausted but now feeling exhilarated by their adventure – and their success in pulling it off.

Will pulled the tarps from the back of the Land Rover and dumped them in a bin on a street corner before they walked up to his flat. "Some homeless guy will find them," he predicted, "and they'll get plenty of use. There'll be no trace of anything we've left on them within a day or two."

Edward looked around the flat, his exhaustion at bay for the moment. "Bit of a tip, isn't it?" he commented, walking around to examine the book left on the table beside the chair, Bronwyn's sketch on the wall, and the tiny kitchen and bathroom.

Will shrugged. "It suits my needs." He dumped his bag on the bed and went to make coffee. "I thought it a great find at the time, right downtown and with a bargain price, too."

"What does Bronwyn think, or has she seen it at all?"

"She's been here," Will admitted. He thought back to her coming for Christmas and smiled. She'd spent the night with him for the first time, but then he'd been called out on a case and missed most of it. She'd been shy and he'd tried to be patient, tried not to push her or to look as eager as he felt. He'd felt cheated when the call had come and he'd had to leave. "I just stay here when I'm on rotation or working an active case, so I don't need much. My chief says he's going to assign me to the cases on the eastern side of the district if he can in the future. That way I'll be close if I'm at the cottage, and if a case requires a presence in the area, the department doesn't have to pay for my lodging."

Edward was watching him. "You're still under the delusion that you'll have a job as of next week?"

"I'm an optimist." The coffee burbled, and Will laid out sugar and milk that was only a couple of days past its sell-by date. Edward lived rough. He wouldn't complain.

He left Edward with strict instructions to shower before climbing into Will's bed and headed to the station, intending to arrive by half-seven. That was early for him, but he'd had time to shower and dress in fresh clothes, and he wanted to get it over with. He hoped to get a few minutes with Bowers alone before his meeting with Notley. He had no idea what to do about Notley now, but he supposed he could come up with something off the cuff as they talked. He hadn't given Notley much thought the past few days. He felt his nerves returning, his stomach rebelling after a breakfast of black coffee and nothing else.

The station seemed quiet when he walked through to his desk. Jay nodded at him, and Quigley glanced up sharply, but neither stopped him to chat.

Beth Holway was a different story. She gave him a smile and rolled her chair over to his desk. "How's the case?"

"It's at a standstill for the moment," he replied, grasping the mouse of his computer in an effort to make her think he had work to do. He liked Beth, but she tended to want a closer relationship than he did.

She leaned closer. "You and Bronwyn still at odds?"

He had to let her think so. "Yeah, it's not looking good for us." He tried to look downtrodden, but thought he'd failed. He had too much on his mind to concentrate on faking emotions he didn't feel.

"If you're going to be around later, I could make us some dinner," she offered. "My mum has her reading group tonight, and Liam is always happy to go out with his friends if I give him money to spend."

Will shook his head firmly. "Thanks, Beth, but right now I don't think I'm very good company. Besides, this case will probably have me on the road again by this afternoon."

"Well, if you change your mind, just let me know." Will didn't miss the disappointment in her voice. "It's just…sometimes you need a friend to talk to, and I'm here."

When he didn't answer, she rolled her chair back to her desk. A moment later, Bowers strode up, giving her a critical look. "Cooper, I'm glad to see you in early this morning. I'd like to see you before you meet with Notley." He hesitated. "Let's walk across the street and get a coffee. You look like you could use some caffeine."

"I could do, sir." Will stood up and pushed his chair away. "Now?"

"Yes, just let me get my jacket and we'll go. I imagine Sean will be in and ready to go soon."

Will waited by the door until Bowers joined him, and then they walked out together.

"Have you heard from Sean, sir? Has he found anything?" Even though Bowers had agreed to send Notley on a wild goose chase, Will wondered now if he'd figured out the drugs connection. Notley was annoying, not stupid.

"He reported in a lot more often than you did," Bowers said with the grimace that passed for his smile. "He hasn't figured it out, if that's worrying you."

"It was worrying me a bit, sir," Will admitted. "Notley's smarter than I usually give him credit for."

They went into the coffee shop and stood in the queue to order drinks. "I've heard from Mathews," Bowers said quietly, watching Will's face for a reaction.

"He complained about me?" Will had hoped to escape Mathew's notice, but obviously that had been a false hope.

Bowers shook his head, but then they arrived at the front of the queue, and the conversation was disrupted. Will ordered a café Americano black, and Bowers indulged himself with a latte. Will fidgeted impatiently as they waited for the drinks to be made, not wanting to push Bowers to reveal anything until they were in a more private space. Finally, they made their way to an empty table in a corner.

"I was told to keep away from Morys Howell," Bowers explained once they were seated. "It seems someone noticed when we pulled his file and whoever it was went into panic-mode."

Will looked at him in surprise. "Did they explain at all, or just warn you off assuming you'd just follow orders?"

"He said that Howell is one of their confidential informants, and we need to keep a distance in order not to compromise him."

"This was Mathews himself?"

"Yes, Mathews called me."

"Do you believe him, sir?"

Bowers took a sip of his latte. "When you first came to me with this theory, I wasn't sure what to think. It seemed crazy, but at the same time, it made sense. I was leery of getting involved, but you intrigued me enough that I was willing to let you go ahead with it on your own." He paused, and Will waited. "Now, though, I've come to believe you're right. I can't stop thinking about it, and everything seems suspicious all of a sudden. Why is the quantity of drugs increasing despite some pretty significant busts? Why is Mathews so adamant that I keep you away from any case that's drug-related when you've obviously got experience that would help solve drug-involved crimes? Why would they let someone off a double homicide just to become an informant? The answer is that they wouldn't, not in my experience. They can get someone else to inform who's wanted for something drug-related, not murder. They should want you to assist when there's drug activity up here in the north. There shouldn't be so many drugs on the streets if they're doing their job properly. I think Mathews is involved up to his teeth, and so is Howell."

Will felt a thrill run down his body. "I really thought we were onto something with this, sir, but it's good to hear that you see it, too."

"The thing is, Cooper, you need to watch your back. These are powerful people with nearly unlimited resources. I know you're careful, but this is out of your league."

"Someone has to take them on, sir."

"I admire your courage." Bowers took another sip of his latte. "Just don't let down your guard, even for a moment."

"I'll be careful."

"I'd like to help you, but my hands are tied. I'm sure you realize that. I can't check files without it being noticed. I can't run pictures through facial recognition or watch CCTV cameras for vehicles without drawing attention to what I'm doing."

"Maybe it'd be good to put pressure on them," Will suggested. The relief at having Bowers on his side nearly bowled him over.

"I'd thought of that, but if we scare them off, we won't catch them. *You* won't catch them," he corrected himself. "What's your strategy, if I may ask?" His unsure look told Will that Bowers knew he, himself, wasn't above suspicion.

He considered how much to trust Bowers. "We haven't got a firm plan," he said at last, "and that's not just me avoiding your question. We thought if we could find out when the shipment is coming in somehow and if we were lucky enough to find at least some of the individuals involved, we could try to disrupt their usual distribution plan, maybe draw out whoever's in charge by taking out some of the underlings."

"They'll be cautious. They may prefer to lose the shipment rather than putting themselves at risk."

Will hadn't thought of that. "We don't know what else to do."

"The two of you can't take them on by yourselves. They'll be ready to protect themselves, if it comes to that. They'll have guns, and you don't."

"I know, sir. We haven't figured it all out yet. Our best idea at the moment is that we could just film the whole thing and turn it in to someone higher up than they are."

"If I knew when it was happening, I could have a team on standby in the area. Maybe even call in Scotland Yard, if we're sure it's happening like you think it will."

Scotland Yard. Surely, no one there involved in this organization. That should be safe. "Can I let you know as things develop, sir?"

"Of course." Bowers glanced at his phone. "We'd better get back, or Sean will think we're talking behind his back."

He would. Notley was nothing if not suspicious when it came to his relationship with Will. "Thank you, sir," he managed say as they walked toward the door. "I appreciate your support more than you know."

Bowers nodded. "I know, Cooper. No thanks are necessary. Just let me know if I can help."

"Keeping Notley busy would be a huge help."

"I'll see what I can do," Bowers promised, laying a bill on the table.

They met in a conference room, Will bringing a portable whiteboard with him to write on. Bowers joined them, to Will's relief and Notley's surprise. Will suspected he'd need backup to continue keeping Notley on a false trail. This time he'd have to outright lie to him; otherwise, Notley would see no reason to continue looking for Davies up by Liverpool.

"You can go first," he offered once they'd sat down.

Notley frowned at him, and then he stood up and directed his gaze to Bowers. "Before we get started, I want to lodge a complaint."

Bowers raised his eyebrows, his face patient. "What's going on?"

"I tried calling Cooper several times during the past few days. He didn't bother taking my calls. It makes me wonder why." His voice was venomous.

Will's mind raced, but he stayed silent. He had no excuse for not taking Notley's calls when they were supposedly working a case together. It was a serious complaint. He'd had to turn his mobile off so it couldn't be tracked, and this was one result of that he hadn't considered.

Bowers glanced at him. "You were so busy you couldn't take Sean's calls?"

He'd thrown the ball back into Will's court. He had to come up with some excuse on his own, then. "I'm sorry, Sean. My battery ran out, and I left my charger here so I didn't have a chance to charge it. My mobile's been dead for most of the past day and a half. I thought we'd catch up here."

"What if I had important information?" Notley persisted. "What if I found Billy Davies? You'd have wasted department resources if you continued your investigation when the case was already solved."

"That's true," Will said, trying to look contrite. He directed his gaze at Bowers. "I'm sorry. I'll make sure it doesn't happen again."

Notley stared at him for a long moment, suspicion twisting his face into a snarl. Finally, he turned and wrote on the whiteboard. "I started furthest north and interviewed Billy Davies' mother again. She insists that Billy has come clean and is shocked that he is wanted in the two murders. I pressed her on Billy's relationships. She knew about Catherine Baines and gave me a couple of names of friends Billy had talked about."

"Was Morys Howell one of them?"

Notley was referring to a list as he wrote names on the white board. "I asked her directly about Howell, and she said absolutely not, that Billy was too smart to get involved in Howell's schemes again." He gave Will a smug smile. "That's how she put it. Too smart."

"That doesn't mean he didn't turn to Howell after the murders," Will pointed out. "Of all the people he knows, Howell is probably the dirtiest. It wouldn't be out of line for him to ask for Howell's help when he realized what a mess he'd made of things."

Notley ignored him. "While I was in the area, I went out to Wirral and talked to William Bruce, the owner of the place where O'Connell was murdered." He consulted his notes. "He seems a stand-up guy, inherited the farm and is trying innovative ways to make it more profitable. I got the impression that he didn't know O'Connell well. He had a couple of names he'd gotten as references when he rented him the place, and I followed up on those. They turned out to be co-workers at the pub where he worked as a bartender. That's where it got interesting."

Will watched him closely. "In what way?"

"Rumors were that O'Connell was selling drugs on the side. Nothing big time, but a few here and there to customers who knew how to ask."

Will decided to take a risk. "How does that relate to Billy?"

Notley shuffled papers. He handed one to Will, the forensics report on the stock trailer. Will wished he'd seen it before. "The stock trailer showed an irregularity. While the edges of it showed filth from the sheep, the center part was clean. It looked to the technicians as if something had been stacked there in the middle, with the sheep on the outsides to hide whatever it was."

"You're thinking boxes of something illegal, say drugs, in the center of the trailer?"

"That's what I'm thinking. I don't know where Davies got them, but I think he was transporting them and selling them to O'Connell, who then sold them on to his customers."

"Boxes of the stuff would attract more attention than this," Will said, thinking fast. "His co-workers said he was a small-time dealer, not a major player, right?"

Notley's smug smile faded. "Maybe they got it wrong. Or maybe O'Connell was selling some himself, but selling most of it in quantity to someone else."

"That looks like something to follow up on," Will said. "You're not thinking it's domestic violence any longer?"

"One should always look for a possible alternative," Notley quoted, "and provide against it. It is the first rule of criminal investigation."

Will rolled his eyes. He couldn't help himself. "You've already used that quote during this investigation, Notley. You're repeating yourself."

Notley glanced at Bowers, but his face remained impassive. "If it's appropriate, then I'm going to say it." He waited for a reaction, but when none came, he went on, "I also paid another visit to Peter O'Connell's parents. They tell me he was thinking of emigrating to Australia."

Will's eyebrows shot up. "Australia? They might have shared that when we were there before."

Notley shrugged. "We didn't ask a lot of questions that night."

"So he'd need money for the move," Will concluded. "Hence, the drug sales to augment his income."

"It seems logical to assume that's the case."

Will didn't know how that information would be useful, but he filed it away for later thought. "Did you get to Carlisle to talk to Davies' brother?"

"I did. He's also interesting in that he owns a car dealership. Guess where Davies bought his Ford Kuga?"

"The brother confirmed that he paid cash?"

"He did. He said he hadn't heard from Billy since he'd bought the car, but he thought he was doing well with the farming. I asked him about Billy's friends, specifically Morys Howell, and he knew the name, but he didn't think they'd been in touch recently."

"If he didn't talk to Billy much, he might not have been aware. He didn't think it strange that Billy had that kind of money?"

"He said Billy told him he'd been saving it up. He'd got a good price on the lease of the farm since it was so remote, and he'd made money on it."

"What are you thinking?"

"I think that Billy was involved in the drug trade. That's where he made his money."

"Okay. That's it?"

Notley handed Will the dry-erase marker. "Your turn."

Will tried to think it through on the fly. He should have come more prepared, that was a given. He'd been too busy thinking of the dead body in the back of the Land Rover to focus on much else, and there wasn't much he could tell Notley. "I've had no luck tracing Morys Howell so far, unfortunately. He's not home in Llandrindod Wells." They hadn't even made it there yet; mentally, he put it on the list for that afternoon. Howell would now be a priority for Edward and Will after Bowers had been warned away from him. "The coastal villages are small, though, and I've had some credible sightings of Billy Davies in a few of the pubs along there." It was a total lie, of course. Billy was lying dead in a field in northeastern Wales. "I showed his picture around, and he's been seen."

"How recently?"

"In the past couple of days. It makes sense that, after he killed Peter O'Connell, he fled from that area, and he does have a contact there in Morys Howell." Will didn't dare look at Bowers.

"That's it, then?" Notley spat. "That's all you have? I've made contact with Davies' family and figured out the drugs connection, and all you've done is show his picture around some pubs?"

"You had leads to follow. I had less to go on. Just Morys Howell's name, that's it."

"What you do in this world is a matter of no consequence," Notley growled. "The question is, what can you make people believe you have done."

"Your stupid quotes don't help right now," Will shot back. "I've accomplished as much as you have. It's not my fault you had the forensics report on the stock trailer before I did. Maybe if you'd shared that information, I'd have had a better focus on what to search for."

"I'd have shared it if you'd answered your mobile," Notley shot back. "Maybe you shouldn't be trusted to go off on your own, Cooper. Maybe you're just wasting department resources with no one along to keep you accountable."

Bowers stood up. "This isn't getting us anywhere. Sean, you need to be respectful, and Will, you need to keep your temper under control." He glared at Will, and it looked real, not faked. "This is what I think you should do. Sean, I want you to catch up here in the office the rest of today. Do your paperwork and get in some research, something that'll help you figure out where Davies is hiding. If you find anything credible, share it with me and, if I think Will needs to be involved, I'll call him back."

"Where's he going to be?" Notley frowned, obviously annoyed.

"I'm sending him back to Fishguard, to the coastal villages there. If Davies has been seen there, he needs to be on his trail."

"I should be there, too," Notley protested. "There have been no sightings of Davies anywhere near Liverpool or Carlisle."

"I want you in the north again," Bowers insisted, his voice indicating he was not to be argued with. "I want you to follow up on any tips we've gotten there, and I know there have been some because I checked. Once the media put it out that he was wanted for two homicides, people have been calling. On Saturday you can attend Catherine Baines' memorial service, and on Sunday, Peter O'Connell's. They're scheduled back-to-back, and you know someone needs to be there in case Davies shows up."

"I thought Cooper was our guy in that part of the district. Free lodging and all that."

"His home there is a thing of the past, apparently," Bowers told him.

The triumphant look that flitted across Notley's face made Will cringe. Poor Notley wouldn't be laughing once he learned how he'd been misdirected and used.

"Don't celebrate my break-up too soon," Will said. "Maybe we'll work things out."

"I wouldn't hold my breath," Notley snorted. His reluctance to work the case alone had disappeared.

"You two keep in touch through me," Bowers told them in conclusion. "I want to be informed every step of the way." The look he gave Notley was tinged with guilt, but the one he sent Will's way was stern. "Call me."

Chapter Sixteen

Edward was waiting when Will opened the door to his flat. He put his finger to his lips and pointed at the radiator, and Will raised his eyebrows in shock. He pointed toward the bathroom, miming a shower, and Edward nodded. Will had showered when they'd first arrived, but the stink of the corpse was still in his nose and he felt like everyone he came into contact with would notice.

What had he and Edward said when they'd first gotten there? He fought to remember, but his mind was fogged with exhaustion and he couldn't bring it up. Whatever they'd said, someone knew the two of them had been together. Truthfully, he was surprised no one had been around to stop them by now. Maybe they'd been waiting for him to come home so they could trap the two of them together.

He changed his mind about the shower. "Let's go," he mouthed, and Edward nodded. He stopped to throw clean clothes in his kit bag, scooped a box of biscuits and two bags of crisps into a carrier, and grinned when Edward picked up a flask he had found in the cupboard and thoughtfully filled with coffee.

They fled down the stairs and out the door, where they paused and looked around. Nothing seemed out of place. People strolled by on their way to shop or work, and a woman walking a dog dodged around them.

They'd parked around the next block, just to be safe, and now Will was grateful for his caution.

He kept an eye out as they walked back to the Land Rover and got in, locking the doors. "Did you see anyone following us?" he asked Edward as he fastened his seatbelt.

"No, but that doesn't mean they weren't there. They might want to follow us, to see where we go." Edward scratched at his chest. "Can we open the windows? It smells a little funky in here."

"Bronwyn's going to kill me," Will moaned. He hit the buttons and the windows slid down, and then he pulled out of his parking space. He merged into the traffic and turned at the next corner, pulling over again to the side of the street. They watched the traffic go by for a long minute, and then he repeated the process three more times before he felt secure in thinking that no one was following them.

Will filled Edward in on his meeting as they followed the A470 south. He felt bad having to lie to his friend about his conversations with Bowers, but it didn't really make any difference in the direction their investigation would take them now.

"Morys Howell is definitely a person of interest," Edward concluded. "We couldn't be lucky enough to have stumbled onto our man in charge, could we? Not the mastermind behind it all, but his lieutenant who runs the whole show for him?"

"Maybe," Will hedged. "If we have no one else to chase, then I guess we'll plant the drugs on him and see if that draws anyone else out. I have to think he's fairly important to them, if they managed to erase a double murder charge in order to recruit him."

"It has to be him," Edward insisted after a moment's thought. "Getting off on a major crime, evidence disappearing…they wouldn't take that risk for just a guy transporting stuff for them."

"I hope you're right." Will signaled and changed lanes, watching his rear-view mirror. There was a silver sedan behind him that he didn't like. He slowed, but it passed by and continued on. *Paranoid*, he told himself. He didn't know how they'd fail to follow him and Edward if they knew the two of them had been at Will's flat together. Maybe they'd thought they'd have more time to get someone there. Whatever, he was glad for the good luck, if it were truly that.

They'd decided that finding Morys Howell was a priority, so he bypassed the turnoff for Aberystwyth and headed inland toward Llandrindod Wells. Now that they were forced to drive more slowly, the countryside wasn't such a blur, and Will found himself noticing the various greens of the pastures and hillsides when he caught a glimpse of them through the overgrown hedgerows. Cattle grazed alongside sheep here, crumbling drystone walls only partially effective in containing them within. He was forced to slow even more as they drove through small villages on the way that reminded him very much of Llangynog, just a few houses and maybe a church and a pub.

Llandindod Wells proved to be a mid-sized village with a medieval look that reminded Will of the walled cities he'd seen, and Conwy in particular, except without a castle. It did have a lovely old stone church with a cemetery reminiscent of St. Melangell's, and pubs and shops enough to satisfy the appetites of the residents not only of the village itself, but also of the farms and small villages nearby.

He parked in an empty space in the downtown area, and they sat in the car to plan their day. It was already nearly noon. Will had an address for Morys Howell, so their first priority would be to use Google maps to find it. They'd need to know his habits and what his vehicle looked like if they were to arrange to get him arrested, especially if it ended up being last minute. It all depended on them finding out when the shipment was coming over.

"If we can't find out when it's coming, we'll call in a tip on Saturday morning. That should keep him in jail until Sunday," Edward commented.

"If the shipment isn't already in transport, they can just postpone it until he's available," Will pointed out.

"What's our alternative?" Edward's exasperated tone told Will he'd better keep his opinions to himself.

"How about the tough guys in Aberstwyth?"

Edward's eyes lighted. "We can find them tonight. They'll be at the pub. It's got to be their local. We'll follow them and see what they're driving or where they go, and then we can wait for a time when we can plant the stuff on them. It'll probably have to be tonight or tomorrow. We can't manage it all last-minute."

"No matter, it'll disrupt their plans. We'll set them up with too much for it to be personal use, and that'll be good until they get a barrister to plead their case and get them out. We'll save most of it for Howell, if you really think he's our main player."

"I do think so." Edward turned to look out the window. "We need to watch the warehouse, too. It's got to be where they take the stuff to divide it up. If we're wrong about that, it's going to be tough to make this work." He sounded worried. "I wish I could have followed Davies longer. I got onto him from Peter O'Connell's dealing." He turned back to Will. "I don't think I ever said. I followed O'Connell and got onto Davies because that's where he got his product. I thought I could follow Davies back to where he picked it up, but then they came to his house and shot Catherine Baines and threatened Billy, so it all fell apart. He would have taken me back to the warehouse, or wherever they are taking the loads when they arrive."

Will was worried, too. "You can't change the past, mate. Best -laid plans and all that. If all this falls through, though, we're in some deep trouble."

"I know, I know," Edward snapped. "No one will really know we planted drugs on our suspects and called in tips. No one will know we suspected our bosses are major drug importers. We can just disappear."

Bowers knew, most of it, anyway. "No one knows we concealed a dead body," Will couldn't help adding. "I'm pretty sure we'll disappear if we can't make this work, but maybe not by our own choice." He wondered if his last thoughts would be of Bronwyn.

They programmed Google maps on one of the mobiles to take them to the address they had for Morys Howell. Quigley hadn't gotten a place of employment for him and he probably wouldn't be home, but they'd find it, maybe talk to a neighbor or two, and keep an eye on it.

Howell's home, when they found it, turned out to be a row house in a string of attached homes stretching an entire block. They parked across the street and gazed at it. The homes were gray stone, with concrete steps leading to black doors. They were narrow, but probably three stories high, and, without exception, they'd been well-maintained.

"It's strange that no one wonders where Morys Howell is getting his money, "Edward commented, starting at the houses. "I can't afford something like that, and I've seen your places, so I know you can't."

"Maybe he inherited money. I didn't get much chance to check into his family situation before I had to stay off the computers."

They watched the house, sitting in the Land Rover. Parked cars lined the street in front of the houses, but a sidewalk ran between them and the tiny front gardens. Howell's house featured a neat lawn with tulips alongside the short walkway to the steps. A pot of mixed flowers decorated the stoop.

A woman stepped out of a house three doors down. She had a little white dog on a leash, and she locked the door and then descended the steps to the sidewalk, setting off at a brisk pace toward the village shops. They watched her until she rounded a corner at the end of the row of houses.

A few minutes later, another woman pushing a baby's pram came around the same corner. Carrier bags hung from the handles of the pram, and Will assumed she'd combined exercise with necessary stocking-up on supplies and was now returning home. He glanced at Edward. "Are we just going to sit here, or are we going to ask some questions?"

Edward shrugged. "What if she goes into Howell's flat? We don't know. Maybe he has a wife and a family."

"I'm going to find out," Will said firmly. He slid out of the car and walked slowly toward the woman, not wanting to startle her.

She saw him coming and moved the pram to the side of the walkway, and then she flashed Will a quick smile and said, "Hello."

He nodded and slowed. "Do you live here?"

The woman stopped. She didn't seem concerned, but rather curious. "Just there." She pointed at the door next to Howell's.

Will flashed his warrant card at her. "Can I ask you some questions?"

Her eyes widened. She glanced at the row of houses, and then she nodded quickly. "If it won't take long?" She made it a question. "Boss Baby is about to wake up, and I'll need to get some lunch in him before long."

Will smiled, trying to set her at ease. "Sure, I'll be quick. I'm wondering about your neighbor, Morys Howell. Do you know him?"

She hesitated. "Only to greet when we walk out at the same time. I know his wife better."

"I didn't know he was married." Will thought if he kept it brief, she'd elaborate more.

She did. "Yes, Jill is her name. Jill Howell. They've been married just a little over a year."

"Does Jill work?"

"She works down at the garden centre during the season. She'll be working now."

"Do you know what kind of work Morys does?"

The woman thought for a minute. "I'm not sure. He works from home most of the time, but I know he has business trips that take him away for a day or two, sometimes longer."

"Do you know where he goes?

"No, I'd have no idea. I only know that Jill is home alone sometimes."

"Is he home now, do you know?"

"I'm not sure, but I would think so. His car is just there." She nodded toward a Mercedes sedan and then looked at Will curiously. "I know Morys has something of a past. Jill told me once when we'd had a glass of wine too many. But now he's a successful businessman, with a nice house and a nice wife. What is it you think he's done?"

"Just a minor offense," Will assured her. "I'd appreciate it, though, if you wouldn't mention that we'd talked. I can't say much, but I do think it'd be safer for you if he doesn't know."

Shock took her back a step. "What do you mean?"

Will didn't want to frighten her, but he did want her and her baby safe. "You said you know about his past. I'm not sure what he's capable of, but if he thinks we're checking into him, he might take it badly."

She gave him a horrified look and then pushed the pram toward her own stoop. "You should be ashamed, putting a woman and her child in danger." She paused and looked back at him. "Anyway, Morys isn't a bad man. He's changed his ways, obviously, or he wouldn't be living here where he does."

She'd attracted the attention of another passerby, a man jogging who slowed to a walk and then stopped beside Will. "Everything okay here?"

Will tried to look inoffensive. He held out his warrant card again. "Just checking on one of your neighbors." He nodded toward Howell's house. "Do you know Mr. Howell?"

The man shook his head. "I see him coming and going some, is all. I think he's in some kind of export business. He's at home most days, but then I'll see him going off with a suitcase and then he won't be around for a few days."

"Why did you think export business?"

"Is he in some kind of trouble?" The man suddenly seemed to grasp the implication of having police questioning him about his neighbor. "Price gouging? Money laundering?"

"Not that we're aware of. We're just curious how a former felon can afford a nice house like this," Will explained, trying for a reasonable tone. Surely, the police did this with every former criminal, didn't they? He hoped the man wouldn't realize the absurdity of it all.

"I wondered that, too," the man said, surprising Will. "Not that I knew he had a criminal past, mind you. Does he?"

Will nodded, hoping not to have to elaborate.

"I just thought it must be a nice, cushy job he has if he can work right from home and get to travel and come out of it with plenty of money to spend. I did wonder what he did for a living."

Will ambled back to where Edward waited in the Land Rover. He slipped back into the driver's seat and told Edward about the conversations. "What do you want to do now?" he asked when he'd finished.

"We could stay and watch the house, see if he goes anywhere and follow him," Edward said. "We might be better off following him around than watching the warehouse. It's really looking like he's involved up to his eyeballs. They're not going to pay just anyone enough to afford a house and a car like this. I think someone's put him in charge of it all, and that means he knows who that someone is. We could jump him and ask him questions."

"And get ourselves arrested. You know Mathews isn't going to let that go, if he finds out. He wants Howell protected so he can do his job."

Edward squinted toward the house. "That's if Mathews is even involved. I wish I knew for sure." He focused hard. "They probably know we're onto him. I bet there's a camera right on his front stoop that recorded both of your conversations."

Will glanced around uneasily. "Let's head into town, then, get some lunch and maybe catch a little sleep, if we can. I don't know about you, but I'm about all done in."

"I want to try to follow those two thugs from the pub later."

"And we should keep an eye on Howell, too. We're this close. I don't want him getting onto us and slipping away somewhere."

Edward grinned. "You did well, mate, getting information. I don't want to jinx us, but it was almost too easy. I think we're ready to get started with our disrupt and confuse plan. Tonight, we'll follow our two friends from the pub and plant something in their car or their flats. We'll have to see how it works out, but I want the drugs planted by tomorrow morning. Then we'll call in a tip and see them taken in."

"Once that's done, we follow Morys Howell?"

"I'm thinking he'll lead us where we need to be, but if the timing gets tight, we'll have to get him arrested and then hope the warehouse is the right place or that we can find the right lorry to follow from the ferry. That's where it gets harder, but without Howell to run things for them, they'll be scrambling and hopefully make mistakes."

Will nodded. "That's our plan then. Let's go find something to eat. I'm fading here, and I don't think I can go much longer on no food and no sleep."

Edward laughed, and Will remembered the easy charm that made him so good at undercover work. "You've gotten soft, mate. We used to go without for days at a time when something big was happening."

"Well, now I've discovered there's another way to live, and I've found I like it quite a lot."

Llandindod Wells offered a good variety of pubs and restaurants, but Will and Edward decided a bakery with sandwiches on offer was the perfect way to obtain a decent lunch without putting themselves into a corner, just in case someone was now onto them. They bought two sandwiches each, thinking to save some for their dinner, and bags of crisps. Will pulled up to a dash-and-carry afterwards, sending Edward inside for bottles of water and apples. He came out grinning and waving a packet of chocolate biscuits. They were set for an evening of activity.

They drove out away from the village on the first B road they came to, weaving through the nearby farmland until they found a country lane that was so narrow and grass-filled that they worried about getting stuck between the tree trunks that lined either side. When they rounded a corner and found a lay-by, they decided they'd found their home for the afternoon. They ate their lunch sitting comfortably and chatting, and then Edward moved to the back seat and Will reclined his front seat. It was time to try to sleep.

Will wasn't as good at daytime sleeping as he used to be. He shut his eyes, but the window he'd left cracked at the top let in the sound of a buzzing insect just outside. He squinted to see a large wasp, raised the window to keep it out, and then shut his eyes firmly again. He tried to relax and empty his mind, but he was restless. He shifted in the seat, feeling too warm now without the window, so he reached out blindly and cranked it open again.

"Hey, I'm not getting much sleep here with all your racket," Edward complained from behind him.

"Sorry. I'll try harder," Will said. He took a deep breath and then another. What did Bronwyn do? He concentrated on his sense of hearing. He could hear the wind stirring the trees outside, and a bird singing somewhere nearby. That was a good sign, wasn't it? If someone were stalking them, the bird would surely fly away. He re-focused. Now he could hear the wind again, the tinkle of a loose wire on the nearby fence, the bleat of sheep. He could smell the sheep, as well, an acrid scent that he didn't think he could ever grow to ignore, no matter how much time he spent in Llangynog. He took in deep breaths. The sheep stink covered anything else he might be able to smell.

Finally, he drifted off into a restless sleep, waking to look out the windscreen and then relaxing back into a doze. He could hear Edward snoring from behind him, and he tried to match his breaths to Edward's so it wouldn't be so disturbing. He drifted off again, and this time no dreams startled him into wakefulness.

Edward woke him some time later. "Hey, mate, it's getting on eight o'clock. We'd better head back into town."

Will shook himself mentally. Had he actually slept away nearly six hours of daylight? He opened the car door and stepped outside into the dusk to relieve himself, and then he stretched his arms toward the sky, arching his back to try to work out the kinks. He didn't feel rested at all, but maybe once they got busy, the achiness would fade a bit. He hoped so.

They hid part of their drug stash beneath a rock beside the lay-by and drove back into town, pulling into a parking space a half-block from the pub. They sat in the Land Rover and ate the spare sandwiches and crisps, washing them down with bottles of water. By then, Will was starting to feel more awake and able to face the night's work. With luck, it wouldn't involve anything more than following the two men and probably breaking into their vehicles.

But their luck seemed to have changed. The pub did a brisk business, but neither of the two men who'd attacked them walked through the door, in or out. They waited, chatting aimlessly, keeping an eye on the door and trying to avoid the notice of people passing by on the sidewalks, with little success. Although most passersby were too absorbed in conversation or their mobiles to see them, those who did couldn't help but be curious about the two men sitting in the Land Rover apparently doing nothing.

At ten, Will shook his head at Edward. "They're not coming."

"I was sure they'd be here. Maybe we should wait another hour?"

"It was early when we saw them before," Will pointed out. "Maybe they were here before we got here. Afternoon drinks in the pub."

"What do you want to do, then? We can't do much disrupting unless we find them."

Will looked toward the pub. "I'll just go in and have a glance around. If they're not there, we'll drive by the warehouse to see if anything's happening there and, if it's quiet there, too, we'll go watch Morys Howell's house."

"An all-nighter, no matter what," Edward groaned. "I'll go check the pub. It's my turn. You drive around the corner and hide the Land Rover, in case they're lying in wait for me."

Will nodded, and Edward slid out, running a hand through his unruly curls. With a grin, he set off for the pub up the block, while Will started the Land Rover and pulled past him and around the next corner and then the next one after that, for good measure. He parked and walked back to the main street, edging around the corner of a stone building to see if Edward had stirred up any activity in that few minutes.

He had. He saw Edward walking fast toward the corner with four men in obvious pursuit. None of them were running, but he turned and ran back to the Land Rover, seeing Edward over his shoulder break into a run as he rounded the corner behind him. He started the car and slammed it into reverse, backing up the empty street to the corner just in time for Edward to leap inside, the men right behind him. One grabbed at the door as Will floored the gas pedal, swinging away as it dragged him a few feet. In the rearview mirror, Will saw them milling around in obvious frustration.

He glanced at Edward, who was grinning. "We've got them now," he told Will, and Will supposed he was right.

They rounded several corners and drove up side streets before parking the Land Rover and walking back to the main street, keeping a watch out as they went. The men would know about the Land Rover now, and he was sorry to have given that secret away. Now they could be easily tracked with CCTV cameras, and if whoever was in charge was law enforcement, he would be aware of all their movements. Nothing they did now could be done in secret unless it was done on foot.

Hugging the wall, they saw the men scattered up the street, peering into dark side streets and into the few shops open at that time of night. Someone screeched up in a red Ford Focus, and Will and Edward exchanged glances. It would be good news and bad. That car would be their target later that evening, but if one of the men was driving around, he'd find the Land Rover and they'd be without wheels.

Then Edward grinned, and Will caught his idea almost at the same moment. "They're going to vandalize the Land Rover." Guilt and euphoria fought for his brain. Edward pulled a phone from his pocket and pushed it toward Will. "You'll have to hang around the Land Rover to give your report, so I'll take care of the rest."

Will took the phone and peeked around the corner again. The Fiesta flew down the street and careened around the first corner it came to. Obviously, the driver had spotted the Land Rover, and he and his buddies were headed toward it. Will turned back and took the shorter route toward the car, stopping behind a spot where a large stone staircase protruded near to the sidewalk. He squatted down and watched.

The Focus drove up cautiously, bypassing the Land Rover on its first pass. Will could see at least four occupants, and he crossed his fingers, hoping they had all come. The Focus did a U-turn at the far end of the street and drove back toward his hiding place. It bypassed the Land Rover a second time, but stopped a half-block further up the road. The doors flew open and the men tumbled out. Will now counted five of them. They opened the boot and grabbed things; Will couldn't see what, but he supposed a tire iron at the least and probably other lethal weapons. Another twinge of guilt raced through his brain. There was nothing he could do at this point.

As the men approached the Land Rover, he dialed the local police station. "I'm watching a group of men vandalizing my Land Rover," he told the operator. He gave her the address and urged her to hurry.

"Are you in a safe location?" she asked.

He thought of his former girlfriend Lesley, a 999 operator in Cardiff. "Yes, I'm safe, but I'm afraid my vehicle will be badly damaged. Please don't use sirens. I'd like these men caught."

He heard the windscreen shatter as he hung up. He peeked around the stone pillar. The men had gathered around the Land Rover, laughing now and daring each other on. One of them swung at the vehicle with the tire iron, and Will winced as the driver's side door caved in. He felt bad about the damage, and he hoped the men would be too occupied in their task to notice the patrol cars that'd be there quickly. He really wanted them caught, and not only for the reasons they'd planned. Now, they'd made it personal.

A noise behind him startled him, and his heart lurched as he jerked around to see Edward squatting down beside him. "Idiots," he said. "They left it unlocked."

Will let out a breath of relief. Now things really were swinging their way.

A patrol car swung around the corner, and they turned back to see another coming from the opposite intersection, blocking the street in both directions. Officers slipped out quietly, any noise they made masked by the shouts of the men and the crash of metal on metal as they beat on the Land Rover. The newcomers approached the crime from both directions. When they got near enough, one of them shouted out, "Drop to the ground. You are surrounded."

The men panicked. One dropped down, while four others took off running. One of those was tackled immediately, and another stopped short when he saw the patrol car blocking the street, raising his hands and dropping to the tarmac. The officer still inside the vehicle turned on his blue lights at that point, and another man dropped onto his chest on the street. The last man sprinted fast past the patrol car, only to be tackled by another officer just the other side of it. It was over very quickly.

Will and Edward ventured out, hands raised, and the four officers turned toward them. "My car," Will called out. "I'm the one who called it in."

One of the constables stepped forward. He kept a cautious eye on them as they stopped in the street, hands still raised. "Are you armed?"

"No," Edward spoke up. He held his hands higher, and the officer reached out and patted him down. He did the same with Will afterward, and then he relaxed a bit. "Tell me what happened here."

Will waited for Edward to concoct a story. "We met two of these men last night, sir. We went into a pub down on the main street and enjoyed dinner and a drink. When we left afterwards, the men were waiting for us. They attacked us in the street outside, and we fought them off as best we could. I'm sure there were witnesses who could verify that fight. We drew a crowd. When we felt we could leave without them pursuing us, we left. The pub's CCTV should show that happening, too, sir."

So far, everything Edward had told them was true, and it could be proven by the cameras. Will liked that.

"Why would they do that?" The constable looked skeptical. Behind him, his partners had handcuffed the five men and were putting them into the patrol cars. "People don't usually just attack strangers in the street. You must have provoked them somehow."

"They said they didn't want people like us in their town, that they found their workers in their own way. That's a direct quote, sir."

The constable tilted his head to one side and frowned. "You were looking for jobs?"

Edward shook his head. "We're just on holiday here, but I took it to mean they'd mistaken us for someone else." He glanced at Will, his look pure innocence. "We thought they were dealing drugs, and they'd thought we were here to break into their business."

"Were you?" The constable watched them closely.

"No, of course not. As I said, we were just in the area on holiday for a few days. We used to work together, but now Will works in Caernarfon and I work in Cardiff. We don't see much of each other." He paused, and then elaborated. "Actually, it had been more than a year since we'd seen each other. We decided to meet here halfway between for a couple of days, just to catch up." He paused, letting that soak in. "I really think they mistook us for someone looking to get in on something illegal. That was the impression I got." He looked at Will.

"They drove up in a red Ford Focus," Will joined in the story. "That one over there." He pointed up the block.

"What drew them back to you tonight?" The constable was still suspicious. "If you'd left after the previous encounter, why would they go after you a second time?"

Edward shrugged. "We didn't want to get into another battle with them, sir, so we bought sandwiches from a bakery earlier and ate on our own."

"The wrappers are in the Land Rover," Will helped with details. "We were trying to avoid another encounter."

Edward nodded. "We thought we'd like a beer, though, so I just peeked my head into the pub to see if the coast was clear, and one of the guys spotted me. I left in a hurry, but they drove around until they found the Land Rover and went for it, since they couldn't find us."

"We were hiding behind those pillars," Will pointed, "and when we saw what they intended, we called you."

"Have you been drinking?"

"No, sir. That's why we thought we could duck into the pub for a beer before we retire for the night." He paused, making it look as though he was thinking it through. "No drugs, either, sir."

The constable was nodding. "I'll need your names and contact information," he said.

"The Land Rover belongs to my girlfriend," Will said. He knew they'd call in the registration; probably already had. "Her name is Bronwyn Bagley. She'll verify that I borrowed it. I can give you her mobile number."

"That would be helpful," the constable said drily. He probably still thought they'd instigated the attack in some way, but he had little choice but to accept their version of things. The men might say something else, but cameras would support their version, and he knew it. "I'll need you to come into the station and sign some statements."

"Yes, sir, we can do that." Will wanted to look cooperative. They'd probably be breathalyzed, checked for drugs, but they'd come up clean so it wasn't a problem. The only problem he foresaw was…"Sir, could I ask a favor?"

The constable looked at him.

"When you call Bronwyn, could I talk to her after you're done?" Will's abashed look wasn't all fake. "I'll need to do some fast-talking after what's happened to her car."

The constable smiled. "Women, yeah? You'll be in some trouble when she sees what it looks like now." He kept smiling. "Come on back to my patrol car with me. I'll just check on the registration and then we'll give her a call."

"Thank you, sir." Will meant it. He could see activity back by the Ford Fiesta, and he wanted to smile, too, but he suppressed both that urge and the one to look at Edward. If it were true that these men were involved with the drugs operation, they'd managed a good bit of disruption that night.

Chapter Seventeen

Bronwyn's week seemed to drag on forever. She tried to keep her mind on her work, to be pro-active about the St. Melangell's Day events since she would be out of the office the next week, but thoughts of Will crept in and she'd find herself sitting blankly at her desk, gazing into space. She really wanted it to be all over so that he could drive with her to the Brecon Beacons, but even more, so she'd know he was safe.

In the evenings, she'd go to her parents' house for supper, helping to wash up afterwards and then wandering out to the barn to watch her dad with the lambs. She'd feed her pony Hobbs apples and carrots, and then she took the time to wander out to the pool of water in the wooded area behind the pasture, the place where her visions occurred. Nothing showed up in the still, dark water, but Daisy had a jolly time sniffling in holes and chasing squirrels and birds that teased her from high on branches. Afterwards, she'd leave feeling more relaxed, although Will was always at the forefront of her thoughts.

She'd had an idea for some time about planting a vegetable garden by the cottage. Now, encouraged by talk of the organic garden her mother and Mai were working on, she decided if it was going to happen, it was time. It would give her something to take her mind off Will, at the least, and if anything grew, they'd have fresh veg for their summer dinners. She called the owner of the cottage and asked for permission to dig up a patch of lawn and fence it to make a garden, and the owner gave her his blessing. "It's not going to sell in the near future anyway," he commented, "so you'd might as well make it your own. Just keep it looking nice, will you? No weeds?"

Bronwyn promised to do just that. She had an idea that the owner hoped she and Will would eventually purchase the house outright, so he would be motivated to encourage them in any way he could. It tended to work to their advantage.

She stood outside the back door of the cottage on that Thursday evening and looked the situation over. There was a sunny patch of lawn just at the back of the cottage near the conservatory that she thought would do nicely for a garden. She dragged a shovel out of the garage and stuck it in the soil tentatively. The turf was tough, the shovel barely made a scratch in it, and she felt disheartened. She'd never be able to dig it up on her own. Perhaps Maddock would come over with his cultivator and dig it up for her? Now that she thought of it, Maddock would probably have to help with the fence, as well. Will, for all his great traits, was not very handy around the house. The lawn mower situation had shown her that. She smiled fondly. He hadn't even known how to start it up.

When it was too dark to see, she moved back inside, having sketched out a garden plot with a can of spray paint she'd found in the garage, left from the previous tenants. Once indoors, she called Maddock and begged him to come help her prepare her garden plot. She could hear the grin in his voice as he teased her about Will. "What? Your big, strong detective can't dig up a garden spot for you?"

"You've got the machinery to do it," she retorted, "so why make him dig it by hand?" She suggested that he loan them the cultivator, knowing he'd refuse, and he relented then and agreed to come over the next day and get it done. "You'll have to build a fence around it, too," she told him.

"Of course, I will," he moaned in mock agony. "Your detective is useless, Bron. You'd better look for a nice farm boy to fall in love with instead."

She hung up on him, not mad, but left without words. He loved to tease Will, and he teased *her* about Will, too, but she knew they liked each other well enough. He only meant it as a bit of fun, and that's how Will took it. He had no delusions about his failings as a home repairman/mechanic/fix-anything-himself guy. He'd grown up paying someone else to do those things; he felt the inadequacy now, and he admitted it freely.

She was deeply asleep when her mobile rang out in the late night. She grabbed it from the nightstand, her heart leaping with fear.

"Hello, this is constable Rhys Jones from Aberystwyth Constabulary. With whom am I speaking?"

"This is Bronwyn Bagley," she managed, her voice squeaking with terror. She wanted to ask if Will was okay, but she couldn't make the words come out. *Why else would he be calling? He had to be calling to tell her Will was hurt, or worse.*

"Ah, then I have the right number." He sounded too cheerful to be delivering a death notification. "I'm calling about a vehicle registered in your name, Miss Bagley, a 2008 Land Rover. Do you own this vehicle?"

"Yes, it's mine," she said, "but…"

He interrupted her. "Do you have it there with you?"

"No, I…my boyfriend borrowed it a few days ago." She hesitated, trying to make thoughts form in her sleepy mind. "He was meeting up with a friend for a few days, and we thought it'd be a better vehicle for them than his little MG. Is he okay? His name is Will Cooper. He hasn't had an accident, has he?" Suddenly, the words came tumbling out fast; she seemed unable to stop them.

"Your friend is fine, Miss Bagley. He's standing right here, waiting to talk with you after we finish. He wasn't in the vehicle when it was damaged."

"Oh, thank God." Relief flooded her, and she suddenly felt wide awake. "What happened?"

"The vehicle was parked on a side street here in Aberystwyth, and some vandals decided to take a tire iron to it. They smashed the windscreen and put a sizeable dent in the driver's door. We have them in custody now, but there was some confusion about who the vehicle belonged to."

"It's mine. Will borrowed it, is all."

"Okay, that's all I need to know. I'm going to let Mr. Cooper talk to you, but keep it brief."

She waited, and then Will's voice came through. "Bronwyn? I'm sorry about your car."

"No, it's okay, as long as you're not hurt. That's all that matters."

"We're fine. For some reason, these men took a disliking to us and decided to take it out on the poor Land Rover. Everything's going well for us otherwise."

She supposed that meant they were accomplishing what needed to be done. He couldn't say much with the constable standing beside him, listening. "Everything's fine here, too. I miss you, and I worry, is all."

"I'll see you in a couple of days." There was a moment's silence. "I might not be back in time to drive you down to the Beacons. I'm sorry about that."

"I can manage." Disappointment bit at her, and she couldn't stop herself adding, "How about meeting your parents?"

"I can't promise anything. You know how it is. If it doesn't work out next week, we'll do it soon. I won't keep letting it go."

He didn't mention his job, but she supposed he didn't want the constable standing there to know why he was in Aberystwyth. She thought she'd done well in saying he was on holiday with a friend, especially considering she'd been woken from sleep and had to think on the spur of the moment, but he probably couldn't compliment her on her quick-thinking, either. She decided to be gracious. The damage to the Land Rover was a relief, when she'd thought it was Will who was hurt. "I love you, Will."

"Thanks for not being mad about the Land Rover," he said in return. "It really wasn't my fault. I wasn't even in it when they went for it."

And then he was gone, the mobile obviously handed back to the constable and the call terminated.

At least I heard his voice, she tried to console herself afterwards as she cried into her pillow. *At least he's safe.*

Friday seemed endless. She re-checked her notes for Daryn and Janice, going over every eventuality in her mind so that she felt comfortable that nothing could go wrong while they covered for her. The registrations for the St. Melangell's Day celebration had slowed, but she entered the information from those few that arrived into her spreadsheet and then filed them in the folder. She could spend a few days catching up when she returned before she had to send the tee shirt order off to the printer. Truthfully, it wouldn't set her behind much at work to be gone the few days. It was the conference itself that worried her.

She googled the directions to the Brecon Beacons, printing exact instructions for driving to the lodging booked by the conference for its attendees. The little MGF didn't have sat nav; such a thing didn't exist in 1996 when the car was new. She could use her mobile, though, to give her instructions with Google maps. She liked a print-out as backup, and she planned to buy a road map when she filled up at the petrol station in Oswestry on Saturday when she finished work. Only then would she feel truly prepared, having covered every base she could think of. She planned to leave plenty early on Sunday so as to have the entire day to navigate to her destination.

Although the whole idea of the conference was daunting, she did look forward to seeing the Brecon Beacons. Her family had never traveled. Going to university in Wrexham had been more an ordeal than anything else. Desperately homesick for her family and missing the mystical connections she had in Llangynog and Pennant Melangell, she endured only a brief few months before fleeing back home. When Will came into her life, her world had expanded. He'd taken her to the seaside once for a picnic, and she'd visited him in Caernarfon, driving herself there as a surprise and managing just fine. She knew the conference was important, but if only Will could have accompanied her, it would have been so much more fun.

She left the centre to drive back to the cottage at lunchtime to check if Maddock had come to work on her garden plot. Navigating the little lane in the MGF with the pheasants fluttering ahead of the car made her smile, despite her anxiety. Beside her, Daisy sniffled the air excitedly. She loved riding in the convertible, and Bronwyn supposed any hair she left behind on the seat was a fair trade for the damage done to the Land Rover while Will was borrowing it. It had turned into a fine, spring day, with sweet woodruff blooming alongside the verge and glimpses of new lambs in the field in the openings between the hedgerows. She would have walked the lane that morning except that she wanted to check on Maddock midday to see if he'd shown up to plow her garden spot. It was the only time she'd taken Will's car out of the garage. She knew he didn't want it common knowledge that he'd left it there, but now it seemed a moot point. They obviously knew he had her Land Rover, so it was a reasonable assumption that she had his MGF.

Maddock's Ford truck was parked in the drive at the cottage when she drove up. She hurried out of the car and around the back of the cottage, Daisy running ahead to greet Maddock. He was stooped down talking to the dog when Bronwyn saw him and called out a greeting.

"It looks great," she enthused as she took in the freshly-tilled soil.

He bobbed his head. "It didn't take more than an hour. Is it the right size?"

"It's perfect," she said. "I can rake it even this afternoon after work. You don't need to bother with that."

He scratched his head. "Now you need a fence or the rabbits will eat everything you plant. I don't suppose Will could manage that for you?"

She gave him a wry look. "What do you think?"

He laughed. "I can probably get it done next week, if you're okay with livestock fencing. Otherwise, you'll have to buy whatever you want."

"Livestock fence is perfect. It'll keep the rabbits out, at least."

"That, it will, unless they burrow under." Maddock grinned at her. "Is lunch on offer?"

She nodded. "I'll put something together for us. I have a group in today, but they should be okay for another little while."

She went inside and busied herself in the kitchen, grilling cheese and apple sandwiches and then putting them on plates with crisps. She could see Maddock out the window, loading his cultivator onto the truck.

He came in as she finished and stopped to wash his hands in the sink. "Got a beer for me?" he wanted to know.

"Look in the fridge," she told him. "Will won't complain if you drink one of his since you saved him the trouble of digging up my garden."

"It'll be a fine garden spot," Maddock said, following her to the conservatory and taking the chair opposite hers. "You can watch it grow from in here." He took a bite of his sandwich and chewed thoughtfully.

"Something's on your mind," Bronwyn observed, suddenly wary. "Is it Maegan again?"

Maddock swallowed and took a sip of his beer. Bronwyn noticed it was one of Will's local brews he was so fond of. "In a way, yes." He hesitated, not quite meeting her eyes. "I know it's not something you like to talk about, but would you tell me about them? The fairies, I mean? It's just, Mai and I would like to know more about it so we can understand and help her, if we need to. You said they are real, but are you sure? Couldn't it be that you just imagine them?"

"And Maegan imagines them, too, I'm guessing?"

Maddock had the courtesy to look embarrassed. "In the best of all worlds, yes, that would be it. Maybe she got the idea from a book or a show she watched. But it'd be quite a coincidence that both you and Maegan have the same experience, wouldn't it? I mean, if they weren't real."

"You're saying you believe us, then?"

"I think so." Maddock looked so downtrodden that Bronwyn's heart broke for him. It wasn't easy to deal with a child with the sight, to protect that child from the bullies and disbelievers and the people who would look at her as if she were tainted, somehow.

"There are multiple ways to experience the mystical world," Bronwyn said slowly, and then she looked at him sharply. "You aren't to tell Will any of this, ever. Do you promise me that? Because I won't have him thinking me odd or deranged or something."

Maddock nodded. "You said he knows some of it, though."

"I couldn't stop him knowing," she admitted. "I see things in that pool of water in the woods behind the house. Not all the time. Not often. But sometimes I have visions. Our ancestors used to call it scrying. You know about that?"

"I do know about scrying. You don't grow up in Wales without knowing something of its magical side. This is the country of Merlin, after all."

She smiled, despite her reluctance to discuss this part of her life with him. "Will saw me once. I go into a trance, more or less, and he saw me doing it and realized where I was getting information that I gave him about his case. He's pretty good at putting two and two together, even if it is a pretty outlandish thought. He asked me about it, and I had to admit it." She looked at her brother across the table, watching her with total concentration. "That's all he knows, though."

"I won't say anything. I promise." He seemed to have forgotten his lunch. "How does it work?"

"I really don't know. I just sit on the rock and look into the water, and sometimes images appear. They don't stay long, and then they fade away as if they were sinking into the depths." She saw him looking confused and decided she had to be more specific. "Last winter, I saw a drowned man in the water. He almost looked like he was floating in the pool of water, except I knew he wasn't real, not there anyway. I could see details, like the ice rimming the pond where he really was. And then he sank down into the pool until I didn't see him anymore." She shook herself from the memory. "I called Will, and they were investigating a drowning, but it wasn't him. They found him later, just like I'd seen him, same clothes and everything. That was Doctor Marks."

Maddock let out a breath. "That must feel so weird, to see something that happens later."

"It does. I didn't used to see things as often as I do now, but I wonder if it's because I help Will, because there are things he needs to know so they come to him through me."

Maddock let that process for a minute, and then he took another bite of his sandwich, chewing thoughtfully. "That doesn't seem too odd, I guess. Tell me about the fairies."

Bronwyn nodded, almost to herself. "When I was little, Maegan's age, I'd see them around here and there. They'd be in the pasture playing games with each other or up in a tree, watching us down below." She pondered it for a moment. "They talked, but in their own language so I couldn't understand them. They are all different, some tiny like a little insect and others as big as one of Maegan's LOL dollies. They dress in flower petals and leaves and acorns, and some have brilliantly-colored hair and wings, too. They can be beautiful, or they can be really ugly. They appear and disappear out of nowhere, like magic."

"They aren't scary for her?"

"No, I never felt frightened of them. I thought them fascinating, like living dolls that I could watch and play with, not that I could ever catch one. But I spent a fair amount of time chasing after them trying to catch them." She smiled in reminiscence. "Just in the past year or so, they've started talking to me in language I mostly understand. I don't know why." She didn't know how to explain about being the guardian. "It started after Granny Powers died. I think someone here is meant to carry on the role of St. Melangell through the years, and maybe it was my turn. It has to be someone who is able to cross the lines between worlds, which are thin here, especially in Pennant Melangell, and I could do that. Then whatever is happening to me, whatever I'm worried about, they try to help me. What happens is, they just suddenly appear to me, and they walk in a circle around me. There are mushrooms where their feet land. They take turns telling me things, usually three phrases, in a mix of modern and medieval English. Then they count, 'once, twice, thrice,' and they disappear. The mushrooms are still there to show where they were."

Now Maddock was staring at her, and she knew he was struggling to believe her. "And you tell Will."

"Not all the time, but if it helps him solve a case, then yes, I do, but I pretend I've gotten the information from a vision. I really don't want him to know about the fairies." She shuddered in mock horror, but she meant her words. "I look up the phrases and translate them into something understandable, and then I tell him. Or not. Sometimes I just think about it over and over, and I worry about what they are trying to tell me."

"But it'll be a while before Maegan understands what they say?"

"I think so. Like I said, it was just about a year ago that I first understood them."

He thought that over, chewing slowly on the last of his sandwich. "Is there anything else?"

Bronwyn wasn't sure how much he could handle, but she couldn't ignore Pysgotwr, one of her earliest friends. "Yes, there is. There's the green man. Do you know about him?"

"Dad used to tell us stories about him. He's like a forest spirit, right?"

"Yes, that's right. He's huge, and he looks like a tree, only he wanders around instead of being rooted in the ground. He likes to fish, and he has a dog with him, a little spaniel. He's always talked to me, even when I was really young, and he says wise things that you have to think about afterwards. There's nothing frightening about him. He's just odd, and even though I see him in open spaces sometimes, other people don't seem to notice. He kind of blends into the forest. I think of him as a protector, of creatures, the land, and me."

"Nice." Maddock was nodding. "I guess that makes me feel better, although I don't know about a big man being my little girl's best friend."

"He's a protector, not a friend," Bronwyn pointed out defensively. "It's different."

Maddock leaned back in his chair and gave her a wry smile. "Thanks for this, Bron. I know you guard your secrets even from us, but I'm glad that you love Maegan enough to open up about them if it helps her. I know you said to be accepting, but to teach her its private stuff. That's what we're trying to do."

"Does she know about me?"

"Do you want her to?"

Bronwyn considered that. If she'd had someone else who shared her abilities to talk to, it would have made her path much easier growing up. But if Maegan knew, as young as she was, she might let it slip, and then Will would know. "Let's wait a bit. If she has questions later, I'll talk to her about it all. Right now, she'll just think it's a fun secret, if we're lucky."

Later, after dinner, she walked out and clambered over the stile, heading for the pool of water. The evening was warm for the time of year. She shrugged off her jersey and left it dangling from a fence post to pick up on her return trip. Tiny bluebells bloomed beneath trees where finches twittered noisily, and maple pinwheels twirled in a whirlwind around her whenever a gust of wind blew the treetops into swirls of motion. Her footfalls and Daisy's were quiet thuds on the muddy path, making her grateful that last fall's fallen leaves soaked up the worst of the muck. Overhead, a whir of hawk's wings drew her gaze upward, where scudding clouds raced across a mostly-blue sky. A storm was blowing in on the spring breeze. She could feel the change in air pressure. She took a deep breath, smelling the mud and the sweetness of blooming trees.

She sat on the rock in the fading light, seeing nothing in the pool's dark depths. She watched for several minutes, Daisy lying quietly beside her, but the pool offered nothing but dark, still water. Taking a breath, she closed her eyes and tried to feel herself a part of nature. "Please," she whispered, "please give me something to help Will. I know what's happening is far away from here, but what happens in other places affects us, too. You must have connections in other parts of Wales. Please, help me to help him."

She waited, but only the quiet of dusk answered her plea. Even the birds had fallen silent by then, a scurrying squirrel the only interruption in the quiet sanctuary of the forest as it leapt up the trunk of a nearby tree. She sighed and slipped off the rock. It was time to go home.

"They will help you if they can." The deep voice froze her into place. She turned and saw Pysgotwr standing behind her, near the rock she had just abandoned.

"Will is in deep trouble," she told him, fearing he'd leave before she could get answers from him. "You know he needs information so he can catch whoever's importing all those drugs. They do a lot of damage, cause all sorts of crime, disrupt what is meant to be."

"The world has changed," Pysgotwr acknowledged. "What was once isolated, is now overrun. My world is fading."

She didn't know what to say. "Wales will always be a mystical land, and there will always be thin places like Pennant Melangell, places where people like me can cross over the lines between worlds."

"Only time will prove you right or wrong." He loomed over her, tendrils of spring vines and wildflowers crowning his dusky hair and framing his wizened face. He wore a tunic of thin bark, with overlapping leaves coloring the chest part deep green. His skin looked leathery, or perhaps even bark-like, too. She'd never touched him to find out. "They will come to you soon."

Her heart quickened. "Tonight?"

"I cannot say. When they know, they will come."

He turned to walk away.

"Wait!" she called out. "What about Maegan? Does she know you?"

"She is very like you," Pysgotwr, as usual, evaded a direct answer. "She, too, will find joy in the connections that join all of creation."

She watched him walk away, encouraged by his words despite his obvious pessimism, yet saddened, too. Had his pronouncement that his world was fading come about because she'd asked for information from places away from Pennant Melangell? Was it because the world was no longer made up of isolated communities, but because she'd pointed out that all was interconnected in this modern world?

They came to her as she was walking from the car to the front door of the cottage. Daisy saw them first; she froze and then lowered herself to an alert sit, obviously confused.

They circled her, their feet silent despite that the wind had died with the sunset. Hideous and comely, delicate and hardy, scowling and grinning, welcoming, yet off-putting at the same time, they were the Twlwyth Teg, the Welsh fairies, come to bring her what scraps of information they had managed to gather. She waited, delighted to see them and unable to keep her excitement in bay. She reached out to grab Daisy's ruff, holding her still as the fairies hovered.

"The lion rampant sails over the whales' road," shrieked the creature nearest her. She jerked her head to see a stick-like being with flowing green hair sprouting from its head. It wore a shift made of spring leaves and blinked at her once with sapphire eyes.

"Look to the portal at vespertine." The second voice was less harsh, more melodic, and she looked to see a rotund little creature grinning at her as it skipped around a mushroom. This one wore a dress made of bluebells that offered little in either fashion or modesty.

"Simples for all on the eve of Beltane," trilled out a third voice, this one high and shrill.

She didn't have time to pick the third fairy out of the gathering before they chanted in unison. "Once, twice, thrice!" and disappeared.

This is it, she told herself, *exactly what Will needs to know.* She didn't know all the words they'd given her, but most of it she could figure out and Google would help with the rest. She released Daisy and hurried out of the circle of mushrooms in the lawn, almost running to the front door.

A lion rampant – wasn't that a lion on a shield, maybe rearing up, ready for battle? Whales' road must be the sea. She didn't know how the two things fit together, but maybe it'd mean something to Will. A portal was an entrance. It was where the word 'port' came from, so a port. Vespertine was a word she didn't know, but she repeated it firmly every few seconds so that she wouldn't forget it before she looked it up. Beltane was a pagan spring festival. She'd double-check, but she thought it was the modern May Day, the first of May, which would be Sunday. The eve of Beltane would be Saturday night, and she knew what simples were.

Will would be so pleased. She smiled at the thought. She was pleased, too. If the drugs were coming on Saturday night, maybe he'd be there on Sunday to drive with her to the Beacons. The Twlwyth Teg had been kind to her. They'd come through when she'd begged them to. Maybe they weren't as awful as she sometimes thought they were.

She used the internet on her mobile to check on 'vespertine.' It meant dusk, just after sunset, so it was also a time. Her fingers tangled as she typed 'Beltane;' she was in too much of a hurry. As she'd guessed, it was the first of May, now called May Day. The fairies would know it by its pagan origins. Before she left the website, she typed in 'lion rampant.' Again, she'd guessed right. It was a lion, usually pictured with a crown, standing on its rear two legs and pawing the air with the front legs. Connected with heraldry, it was most known as a symbol of Scotland. *Scotland?* She didn't know what to make of that, but maybe it didn't apply. The lion rampant was a common sign in ancient times. Or maybe the shipment wasn't coming from the mainland, after all, but from Scotland?

279

Unconscious with excitement, she plopped on Will's chair and looked at the pre-paid phone. He'd put two numbers in: one for him and one for Edward. She took a breath and pushed the green call button with his number on the screen.

"Bronwyn!" She could hear excitement in his voice.

"I have information for you." She wanted to shout it out, but she kept her voice low in case it could be overheard on his end of things...or hers. As that thought occurred to her, she got up out of the chair and slipped outside into the dark, Daisy at her side.

"Are you still there?" Will's voice was anxious now.

She'd been silent too long. "I just thought I should go outside in case someone is listening inside."

"Yes," he said. "That's smart."

"The shipment is coming in at sunset on Saturday night," she said without prolonging it further. "Over the water, so I assume there's a ferry that arrives in the evening?"

"I don't know, but we'll check." She could feel the excitement through the phone. "How do you know it's Saturday night?"

"Beltane Eve," she blurted without thinking. How would she have that from a vision? "Beltane is the pagan festival that's May Day now." If she didn't explain, he wouldn't ask. She suspected that he really didn't want to know. "There's something about a lion rampant, too. Do you know what that is?"

"It's a symbol in heraldry. I've seen it on pennants at castles sometimes."

"I don't know what it means," she apologized. "It's traditionally a symbol from Scotland, so maybe the drugs are coming from there, or it could be part of a coat of arms for a person. Are any of your suspects minor royalty?"

"I don't think so, but they wouldn't have to be, would they? Clans and families who aren't royal have coats of arms, too, I think."

"I don't know much about it. Do you want me to research it and get back to you?"

"No, that's okay. Really, you're brilliant, sweetheart. This helps a lot. Now that we know when the shipment is coming, we can time our activities to disrupt them as much as possible. If we make it hard enough for them, we think whoever's at the top of the chain will be drawn out. That's really what we need. I'll try to figure out the lion rampant part, but even without that, this puts us a big step forward."

She wanted to ask if he'd be back on Sunday, but she didn't want to look like she was pressuring him. Finally, she settled on, "I'll be glad when this is all over."

"So will I. I just want my regular, hectic life back." He was quiet for a moment. "Thanks for understanding about your car. You were perfect, talking to the constable."

"I tried to think what to say other than that you were working there. I wasn't sure if you'd told him you were detectives, if you'd want him to know."

"We didn't. If we'd told him that, he'd have had to call our stations to verify it, and then they'd know what we were doing and where. They probably know by now anyway, but it still disrupted their plans. Those men not only had illegal drugs in their car when it was searched, but they also had unregistered firearms. They were total idiots. They won't be released soon unless whoever's pulling the strings is more powerful than even I think they are."

"I wish I could be there to see how you manage it all."

"No, you stay safe there in Llangynog. I don't want you anywhere near this."

"I started a garden today." It was time to move to safer topics. She wandered back to the house, pushed the door open with her free hand, and went inside, locking it behind her. "Maddock came over and took out the sod and plowed it up for me. He's going to put a fence around it this weekend sometime."

"What are you going to grow?"

"I haven't decided yet. We'll talk about it when you come home. You can tell me what vegetables you like best, and that's what I'll plant."

"Is beef steak a vegetable?"

She tried to laugh, but knew it sounded faked. He was trying, but she could feel a distance between them that hadn't been there in a while. She was used to talking over his cases with him; this time, he had Edward for that. He wouldn't want to talk about the visit with his parents either.

Every time he had, she'd felt his reluctance, blaming herself for that. Things seemed strained.

He felt it, too. "I've got to go, love. We've got a lot to do before tomorrow night. I probably won't be able to call you again until after it's all over, but I do miss you. I wish we were sitting together in the conservatory, sharing a bottle of wine and talking over this case. I promise you this isn't what our life is going to be like. It's just this one time."

The lump in her throat threatened to silence her. "I know, Will. It's okay."

Later, she relaxed on her bed, Daisy snuggled against her hip and her mind swirling from one thought to another.

She could tell that Will had been happy with the information she'd given him, and that was one up on Edward, who despite his charm and his history with Will, couldn't come up with a source that could give him something that specific. She only hoped that the information did turn out to be accurate; otherwise, it might throw the entire effort off and put the two of them in even more danger than they already were in. That worried her. The Twlwyth Teg had always been right on target before, but sometimes she'd misinterpreted their messages and gotten the meanings wrong. This time, that could not happen. It just couldn't. She thought back over their words and, other than the lion rampant, she couldn't see how she might have made a mistake.

Thinking of the Twlwyth Teg brought another thought into her mind. She'd begged Pysgotwr to make them see that the world had expanded, that whatever was happening in the rest of Wales affected what happened right there in Llangynog. She was sure that other places, not just in Wales, had a mythology that included fairies and other mystical beings, but too often people had grown away from those stories from the past. They had the internet now, and television and movies and vehicles that could carry them around the world in a day. They didn't have time for the otherworld, and so it faded into obscurity. If the Twlwyth Teg didn't want to fade away with the others, perhaps they would need to adapt to the changing world, to expand their connections and to reach out further than just Pennant Melangell. Maybe she'd gotten that message through to them. Maybe they'd thought her words made sense. If they were determined to survive, maybe she'd forced them to take a step toward that goal. Fishguard was far away, yet, somehow, they'd 'seen' information that Bronwyn needed. Information that would keep her there with them and in contact with them.

There'd been a strain between her and Will. She knew he had taken a big step in renting the cottage and committing to the commute to Caernarfon, and she'd tried to let him see how happy it made her to share their lives this way. Still, she'd pushed him about his parents, and she felt badly about it now. There was an awkwardness again that she hadn't felt for a while, and that brought a discontent that she couldn't quite shake. She just didn't know how to make it better.

When she finally fell asleep, it was to restless dreams of the Twlwyth Teg. Maegan was a part of them, but so was Will, and she jerked awake feeling horrified that he had discovered her secret. But he hadn't. *It was just a dream*, she thought as she drifted off again.

Chapter Eighteen

Although Will and Edward were happy with the way the arrests of the men went, they didn't know for sure if the individuals they'd taken out were involved in the drugs operation, or if they'd just taken against the two strangers in the village for other, unknowable reasons. If progress had been made toward disrupting and drawing out the people at the top, they would have to wait to find that out.

The night had been long. They'd had to go into the local constabulary to write statements about the incident, and then they'd been driven back to where the Land Rover waited, still drivable, but in sad shape. Will found the insurance information in the glove compartment and set it aside for a call the next morning, and then they drove back out to the farm lane where they'd had their lunch, checked on the rest of the stash they'd hidden there, and tried to sleep. After the night's events, they worried about being followed, figuring that if the men were valuable to the operation, someone would be wanting revenge. They thought they'd be woken by the sound of an approaching vehicle on the dirt track, but if someone were to note their tyre tracks and circle around to surround them on foot, they'd be caught unawares. Doubtlessly, considering the stakes, if that happened, they'd never be heard from again.

So, they took turns sleeping fitfully, and as the sky lightened toward dawn, they roused themselves and drove back toward the town. They reasoned that, even if they were more visible there, the fact that there were other people about would protect them better than isolation. They decided that they would hunker down and sleep in the Land Rover on the main street that next night unless the shipment came sooner than the weekend. A Friday night should keep the streets busy late, so they'd have plenty of company in the downtown area.

They debated what to do over bacon rolls bought in the same bakery where they'd gotten the sandwiches the day before. So far, luck had been with them. They'd managed to locate Morys Howell and to put the men they hoped were the guards out of commission. They still had a vehicle to drive, and most importantly, they were still alive and free.

It was as they were congratulating themselves on their accomplishments that things suddenly went south. Or more accurately, north.

One of the pre-paid mobiles sang out from the centre console, jolting them into action. Will grabbed it out and answered, hoping it was Bronwyn.

It wasn't. Bowers' voice whispered from the other end. "Cooper?"

"Yes, sir, it's me." He kept his voice low, too, but he knew that he'd have to admit his lie to Edward once the call was finished.

"I'll keep this short. I've had a call from Chief Inspector Mathews. He's instructed me to cancel the alert for Anglesey."

Will tried to think fast. He'd have only a minute or two to ask questions. "Did they switch it to somewhere else? Fishguard?"

"No, it's only been cancelled entirely." There was a pause. "You must have drawn some attention, is what I think. If they'd changed the alert to Fishguard, you'd guess the shipment has been diverted to Holyhead. By cancelling it entirely, they'll know you'll have to choose which one to concentrate your efforts on. Or maybe they're just going to lay low for a while and bring it in later, after they've had time to get you off their backs. It's hard to know."

"It could be another port just as easily as Holyhead or Fishguard," Will mumbled, upset at the news. "Pembroke." Two of the three left from Rosslaire; maybe they should just cross to Ireland and watch from there. But they'd have no way of knowing which lorry was their target or, as Bowers had said, if the shipment really was to be delayed until he and Edward were taken out of the picture. This really threw a wrench in things. "Did he say anything else, sir, that might help focus our efforts?"

"No, I'm afraid not." Bowers sounded apologetic. "Where are you? You're obviously stirring the pot, making him change the plan."

"You're sure it's him, sir?" Will caught the implication.

"It's pointing that way," Bowers said, after a moment. "I hate to think it, but he's giving me little choice. The only other conclusion is that it's the commander giving us both orders, and that would make Mathews as innocent as I am. But, honestly, I would think the call would come directly from him if that were the case. It seems Mathews thinks I am easily fooled." He sounded bitter.

"We'll show him otherwise," Will promised, hoping he was right. "We're in Aberystwyth. That's where we've been concentrating our efforts so far. We have a suspect we think is in charge when the shipment comes in and is divided up, and last night we managed to get five men arrested for vandalism, drug possession, and possession of illegal drugs. We think they're some of the muscle who guard the shipments as they're being divided and sent in various directions. With Davies out of the picture, that takes out a driver, as well. We're disrupting their chain as best we can, sir."

"You've been busy," Bowers observed. "Is it Morys Howell?"

Will hated to give him specifics. "Yes, it is."

"I wish I could help, but I don't trust them not to be monitoring our actions here. That's what I'd do in their place." He went silent for a minute. "Have you thought if you could use the press in any way? I know you and your partner have the experience, but I've been thinking that the press is aggressive here and maybe you could use that to your advantage somehow."

"We'll toss that around, sir, see if it gives us any ideas. Thank you." Will tried to think. "How's Notley?"

"Not happy. He isn't making any progress, and he resents that he has to attend the memorial services and you don't. You're taking his calls?"

"I can't, sir. If I turn on my mobile, they'll track me. I know that'll make him mad, but by the time I see him again, hopefully this will all be over." He paused. "I hope he finds Davies," he went on, hoping Bowers wouldn't hear the lie. "That'd give him some satisfaction, at least."

Bowers must have realized the truth. "He's not going to find him, is he?" He waited, but only a second or two. "Don't answer that. I don't want to know. Listen, I should go. It shouldn't take long to get a coffee; I'll be expected back. Take care of yourself, Cooper."

"I will, sir."

"I know you can't let me know what you're doing, but if I can help, let me know." There was another moment of silence. "Other people here would help you, too, Cooper. Quigley, Mehta…"

"I don't want to involve more people than I already have, sir. This isn't going to lead to any promotions, after all."

"No, you're right. Take care, Cooper. Good luck."

Will hit the end call button and turned his eyes to Edward, who was staring at him, shock in his eyes. "Edward, listen, let me explain."

"You told your chief what we were doing? How could you? How the bloody hell could you, after we agreed not to?" Edward was spitting mad, his words brittle and biting. He turned to the passenger window and looked out, then swung his head back to glare at Will. "Why would you do that?"

"I didn't do it to betray you, mate," Will tried to make his voice soft and reasonable. "It was the only way I could get off without Notley tagging along. Don't you see? We were assigned to the Catherine Baines case, and then we tracked Davies to find Peter O'Connell, too. In our department, partners work together nearly all the time. I'd already gone off on my own with that first major case with Notley, so I couldn't do it again without Bowers' support. I had no choice." Despite his intentions, his voice had a begging tone. He didn't want Edward mad at him. "I told him what we were going to do, and he gave me his blessing. He sent Notley back to Liverpool after Billy Davies and told him I was going to go south to try to find Morys Howell. He made it sound reasonable that Davies might hide out with Howell, them being partners in the armed robbery."

"What if his office is bugged? They probably know exactly what we've been doing." Suddenly, Edward's temper flared even more. "Are you keeping him informed?"

"No! No, I'm not. This is the first I've talked to him since yesterday morning, and before that, it was only on the Tuesday when I first left to meet you. I don't call in and report. And, just so you know, we never talked inside the station building. Strange as it looked, we went to the coffee shop across the street together and talked. God, what do you take me for?"

"I don't know anymore." Edward turned away again. "I thought I could trust you."

"You can trust me." Will's voice was soft again. "I trust Bowers, as well. He's always been good to me, and I really think he's honest." He paused. "I *know* he is. Why else would he call and give us information? He didn't have to do that."

"Unless he's misdirecting you, trying to push us away from our big bust."

"He's not doing that. Think about it. If he was misdirecting us, he'd send us somewhere specific."

"And he didn't?"

"No." Will told him what Bowers had said, trying to be as accurate in the details as he could be. "It leaves us in a lurch," he concluded at the end. "Now we don't have a good guess as to where the load is expected, if it's even coming in at all. It could be any of the three ports...or somewhere further north in Scotland, I suppose."

"No, Scotland wouldn't be manageable. It's Welshmen running this show, so it has to be Wales, at least. That gives us three ports. I don't see how we can watch all three."

"Two have ferries going out from Rosslaire," Will pointed out., abandoning the idea of Scotland. "Maybe we cross over to Ireland, watch from there. If we see a lorry that's been given an okay without an inspection, that'll be the one."

"It'll arrive just at the last moment," Edward said. He seemed to have forgotten his anger for the moment. "But the logistics are impossible. Even if we see one that looks suspicious, we'll have to cross with it on the ferry and then – what? – follow it from there?"

"Why not? It's as good as anything else we've got."

"That won't give us time to get Howell arrested, to draw out whoever's in charge. And we wouldn't know which port to leave the car at."

Will sighed. "Then what do we do?"

"I guess we could plant the drugs in Howell's car or house before we go, and then we could call in the tip from the ferry terminal in Ireland."

"If we get the wrong lorry, we'll have gambled away our whole plan."

Will remembered something. "Bowers suggested using the press. Is there any way of involving them that might help?"

Edward slumped back in his seat, watching a couple walk by. The woman was pushing a pram, and the man touched her arm and pointed into a shop. "What if we spread a rumor that there are dirty customs officials at the ports? If the press picked up on that, it'd make it harder for the lorry to get through without an inspection."

"If the rumors were specific, say Pembroke and Holyhead, then that'd leave Fishguard as the only option they had left."

"It might work." Now Will could hear excitement in Edward's voice again. "It's like hunters who have beaters chasing the creatures toward the shooters. The press will be our beaters, and we'll be the shooters."

"I like it."

"Except we're shooters without weapons," Edward pointed out, his voice losing some of its excitement. "And we need a tip about when that shipment is coming, at least. It'd be even better if we knew what lorry we were looking for."

Will faked a chuckle. "If wishes were horses, and all that. You know we have to make do with what we have and just hope for the best."

Edward looked over at him. "I've had another idea I've been thinking about the past day or so."

"Yeah, what's that?"

"Our major problem here is lack of personnel, right? If we had more feet on the ground, we'd have a better chance of tracking them and drawing them out and even capturing them at the end and keeping those drugs off the streets. You know as well as I do that the two of us have no hope of confronting them. The best we'll be able to do is to film the thing and turn it in. The drugs won't be stopped. Some of them will get away."

"Short of calling in Scotland Yard, I don't see another alternative. We can only do as much as we can. Your goal is to catch whoever's the top man in charge, isn't it? We can do that with filming it, if he's present."

"What if – I'm only suggesting this – what if we called in other favors?"

Will couldn't help staring. "What favors?"

"Well, not favors exactly. What if we approached the former cartels?" Edward had the grace to look ashamed. "I guess they aren't really 'former,' but the ones who've been hurt by this new operation. What if we got in contact with them somehow and gave them the chance to help us out?"

"Not a good idea," Will objected. "They'd give us up to the very people we're after in hope of getting something bigger in return, maybe a partnership or something. And, if they didn't go that way, they'd come in guns blazing and destroy everything." He shook his head. "It's a bad idea, Edward."

"I know." Edward gazed out the window, but Will knew he wasn't seeing the scenery. "I'm that desperate to get these guys, though, I'd probably give it a try if you were on board."

"I'm not, at least not now. And don't go thinking that because I confided in my chief, that you might go behind my back on this."

"No, I wouldn't." He cast Will a half-smile. "At least one of us is trustworthy."

"Let's try the press, try to squeeze them into one port that we know for sure they're using. Then we'll reevaluate."

"Yeah, sounds good." Edward looked at Will and grinned. "Your boss did help us. I'll admit it. Maybe he's one of the good guys, after all."

They drove up the coast, not wanting to bring the press in from too near Fishguard. It felt like they were shirking their jobs, driving off away from it all, but Will knew he was right, that the press was their only hope of funneling the operation through a definite port. He was grateful for Bowers' tip. If he hadn't called, if Will hadn't confided in him, they'd probably have missed the shipment entirely and all they'd done would have been in vain.

They decided to drive all the way to Caernarfon before making the first call. Will planned to stop by his flat to exchange some of his dirty laundry for fresh clothes, and he thought a stop at the station wouldn't be a bad idea. If their adversaries were watching either place, they'd see Will checking in and, hopefully, think their strategy had worked. They might even conclude that he'd ended his search for Morys Howell, as had been requested. He could also check his mobile for calls from Notley so as to deter more suspicion from that quarter. Edward would remain in the Land Rover, keeping a low profile in order to keep their enemies guessing.

They found a parking space near the flat, and Will jogged up the stairway, keeping an eye out as he did. Nothing looked different. He opened his door and peered inside before entering. Again, nothing looked disturbed. He wouldn't stay long. He opened his kit bag and tossed the dirtiest clothes into the laundry hamper, and then he filled it again with a clean pair of jeans, three tee shirts, and another jacket. He was running out of clean clothes, and the swampy smell of the ones he'd worn at Hoylake gave the entire flat a musty smell that'd be hard to get rid of, but there was no time to do a load of wash. He'd deal with it later. He stopped at the kitchen cupboard to stuff re-sealable bags into his duffle; they'd already wished for a few of those in the past couple of days. He looked around, trying to think what else they might need, but nothing came to mind. Most of his belongings were now in Llangynog, at the cottage.

Before he walked back out and locked up, he pulled out his mobile and pretended to scroll and then push a call button. Unless there was a camera perfectly positioned, it would appear to anyone watching or listening that he was making a legitimate phone call. "Hi, love," he started, wishing it could be a real call, and then he made up one side of a brief conversation in which he told her they were still searching for Billy Davies, that the search was headed back up toward Liverpool, and that he'd be busy for several more days. He ended it with a declaration of his love and his hope that they could mend things between them, and then he pretended to end the call.

He made Edward duck down low as he drove from there to the station. Will parked in the employee lot, got out, and locked the car door, leaving Edward hunkered down in the passenger seat. He hoped no one would glance inside, curious about the damage to the windscreen, but that was a chance they'd have to take.

He strolled through the station and past his colleagues' desks, pausing to greet Mehta and Beth. He took time at each of their desks, telling them that he was still in search of Billy Davies, that he was headed back northeast to join Notley for the two memorial services, that the investigation had stalled, but he still had hope of finding Davies sooner or later. He was near enough to his desk that any bugs planted there would pick up the conversations, which was his purpose. He wanted his location firmly established so that no one would suspect he was headed back to Llandrindod Wells that afternoon.

He left the station a few minutes later, having successfully avoided the notice of Bowers, who he'd have liked to have seen and thanked, but couldn't without giving both of them away. He got back into the Land Rover, looked at Edward who gave him a thumbs-up, and drove out of the lot and onto the street.

They couldn't call the press from Caernarfon without tipping someone off that it was Will, so they drove on to Bangor, which was big enough and near enough to Anglesey to alert the locals that one or more of their customs agents might not be acting in good faith. They had to drive around a while before they found a rare call box, and then Edward got out and made the call, an anonymous tip that the reporter who took the call seemed at least somewhat interested in.

That task accomplished, they got on the A470 and cruised fast back toward the south coast, detouring past Llandrindod Wells toward their other target port, Portmouth. Time had gone fast, and they were in a hurry now to get the second call done so they could return and watch Morys Howell for activity. As they passed through the little village of

Llandielo, Edward pointed out a phone box alongside the road and they decided it was near enough to do the trick. This time Edward was more specific in his story, telling a reporter that someone in Portmouth was allowing uninspected cargo into Wales. They hoped they hadn't left it too late, but the warning from Bowers hadn't come soon enough to do anything else. They were being squeezed, too.

"Suppose the shipment comes in tonight," Will ventured as they drove back toward Llandrindod Wells.

"That's the worst-case scenario for us," Edward drawled. "There'd be no time for the press to act, and we'd have no time to frame Howell for drugs possession and take him out for a few days. It can't be tonight. Tomorrow would improve our odds of success by at least fifty percent, and by Sunday, things would all be in place."

"It's not a perfect world," Will said. He signaled and left the motorway. "If we stayed somewhere tonight, we could watch the news to see if we've made any impact."

"We're surveilling Howell tonight." Edward shifted in his seat. They'd been in the Land Rover too many hours over the past several days, and both of them were feeling the strain. "Since we don't know when to expect it or what vehicle the load is coming over on, he's our only hope for catching them. With him still in play, we'd miss whoever's at the top of the chain, but I'd imagine it'd be a major disruption for them anyway if he was arrested, and maybe he'd talk to save himself."

Will glanced in the rear-view mirror. He'd had a feeling of being followed since leaving Caernarfon, to be honest. It wasn't anything specific, just an intuition of something not quite right. "Do you want to go back to our farm track?" he asked Edward. He wouldn't share his suspicions yet, but going back to that remote area would expose anyone tracking them. "We'll need to raid our stash of illegal drugs if we're going to plant them on Howell."

"No, let's get to Howell's." Edward dashed his hopes. "It's later than I wanted already. We'll stop at a shop and get some supplies. Food," he grinned, "and water, maybe even a beer if you're lucky. Then we'll get to his house and start watching."

"No definite plan?"

"Not yet. We're playing this one by ear."

Luck struck while they were inside the shop, waiting for their sandwiches to be made.

One of the pre-paids vibrated in Will's pocket, and he snatched it out quickly, waving Edward toward the counter to wait for the sandwiches while he ducked away out the door to take the call.

He knew it was her the minute the call connected. "Bronwyn!"

"Yes, it's me," she answered, and then the phone went dead still.

He kept trying, wondering if the phone was defective. Passersby looked at him askance, but he ignored their curiosity. He leaned against a wall and then stepped away from it, agitated.

Finally, she came back on and explained that she'd remembered to go outside, in case the cottage was bugged.

Brilliant girl, he thought. He knew she had news. He'd heard the excitement in her voice the moment she'd first spoken. "What is it?" He looked around to make sure they weren't being overheard. He still felt eyes watching him.

She came through beautifully for them. She had the day of the drugs shipment and even the time. They could check the ferry schedules for one that arrived around sunset on Saturday night, and now they could set Morys Howell up to be arrested near to that time, taking him out of the picture and, hopefully, forcing someone else to step up and take his place.

A thrill of excitement ran through him, and he remembered what it had been like in the old days, when he'd worked drugs and alcohol with Edward. The major crimes force was good, but there was nothing like the thrill of knowing you'd worked undercover and your efforts had led to a major bust, the takedown of a major player in the illegal drugs trade.

Edward came out carrying the bags as Bronwyn was telling him about her gardening plans. He smiled to himself, wondering how he was going to get around telling Edward how Bronwyn got her information. Edward would be worried that it wasn't accurate, but he knew it would be. She'd never led him wrong before. He felt bad cutting her off, but there were things to be done, and time was wasting away. He told her that he had to go, and reluctantly, ended the call.

294

Edward nodded toward the Land Rover. "I can see you had another tip from your sweet lady friend. You can tell me about it while we're walking. I assume the plan hasn't changed?"

Will shook his head, and then he told Edward, keeping his voice low, about the day and time of the shipment. "There was something about a lion rampant, as well," he finished. "She didn't know what that meant, but it's something to keep in our minds."

"You know for sure this information is accurate?"

"She's never been wrong before. I can't imagine that she is this time."

"You know what this means?"

"It means we can work on getting Morys Howell arrested tomorrow late afternoon. How long does the ferry take? An hour or two? We'll want to check the schedule and then time Howell's arrest for just after it sets off from Ireland, too late to stop the shipment."

Edward had stopped walking. He hesitated, and then spoke with reluctance. "You know what else this means, Will. It means that she's involved. There's no other way she could have this information."

Will stopped and faced him. "She's not involved." He stalked over to the driver's side door, checking traffic.

Edward followed him. "You can't keep denying it, mate." He grabbed Will's arm, forcing him around to face him. "Look, first she knew where Davies' body was, and now she knows this?" Edward kept his voice low, but his eyes were fierce and his mouth set in a firm line. "What? Is she playing both sides? Pretending to be part of their operation, but just doing it to get the information she feeds to you?" He blinked. "Is she undercover, too?"

Will yanked the car door open and pushed inside. He sat, hands on the steering wheel, and waited for Edward to get in.

The passenger door opened, and Edward slid in, slamming the door. "Did I hit a nerve there?"

"She's not undercover, Edward." He stared through the broken windscreen, avoiding Edward's eyes.

"Well, it has to be one or the other. There's no other choice. Either she's undercover, or she's working with them. Which is it?"

295

Will took a breath, letting it out slowly. He closed his eyes. Bronwyn would kill him. "She's fey. Do you know what that means?"

When there was no answer, Will opened his eyes and threw a glance Edward's way to see how he was reacting.

The pronouncement seemed to have left him speechless. He struggled for a moment, and then he swallowed. "Like away with the fairies or something?"

"It took me a while to get used to," Will admitted. He didn't want to look at Edward, afraid of seeing ridicule or, worse, pity on his face, so he looked at the cracked windscreen, seeing patterns in the shattered glass. "She doesn't like people knowing. It's not 'away with the fairies,' like you said. She sees visions in a pool of water."

Edward shook his head. "That can't be true. No one can do that. Not really."

"People used to believe it. They called it scrying." He hesitated. "I've seen her do it, mate. She goes into a trance and then she knows things, and they're never wrong. That's why I believe her." He chanced another glance Edward's way, and to his surprise, he saw the beginning of acceptance.

"She's like a witch, then?" A grin flirted with the corners of Edward's mouth. "Did she put a spell on you?"

Will swallowed hard. "She's not a witch. She's more of a seer. She can't control what she sees, but sometimes she sees things that help solve my cases. Mostly, it's just things that are near to Llangynog that she sees. I'm surprised at this one." He was. "And thankful."

"You're sure she's right?"

"Like I said, she's never been wrong."

Edward nodded. "Okay, I'll believe it if you do." He looked at Will. "You didn't answer my other question."

"What other question?"

"Did she put a spell on you? I mean, even you admit that she isn't your usual type."

Will allowed himself a small, rueful grin. "Sometimes I think she did."

They arrived at Howell's house just past eight in the evening. It looked much the same as before, with a few people strolling past with dogs or jogging, but no sign of activity at the Howell house. The Mercedes still sat parked, although it had been moved to a different parking space. "He's been out," Edward observed as they parked between two SUVs that gave them a modicum of cover. Will checked his mirror again. There were two vehicles behind him on the street, and both passed by as soon as he was out of the roadway. One looked to be a family with children in the rear seat, and the other was occupied by a single woman who didn't give them a glance.

"He probably went over to the gaol to see if he could bail out his buddies," Will said, hoping he was right. If the arrests of the five men the night before had drawn Howell out, they hadn't wasted their efforts. They settled in and ate their sandwiches, watching the house, which remained quiet. Occasionally, a door in the block of row houses would open and someone would emerge, and more often someone would arrive home, on foot or by vehicle, walk up the steps and into one of the other houses, but nothing happened at the Howell home. As dusk fell, lights went on, so someone was home, but obviously they were staying in for the night.

The area grew even quieter as dark descended on the street. A light rain began to fall, pattering on the roof of the Land Rover and lulling Will into a sleepy doze. He picked up his bottle of water and took a sip, trying to shake the lethargy. He still had the feeling of being watched, although nothing happened to make it obvious.

"I'm going to stretch my legs," he announced as midnight approached. The lights inside the Howell home had gone out more than an hour before, and he thought it time he prowled around a little. He wanted to check for cameras and to see if there was an easy spot for a break-in, a place that'd go unnoticed if he and Edward were to plant the drugs inside the house rather than in Howell's car.

Edward nodded, and Will stepped out of the car and stretched, the hours of sitting having stiffened his arms and legs. He'd be glad when it was all over and he could go back to hiking with Bronwyn, to sleeping in his own bed, to being able to relax and not be constantly vigilant. He pulled his mac on and flipped the hood up, and then looked around, trying to look casual. No one appeared to be out, and most of the houses on the street were dark, despite it being a Friday night.

He strolled up the sidewalk, walking all the way to the end of the block, and then crossed the street and walked back toward the row houses, checking inside the cars parked alongside the sidewalk. They all appeared empty, but Will still felt eyes on him. Maybe it was just nerves. He hadn't done this type of work for a long time.

He rounded the block and entered an alley that ran behind the row houses. He counted as he walked, trying to locate Howell's house among all the other lookalikes. When he was behind the one he thought was right, he hopped the fence and crouched in the garden, waiting for the lights to go on inside or an alarm to sound, but nothing happened.

He crept closer to the house, trying to look for cameras on the porch or in the eaves as he stayed in the shadow of the fence and the shrubbery, taking his time. He'd learned long ago that rushing toward a target was the worst way to approach it. Patience and caution got him more results. He was peering at what looked like a possible camera when a rustling in the bushes startled him and he dropped to the ground, grabbing his knees and ducking into a bundle that he hoped looked like another of the shrubs that lined the fence. He waited in silence, holding his breath. The house stayed dark, and the rustling stopped, but he knew something was there. He risked a breathy "whoosh," and a cat stepped out from behind a bush just ahead of him. It stared at him in the dark, the rain matting its fur, and then it leapt up and over the fence.

Will took a deep breath to steady his nerves and stood up. He could see now that a camera in the eaves pointed into the back garden. Squinting, he could see another above the back stoop, and he suspected that he'd see more, if he got near enough, surveilling the entire outside of the house. They wouldn't be getting inside.

He turned and slunk back through the garden, continuing to take his time. If the camera hadn't picked up the cat, it might not pick him up if he went slowly and stayed between the shrubs and the fence. It felt like an hour had passed when he finally reached the back edge of the garden, and he chose a spot between a shrub and the fence to climb back over. He tried to make his leap look cat-like, but suspected he failed miserably. He wasn't as nimble, small, or quick as a cat, after all.

Once back in the alley, he hurried out onto the street. There, he began to stumble and weave, thinking that on a Friday night, a drunk might look less out of place than a regular man walking. He bumbled his way back to the Land Rover, looked around for watchers, and then slipped back inside.

"Well?" Edward wanted to know.

"Cameras everywhere," Will reported. "It'll have to be the Mercedes."

"Tonight?"

"No, he might find them. It has to be tomorrow when we know the ferry has already left Ireland."

"That'll be tricky."

"I know. Do you have a better plan?"

Edward shook his head. "No, we'll have to go with yours."

Chapter Nineteen

Will woke with a jerk. He'd slumped down in the seat of the Land Rover, his head against the driver side window. Rain came down in fits, and the side of his head was damp with condensation from the inside of the window. He pushed himself up and glanced into the back seat, where Edward lay sprawled awkwardly, his knees tucked up and his feet dangling. He'd been snoring, but Will's movement woke him and he sat up fast, alert.

Edward relaxed when he saw Will looking at him between the seats. "What?"

"It's morning, sleepy head. Time to figure out what we're doing."

Edward squirmed to a sitting position, running a hand through unruly hair. "A shower somewhere?"

"Do you think we could chance a room, just for a bit?"

"If we're not sleeping there, just using it to clean up, we should be fine. One of us can keep a watch while the other showers, and then we switch."

Will thought it over. "I've had a feeling of being watched since we left Caernarfon," he confessed. "I've nothing concrete, just a feeling."

"I thought it was just habit, you checking the mirror all the time." Edward grinned.

"I think someone's watching us. They're hanging back, staying out of our way and not trying to stop us doing what we're doing, but they're interested."

"Another cartel?"

"Maybe. I don't know."

"If they wanted to stop us, they had opportunity during the night." Edward stretched. "We've both been sleeping like babes here for the past few hours."

"Yeah." Will was thoughtful. "I've been thinking about your idea of bringing in some help from the cartels who've been displaced by this new group. I think you're right that they'd be eager to take the competition out of the picture."

"You don't think they'd sell us out?"

"Maybe. My thought is that we just use them for small tasks. I don't think it's a good idea to have them there when the load is being divided up, but maybe they'd be willing to help us out as far as Morys Howell is concerned. If they'd agree to help get him arrested while the shipment is on its way over on the ferry, that'd free us up to meet it when it comes in and follow it to its destination."

"I'm liking it." Edward frowned thoughtfully. "I wish I had an informant here who could help me find them. I'm not used to working this area." He glanced at Will. "It's both a blessing and a curse. I've been able to work anonymously here because they don't know me, but when I need a contact, I don't have one."

"All we can do is put the word out and hope someone is interested enough to come to us." It sounded hopeless, but Will was an optimist. He was sure there was someone in the area who felt displaced by this new, highly efficient cartel. If they mentioned it to the right people and, at the same time, avoided police notice, they might just get in touch with someone willing to help them out.

"We don't tell them what we're doing, just that we need Morys Howell out of the picture, and it'd be in their best interests to help."

"I think so. We might even suggest that we're police, just to keep them in line. We don't want them killing Howell, just arranging for his arrest."

They drove into the town centre and parked, getting out and walking to a restaurant, where they ordered full English breakfasts, reasoning that a good meal would go a long way toward clearing their minds so they could focus on what would be a crucial day. After breakfast, they found a small hotel and booked a room, ignoring the speculative looks the receptionist gave them as they filled out paperwork. Will asked for a ferry schedule, and she directed him to a computer terminal for guest use. Edward headed upstairs while Will tried to figure out how to read the schedule.

It looked like a ferry would arrive at 7 p.m., which was just about sunset this time of year. Boarding was at 3:30 p.m., with a travel time of three hours, fifteen minutes. He wondered if one of them should get across to Ireland to watch the lorries board, but they'd left it a little late for that. Still... He checked the outgoing ferries. There was one that left just after 10 a.m., which would be a rush getting to. It might be worth the effort.

When he made his way upstairs to the room, Edward was clean. He'd flung his towel into a corner of the bathroom, put on jeans, and was sitting on the edge of the bed, watching the television. It was tuned to a news channel.

"Whew! You stink," he told Will, grinning. "It feels good, getting cleaned up."

"Any news about the customs agents?"

"It's been mentioned," Edward hedged. "It doesn't look like it's breaking news, but they did mention a tip, both at Pembroke and up on Anglesey. Even if they don't catch someone, just the idea that they're looking into it might prevent the shipment coming in there."

"Then we've been a success." Will gestured toward the bathroom. "I'm going to run in there and make myself presentable."

"I'll head down to the lobby and keep a lookout. Meet you there in a half hour?"

"Make it twenty minutes. I think one of us needs to be on the ferry to Ireland, and the only one that works timewise leaves at 10:15. We don't have much time, so we'll have to hurry."

When they met in the lobby, Will was only three minutes late.

Edward was still tuned into the morning news. "It looks like they're pressuring the port authority to investigate," he reported. He gave Will an assessing glance. "You look better."

"And I smell better, too." Will finished it for him. "You're okay with going off to Ireland?"

"No, I'm not going. You are. It's your turn to take the easy path. I'm the one started this, and you've done more than your share to help me. I'll stay here and take care of Morys Howell, one way or another."

"What does that mean?" Will looked around, but they were alone in the room.

"It means if I can't find someone to take him out, then I'll do it. I'll try to get the drugs into his car and call in a tip, but if that doesn't work, I'll stage an accident or something. I'll have three hours to do it after the lorry is on the ferry, but I'll want it done just after the ferry departs so Mathews has time to rush up here and take charge. The timing is important, but, like I said, one way or another I'll get it done."

"You'll meet me back at the ferry terminal when it comes in?"

"That's my plan. I'll drop you off, head back up here to wait for your call, and deal with Howell, and once he's out of the picture, I'll head back to Fishguard to pick you up. Hopefully, we'll have a lorry to follow at that point." He looked away from the television and toward Will. "Still feel like you're being followed?"

"Not at the moment, but I bet the minute we step out the door, it'll come back."

"We'll catch them on the way to Fishguard. They can't follow us all over the country without giving themselves away."

"I just can't figure out why they haven't tried to stop us," Will said. He'd puzzled over it every waking moment, and he'd come up with nothing. "You wouldn't think they'd want to let us disrupt their schedule, taking out their men and risking discovery."

Edward shook his head. "Maybe it's just you being paranoid."

"Could be," Will acknowledged. He was a little out of practice at this, truth be told.

They took the A497 to Fishguard. Will was uncomfortable with the now hard-to-miss Land Rover, its windscreen shattered almost to the point of blocking their vision and the driver's side door caved in. At least the door still closed. He wondered if they'd have been better off to call it into the insurance and hope for a loaner car for a few days, but it was too late for that now. If someone was watching for it, they'd see it. He wondered if Mathews would be confident enough at this point to ignore them anyway. He probably thought his men had disrupted Will's and Edward's investigation; he'd know that they'd realize he could now track the Land Rover and monitor their activities. Maybe they were both working at the same scheme from opposite sides.

He pulled in beside the ticketing office at the ferry terminal and hurried inside. A young woman dressed in jeans and a hand-knit jumper checked his passport and then sold him a round-trip ticket, looking at him oddly as if wondering why someone would ride the ferry over, only to turn around and ride it right back. He supposed it would seem a wasted day to her.

He gave her a smile. "Going over to meet my girlfriend and bring her back with me," he explained, hoping it sounded reasonable.

Her face cleared of confusion. "It's going to be a fine day for it anyway. The rain's gone and they say the sun will be out in an hour."

Will nodded and thanked her. He walked outside to let Edward know he'd been successful in his purchase. "Be careful, mate," he told him. "Don't take chances. It's not worth it. If you don't get them this time, there'll be another chance at it."

Edward waved him off cheerfully. "This is it. I can feel it, now or never. So, it'll be now." He grinned. "Thanks for everything. I'll see you in about eight hours."

"Make it seven and a half," Will told him. "The sky is going to be clear and the water calm."

Once he'd seen Edward off in the battered Land Rover, Will walked down to look at the pier. Fishing boats of various sizes stood at anchor in the harbour, and he watched a few come in from the morning's work, chugging in slowly and pulling up to the dock to empty out the morning's catch. Voices called out as they approached and nearly always someone scuttled closer to help them tie up alongside the dock. He thought it must be a close community, like the farming communities he'd come to know, where people knew each other and helped out where they could.

As promised, the sun emerged from the hazy fog, and then the skies cleared fast to a dazzling blue. The ferry, Stenna Line, came in on time, and Will watched carefully as it emptied, lines of vehicles – cars, SUVs, lorries, and a few foot passengers – slowly exiting bumper-to-bumper onto the tarmac where the passenger vehicles drove off toward the main road and the lorries lined up for inspections. He studied them as officials asked for paperwork and then opened the backs of some of the lorries to check inside. They were checking most, but not all, he noted, wondering what the criteria was for an inspection.

He queued with the other foot passengers, only three of them, and presented his ticket at the gate. He followed the others up metal stairs to an observation deck, where he wandered toward the outside deck and watched as the vehicles loaded. Efficient workers in orange vests directed each one forward to form several lines on the car deck, passenger cars first, followed by the bigger commercial vehicles. Within fifteen minutes, the vehicle deck was full, barriers were being pulled up, and the occupants of the vehicles were climbing the steps toward the passenger lounge to join him. He went back inside and took a seat where he could observe them.

Soon, the ferry sounded its booming hoot and they began to move. Once out of the harbour, the ferry took on speed and Will was surprised at how fast it moved across the water. He left his seat and wandered back outside where he walked to the back of the ferry and watched the little cottages lining the Welsh shore fade quickly into the distance. A group of fellow passengers took pictures with cameras or mobiles of the receding shoreline and the big wake behind the ferry. Will watched for a few minutes and then sauntered back around to the front of the ferry. He could see nothing in the far distance yet, and he supposed they'd be at least halfway across before the faint line of Ireland's shores could be seen against the horizon.

He strolled back inside and checked out the cafeteria. The food looked pretty fresh, so he ordered a bowl of cream of mushroom soup and a roll. He carried it to an empty table and sat, looking out at the sparkling water and slowly enjoying his lunch. It was surprisingly good, and he resolved to order it again for the return trip.

His mind turned to Bowers. He'd come through with two important tips for Will and Edward, but that didn't prove that he was on their side. Will had tried to be positive while talking with Edward, but he had doubts that he hadn't dared express. It was nothing he could pin down, but the feeling of being watched had begun in Caernarfon, and that made Will suspicious. Weren't the best snares those whose victims didn't suspect they were there? Just because Will couldn't come up with reasons why he felt uneasy, that didn't mean Bowers wasn't setting them up for a clever trap, one they'd never expect until it was too late. He turned it over and over in his mind, trying to see how the information could be used to trap them, but he came up empty. It worried him, but he couldn't solve the puzzle.

Finally, he shook it off. He got up, threw his trash in the bin, and wandered back out the door to the outside deck. He squinted off into the distance, but still he couldn't see a hint of land. He let the sea wind blow in his face until he was cold, and then he went back inside.

Bored, he pulled a mobile out of his pocket, one of the pre-paids. The ferry offered wifi, and he had a good signal. He hesitated for a moment, and then he entered Bronwyn's number. What could it hurt at this point?

She answered immediately. "Will? Did something happen?"

"No, nothing's happened yet. You said tonight, remember?"

"I just thought…well, things can go wrong sometimes."

"No, I'm on a ferry on my way to Ireland to monitor the traffic from that side, and I'm bored watching the empty water go by. All I could think to do was to call you."

"It's perfect timing. Our group today cancelled at the last minute, so I have a free day. I had a call from Bodnant Gardens suggesting that they could use a few more of my sketches in the shop, so I decided to go hiking in search of subjects. Only, it's more fun if I have you with me."

"But then you don't get any sketching done." Will smiled to himself. He'd never actually watched Bronwyn creating her art; he'd only seen the finished pieces. He had the one at the flat in Caernarfon. He'd bought it on a whim the first time he'd gone to Pennant Melangell, when he was investing the murder there a year ago. Little did he suspect that he'd be living with the artist a short year later.

"It's a gorgeous day. Daisy is running all over, sniffling at holes and trees, and I'm sitting beside a little stream of water, doing a sketch. I'll try to find a few other subjects for preliminary drawings, and then I'll finish them up at home when I have time."

"Are you all ready to go tomorrow?" He hated to bring it up, but thought he should ask.

"You won't be back, will you?" He heard her disappointment. "I don't have to leave until early afternoon."

"If this goes off as we plan, I'll be busy with paperwork tomorrow. I'll try to join you on Monday or Tuesday."

"Then we could still go get Lark for the weekend?"

Oh, God...if only that ordeal could be postponed. "We'll see how it goes. Everything's up in the air right now. Truth be told, right now I can't make plans for longer than an hour or two ahead of time."

They went on to chat about inconsequential things then – her planned garden, Daisy's adventures, a hike near Oswestry called Giants of Vernwy trail she'd like to take him on, a possible holiday in the summer with Lark. He relaxed as they chatted, and his optimism returned. She had that undefined ability to give him a sense of calm. That was why they loved her working at the centre, and it was why he loved coming home to her at the end of a few days' work.

As they finished the call, he heard the blast of the horn that signaled an arrival in Ireland, and he watched as vehicle passengers fled down the staircases back to their cars. When the passenger lounge was empty, he stood up and followed them, disembarking onto a gangplank that led to a dock and solid land. For a moment, he swayed a bit until he got his legs back under him. He hadn't been aware of the ship's movements until he'd stepped on land.

He strolled to the Stena Lines office and sat in a passenger waiting area with a crowd of other ticketed passengers. Even most of those with vehicles would wait there until it was time to board, leaving their cars in a queue. Lorries were in a different queue where paperwork was being inspected and, in many cases, the doors opened for an inspection.

Suddenly, one of the lorries caught his eye, and he sat up without thinking. Excitement frizzed through him, an excitement of knowing that a long case was nearly at a satisfactory end. It was a smaller lorry, dirty with road grime and nondescript except for the symbol painted on its side. The words "Royal Transport" named the trucking company, and their symbol, a lion rampant, accompanied the prideful moniker. Will knew, without a doubt, he'd found the right lorry. *Thank you, Bronwyn.*

He watched as the lorry's papers were inspected, but the agent waved it on from there, no inspection requested. He pulled out a mobile and tried to inconspicuously snap photos, zooming in as best the cheap phone would allow. They could be enlarged and improved later. He snapped one of the lorry, a closer one of the driver, and two of the customs agent, adding a third as the man moved nearer to the passenger lounge to inspect the next lorry. He had it, the first real evidence in the case. Now the thrill had him vibrating with energy. He could hardly wait to arrive back in Wales and share the news with Edward.

He glanced around, but no one was paying him any attention. They were occupied with children or watching the activity outside, checking the time to see when loading would begin. *So far, so good.* He pulled out the mobile and entered the number of another of the pre-paids. Why wait for his arrival in Wales when he had the time and ability to call now?

"We've got them," he blurted as Edward's voice greeted him from the other end. He described the lorry in a lowered voice. "It's the right one, I know it."

"It's all falling into place." Edward's voice echoed the excitement Will felt. "You're not going to believe it, but I'm on the road back from Wrexham with Billy Davies' corpse in the back."

Will was confused. "Why?"

"I made a deal with the devil. I found the right person, or I should say he found me. He was interested in anything that'd open the market up again so I explained what we had planned, and he agreed to be a crucial part of it. He's watching Howell's house right now, and when Howell leaves, as we know he will, his guys will rush in and do a quick burial in the back garden."

308

Will felt dizzy with disbelief. "The cameras will pick them up."

"No, they won't. They know there are cameras there, and they'll take them out before they bury the body. Apparently, they have someone in their operation who's an expert at that. He assures me that they can have the body buried and a tip called in within twenty minutes of when Howell drives off. Howell will be followed, and his arrest should be imminent at that point."

"You think he'll leave before the ferry docks."

"It doesn't matter. If not, I'll call and they'll arrest him at his house. That's why you identifying the lorry is such an amazing piece for us. We can follow it from the harbour, no matter where it goes. I don't think they'll divide it up until someone else shows up to supervise, even if they have to wait a while. It's getting Howell out of the loop that'll do it for us."

A nudge of conscience tweaked Will's enthusiasm. "You're sure it's Howell that killed Davies?"

"No, I'm pretty sure he didn't. But I do think he ordered the murders of all three of our victims. You aren't backing out on me now, are you? Because we've got this."

"Just filming it," Will reminded him. "We aren't going in guns blazing because, as you are aware, we have no guns."

"Filming it is enough," Edward assured him. "See you in a few hours?"

"Yeah, I'll be there. I should be able to pick you out of the crowd."

"You can have the Land Rover fixed after, you know."

"But the smell may never leave it," Will groaned as he ended the call.

Loading the ferry was a repeat process from that morning's trip. Vehicles were waved on as the orange-vested workers decided what would fit where. They seemed expert at fitting as many vehicles on as possible, a daily puzzle for them to solve. Every paying vehicle was money in the bank for the Stena Line, so the more adept they were at using every inch of available space, the better.

Will waited until the Royal Transport lorry was beckoned forward, and then he hurried up the dock to the passenger loading zone. He climbed the metal stairs to the passenger lounge and made himself comfortable. He watched as passengers from the vehicles made their way up. He opened his mobile and tried to enlarge the photo he'd taken of the driver, but it blurred before he got it clear enough to see. There was no way of telling which passenger was the driver of the lorry.

Once the ferry was underway, he allowed himself to breathe and to think about the next few hours. Everything seemed to be falling into place, which made him nervous. No operation went perfectly; there were sure to be flaws that would force them to change the plan at a moment's notice. It could still all go wrong, and the next morning could find them without suspects, without the drugs, and without jobs – and that was if they were lucky. He was afraid to relax. After a long period of reflection, he knocked on the wood on the side of his chair for luck and strode over to get his bowl of soup. He was too nervous to eat much, but the soup would fill him up without causing his stomach to churn, he hoped.

He watched his fellow passengers. He didn't recognize any of them from the earlier crossing, so if he was being followed, they hadn't bothered with the ferry. A few of them chatted, but most isolated themselves in family groups or as individuals. He figured the lorry driver would be nervous. Anyone would be nervous carrying a big load of illegal drugs into the country. He chose three candidates, but couldn't be sure without a better photo to help identify his target. It'd do no good anyway. They had the lorry to follow; they didn't need to know who was driving it.

In the end, he went outside and stood on the deck watching for the faint line in the horizon that would be Wales. *Land of magic*, he thought, *traditional home of the famous Merlin. Land of dragons.* Sometimes he found it easy to believe that Bronwyn had mystical connections. They didn't seem out of place in Wales, after all. He regretted the need to tell Edward about it, but maybe it was for the best. It seemed fitting that his best friend should know their secrets if he and Bronwyn were going to try to make a life together, and it made him feel better about himself knowing that Edward was willing to overlook her oddities, as he did.

He was relieved to see Edward waiting at the end of the dock when the ferry arrived. So much could go wrong at that point, and Edward had taken chances he didn't think he'd have had the courage to take. He hurried Will toward a little Citroen in the car park. "Had to switch vehicles," he explained as he used the key to unlock the door. He pushed the button to unlock the passenger door, and they both slid inside, Will having to squeeze his long legs into the smaller vehicle. Even his MGF had more leg room than this ride. "It seemed better to just leave the corpse in the Land Rover until they got rid of it."

"That was trusting of you," Will observed nervously. "They could just turn it in, corpse and all, and say they found it and confiscated it for the police. The locals here are already familiar with us and with that vehicle. It wouldn't take much for us to be in big trouble."

"Sometimes you have to take a chance. You took one when you told your chief super about this." Edward started the car and backed out. "It's my turn this time. Which one is it?"

"The lorry with the lion on it, Royal Transport," Will said. He was watching the line of vehicles as they slowly emerged from the ferry.

"They called the tip in about an hour ago. Howell should be out of the picture by now."

"Did anyone watch to make sure?"

"He wasn't home, so no. We just have to assume he was picked up. The good news is that, at last report, the entire street was blocked off while the dogs did their thing and then the constables did the digging, so I'm assuming that means my new contacts didn't turn on me. Howell's wife was at home when the show started, but she's in custody now."

"I wish we had an ear inside the station here."

"So do I, but we don't, so we just have to cross our fingers and hope for the best."

"How did you get them to bury the corpse for you?"

"I talked to a few people, and I must have hit on the right one. He came to me and basically asked how they could help."

"Not another undercover cop?"

"I'd have known. I think these guys are desperate to get their business back up and running again. They sent a guy over to help me, and the two of us drove back up to north Wales and got the body."

Will shook his head. "You're braver than I am."

"There is some bad news." Edward's head snapped up and he nodded toward the line of vehicles. "That's it, is it?"

"The very one." Will waited while Edward drove toward the line of cars and signaled that he wanted to merge in. A kind older man in a blue Toyota waved him in ahead of him. They were only three vehicles behind the lorry. Luck really did seem to be falling their way.

Or did it? "I was definitely followed when I went to get Billy Davies."

Will's head swiveled to stare at Edward.

"I didn't see him for a long time, but you know how deserted that hilly country is up there. It'd have been impossible not to notice him behind me."

"What happened? Are you sure it wasn't just a farmer checking on his sheep or a tourist who got lost on the way to Conwy?"

"It was a definite tail. I'd pulled over near where we dropped the body, and he went past slowly. You know how it is, looking but pretending not to. I didn't get a good look, but I'm guessing he didn't want me to. He went on up the road, but he pulled over maybe a quarter mile away. We debated what to do, and in the end, we went ahead and got the body. We'd driven all that way up there, and we had a plan. We got out and got it, carried it back, and loaded it fast. The car didn't move, but I'm guessing they were watching us with binoculars. Hopefully not long-lens cameras. Anyway, they didn't try to confront us. They just watched. When we turned around and headed back, they did, too."

Will frowned. "What do you think it means?"

"I think maybe your chief super put a tail on us. You said you'd felt eyes on us ever since we left Caernarfon. Maybe he didn't intend to stop us, but he wants to keep tabs on what we're doing."

Will thought about that. He hated the idea of someone like Jay Mehta or even Beth Holway being told to tail him. He liked them, and he didn't want to feel diminished in their eyes, like some sort of criminal. Which he was, of course. It wasn't exactly legal to hide a murder victim, nor to buy and plant illegal drugs on people. Did it mean Bowers was with them or against them? It could go either way. "What did you do with the drugs we had left?"

"I gave them to our help, a little thank-you."

"How am I going to get the Land Rover back? I mean, what if this all goes south?"

"I told them we'd meet them in the morning to trade back. By then, we'll have our film and be ready to head back and make a report."

"If it goes the way we want it to." Will drummed his fingers on the arm rest. "If we get caught, this will be the vehicle the police find. They can trace it back to them, and they know it."

"They didn't seem too worried, and I thought it'd be better to follow our quarry in a strange car than to do it in the Land Rover," Edward said defensively. "What would you have done?"

"Probably the same. The truth is that, with things going as fast as they are, worrying about cars is the last thing we need to do."

"Right, that's what I thought."

"Do you think whoever's following you knows we changed vehicles?"

"Definitely. I don't know, Will. It might mean they're waiting until they have lots of evidence against us and then they're going to put us away forever."

"We're committed now." Will gazed out the window, blindly watching the countryside go by.

"It's too late to change what we're doing," Edward agreed. "We'll just have to go ahead with it and take our chances, either way."

The transport lorry turned onto the main street and picked up speed. Edward let a few cars get in between them and it, and he fell silent as he concentrated on not losing sight of it. It turned left without a signal, and Edward pulled into the next parking space they found. They waited, tense, hoping they'd made a good choice in not taking the corner behind it. Finally, it pulled back onto the main road two blocks further along. They could see it ahead of them, not speeding, but not driving slowly either. Edward signaled, pulled out into traffic, picked up speed and passed it, watching it in his rear-view mirror. "I don't want to lose him, but it can't look too much like we're following him, either."

The lorry made another turn, this one to the right, and Edward pulled off again, hoping the Citroen wasn't overly visible among the other parked cars. They waited and watched for what seemed longer this time.

Will drummed his fingers on the seat beside him. If they lost it now, then what? They'd head to the warehouse and hope they'd gotten it right.

Edward gave a sudden start. "They're going back the way we came," he announced. He pulled the Citroen out into traffic, took the next right and then flipped the car in a circle, speeding back toward the main street. "He'll be taking the A30," he predicted, but the lorry passed by the entrance to the motorway and continued on south.

"Where the heck is he going?" Will sat forward. "Are we being followed?"

"I can't tell." Edward sped up, following the lorry closer now.

"Maybe we got it wrong. It isn't the warehouse."

"Or he's leading us into a trap." Edward checked his rear-view mirror. "There's something silver that's been behind us most of the way. Or maybe it's just that there are a lot of silver cars, and I can't tell one from another."

They followed the lorry on the A487 past the coastal villages that extended further out on the peninsula. At Haverfordwest, it merged onto the A40 and headed inland. Darkness descended as they watched inlets from the sea and then farmland pass by, and Will felt his nerves ramped up as he wondered where they were headed. There was more traffic as they passed Carmathen, making it harder to decide if they were being followed. The lorry kept a steady pace six cars ahead of them as they tried to track it in the darkness.

"He's exiting," Will announced as they approached a road sign. "Maybe it's Llandrindod Wells, after all."

But it wasn't. The lorry turned off onto a farm lane just past a village called Llandello, and Edward turned his face to Will. "What should we do? We can't just drive up the lane behind him."

Will shook his head. He wasn't feeling good about any of it now. "I guess we park somewhere inconspicuous and walk."

"We'll have to hope it's not far. With our luck, they're just taking a shortcut to another little farm road that comes out on the motorway again."

Hope seemed a distant goal at the moment. If only they'd been able to place a tracking device on the lorry, they wouldn't have to worry what to do.

Edward pulled into a lay-by and parked. He looked at Will, who looked back, and then they both got out. Edward reached into the centre console and tossed Will a small torch. He caught it, flicked it on, and they started up the lane, walking fast. The light had faded with the sunset so that it was nearly dark, but they could see well enough with the torches. Ahead, though, they saw only darkness.

Chapter Twenty

"Stop! Turn off the light!" Edward's warning came suddenly from the dark.

Will nearly bumped into him. He flicked off his light. "What is it?"

"I hear voices."

Will strained to listen. A slight breeze shook the grasses on the verge, and now that their lights were out, stars were appearing above them. He squinted. "I can't hear anything, but it looks like there's a light up there ahead of us."

"I see it, too. Just a crack, like lights on inside a building with the doors closed."

Will glanced around behind them. Now that his eyes had adjusted to the darkness, he could see silhouettes of trees off the road, and rocks, too. Maybe sheep. Something moved behind them, and he wondered. A sudden raised voice echoed through the night, and then was silenced.

They crept on, wary now, feeling their way in the dark and trying not to stumble. Will kept moving steadily. The light in the distance formed itself into a building, cracks around huge doors forming a rectangle of light, making it look like a child's drawing of a house. They'd be inside a barn, he thought. He wondered if they'd left guards outside and figured they weren't stupid enough not to. He reached out and touched Edward's jacket sleeve, then nodded toward the fields.

Edward understood. They split up, leaving the road and its somewhat solid footing for pastureland filled with unexpected holes, tufts of grass, and rocks to trip them up. Will knew that he was on his own now. He and Edward would have to trust each other to work in sync, but each would make his own decisions, for better or worse. If they were spotted, if one of them were captured or wounded, the other probably couldn't risk coming to the rescue. He wondered briefly if the Citroen would still be there after, but shoved that thought away. There were other more important things to think about.

The night seemed terribly quiet now as Will stumbled carefully through the field, trying to stifle curses as he tripped into a hole or stubbed a toe on a rock. Shadows moved to his left, and he hoped they were sheep or cattle. There'd been no fence along the road, but that wasn't uncommon as livestock was often free-range in rural areas. A thought of Bronwyn flicked through his mind, and he had the presence of mind to pull out his mobiles, the two pre-paid ones. He turned one off and put the other on silent mode. The last thing he needed was to get a call in the quiet of the night.

The going got easier as he approached the building. He could see now that it wasn't so much a barn as what the Americans would call a pole building. It was larger than a barn, and much newer, with big double doors that could accommodate a small lorry, as well as farm trucks and stock trailers. He couldn't see the lorry so he supposed it had pulled inside to be unloaded. Outside, one farm truck and two pickups were parked, all with stock trailers attached. Two other vehicles, a black sedan and a silver 4X4 were also parked outside the building. There were no windows in the building, but Will tried to take photos of the registration numbers on the vehicles, as well as of the vehicles themselves. He knew Edward would be doing the same from the other side. Without the possibility of a flash, the pictures would be difficult to see, but perhaps the techs in the lab could make them clear enough to get the numbers and letters off them. It seemed important to try.

Will froze as a man walked around the corner of the building. He'd been caught in the open, but if he didn't move, he thought he might not be seen. It was usually movement that caught the eye when you were stalking prey, not the prey itself, which would be camouflaged. In this case, he'd have to hope the darkness provided enough camouflage that the man wouldn't notice him. He reached up and pulled the front of his shirt over the bottom half of his face and rifled his hair down over his forehead. He could see the man carried a weapon, some sort of high-power rifle, if he had a guess. He couldn't see it well enough to know for sure.

Another man rounded the far corner of the building and stopped to talk to the first man. Will couldn't make out their words, but he noticed that they kept a wary eye as they chatted. Their shift tonight would last only a couple of hours, he thought, so they'd be alert and not burned out or tired. He wondered how many of them there were.

He waited, frozen in place. A third man wandered in from the pasture, and Will thought he'd come from the direction Edward would have been lurking. It worried him that they were patrolling the land away from the building and not just the building itself. Edward obviously hadn't been seen; so far, luck had been on their side. The three men talked for another minute, then they wandered off again, one heading toward Will's direction.

He hunched down, moving slowly until he was squatted down low. He tried to steady his breathing so that it wouldn't be heard. He pulled his shirt up higher to hide his face as best he could. It was awkward and limited his movements, but it seemed necessary to him. He hoped he'd look like a rock or a sleeping ewe. He wished he could lie down, but that was impossible now. His legs ached from squatting.

The man passed by him not more than ten feet away. He was swinging a torch around, and Will held his breath, but again, his luck held. The light flared on an old piece of farm machinery about fifteen feet behind and to the right of Will's position and stayed there as the man approached it and examined it, moving the torchlight from side to side as he examined his target.

He stood up slowly, trying to be silent. He picked up a rock and gripped it tightly, whether to use it to defend himself if necessary or to try to approach the man from behind and take him out, he wasn't sure yet. The only thing he knew for certain was that he couldn't let the man discover him. He stood still and watched as the man crouched down and shone the torch beneath the machinery, probing the dark shadows there. He seemed intent on his examination, and Will knew he could probably creep up behind him with the rock, if he wanted to. But if the man didn't return to the building in a short time, an alarm would be raised. They'd know that someone was outside the building watching and waiting, and that would mean the end of their surveillance. They didn't have enough evidence yet, so it would also mean their mission had failed. He decided to wait and see what might happen next.

He moved silently to the left, further from the torchlight, and he crouched again.

A flare of light startled both the man and Will. The man swung around to see the big double doors of the building slowly raising, and he set off back toward the building.

Will followed him at a distance. He'd be more visible in the light coming from the open doors, but he wanted to be close enough to see what was happening. When he judged that he was as near as was safe, he laid down in the dirt, propped his elbows up, and held the mobile high to take photos.

A pickup pulling a stock trailer emerged from the building. Will got a picture of the registration and watched as it pulled out and stopped, the driver stopping to talk to another man who'd walked out beside the truck. He was on the wrong side to get a picture of the two, but he guessed that Edward would have a better opportunity for that. He snapped a shot of the stock trailer, which appeared to be loaded with sheep. His guess was that they were using the same strategy they'd used with Billy Davies: loading the drugs in the centre of the trailer and surrounding the boxes with sheep so as to appear a simple farming transport. After a minute's conversation, the truck pulled away and headed off down the lane, obviously carrying its share of the load to one of what appeared to be four destinations.

The light flared from the building now that the big doorways were empty, and Will ducked low, burrowing himself into the dirt and grabbing some in his hand to rub on his face to darken it. He didn't know where the three guards were at the moment, nor whether there were more. He could keep a good watch from his prone position, but it would put him at a disadvantage should he be seen. He could hardly fight his way out when he was lying flat, and it would cost him precious time to get to his feet.

He could see the lorry now, and men were grabbing boxes from the back of it and stacking them beside it, ready to load the next truck. He could count three men working, but he thought there'd be more inside the lorry. One man stood with his back to the doors, watching the activity. Will couldn't see his face, but he thought he could be Chief Superintendent Mathews from the size of him and his stance. He hoped the man would turn around so he could see his face, but it didn't happen. If Will could get a picture of him, that would be enough. He and Edward could withdraw and call it in. Or could they? The local constables would have no firepower strong enough to confront the guards with their high-power rifles. They wouldn't want to put them at risk, and getting a SWAT team in would take longer than they probably had.

The next truck backed into the building with its trailer. The driver struggled with it, having to pull back out and try again several times before he got it right. As soon as it was fully inside, the doors descended again, leaving them in darkness outside. Will breathed a sigh of relief. At least for the moment, he felt invisible again.

He stood up slowly and inched toward the machinery the guard had been checking out. If he thought he'd been thorough in his search, he might not return to it for a while, so Will thought he'd be safe to use it as cover. He kept an eye on the building as he moved. As soon as the doors were down, the guards resumed their patrols. There seemed to be only the three of them, but now two moved out away from the building with their torches and only one remained to walk around the building itself. A bigger problem for Will and Edward.

One of the guards headed in Will's general direction, but his trajectory was more to the west of Will's position. Unless he altered his path, he shouldn't be a problem at the moment. As he moved, he turned slightly away from Will. Will watched him circle around, pointing the beam of his torch in a wide arc, and then he turned back and wandered toward the building again.

Minutes passes slowly. When about twenty minutes had gone, the doors whirred open a second time, and the second truck and trailer pulled out. The three guards joined the other men at the building's entrance to watch this process, and even the man who'd had his back to the door came forward to oversee what was happening. A thrill of excitement ran down Will's spine. He was sure now it was Chief Superintendent Mathews, waving his arm and directing the men. He snapped pictures of him, his phone silent and dark but recording what he hoped would be a clear enough picture of the man. He swung it and got pictures of other faces.

And then something tapped his back and a voice said, very softly, "Freeze."

He spread his hands to his sides as a flood of thoughts raced through his brain. Could he drop the mobile, try to salvage the photos for someone to find later? Where was Edward? How could he have been so careless as to let this man sneak up on him? Surely, he'd have heard his footfalls. They must have been masked by the commotion at the building, or he was simply distracted by the excitement of recognizing Mathews directing the operation. His heart thumped. He'd assumed there were only the three guards; that's all he'd seen before. Obviously, they'd had backup. He'd been lax. He'd relaxed his guard, just for the moment, but that's all it took. He was caught, and that probably meant he was dead. He swallowed, his throat suddenly dry.

"Stand up and put your hands behind your back," the man instructed him. He pictured the rifles he'd seen and obeyed, dropping the mobile phone into the dirt as he did so. He tried to tell himself that it was good that the man hadn't shot him immediately, but he suspected that status would be short-lived. They'd want to question him first. His hands were yanked back hard and bound tightly with a zip tie that cut into his wrists. The man stooped to pick up the mobile phone and then pushed him forward with a hand thumping the middle of his back. "Walk to the building."

Will walked. The man hadn't turned on a torch, and Will wondered if he wanted both hands free in case he needed to use the gun. Or maybe he just wanted not to be seen. A torch might allow Edward to see them, and the man would know Will wasn't alone. He stumbled over a rock, and the man grunted. He tried to look for Edward, but he couldn't see much. "Who are you?" he asked the man.

"Quiet," the man barked, his own voice kept low. "Just walk."

Will walked. They emerged into the light of the building as the second truck drove away up the farm track, and heads swiveled as the men scattered there took notice. Mathews stared for a moment, and then he grinned. "Can't shoot him now or we'll draw attention," he grumbled. "Bring him in. You can take care of him when we're finished here. He's been nothing but a pain in the arse for a long time, but tonight will end that. Where's your partner, huh?"

Will clamped his mouth shut. They'd kill him anyway so there was no need to answer the question.

"Not going to tell me," Mathews seethed. "No worries. We'll find him soon enough. Maybe if we wait to shoot you, he'll come to your rescue and we'll get him then." He turned to Will's guard. "Get the others and check the pastures."

Will was pushed into the building and off to a corner, where he was shoved to the floor. He sat awkwardly, with his hands behind his back, his wrists stinging and his shoulders already aching. As he watched, another truck was backed into the building. The men returned to their labor, and the doors came down again. He wished they were a little less efficient.

Where was Edward? He was surprised Mathews hadn't questioned him more, but he was just as sure that Mathews knew Edward was nearby, and that the two of them were alone. He'd been following them; that much was obvious. They'd known someone was watching them, and now there was little doubt who it was. It wouldn't have been hard for Mathews to keep tabs on them all along with unlimited access to police resources at his disposal. He'd have looked at what vehicles they had available, including Bronwyn's Land Rover, and he'd have tracked them using the CCTV cameras that filmed every spot in the whole of the U.K. He'd have assigned people who were very good to do that for him, without needing a reason why. And now they were done for. There'd be no point to Mathews arresting them for the murders of Catherine Baines, Peter O'Connell, and Billy Davies, even though he absolutely could make it look as if they'd been responsible. He couldn't take the chance that, somehow, they'd have a tiny piece of evidence that would turn the accusations back onto him. They'd been careless despite their efforts, and now it was over for them.

Except they didn't have Edward yet. He had to assume that Edward had seen him captured. How could he not when they'd marched him right into the light? If Edward was still out there somewhere, he'd know that he couldn't come to Will's rescue, but, surely, he'd go for help. He'd abandon all his plans for taking this group down and try to save Will. Of course, he would. He could make a 999 call, and the local constabulary would respond. Will's spirits sank at that thought. They'd have no chance, however, against the firepower Will saw in evidence. Edward would realize that and not want to put more lives at risk, even to save Will.

If not the local police, then, maybe Edward could rally the guys who had the Land Rover, even if it led to a bloodbath. Those men wouldn't care, and at this point, neither did Will. The only problem with that idea was that it would take time, and time was something he was nearly out of.

Will sat back and allowed his thoughts to wander to what would happen later, after he was dead and maybe Edward, too. Bowers would know most of it, so maybe they hadn't failed, even if it cost them their lives. Maybe Bowers would see it through to the end, to the arrests of Mathews and all the rest of them, whoever was involved. Bowers didn't know it all, but he knew enough, Will thought. Bronwyn knew, too. She'd go to Bowers, or more likely he'd go to her, and they'd fill in the blanks together. He felt a sad sort of triumph when he thought of it. Unless Mathews got to Bronwyn before Bowers did, something could be salvaged from their sacrifice.

Before, time had seemed slow. It had felt like the minutes crawled by as he waited in the dark for something to happen. Now, though, the minutes raced. The stock trailer was filled quickly, and then sheep were herded up the ramps and allowed to arrange themselves around the boxes that occupied the middle before Will felt like he had time to think it through.

The doors opened, and the truck drove out. Now only one more trailer remained before they'd be finished dividing up the load, and then they'd shoot Will and scatter to the wind before the shot was noticed and checked out.

Before the last truck was in place to back inside, though, there was another commotion. Will's heart sank as he saw Edward being escorted into the building, just as he had been a short time before. The faint hope that Edward had fled and gone for help faded, leaving Will shaken. With Edward's capture, there was no one left who could save them. He tried to breathe, to hold onto what minutes of life he had left, but all he felt was terror. His heart was pounding, and a dizzy blackness threatened to topple him into unconsciousness.

Edward was pushed to the floor beside Will. He was sporting a reddening bruise on his cheekbone that would turn into a black eye if, somehow, he lived long enough for it to develop. He'd tried to fight, then, and Will felt a little remorse for his own easy surrender.

Mathews sauntered over. "You two were always someplace you shouldn't have been and doing something you shouldn't," he said, a gloating smile on his face.

"We were good at what we did," Edward told him defiantly.

"I'll give you that. But you weren't at the top of your game this time. This time you came up against something bigger than even you could handle. I won't lie to you. This mistake is going to cost your lives."

"We have backup," Edward blurted.

"I don't think so." Mathews leaned back against the wall. Behind him, men were busy loading both the farm truck and the last trailer. "Everyone else is accounted for. They're doing what they're assigned to do. It's only the two of you who disappeared, who went rogue. You're all alone."

"There's my partner," Will pointed out, desperate to help Edward create some doubt in Mathew's mind. It might buy them a little more time. But it'd do them no good. No one was coming. No one knew they were there.

"Your partner is in Liverpool. He attended Peter O'Connell's memorial service this evening." Mathews shook his head. "No, you two are without friends here. It seems fitting, doesn't it? You were partners before, and here you are, partners again, at the end of things."

Neither of them spoke. There was nothing else to say.

"I suppose you thought taking Morys out would stop us," Mathews gloated then. "Morys will be cleared and out within a couple of days. I take care of my own. I'm glad you got him arrested, though. Otherwise, I wouldn't be here to see the end of you two."

Will stared at the floor. He supposed Edward was doing the same.

Mathews shrugged and turned away, looking out at the farm truck. "They're nearly done."

Regret flooded Will's mind then. He'd never see Lark grow up, never see how she'd take the world by storm. She was precious, smart and confident and curious, and he knew she'd make her mark as an adult. He just wouldn't be around to see what that mark would look like. And Bronwyn...they'd just met, really, just established a comfortable relationship. He'd never get to see what life had in store for the two of them, whether they'd stay together. She'd mourn him, he knew that. But it wouldn't last, and someday she'd meet someone else, someone who'd stay with her and not waste his life chasing demons. He blinked away tears, determined to deny Mathews that sight.

Will pushed thoughts of Bronwyn and Lark from his mind. It'd do no good to think of them, despite it being his last moments on Earth. They were safe, and he supposed life would go on for them. But his mind looped back to them, despite his efforts. Bronwyn would find her calling at St. Melangell's, guiding people to more peaceful lives. Lark would go off to boarding school, where she'd excel. They'd remember him for a while, but less so as time went on and they made new lives without him.

He pushed those thoughts away a second time. He intended to accept his fate now that it was certain, to face death with dignity. He breathed in and out slowly, trying to stop himself shaking. He was determined to remain defiant until the end, and he didn't want to give Mathews the satisfaction of believing him fearful. He wondered what it would feel like. A flash of intense, unendurable pain, he supposed, and then nothingness. He glanced at Edward. The look of defeat and despair on his face dispelled any glimmer of hope Will might still have clung to. It was over.

They watched in silence as the last of the lorry's load was arranged in the farm truck and its trailer. A final group of sheep was herded from a pen and the men funneled them onto the trailer, slamming the gate shut behind them. The truck started, and the doors rolled up.

"Will," whispered Edward, "thanks, mate, for coming with me. I'm sorry for…"

And, at that moment, the world exploded. A huge flash of light blinded them, and something blew up in front of the farm truck, halting it in its tracks and shaking the building. Immediately after, a spat of gunfire deafened them. Men in body armour flooded in through the open doors, screaming commands and warnings that registered with Will only after he'd had a moment to regain his senses.

Edward was faster. "Scotland Yard!" he screamed, and they both flopped over on their sides and tried to disappear into the cement floor as men raced through the doors, guns firing as those inside defied the orders and tried to fight their way out.

From the corner of his eye, Will saw the truck driver fling himself out of his truck and dive to safety behind it. He crouched there, obviously unarmed and unwilling to put himself in the line of fire. One of the armed guards charged forward, bellowing defiance before crashing to the floor in a spatter of blood. Another took his place, leaping toward the attacking force, only to be taken out by a shot to his leg. His gun skittered across the floor and was kicked aside by one of the heavily armed attackers.

On the other side of the building, behind the truck, Mathews stumbled toward a side door. He was hobbling, but making good time as the door was yanked open by another man running ahead of him, and Will saw him slip out. Two of the newcomers plowed through the confusion of men and guns and ran out behind him, pausing carefully with weapons drawn before shouting out orders and continuing their pursuit outside.

Will ducked as a bullet flew over his head and imbedded itself in the wall above him. He curled into a ball then, trying to protect his head as well as he could with his arms contained behind his body. Beside him, Edward was yelling something, but he couldn't make out the words with all the noise around them. He saw feet rush past, hesitate, and then hurry on.

Then, suddenly, it was quiet. Men's footsteps rustled on the dirty floor as they walked carefully around, looking inside and behind the lorry, the truck, the trailer, and the pens where the sheep had been. Will lifted his head and rolled to his side, watching, his arms aching and his wrists burning with pain. Men, more than he'd anticipated, lay on the floor, some outstretched on their stomachs in surrender and others bloodied and gasping or crying with wounds. Two lay still, the one he'd seen fall and another, their weapons kicked away from lifeless hands. The attacking force wore protective gear and carried weapons, and there seemed to be a lot of them, too.

Two of them approached Will and Edward. They stood over them, gazing down, their guns held loosely. "You're not hurt?" one of them asked, and Will answered in the negative. The man stooped down and grasped Will's arm, strong arms pulling him to his feet, and his companion did the same for Edward. "I'm placing you under arrest," the first man told them. "Detective constable Jim Williams, Scotland Yard. This is my colleague, Kiernan Chesterfield."

"But we're obviously on your side," Edward argued, turning slightly to wriggle the hands that were still tied behind his back. "We were surveilling them, and they figured it out. If you'll just untie my hands, I'll show you my ID. Edward Smythe. I'm an undercover agent from Cardiff drugs and alcohol."

"That may be," Williams said, "but until we sort it all out, we're arresting everyone. At the least, you're wanted for the illegal transport of a corpse and for drug possession, no matter who you are."

So that's who'd been watching them. He'd been so wrong. Thankfully wrong. Relief made him dizzy again, and he swayed on his feet.

"You're Cooper, right?" Chesterfield surmised, nudging him with an elbow to make him look at him.

"Will Cooper, sir, detective chief inspector from Caernarfon major crimes." *We're alive.* Will felt exhilarated. He had no idea how Scotland Yard had known to be there, who had called them in or even why, but he felt over-the-top grateful. He didn't care if they were charged or if they ended up in prison, he suddenly wanted to whoop with joy. "Who called you in?"

The man shook his head. "Come on. Let's get you in a car and in an interview room, and then you can ask your questions."

The other man grinned. "We may not answer them, though. When you go off on your own, without authorization, you get treated like any other criminal."

"Where are we going?" Edward planted his feet. "I'm not moving until you tell us that much, at least."

"We can't exactly take you to Cardiff, can we?" Chesterfield observed. "It's Caernarfon we're headed for."

Caernarfon. Will felt his exhilaration deflate. *Caernarfon.* He'd be paraded through the station, past all of his colleagues, his friends and not-friends, with his hands tied behind his back and at least two Scotland Yard detectives as escorts. No matter that their efforts had probably succeeded in stopping a major criminal enterprise headed by at least one of their own chief superintendents, the immediate effect would be shame. Some would look at him with pity; others with speculation, and some, like Notley, with delight, but none of those reactions would make it less painful. "Do I get a phone call?" he ventured.

"From the station," Williams said. He reached out for Will's arm and nudged him forward.

Will stared around the building as he stumbled slowly toward the big doors. The two dead men lay sprawled on the cement floor, blood spreading in irregular circles beneath them. Already, yellow crime tape marked out the areas surrounding each of them. No one would be allowed to approach them until the crime scene technicians and the coroner had examined the areas in detail. Most of the other captives had been taken out of the building and were being loaded into panda cars that had, somehow, magically appeared outside the building. Will hadn't heard them drive up, so he supposed they'd come without sirens and lights. In the confusion after the initial flash explosion, much could have happened that he'd missed. Two men lay wounded outside, being tended to by emergency responders in a glare of floodlights. It looked to Will like they had gunshot wounds that probably weren't serious enough to kill them. He wondered about Mathews. He guessed that a team had surrounded the perimeter of the site to capture any of the suspects who tried to flee, as Mathews had. He'd be caught.

If it embarrassed him to be marched through the station, imagine how Mathews would feel. The thought comforted Will a little. At least he'd done what he had for good cause. He thought much of the attention would be on Mathews, one of their own who'd used his position to build a thriving criminal empire. He still wondered if anyone else was involved. *Not Bowers*, he thought. Bowers would have been the one who'd brought Scotland Yard in. Now that he could think clearly again, he was sure that was how it went. He was also sure about who had been following Edward and him the past few days. Bowers must have taken him seriously enough to call them in. They'd followed at a distance, just watching and letting them do their thing, until it came to the final moment. Thank goodness they'd come in before that last truck had driven off, or Will and Edward wouldn't be there to give them their side of the story.

He wondered about the Citroen. The detectives would know Will and Edward had used it to follow the lorry. They could trace its registration and find whoever it belonged to. Would that person be charged with a crime? He guessed so, considering that whoever it belonged to had been a willing participant in the moving of Billy Davies' body and its subsequent burial in Morys Howell's garden. There was no help for that now.

When they arrived at one of the panda cars, Williams grabbed Will's shoulder and turned him around so his back was to him. Will felt a tug on the zip tie around his wrists, and then it fell free. He turned around and gave Williams a grateful look.

"That was all show so my mates don't get the idea I'm soft." Williams winked at him. "You're still in a lot of trouble, but I don't think you need your hands confined behind your back."

"Thank you," Will blurted. He didn't know any of the Scotland Yard detectives. Maybe that was a relief. He opened the rear door himself and settled in, rubbing his wrists to try to restore circulation in them. Deep grooves marked where the zip ties had been pulled too tight, and there was blood where the ties had embedded themselves too deeply. They'd need to be cleaned and maybe stitched. He glanced around, having never been in the back of a panda car before. The door had no handle from the inside, and bars separated him from the driver and Williams, who climbed into the front passenger seat.

Williams turned around to look at Will. "Don't thank me too soon. You have a lot of explaining to do, and it won't go easy on you. You didn't exactly follow department guidelines. They'll probably hit you with conspiring to pervert the course of justice and willful obstruction, at the least, even if your intentions were noble." The car started up and began pulling away down the farm track.

"I knew that from the start," Will told him, "but we thought it worth the sacrifice to get this operation stopped."

Williams studied him for a minute and then nodded. "I wouldn't say anything about it just now," he warned. "You'll want a solicitor present."

"Yes," Will agreed. He felt overwhelmed at the moment, but underlying that was the joy of knowing he'd survived it. Nothing else mattered. He could survive the loss of his job. He could survive prison, too, if it came to that. He'd thought himself a dead man a short time ago, and it was as if he'd been given an unexpected and wonderful gift when they'd been rescued. He'd have liked to talk to Edward, to know his thoughts and maybe even celebrate their survival, but that was obviously not possible. He didn't know when he'd see his partner again. It could be a long time, and certainly not before they'd both given their statements and been thoroughly questioned.

"Here," Williams interrupted his thoughts. He was bent around toward the back seat, holding a mobile phone between the bars that separated front from back. "Make your call. It's my personal phone, so this one won't count."

An amazed gratitude poured over him as Will reached for the mobile. He settled back into the seat and watched for a moment. Emergency response vehicles littered the entire length of the lane, surrounding each of the pickup trucks with their trailer loads full of drugs. They must have been waiting for the first truck, checked to see that it was, indeed, carrying some sort of illegal cargo, and then moved in. An ambulance edged ahead of the car Will was in, weaving around the other vehicles.

He looked at the mobile, touched the phone button, and inputted Bronwyn's number.

"Hello?" she answered quickly, her voice agitated. She'd waited up to see what happened, then. *Of course, she would.* She'd known when it was going down. She'd worried over him, and he knew it.

He felt dizzy as a wave of emotion washed over him. He couldn't say much, not with Williams right there listening. "Bronwyn?" he managed at last. "It's over, love. I'm safe. It's all over."

Chapter Twenty-One

Bronwyn opened her eyes and reached for her phone on the nightstand. Nearly 5 a.m. She hadn't slept well in the strange bed, nice though it was. It reminded her of her university days. She'd never felt at home there either.

The sun was just beginning to light the sky. She rolled out of the bed and looked out the window. Clouds made the sunrise dim, but there were a few breaks between them and once the sun rose just a bit more, it would be beautiful. She picked up the phone and looked again at the time. She'd might as well just get up and out.

She showered and put on jeans and a brown jumper over a tee shirt she'd bought the day before. She'd been tired of driving and needed a break so she'd stopped in a little village full of tourist shops to wander and stretch her legs. She'd seen the stack of shirts and been attracted to them, deciding that buying one as a souvenir of her holiday wouldn't strain her budget too much.

Outside, she walked to the garden that was one of the hotel's best features and used a washcloth she'd thought to bring to dry a bench attached to a picnic table. The garden was an open space surrounded by trees and flowering shrubs, beautiful this time of year, and she knew this was where the seminar would at least begin. She looked around, trying to notice the small things: a rook cawing from the top of a tree, doves cooing from the hotel's roof, a pair of brown rabbits nibbling on the grass

332

nearby. The sweet scents of lilac and flowering plum nearly overpowered the smell of baking pastries from the hotel kitchen, and she could hear a faint clattering from inside that spoke of early activity. She'd get a breakfast free in the hotel later in the morning and, if she'd wanted, a cup of tea now, but she'd wait a bit. She wanted some time alone to think about the past few days before turning her mind to the seminar.

Will's call had brought her immense relief, but not peace. He had survived the operation, and that was the most important thing to her. He'd been brief, had told her 'it is over' and not much more than that, but his voice had sounded great, almost exhilarated. He'd said that he and Edward were on their way to Caernarfon, so she assumed they'd be interviewed about their activities and be kept busy with paperwork, at the least. She tried to imagine what all would be involved, but she didn't know enough about police procedures to hazard a good guess. He'd said he would be busy for several days, a great disappointment. He'd not make it to the Beacons, then, and nor would she be meeting his parents, as they'd planned. She'd hoped for another phone call the next morning, but he'd been silent since that midnight call. She wondered why.

She tried to picture how it would have gone down. She'd watched the news on Sunday morning and again on Monday. It had taken place in a remote farming area near a village called Llandello. She'd looked it up. It was down southeast of Fishguard, still on the peninsula. Sunday's headline had been about a big drug bust, millions of dollars' worth of pharmaceuticals that now wouldn't flood into cities and towns across Wales and England. It gave the credit for the investigation to some unnamed 'undercover agents'', which she guessed to be Will and Edward. Scotland Yard had carried out the actual operation, though, and she didn't know how they'd come to be involved. There were two deaths and several wounded, all suspects. By Monday, the news media was naming the chief superintendent from Cardiff drugs and alcohol, Llewellyn Mathews, as the head of the drug cartel. Edward had been right about that. She was glad the others he'd suspected were, apparently, not involved.

The trilling of a chaffinch interrupted her thoughts, and she roused herself and walked inside to find an urn of hot water in the hotel lobby.

She filled a cup and chose a tea bag, and then wandered back out to the bench. The sun was starting to beam through the trees, drying the dew that sparkled the lawn and dampened the furniture. It promised to be a fine day for the seminar, and she had high hopes that she'd come away inspired.

She'd left Daisy at her parents' place, assuring them that she'd be fine making the drive on her own despite their obvious concern. They'd seen the news, too, of course, and they were alternately awed and disconcerted by Will's part in something that big…and dangerous. They hadn't said anything specific, but she knew they worried about her and Will. He obviously wasn't the strapping farm boy they'd pictured for her, but it was her choice, not theirs, and they knew it. She hoped Will's parents would be as accepting.

And now her thoughts turned to that cancelled outing. She'd been nervous about meeting them after all Will had said about them, but determined to make it happen. She'd geared herself up for it so much that, now it was cancelled, all she felt was disappointment. Even more, she felt sad that Lark wouldn't get her long weekend with them. She'd looked forward to taking her shopping for things to decorate her bedroom in the cottage and to watching her ride Hobbs again. She hadn't been able to visit for a long time.

She heard footfalls and turned to see another of the guests approaching, her own cup of tea in hand. She smiled at Bronwyn. "Can I join you?" She was tall and slender, willowy, with dark hair, fair skin, and a scatter of freckles across her face. Like Bronwyn, she wore jeans and a warm jumper against the chill of the morning.

"Of course." Bronwyn snatched up the washcloth and held it out. "You might want to dry the bench a little before you sit. I'm Bronwyn."

"Sarah," the woman responded. She dried the bench and sat down, cupping her hands around the tea mug for warmth. "What a beautiful morning!"

"It is." Bronwyn felt herself warming to Sarah, feeling an immediate camaraderie. "Where are you from?"

"I'm a hiking guide in the Lake District," Sarah told her. "You're here for the certification, too, aren't you?"

"I am. I work as a coordinator for the counselling centre at St. Melangell's. Have you heard of it?"

Sarah shook her head. "Tell me about it."

Bronwyn launched into an enthusiastic description of the centre and her role there, digressing into the history of St. Melangell as Sarah showed interest. "I feel like we are carrying on her mission more than a thousand years later."

"It's always been a sanctuary for women?"

"For well over a thousand years. And not only for women, but for nature, as well. Wales is pretty scarred up from all the mining through the industrial years. Part of my intent going forward is to enable healing and to promote protection for the environment. Pennant Melangell is fairly remote, but we draw people from all over North Wales who are seeking a place of refuge and peace."

"I'll have to visit," Sarah said, "and you'll have to come to the Lake District, too. There's beautiful hiking there. Do you like to hike?"

Again, Bronwyn felt herself drawn out into conversation with an ease she didn't usually feel. Sarah was as enthusiastic about exercise and nature as she was, and they spent a happy hour describing their favorite hikes and telling tales of their adventures.

"You have a boyfriend, then?"

Bronwyn had mentioned Will. "He's a detective at North Wales major crimes."

Sarah was impressed. "Major crimes! That's something. My boyfriend works at one of the hotels. He's a bartender right now, but we have plans to make our own small group touring business. We'd like to offer hiking, of course, and now the forest bathing, too. That'd be my part. Luke wants to offer boat tours, just smaller groups, not like the bigger tour companies, and maybe bicycle touring."

Bronwyn was busy asking questions when the woman in charge of their training scurried toward them. "Come and have your breakfast so we can get started on our first session."

Sarah looked at Bronwyn. "This is going to be good."

"I think so."

To Bronwyn's surprise, breakfast wasn't a full English or a continental. The ten participants in their training group found themselves split into two groups at tables inside a pleasant dining room. Glasses of green liquid waited on the placemats, which they were told contained fresh fruit juice, spinach, and ginger. Bronwyn tried hers and found it nice. She couldn't really taste the spinach; it tasted like spiced fruit.

Wait staff brought bowls and plates. A granola cup contained yogurt and blueberries, while a baked frittata featured asparagus and locally made goat cheese. Baskets of whole meal scones sat on the tables, and Bronwyn found herself eating far more than usual as she chatted with Sarah and three other women who introduced themselves as Lucy, Emily, and Molly. Emily and Molly were old friends in their sixties, both dressed in jeans and colorful blouses. They were from York and planned to conduct tours in the Dales National Park on a volunteer basis. Lucy was the youngest of the group, only nineteen. From Cardiff, she told them she didn't yet have a plan for how to use her training, but that she hoped something would 'just turn up.'

After breakfast, the dishes were cleared away and their instructor, Priscilla Jonas, began the first session. Before they were to be taken outside to experience what they were learning, she wanted to explain the background of the movement and some of its features. Bronwyn took notes on a yellow pad as Jonas talked, her voice melodic as she detailed the history, health benefits, and basic structure of the exercise. "A lot of people think of it as meditation," she told them, "but it's not really that. It's a mindfulness exercise. A guide is not necessary to do it, but people usually find a guide helpful in teaching them to take their time as they do it. We are used to a frantic pace in our daily lives, so the slowing down is the hardest part. The idea is to engage slowly and intentionally with nature, to really connect with the natural world."

They listened and took notes for the first two-hour session, and then they were served lunch before going outdoors for the actual experience. Like breakfast, the food was natural and organic: a wild greens salad and a banana oatmeal cookie. Herbal tea accompanied the meal.

"I'll give you all the recipes on Wednesday," Jonas promised them. "It's nice to end a session with a tea that you've concocted from things gathered on your walk."

They were given a free half hour before the afternoon session. Bronwyn sat in the garden and checked her phone for messages. Still nothing from Will. She swallowed her disappointment, but couldn't entirely dampen her concern. *He'll call when he can*, she told herself firmly, determined not to let his silence ruin her enjoyment of the training. *He's being kept busy with interviews and paperwork.*

The afternoon session dismissed her concern about Will and overwhelmed Bronwyn with happiness. She felt entirely in her element. Despite her prior experience with nature meditations, she found herself learning new tricks to use and new ways of looking at nature. They walked slowly through the trees, stopping to feel rough bark, pine needles, and soft leaves. They examined the shapes of leaves, stones, and bugs. They dug their hands into the soil, feeling the loam slip through their fingers back to its earthly home. They laid on the ground on their backs, spending a full half hour watching the clouds drift by and the leaves flutter overhead. Bronwyn hadn't done that since she was a child, and she noticed things she'd overlooked despite the meditative walks she was used to taking. She found she was seeing the world more clearly than she had ever done. Thoughts left her mind, and she just soaked up the natural world until she felt empty and tranquil.

At the end of the day, she fell into bed renewed and relaxed, at peace with life. She even forgave Will for not calling her.

The next two days were more of the same. Each meal was organic and natural, made with local vegetarian ingredients. Tea was served several times each day, and the participants were encouraged to gather wild greens and flowers as they strolled through the forest, bringing them back to supplement a tea buffet fit for a fairy's banquet. Bronwyn was delighted. She, like the others, experimented with various combinations, trying lemon grass with clove and raspberry leaf or calendula with echinacea, cinnamon, and clove. Bronwyn discovered her favorite combination was raspberry leaf with mint, clover flowers and lavender flowers. She resolved to plant as many herbs and flowers as she could in the little sensory garden at the centre so that her wanderers could gather their own tea ingredients.

Other ideas planted themselves in her mind, as well. They ventured away from the garden and into the park, trying a new location each time. She loved the areas that included water, both for its sound and for the opportunity to take her shoes off and immerse her feet in it. She thought about the fountain in the sensory garden, which had turned into a bird bath as its battery-run pump was always flat. Sarah laughed at her. "You can get a solar one." Feeling foolish, Bronwyn wrote it in her notes: solar fountain.

On Tuesday evening, she went to a pub with Sarah and Lucy. There, she discovered a chain downspout that would make beautiful chiming sounds when it rained. She added it to her growing list, as well.

By Wednesday afternoon, she had written pages of ideas and collected a sheaf of recipes for natural meals and teas. All thoughts of Will had diminished as he'd failed to call her and her excitement about the workshop took over. By the time she was handed her certificate, she was almost happy that she'd be able to return home right away and start developing her ideas rather than going to Gloucester to get Lark.

She sat at the table in the garden, chatting with Sarah, after they'd gotten their certificates. She was reluctant to leave her new friend, but they exchanged mobile numbers and promised to keep in touch, to report on the success of their ventures. The session had ended at noon, so she had all day for the drive back to Llangynog. Still relaxed from her experience, she felt in no hurry to get started.

When she finally said goodbye to Sarah, she turned to walk back to the hotel room and stopped in her tracks. Against the whitewashed wall of the hotel stood Will, leaning back and watching her. When he saw she'd noticed him, he grinned and held out his arms.

She ran to him without thought, joy flooding her mind.

He wrapped his arms around her and held her tight to his chest. "Sweetheart," he murmured, his voice husky, "I missed you so much."

338

He didn't let her go. "I just want to go home and sleep for three days and be with you. That's it. That's all I need to be happy right now."

She felt guilty, having enjoyed her training so much while he had been through God knew what back at the station. "Are you okay?" she whispered into his chest.

"I will be." He stepped back then and held her hands, seeming to need to touch her. "Did you have a good time?"

She nodded. "It's been great. 'll tell you about it later. How long were you standing there, watching?"

He looked down at her. "Maybe ten minutes. I liked seeing you happy, beautiful, enjoying the day."

"I wish I'd seen you sooner, though."

He gathered her in close again. She could feel a quiver in his arms around her. "It doesn't matter. I liked watching you from a distance." His voice was soft, with that roughness to it. He seemed tired. He bent to kiss her, a gentle kiss.

"Shall I gather up my things so we can go home?" She tried not to let disappointment creep into her voice.

"When are you supposed to check out here?" He let her go. She could tell he tried now to make his voice natural. "It's only an hour and a half to Gloucester. I told my mother we'd be there for dinner at seven. We have plenty of time."

"I…you said you just want to go home. I thought you meant the cottage."

"I did mean the cottage." He smiled, a tired smile. "I was only dreaming when I said I just wanted to go home. I promised you we'd get Lark and meet my parents, so we're going to do it." He held up a hand to stop her protest. "I already called mother. We're committed now."

"We could go another time. It doesn't have to be today, if you're tired, Will."

"No, I want to go. Lark is excited about it, and I want to get her away for a bit. You don't mind, do you? Having Lark with us for the weekend after we've been apart for the past couple of weeks?"

"I love being with Lark. She's never in the way." Truthfully, she'd rather have Will to herself, but she wouldn't admit it to him. She knew he felt the same, but he was trying to keep his promise to take her to Gloucester, and she loved him for it.

He squeezed her hands. "It looks like I'll be with you at the cottage a lot more for a while anyway. I got suspended again. We'll get plenty of time, just the two of us, after Lark goes back home."

"Oh, Will, I'm sorry. I thought you were the hero."

"They're still trying to decide whether it's a hero or a villain. It'll take some time to sort and, meanwhile, I'll have the next four days to be with you before I have to go back."

She chewed that over in her thoughts. It'd probably be inappropriate to be happy about it, but she couldn't help feeling a tiny surge of contentment. "I thought you were suspended. That's not a very long suspension."

"No, I'll still be on suspension. They're going to have a hearing to decide my fate. It starts on Monday."

A hearing? "What does that mean?" It sounded ominous.

"We'll have to testify before a magistrate about our activities. There'll be witnesses to back up or refute what we say. It'll be for all three of us, Edward, Bowers, and me, to decide whether we're guilty of anything."

"They'll decide how long your suspension will be?"

"Something like that. I don't want to talk about it now. I'm here with you, and that's the last thing I want on my mind. Did you say when you have to check out?"

"I have to check out by one. They gave us extra time because of the workshop."

Will pulled his mobile from his pocket and consulted it. "That gives us about twenty minutes. Have you had lunch?"

She shook her head.

"Then let's get you checked out and find someplace to eat. We can take our time over lunch, and then I want you to show me some of the places you went while you were here. Did you think it beautiful?"

"Yes, it's gorgeous here. Will we have time?"

"Plenty of time. If we leave here by four or five, we'll be on time, even if there's traffic. It's not that far. Come on, let's go."

They went back up to her room, and she stuffed her things into her kit bag and then stood on her toes and kissed him, wishing she had the room longer. She didn't recognize the new Will, this one who seemed exhausted and slow and resigned. "Are you sure you don't want to keep the room an extra night, Will? You could sleep now, and then we could get an early start tomorrow and have breakfast with your parents instead of dinner."

"My mother isn't that flexible," he told her. "Besides, I'm not physically tired. I got some sleep over the past couple of nights to make up for what I lost before. It's more…" he hesitated, "I'm emotionally tired, I guess. It was hard, all of it. We were chasing down clues and trying to decide what to do, and we didn't sleep or eat much. We had to be vigilant, pretty much every moment of every day. And then…" he interrupted the flow of words as if suddenly aware of what he was confessing, "then it was over, but it wasn't, really. We had to answer question after question, and they kept at it for days, hammering us with everything you can imagine and more. I'm sorry I couldn't call you. They took my mobile away." He paused, closing his eyes and then opening them again slowly. "I'm just worn out from it all." He reached out and tucked a lock of her hair away from her cheek. "I want to wander in the forest with you this afternoon before we go. I want you to show me what you learned and do it with me, to take me through it, to help me relax. Most of all, I want to see you when your face is all alight with the happiness I saw earlier when you were talking to that girl. I need the peace you share with me." It was a long speech, and he grinned self-consciously at the end of it. "Sorry. I wasn't going to talk about it just now."

She knew he'd left some of it out, probably much of it. "That's okay. I want you to tell me more as you feel the time's right. For now, though, I'll show you one of our paths and take you through a mindfulness exercise, if you want to."

"Perfect," he said.

They took the MGF. Will obviously enjoyed driving it more than the Land Rover, which they left in the parking lot of the hotel. She took a moment to examine the Land Rover, Will watching anxiously. The windscreen had been replaced, so it looked better, but the big dent in the driver's door would take more time and have to be done later, and there were numerous other dents, as well. "The story for my mother is that we hit a deer on the roadway, if she asks about the damage," Will told her. "My parents already disapprove of my career choice, so they don't need to know this damage was work-related."

"I won't tell."

She directed him to her favorite of the trails they had explored during the workshop. He relaxed into the drive, taking the curves faster than he should, glancing her way to see her reveling in the wind as it blew her hair into tangles. She was wearing the new tee shirt with the Brecon Beacons logo. He hadn't mentioned it. Maybe he hadn't noticed, but she didn't care. She had him back, and that was all that mattered.

They parked the little car and locked it, and then Bronwyn led Will to the trailhead. No one else was about, and she was glad to have the place to herself. Forest bathing was easier without the distraction of hikers' voices disrupting the peace and solitude. She hoped that she and Will would get back to hiking again soon, but that would involve more strenuous movement than she had in mind that day. This day was about moving slowly and taking time.

She took Will's hand as they started down the dirt path. The fall's dead leaves cushioned their footfalls as they strolled slowly, and she took time to point out to Will the tiny things she saw: a blue and white moth fluttering over a puddle of water, a water drop still glistening in the centre of a daisy-like wildflower, a fallen feather on the path. She stopped him and urged him to breathe slowly, to close his eyes and listen. She saw him relax as he followed her instructions, talking quietly to her as he strained to hear the rustle of grass in the breeze, the trilling of a bird he couldn't identify, the buzzing of an insect as it passed them. She helped him with details: the bird a garden warbler, the insect a bee. He listened as she spoke softly.

He swayed a bit, and she took his hand, stroking the skin between thumb and fingers. "What do you smell, Will? Anything?"

He concentrated, and she waited in the silence. A whir of wings marked the passing of a hawk from treetop to treetop. She could smell the sweet scent of flowering spring trees, a mix of wild plum, bluebells, and Welsh poppy. He didn't say anything, but stood still with his eyes closed, letting her stroke his hand.

He took a deep breath and let it out quickly. "I don't think I can do this today, love." He looked over at her, obviously not wanting to hurt her. He pulled his hand away, agitated. "I know you're trying, but I've got too much running through my mind to concentrate right now."

"Let's go sit down," she suggested, waving toward a nearby mossy area beneath a big oak tree. She reached for his hand again, pulling him toward the tree despite his obvious reluctance. She stooped down and brushed at the moss, clearing it of twigs and other debris, and then she sat, pulling on his hand.

He sat down beside her. "I'm sorry. I'm trying to do this with you. I know you help other people this way, and I hoped it would help me, too." Tears glittered in his eyes, and he blinked them away.

"Shhhh," she shushed him. "Come here. Lie down and put your head in my lap. We don't need to have any goals, no trying to banish the bad memories or you wanting to please me by trying out my new skills. Just look up at the clouds and the tree, and try not to think about anything, good or bad. Just be, Will. It's not about trying to experience nature, just let go and be a part of it, of the world."

His lips twisted in doubt, but he did as she'd asked, lying down and putting his head in her lap. She stroked his hair away from his forehead and smiled down at him. "Don't look at me. Look at the sky. Smell whatever tickles your nose. Feel the grass beneath you. Breath in slowly and then out. Listen to your breathing. Let yourself feel it and concentrate on that."

"This stick poking me in the thigh?"

"You can move it away," she told him. "Just be still and try to relax." She sat and let her own thoughts wander, trying to clear her mind. Obviously, he'd had a bad week, and she knew he hadn't told her the worst of it. But this was no time to think of that. Now it was time to heal, to let his mind clear itself of worry and regret and stress, to just be a part of the larger world for a few moments before he had to go back and face it again.

In time, she felt him relax, and when she looked down, he was asleep, snoring softly in her lap. She watched him, matching her breath to his and trying not to move, to wake him. She watched a sparrow hawk soar overhead, riding the loft of the wind, and she saw a grey squirrel scurry up a tree trunk and then sit on a limb, its tail whisking back and forth as it watched her. She let herself be mesmerized by them, focusing on emptying her own mind.

She let him sleep for a while, until she felt they had to get on the road to Gloucester. The idea that she was going to meet Will's parents in just a couple of hours terrified her, but she was glad they were going. It was past time. She couldn't imagine they were as bad as he'd painted them to be.

A group of hikers strode by, voices lively in the quiet of the forest. Will's eyes opened, and he stared up at her, and then recognition came into them and he sat up, swiveling around beside her. "I can't believe I fell asleep."

"Do you feel better?"

He thought it over. "How long did I sleep?"

"Maybe a half hour."

"I do feel better. I feel more relaxed than I have in days." He sounded surprised.

They stopped by the hotel to switch the little MGF for the Land Rover in order to have room for Lark to ride back with them. Bronwyn's nose twitched when she got in. *What's that awful stink?* She tried not to react.

"Sorry, love. I'll get it cleaned. I rode with the windows down to air it out, but it's hard to get rid of some smells."

"What is it?" It smelled like rotten meat.

"I'll tell you later."

She let it go and settled back, enjoying the scenery as they traveled through the park and out the east side of it, despite her growing anxiety. What would they be like? She imagined people like her parents, relaxed and friendly. Surely, they would be? She imagined them older, though, and dressed in more fashionable clothing. What would they serve for dinner? She resolved to eat whatever was on offer, vegetarian fare or not. She wanted to make a good impression, and fussing about dietary needs was not a good start. She started to worry about her tee shirt. She hadn't brought anything nice to wear, dressy trousers or a nicer blouse. She hadn't thought they'd be going after Will failed to call her, and now she chided herself for not being prepared.

They arrived in Gloucester after six, and Will drove to the hotel he was used to staying at. It wasn't fancy, but as he said, it provided a place to sleep and that was all he needed while he was there. She wondered why he didn't stay at his parents' house, but she didn't want to ask. They put their bags in the room, and Bronwyn changed into a clean tee shirt. When she fussed about not having nicer clothes to wear, Will told her he wanted her as she normally was, to be herself. "I want them to meet *you*, not some fake person you think you should be." He took a breath, but the smile she expected was absent. His earlier exhaustion and resignation seemed to have returned. "I want them to meet the real girl I've fallen in love with."

When they drove up to the house and parked, Bronwyn felt like taking a step backward. The house stunned her. A detached Georgian that had been kept up through the years, it loomed large and imposing behind an iron fence. This house cost some serious money. She hadn't imagined Will's growing up in a place like this, and it made her take a second look at him, a look that he didn't miss.

"Don't be put off," he said. "I grew up with some money." He seemed a little embarrassed by it. "Whereas, you grew up with love."

She nodded and followed him through the gate.

Lark had obviously been watching for them from the window. The door flew open as they walked up to the entryway, and she ran out, hugging Will around his waist and then Bronwyn. She'd grown since Bronwyn had seen her last, and she looked more mature. Now almost eight years old, she'd emerged into that 'tween year' phase. There'd be no more pink overalls or frocks for her now; she'd be wearing the uniform of the popular girl at school. Today, that was stretch jeans and a loose white jersey with "Hello Kitty" pictured in sequins on the front. It could be worse, Bronwyn thought, although she missed the little girl look of the past.

A woman stepped out behind her, and a man came out a few moments later. Will's mother was of medium height with expensively-styled and colored hair. Her makeup was flawless, and she wore gray trousers with a pale pink silk blouse and pearl earrings. His father was dressed in black slacks and a sport coat, with a pinstriped blue shirt beneath. To Bronwyn, they looked terrifying, and she hung back beside Will, covering her discomfort by fussing with Lark.

"Hello." Will's mother stepped forward and held out a hand. "I'm Elizabeth, William's mother. This is my husband, Charles."

"I'm Bronwyn," she said needlessly, reaching out to grasp Mrs. Cooper's hand. They already knew who she was, after all. She tried to think what they would expect her to say. "Thank you for having me for dinner." *Oh, God, did that sound like they would be eating her?* She blushed.

Will stepped up and took her hand, greeting his parents with a smile. There was an awkward moment of small talk, and then Will's mother gestured them into the house.

Then began what was probably the worst three hours of Bronwyn's life. They went into a living room set with cream-colored sofas and pale green striped chairs, decorated with fresh roses in vases and candles on the fireplace mantel. Will went to a bar in the corner and brought her back a glass of red wine, holding a mixed drink for himself in his other hand. He'd mixed drinks for his parents, as well, which Lark helped serve with some expertise. She perched on a chair with her own cola and watched with delight as Bronwyn's world fell apart.

"Your parents have a farm, don't they?" Elizabeth Cooper asked with a lift of her perfect eyebrows. Bronwyn explained that the farm had been in the family for generations and that they were experimenting with cattle and organic vegetables at the moment. She could see that her description failed to impress anyone, though, and she faltered. "It was a lovely way to grow up," she concluded weakly. She fought for some subject she could bring up that would steer the conversation away from herself.

She wasn't fast enough. "You have a career in management?" Will must have exaggerated that one, and she wondered why. Bronwyn's job as centre coordinator didn't really qualify as management. She described the centre and faltered again halfway through the tale of St. Melangell when she noticed her hostess' eyes glazing over.

"Bronwyn is an artist," Will offered in his own attempt to help carry the conversation. Modestly, Bronwyn explained that her sketches were of local sites and that they were sold in gift shops. She dropped the name of Bodnant Gardens, hoping it would impress, but she got little reaction, and her eyes wandered to the expensive art on their walls and understood why.

Will's father said almost nothing, listening to the conversation with the blank expression of extreme boredom.

Dinner was served in courses. Bronwyn kept an eye on Will to make sure she was choosing the correct silverware and proportions. Wild sorrel soup was followed by a crisp salad, and then the main of baked pork chops, green beans, and scalloped potatoes followed. Bronwyn dutifully took several bites of the pork chop, thankful that the rest of the meal fit into her usual dietary needs. Will kept her wine glass filled, she suspected in an attempt to help her deal with what he had to know was an uncomfortable situation. He'd warned her, after all.

Once the meal was finished, Will insisted that they leave for the hotel. He promised Lark they'd be over early in the morning to pick her up, and he held Bronwyn's arm as they walked out and through the gate.

He opened her door, leaned over to whisper, "Well done, you," and walked around to get in the driver's side of the car. She wanted to cry. If only she could run off somewhere and be alone for a few minutes, she could rail at the world's unfairness and sob her eyes out, and then she'd be okay. Maybe. But she was stuck. Will was at her side, and in the hotel, there'd be no escape. She'd have to make the best of it and pretend it hadn't been as disastrous as it had been.

In the end, he wasn't as clueless as she thought. He closed the door to their hotel room and turned to her. "You can scream if you want to," he said, "or cry or yell at me, or whatever you need."

She felt tears tickling her eyes. "I was a disaster, Will. I'm so sorry." It wasn't that Will's mother had been intentionally rude to her, but that their worlds were so vastly different that she couldn't have possibly related to Bronwyn if she tried. Maybe she had tried, Bronwyn thought. But in her world, people didn't have farms; they had estates.

They didn't grow organic foods; they spent large amounts of money to eat them. They didn't create art; they collected it, and not the sort that was sold at a touristy gift shop.

He strode over and put his arms around her. "You're never a disaster, love. I told you. It's them. I knew how it'd go, and that's why I put it off for so long."

"They'll never think I'm good enough for you."

He shrugged, arms still around her, and looked down. "It's rather I don't think they're good enough for you. I tried to help, love. I kept your wine glass filled."

She smiled and blinked at the tears. "Thank you. I'd have never made it otherwise."

He released her and nodded toward the bed. "Come on, let's take our minds off all of our problems tonight. I won't rehash my mistakes of the past week if you'll forget and forgive my mother's inquisition, at least for tonight."

"It's a deal," she said, and she stretched up to kiss him..

Chapter Twenty-two

They got a late start the next morning, both feeling lazy and self-indulgent after the stress of the past week. They ordered room service and sat by the window, looking out at the long boats on the river as they slowly ate their way through full-English platefuls. As she scooped the bacon and sausage off her plate onto Will's, she had a fleeting memory of the healthy, organic meals she'd enjoyed during the training and vowed to make an effort to serve more healthy options at home. Now wasn't the time for restraint, though, so she emptied her plate and noted that Will did the same.

Feeling content again, she made a conscious effort not to dwell on what she thought of as the fiasco of the night before. She hadn't imagined Will's mother to be so inquisitive, and she tried to remind herself it wasn't purposeful, that she'd just asked the same sort of questions she'd have asked anyone Will brought home. She knew she hadn't measured up very well, but Will didn't seem to care.

When she tentatively apologized again as they finished their breakfast, he brushed it off. "No worries, love. I knew how it'd go. They don't approve of me, either, so we're in it together, at least." He smiled across the little table. "Lark loves you to pieces, and Edward thought you were brilliant, so you've been a rousing success with everyone who matters."

"My family loves you, too," she told him, thinking it was true. Maddock teased him like a brother, and her parents, although a little put off by their living together, mostly approved of him.

Will didn't mention the case, and Bronwyn left it for him to bring up when he was ready. She knew the basic details from the news reports, and when he was ready, he'd tell her the rest.

Lark was waiting when they parked in front of the house. She ran down the walk to meet them, chattering excitedly. "Will we get there in time to ride Hobbs today? I brought my gear. I wouldn't go without my helmet," she said with a sideways glance at her grandmother. "Are we going anywhere else? I need to know if I packed the right things."

"Do you have your pajamas?" Will queried her, grinning. "That's really all you need."

She grinned back. "I have mine, if you have yours."

Bronwyn blushed and glanced to see how Will's mother was taking the banter. She'd come out onto the porch and stood, watching them, neither smiling nor frowning. There was no sign of Will's father.

To Bronwyn's relief, they made a quick getaway, and she thought they'd be home by early afternoon. They stood in the entrance hall while Lark retrieved her bags, and then hurried her into the back seat and merged onto the M5, which would take them a short distance before they diverted onto something that would take them into Wales. Lark chattered for a little while, obviously excited about the weekend, and then fell quiet. Bronwyn looked back to see her holding a hand-held gaming device in her hands, concentrating on it. She swallowed, glancing at Will, who shook his head. Lark had matured in other ways besides her fashion sense, it seemed.

With Lark along, they couldn't talk about serious issues, so Bronwyn looked out the window and watched the scenery go by. She sat up and stretched to see the river far below as they cruised over the Severn Bridge, crossing into Wales. "Someday I want you to take me to Tintern Abbey," she commented as they passed a sign, and Will signaled and took the next exit off the A466.

"We have time today, unless you want to be home early," he told her, glancing in the rearview mirror at Lark. "Hey, are you up for exploring something different?"

She set the game set aside. "Not a castle?"

"There's a castle just up the road a bit," he said, "if we have time. But I don't think we need to be in a hurry today. Hobbs will still be there tomorrow. Can we spend an hour or two at the abbey, and then maybe check out the castle, too? Chepstow, is it?"

Bronwyn consulted her phone. "Yes. It's really close by, Will."

"I know. Lark and I stopped there once before, and I think she'd like a return trip. Today is as good as any other for that." He glanced at Bronwyn and grinned. "Let's make today a holiday."

Will parked the Land Rover and they paid their admission in an interpretive centre and gift shop. Ignoring the museum displays, they hurried to the abbey grounds and stood still, craning their necks at the arches soaring above them into the sky. Much of the structure remained, its setting idyllic in the peaceful valley next to the River Wye, and Bronwyn imagined long-ago monks conducting their business and singing their prayers of supplication and gratitude within its beautiful walls. Those majestic gothic arches, more than a thousand years old, stretched toward the absent roof, which opened to beams of sunlight that felt as if sent from Heaven itself. It had a spiritual feel, which had of course been its creators' purpose. They'd lived in hovels and huts, but they'd splurged on God's house.

Will took Bronwyn's hand and they wandered slowly through the ancient structure, their eyes drawn upward toward the sky. Lark explored on her own, climbing on a stone bench here and passing through a doorway there, and Bronwyn stopped occasionally to snap pictures of her with her mobile, her reddish curls bright against the aged stone arches. Lark returned the favor, stealing Bronwyn's mobile to snap pictures of Bronwyn and Will as they gazed upward or paused for a kiss inside an arched doorway. Will read the informative signs, calling Lark over to summarize the information from time to time, and they stopped finally to sit on a bench left from a thousand years before.

"It feels like Pennant Melangell," Bronwyn murmured wonderingly. "I didn't think anywhere else would feel like that."

"Someday I'll take you to Stonehenge and Avebury, maybe to Glastonbury, too. I know what you're talking about. There's a spiritual feel to certain places." He hesitated. "Maybe not spiritual, exactly, but you know what I mean. There's a power here that can't be explained."

She nodded. "Ancient people felt it and made them into places of worship. I didn't know you felt it, too. I thought only some people could."

"I'm getting in tune with my mystical side," he teased her, and then he sobered. "I had to tell Edward about your visions, love. I tried not to, but there was no other way he'd believe me. I had to convince him it was worth putting all our efforts on that one ferry landing. I'm sorry."

She couldn't breathe. If she hadn't been sitting down, she'd have collapsed to the ground.

He hurried on. "I know you trusted me to keep it secret, and I always did. But I couldn't this time. Edward was convinced you were part of the drugs operation and that's how you knew the things you did. He thought you'd lead us into a trap. I had no choice, and I promise never to put myself into a position where I have to do it again." He looked sideways at her, and she saw worry in his eyes. "Will you forgive me?"

She put her hands up to her face and rubbed at her cheeks. She felt betrayed, all the peace of Tintern Abbey dispelled by his words. If she couldn't trust Will with her secrets, she couldn't trust anyone. "What did he say?" she asked in a small voice.

"He believed me." Will took a deep breath. "I think, in the end, he was as grateful as I was to have the information you gave us. If not for that, we wouldn't have caught them, love. Finding Billy Davies wasn't crucial, but knowing when the load was coming in on the ferry was. We'd identified what we thought was the first destination for the shipment when it entered Wales, and we got it wrong. If I hadn't known about the lion rampant, we wouldn't have been able to follow them. They'd have gotten away with it."

"What if Edward tells them that I gave you that information?"

He glanced upward at the arches. "He won't. I swore him to secrecy, and he won't betray my trust. I know that, as well as I know anything in life. We agreed that we'd already identified the lorry as soon as it was on the ferry. We said we'd gotten information from a confidential informant, and they'll believe it because we pulled in people from another gang to help us get Morys Howell arrested and unable to direct the dividing up of the load. It'll all tie together, and I know for a fact that anyone who could say otherwise won't be found to talk."

Her head snapped toward him. "What does that mean?"

He blinked and realized what he'd said. "The gang members, love. They won't want to talk about their part in what we did, so they'll just disappear underground for a time. All the investigators will have is my story and Edward's, and we've agreed that it was a CI who told us when and how the shipment was arriving."

She was upset, but she knew he wouldn't have given away her secret lightly. Thank goodness he'd thought it was a vision, and not fairies that had given her that information. She'd have to let it go. "It's okay, Will." She'd be shy with Edward now, but maybe she wouldn't have to see him much.

Lark skipped over then. "Can we go to the castle now?"

Will looked at Bronwyn. "Ready?"

She nodded, still upset with him but accepting that it was too late to change things.

Chepstow Castle was more up Lark's alley, although it lacked the mysticism of Tintern Abbey that drew Bronwyn in. Lark ran up the long walkway and waited impatiently for Will to stroll up and pay their admittance. Rounded towers gave the castle a medieval look, while steep walls dropping to the river below would have made it easy to defend. Lark again took off to explore on her own, and Will allowed it, considering that there were only a few other people on the grounds. He gave her strict instructions to stay away from the cliff edge, and then they watched her skip happily away.

"She'll remember being here before," Will explained, "so she knows what's allowed and what's not."

Bronwyn hadn't had the free time to visit many historical sites with Will and Lark, and now that she was seeing firsthand how excited Lark was, she understood why Will loved to do it. She reached for his hand, and he squeezed hers in return.

"Do you want to walk around or just find a place to sit down while Lark wears herself out?"

"I want to see it," she said, so they strolled through the grounds, walking through open doorways and leaning out through windows to see the steep drop to the river. She could imagine medieval knights and ladies, but also artisans and all the workers it would take to keep a castle like that working. "My ancestors would have been the peons in the fields," she observed.

"Mine made the barrels they put the beer in," Will responded in kind. "Cooper. That's what coopers did. They made barrels."

When they'd finished exploring, they went into the little gift shop, and after they browsed through the things on offer, Will bought Bronwyn a small tapestry table runner and a jar of cherry curd. The shop had samples of the curd for customers to try, and both of them tasted it and knew it was a sale.

"Ah, yes," the cashier commented when she saw their other purchase. "This is the tapestry with the rabbit motif. Very traditional."

Bronwyn smiled, and Will gave her a knowing look. She felt honored that he knew her well enough to guess she'd like one that reminded her more of Pennant Melangell than of Chepstow.

From there, they had to detour inland, adding hours to the drive, but giving Bronwyn a last look at the beauty of the Brecon Beacons with its rugged terrain and sandstone peaks. As much as she'd enjoyed Tintern Abbey and the castle, Bronwyn regretted not having time to get out and hike to one of the lakes. The lessons from her training session were still fresh in her mind, and the feeling of peace eased back as memories of meeting Will's mother faded into less of an obsession.

Will left Bronwyn and Lark to drive the Land Rover back while he led the line with his little convertible. Bronwyn was surprised that Lark insisted on riding with her, and flattered, as well. Now that she had Lark to herself, Bronwyn chatted with her about how she might want to decorate her bedroom at the cottage. Not surprisingly, Lark had already given it some thought and had definite ideas about what she'd like, most of which they couldn't afford. Also, not surprisingly, a horse theme was in order, and Bronwyn's mind spun with money-conscious ideas of how to accomplish the look Lark wanted without spending money they didn't have.

They arrived at the cottage in the early evening, too late for a ride on Hobbs, but still in time for dinner at the Tanat Inn. "This is a one off," Will told them as he paid for their order. "I've been suspended without pay, and that situation may last for quite a long time. Money could be tight for a while."

Bronwyn felt a twinge of guilt over the tapestry. "I can pay you back for the tapestry when I get another check from Bodnant Gardens. Tourist season will pick up soon, and I usually sell a few sketches right away."

"No," he told her, "that was by way of thanking you for the tip. I told you, without that, we'd have failed. I'll make Edward chip in on it when I see him next."

After dinner, they walked up the main road through Llangynog to the farm to retrieve Daisy from Bronwyn's parents, flashing torches through the darkness to light the way. "Can I take her on her leash when we walk back?" Lark wondered.

"That's a great idea," Will answered her. He seemed, to Bronwyn, to be more relaxed again now. She didn't know if that was down to her efforts with nature meditation or to the fact that the ordeal of her meeting his parents was behind them. Either way, it made her happy to see him more like his usual self.

Daisy romped out with the sheepdogs to greet them when they walked up the driveway, racing in excited circles around them all. They stopped to pet her, and then went on to the house, where Bronwyn's mum and dad were sitting on the stoop with Maddock, having an evening drink.

"It's the conquering hero back from saving the world from illicit drugs," Maddock greeted them. "It took you too long, but I guess you got it done in the end."

355

Bronwyn didn't want Will reminded of what she'd tried so hard to dispel. "He can't talk about it, Madd."

"Top secret, that," Maddock said, with a grin. "You had our Bronwyn scared near to death."

Will glanced at her. "It was a one-off. Most of my assignments aren't anything like that one. It's just a relief to have it done."

"I'm guessing you're on suspension while they sort it all out?" Maddock pressed.

"Something like that. They're still deciding whether to thank us or lock us up."

Bronwyn's mum stood up and beckoned to Lark. "Bronwyn doesn't want you reminding Will of all that," she scolded Maddock. She bent down to address Lark. "I hear you're going to decorate your own room at the cottage."

"Uncle Will said I could do it however I want," Lark bubbled. She hopped from one foot to the other, back and forth, her curls swinging. "I want horses."

Bronwyn's mum straightened and beamed a smile toward Bronwyn. "So did Bronwyn when she was your age. All she thought about was ponies."

It wasn't all I thought about, but maybe Mum encouraged the horses bit rather than the fairies. "I did," she said. "I even had a comforter on my bed that was horses."

"I still have it in the attic closet," her mum said, surprising Bronwyn. "Maybe Lark would like to see it. She could have it if she wants."

Bronwyn nodded, and Lark skipped happily ahead of her mum into the house.

Lark had never seen the cottage, so it was with some excitement that they led her inside and showed her around, ending with her bedroom.

"Can we decorate tonight?" she begged. Bronwyn's mum had come up with a whole box of things from Bronwyn's childhood she'd saved, along with the comforter.

Bronwyn looked at Will, who shrugged, his face worn. He'd had a stressful couple of weeks, followed by the awkward dinner with his parents and then the long day's drive back to Llangynog. He had to be knackered. "You go have your drink and relax," she told him. "Lark and I will get the room done, and then you can come see after you've rested a bit."

She felt energized again. She couldn't help a feeling of pride in her family, seeing how her mum had taken Lark under her wing that evening. Even Maddock's teasing seemed friendly, rather than mean. A thought nagged at her, though. Why did Will seem to fit so neatly into her world while she was a complete failure in his? She pushed it aside to ponder later.

Will squeezed her arm in thanks, and left them to it. Bronwyn opened the big box, finding newspaper-wrapped memories from her childhood. There was the Staffordshire draft horse, a creamy chestnut colored treasure that was probably a rare collectible these days. A trio of bay-colored Beswick foals frolicked next to a Beswick bay mare on the windowsill once she'd unwrapped them. She nearly cried aloud when she opened the next package: a rearing hunter carrying a red-coated rider. It had been her favorite. She scrambled in the box, opening smaller treasures fast until she came upon the fox that matched the hunter. She'd loved those as a child, and seeing Lark's rapt eyes, she knew that she would treasure them, too.

They spread the comforter on the bed, and then Bronwyn encouraged Lark to put on her pajamas. The bottom of the box had been filled with Bronwyn's reading treasures, and Lark was eager to start on one of the easier chapter books there.

Bronwyn left her and called Will in to bid her goodnight. She watched from the doorway as he admired the horse collection that had now been passed on to the next generation and then kissed a forefinger and touched it to her forehead. "Sleep well, love."

He joined her in the doorway for a moment, looking back to see Daisy curled up beside Lark, both of them content, and he gave Bronwyn a look that told her she'd done it all just right.

The next morning Lark was up early and eager to ride Hobbs. The pony was old now, but that made him perfect for a child to learn on, and

Bronwyn thought he enjoyed the extra attention. She watched as Lark brushed him, pulling out the last of his winter coat and unsnarling his mane and tail, and then she instructed her as she helped check his feet for stones. Lark was strong enough now to lift the saddle on by herself, and Bronwyn stood by as she tightened the girth, helping with the final tug.

They led him out to the pasture, and Lark got on. Will watched from the gate as Bronwyn walked beside the pony, making sure that Lark held the reins correctly and sat up straight. They did two loops and then Bronwyn came to stand beside Will, allowing Lark to ride on her own. She did it well, turning the pony this way and that and urging him into a trot.

"I remember another little girl doing that." Bronwyn's dad had come up behind them.

She smiled. "One of my happiest memories."

"It's good to see another generation enjoying that old pony. He was getting fat, just grazing the pasture all day long." He opened the gate and came through. "Your mum says you are invited for dinner tonight, if you're free. Maddock's group is coming over, too."

"We'd enjoy that," Will spoke up.

Bronwyn was glad he had. She hadn't enjoyed dinner with his parents, but she liked to think that he enjoyed time with hers, and the sense of pride she'd felt the night before was still with her. "Lark will want to ride again after dinner," she warned him. "And Maegan, too."

"That's okay. We didn't have anything else planned." He was watching Lark on the pony, his face relaxed into a smile. "Giving her the riding gear for Christmas was a great idea. She loves it."

She looked a little overdressed for the pasture, but she was at an age where she was probably pretending to be riding in a show ring. Her copper curls bounced as Hobbs trotted, and Bronwyn felt content. Maybe she should get a horse for herself, she thought. Then she and Lark could ride together. It would give them something concrete to bond over.

Maddock came out of the barn and saw them. "Hey," he called, "I might have some free time this afternoon. I thought I could help Will build a fence around that garden patch, if he's willing. Not that he'd need my help."

Will grimaced. "That'll be a dream come true, you building the fence and me pretending to be useful."

Maddock laughed. "I could show you again how to start the lawn mower, too."

Bronwyn listened to them, happy that they enjoyed sparring over silly things. *Like brothers*, she thought, quickly banishing the thought. She was getting far ahead of herself on that. Will was a boyfriend, not a husband, and if he and Maddock teased each other, they did it as friends, not family.

After a bit, Lark turned Hobbs toward them, the grin on her face a treasure in itself. She sat on the pony, asking Bronwyn questions about horses that she could mostly answer, with an occasional query to Google.

Her dad watched, amused, as he worked nearby. Finally, after a question about the history of the Welsh pony breed had been thoroughly explained, he interrupted them. "Hobbs probably needs a little break and a bite to eat. I have two lambs that need feeding, Lark. Would you like to help me with them?"

Lark's eyes lit up. "Can I?" she addressed Will.

"Sure, why not?" He sent a calculating look in Bronwyn's dad's direction. "Maybe Bronwyn and I could go for a little walk meanwhile?"

"You go wander on that trail of Bronwyn's," he replied easily. "Leave this young lady to me. She and I will get Hobbs unsaddled and feed those lambs. Maybe she could help me check on a couple of other newborns in the pasture, too."

Feeling grateful to her dad, Bronwyn set out with Will and Daisy across the pasture and over the stile. Spring was in full splendor that morning, with sun shining between puffy white clouds and a warmth on her cheeks that promised summer days to come. Oak worms littered the path, softening their footfalls, their slight woody fragrance just barely discernable. No wind scattered them down, and most had already fallen. Rowan trees almost glowed with their white blooms, and the evergreens had taken on spring hews of bright, almost lime green edging darker boughs. Bluebells lined the path. If she looked further away, Bronwyn saw tiny Welsh poppies and butterwort in bloom. A dragonfly buzzed by, low to the ground, and birds trilled their songs from the trees. Daisy dashed to and fro, chasing shadows and smells.

She didn't stop Will until they came to the rock beside the pool of water. She climbed onto the rock, and he followed her, settling across from her, legs folded beneath them.

"Now I see how you grew up," he commented as he reached out for her hand, holding it in both of his. "It's a beautiful life."

She met his eyes. "It's not all riding your pony and feeding the lambs. Someone has to muck out that barn and weed Mum's flower beds and clean that big old house. We had chores, lots of them. And school here wasn't so much fun. You have to ride the bus for hours, and there aren't so many kids so it's harder to find some who share your interests." No one else saw the Welsh fairies; she was bullied for that until she learned to keep her secrets close.

"But you grew up close to nature. Things move slower here. You have more time. Your parents have more time to spend with you."

"Will Lark go to boarding school someday?"

Will nodded. "She'll probably go this next year. We all went when we were eight."

"I can't imagine it." Bronwyn couldn't. To be sent away so young, to live communally while still a child…it was unthinkable to her.

"I don't suppose you can. But like I said, your situation was different. It would be harder to leave when your family was so involved. I can't explain it well, but it was different for us."

She squeezed his hand and looked down into the pool of water, seeing nothing there but the stillness of the bright day, the sun's reflection making the dark water look bluer. She waited, hoping Will could tell her about what had happened. He'd been reluctant so far, but now they were alone, without Lark, and in this remote place, perhaps it was time to let more of it out. "What's going to happen, Will?" she encouraged him finally, when he remained silent too long.

"To me? My job?" He dropped her hand and looked away, and then he started to talk, detailing everything he and Edward had done.

He started calmly enough, telling her about going into the station, researching Billy Davies and Morys Howell, realizing that Howell could be an important man in the operation they wanted to stop. He described his impulse to confide in Bowers, and she could see him grow more agitated as he described the mixed emotions going through his mind.

"I can see why you did it in the end, though," she told him, wanting to be supportive of the decisions he'd made.

He looked at her earnestly. "It was the biggest decision I had to make," he said, "but if I didn't tell him what we were doing, there was no way to get Notley out of the way. You know Notley, how he feels about me. If he'd suspected that I was working with Edward, off the record as it was, he'd have done whatever he could to see me fired from the force, even dead, if it came to that. So, that's what did it in the end, figuring out how to get Notley out of the way. Bowers had to support me in that, had to send him off on a fool's errand to keep him busy elsewhere. It was the only way it would work. But I took a chance. I knew Edward suspected Bowers, too, and if Edward had been right, we'd be dead right now, both of us. Edward told me not to say anything to anyone, and I did it anyway, in the end."

"You made the right choice, Will. It came out okay."

"I was lucky, that's all. In the end, Bowers had to admit that he knew what we were up to. Otherwise, he couldn't have brought in Scotland Yard." He paused, thinking, and Bronwyn knew there was more he hadn't yet told her. "He's taken some of the blame away from me that way."

"Edward will forgive you," she said softly.

"He already has. He had no choice. If I hadn't talked to Bowers, if he hadn't called in Scotland Yard, we'd be dead. I wasn't exaggerating about that. It was a close call, just minutes before it'd have been too late."

His words fell between them, hard and terrifying. She didn't dare breathe.

His head jerked as he realized what he'd said. He looked at the sky, silent, not wanting to meet her eyes.

She waited. Maybe he was making it sound worse than it was, but she didn't think so. "Will?"

He turned his head away. "I can't talk about that part yet, not while the investigation is still going on."

It was an excuse, and they both knew it. He'd never kept anything like that from her before. "It's okay, Will." She didn't have any other words for him right then.

He was silent again for a moment, and then he looked down at the rock they sat on. "There were these two guys," he began, and then he told her about the men who'd confronted him and Edward, how they'd gone back the next night and set them up. "They were the ones who beat up the Land Rover."

"But they didn't hurt you?"

"No." The awkward moment had passed, and now he was comfortable telling the story again. "They were all muscle, no brains. Edward and I handled them just fine." He told her about their arrest and how it helped, but didn't really draw out the person they really wanted to catch.

She smiled encouragingly, and he shifted on the rock. "Hard seat, this," he said.

"I sit here all the time," she told him. "This is where a lot of my art comes from."

"I know. I've recognized it." He paused. "It was your tip that made the difference, love." He leaned over to look down at the pool of water. "You saw a lion rampant there, and then I knew who to follow." He didn't ask how she'd known what day the shipment was coming over on the ferry or what time, and she knew he wouldn't. He'd given her space and hadn't questioned things she told him that she'd have to have heard, not seen. Maybe he really didn't want to know.

"I can't say much more," he told her then. "They actually arrested us, Edward and I, and kept us locked up for a few days while they questioned us over and over. That's the real reason I couldn't call you, and that's why I was so tired, that and the fact that we didn't get any sleep while we were on the case. We couldn't use a credit card or an ATM, and we couldn't risk checking into a hotel anyway. There are cameras everywhere, and Mathews had people monitoring them. We suspected it then, and now we know it for sure. We slept in the Land Rover when we could, and we ate takeout or things from the supermarket. But it was being questioned over and over again afterwards, the mental strain, that really got to me. I didn't know what

Edward was saying, and I didn't want to give away more than I had to."
He looked at her. "Some of the things we did were illegal, and a lot of it
was unethical."

"They let you go, though. That has to be a good sign."

He nodded. "Maybe. They let me go, but not Edward, not yet.
Maybe Bowers was responsible for that, I don't know. I'm not allowed
to talk to him, nor to Edward. When I go back in next week, they'll talk
to me more after they've done the initial investigation. They have to see
if evidence supports my statements, and I've told the truth as much as I
can, so it should."

His job was his life. "I'm sure they will know you only did what
you had to," she assured him, but she wondered. This was his second
suspension in a year. They wouldn't overlook it this time.

"After that, they'll have the hearing to decide if there's to be a trial.
It's all going to take some time, and I won't know what's going to happen
with my job until they finish."

"That won't take up your weekends. You'll be able to be here with
me?"

He smiled, but he didn't answer her. Instead, he slid off the rock
and stretched. "We'd better get back. I don't want your dad feeling
we're taking advantage of him."

"He'll never feel that. He enjoys Lark; she's like another
grandchild, one that reminds him of me, poor child. But you do have a
fence to build." She slipped off the rock.

"What are you going to do while I'm fencing with your brother?
And yes, I did mean to say it that way."

She laughed. "Lark and I are going to have an art lesson. Since we
have no money for room décor, I thought I'd hang a string and she could
pin up whatever she creates. That won't cost us a penny, and I think
she'll like it."

"So do I," Will agreed. "Thank you for putting up with her this
weekend. I...I'm just going to say this one thing, and then I'll leave it.
There was a moment when I didn't think I'd ever get to see her grow
up." He stopped walking and looked away again, staring blankly at the
trees. "I wouldn't ever get to see how she'd do at uni, or what career
she'd choose, or who she'd someday marry. It crushed me, and that was

the worst of it. I didn't care so much about dying, but I regretted not being here for Lark." He looked back at her. "And for you. All I could think was that I wanted to see it through, to see where life takes the two of us. It was unbearably sad to give that up." He bent forward and kissed her lightly. "I've been given a second chance, and believe me, I'm not going to squander it."

"Every day is precious," she said.

"Yes, it is." He smiled then, and the tension seemed to leave him. "Let's go home."

Chapter Twenty-three

He hadn't meant to tell Bronwyn so much. His emotions were still raw, and the terror of that night haunted him day and night, to the point where he didn't know if his life would ever be what it had been before. Still, for all he'd told her, he'd left out just as much. He didn't see how he could ever give her the details of what had happened. She'd get some of it from the news, but he'd rather she not know just how close to death he'd been or how ashamed he was about the terror he'd felt at that moment. Yes, he'd told her the rescue had come just in time, but without specific details, she'd never be able to actually picture it, to see how hopeless the situation had been, to know that he'd thought the last moments of his life were passing by, to know he'd been unable to stop the tears that had fallen as he'd sat slumped on that floor, helpless.

He'd known before he committed to it that they'd be in danger, but he'd been arrogant enough to think that, with Edward at his side, they would be invincible. He'd missed working with Edward and, he was able to admit it now, he'd created in his mind a partnership even better than the reality of it. He'd thought they might fail; that possibility had loomed large. He'd assumed he'd lose his job. But he'd never thought it would cost their lives. Not once.

And then, suddenly, they'd been waiting for death in that oversized garage, waiting for the last load to be complete so that they could be shot and their murderer gone before someone came to check on the gunfire. He'd nearly lost control when he realized they'd been saved, but he'd retained enough dignity through it all to contain himself until he was alone the next morning, after they'd questioned him initially and let him rest in a cell away from everyone else. There, he'd relaxed and the tears had come, despite his efforts to stave them off. He'd cried without thought then, his mind screaming silently in terror and relief and exhaustion. Then, spent, he'd slept soundly on that hard mattress in the lonely cell, waking the next morning only to find that it all came roaring back. He knew he was seriously messed up mentally, and he only hoped that time would push it away far enough to the back recesses of his brain that he could somehow get past it.

Being with Bronwyn brought him back to a semblance of himself. He knew that. The calmness of her, the connections with nature and the world, created a peace that surrounded her and engulfed everyone who came into contact with her. That was why she was so good at her job at the centre. She gave people what they came for – a sense of tranquility and spirituality that had nothing to do with religion especially, but that calmed and centered them. Of course, she was lovely to look at, but it was that peace of her that attracted him most, if he were to admit it. When he'd lain in her lap and watched the sky and listened to her soft voice murmuring to him, it was the first moment that he'd felt he could somehow, someday, be himself again.

But first, he had to get through the investigation and hope, beyond hope, that they'd give him another chance to prove he could follow orders and work with a partner to solve major crimes. He'd resented his transfer in the beginning, but now he really enjoyed what he did. And he wanted to keep on doing it.

He'd been given a couple of days respite, but he'd been instructed to report back on Monday and then to stay in Caernarfon until the investigation was complete. He'd been greedy, hardly able to take his eyes off Bronwyn and Lark, grateful for a second chance to see where life took them. Both of them. It was funny what a near-death experience did to a person, he mused. He'd known they were important to him, but he hadn't pictured them being his last thoughts in life. Maybe he needed to reflect on his life's priorities. He wanted to ask Bronwyn to come back to Caernarfon with him, but he knew she couldn't, not with having taken the previous week off and the St. Melangell's Day celebration coming so soon. Maybe that was for the best. He wouldn't be good company once his mind was forced back to the events of the past week and a half. He didn't want her at the hearings, either. He just wanted to come home to her each night when the day's trials were over.

Friday and Saturday had flown by, much faster than he'd have liked. Despite his exhaustion, he'd enjoyed exploring the abbey and the castle with his two ladies, as he'd thought of them then. Bronwyn had loved the abbey. He'd been curious to see if other places affected her like Pennant Melangell did, and it seemed they did have an effect. That was interesting. She'd been filled with excitement after the workshop, and he'd tried not to dampen it with his neediness.

Lark loved riding the pony, and he'd loved seeing how well she fit into the life Bronwyn had grown up with. If only he could give her that, he would. Growing up in the country, close to nature, with an extended family who enjoyed and encouraged her…his parents would never agree to it, though, so he knew it was pointless to dream. And he couldn't make it happen, not with him living part time in Llangynog and part time in Caernarfon. Even if he got his job back, and that was a big question mark right now, and even if Bowers allowed him to work from Llangynog, he'd still have plenty of days when he'd be in Caernarfon or off somewhere else working a case. Lark would have to struggle along with his parents, just as he'd done at her age, and he thought she'd turn out fine.

Maddock ended up having an emergency with the sheep, so the fence didn't get built. Will found himself hoping that Maddock wouldn't find the time to get it done before he could come back and do it himself. He wanted to prove to Maddock he could do the manly chores that kept a household running, even if it would have been nice to share the labour with someone who knew what he was doing.

They spent Sunday morning lazily. Bronwyn and Lark cooked him a full English breakfast, and Lark served it to him in the conservatory with a wildflower on the tray and an air of pride on her face. Afterwards, they'd taken her for a last ride on Hobbs, and then he'd had to kiss Bronwyn goodbye, with promises of getting her Land Rover repaired soon and coming back as soon as they released him to do so. At least there was a Land Rover to repair. He'd learned long after the fact that the Citroen had disappeared from the lay-by where they'd left it. A search later by the local constabulary turned up the Land Rover, parked on a side street with the keys under the floor mat.

Lark was quiet as they drove south through Wales, watching the countryside go by and ignoring the video game that had entertained her just a few days before. He was guiltily grateful for her silence. He had a lot to think about, now that the little holiday was over. He'd have given most anything to know what Edward and Bowers had said in their interviews, but he knew he couldn't know until the hearings, when he'd watch their testimony, as they'd watch his. He thought of what he'd told his inquisitors before, at least what he could remember telling them, and he hoped his story had been consistent. They'd called in a solicitor, Owen Gittens, for him, and the man had listened to Will and taken notes, but hadn't objected to him telling them anything. He'd been an older man, well-dressed in a suit with a red and yellow striped tie, and Will assumed he knew what he was doing. When they'd talked alone, he'd spoken of a plea deal. That sounded ominous to Will. He didn't want a plea deal. He wanted to be declared innocent and to get his job back.

He glanced at Lark, concerned by her unaccustomed silence. "Are you okay?"

She turned away from the window to look at him. "Did you like boarding at school, Uncle Will?"

So that was it. "Yeah, it was fine," he told her. "You're going to have an amazing time, but that's a whole summer away. It's too soon to worry about it now."

She gave him a skeptical look.

"No, really, you will love it when it's time. It's like you're living in a world where everyone is your own age, and it's really fun. There are a few rules, but they're easy, and there's plenty of time to play and chat with your friends. On weekends and holidays, you don't have to go home. You'll be invited to friends' houses, and it'll be wonderful. I wouldn't lie to you. You'll love it."

She nibbled at her bottom lip. "It's only, I always thought they'd send me to school, like you did, and I thought it might be fun, like you said. But now, Grandmother says I might go to Canada instead of boarding school, to live with Uncle George."

Will reeled. He gripped the steering wheel tightly and slowed his speed, changing lanes so as to be in the slower lane. "Canada?"

"That's what Grandmother says. I don't want to go."

"Did you tell her that?" Why on earth would they think to send her to Canada, to an uncle she didn't even know? Surely, they could manage summers with her at home and then send her off to school for the rest of the year?

"Yes, I told her. I wanted to call you, but she said no, I shouldn't. She wants to talk to you about it first."

Oh, they'd talk, all right. "I'll talk to her today. Why didn't you tell me this before?" He didn't need to deal with something like this, not when he already had so much on his mind. A surge of anger left him shaking. He gripped the steering wheel harder.

Lark was watching him. "I didn't want to ruin our holiday." She hesitated, and then blurted, "I want to come live with you and Bronwyn." Her mouth was set in a straight line and her eyes were defiant. "Please? I'll be really good."

He hadn't anticipated this. "Sweetheart, I'd love that more than anything. I really would. But my job keeps me out nights and I don't have regular hours. It just wouldn't work. Your grandparents wouldn't allow it, and they are in charge right now." He thought desperately. "Listen, how about if I can talk Grandmother into boarding school instead of Canada, and you come for holidays and weekends sometimes, like you do now? Maybe we can find a school that's nearer Llangynog so it'll be easier and you could come more often."

"Would you do that?" His heart broke at the hope in her voice. "Would we have to wait until summer's over and I go to school, or could I come stay with you sooner?"

"I don't know. I'll check," he promised her, and then his thoughts flitted back and forth between Lark's announcement and the investigation. He was worried.

"Lark, love, why don't you go put your things away? I want a private word with your grandmother." They arrived back at his parents' house just after noon. His father was nowhere in sight, but his mother

369

met them at the door. He pushed past her and walked into the living room. "Can we sit down for a minute?"

Lark cast him a heartbreaking look of hope as she followed his orders, while his mother's face set into firm determination. "Let's go into the study then," she suggested, her voice measured.

He nodded and followed her into the small room off the entry hall, closing the door behind him. Turning to face her, he swallowed, trying to keep his temper from exploding. "Lark tells me she is to be sent to Canada to live with George." His voice sounded steady to him and he hoped it did to her, as well.

"Yes, that's right," his mother answered. "I intended to tell you when you came to pick her up, but you brought Bronwyn along and it didn't seem the right time."

"Why?"

She blinked at him. "Why what? Why didn't it seem right to tell you with Bronwyn at your side? She's a stranger to us, William, that's why. I knew you would react poorly, and I didn't want a scene with her there."

"That's not what I meant. Why send her to Canada? She doesn't even know George. Why would you do that?" He felt his voice rising with emotion, and he took a breath, trying to regain control.

She took a moment. "Sit down, William, please." She gestured toward the chairs by the fireplace.

He swallowed his anger and strode over to the chairs, planting himself in one of them.

She sat in the other and turned toward him. "I haven't said anything, William, because it never seemed the right time to discuss Lark's future." Uncharacteristically, she hesitated, and he frowned, suddenly afraid of what might come next.

"What's going on, Mother? Obviously, it's not just an impulse, sending Lark away. It's something more, isn't it? You've been thinking about this for a while."

She nodded, taking her time despite Will's obvious impatience. She picked up a pillow and turned it over, setting it back in place. "Your father has been having trouble with his memory." Her voice was quiet.

He tried to take it in. "Father? How long has this been going on?"

"At first it was just little lapses, maybe for a little over a year now, but it's gotten bad enough he hasn't been able to work for the past few months."

"But he's always gone when I come by," Will pointed out. "You implied he was at work."

"He goes to the office and they let him consult on cases, just to make him feel useful, I think. He is still an owner in the firm, so they don't exactly know how to handle what's happening."

"Has he seen a doctor?"

She frowned at him. "Of course, he's seen doctors. Did you think we'd neglect his care?"

He sucked in his frustration. "And?"

"He has Alzheimer's, William."

"Alzheimer's." Will felt stunned as he tried to take it in. His capable, ambitious father...he couldn't picture it.

"And as it happens, he will need more and more care as time goes on."

"So, you want Lark out of the way."

"Don't say it like that," she reacted sharply. "We've done our best by her, and we love her, too."

Will waited. He could think of no response to her outburst that wouldn't anger her more.

After a moment, she went on. "We thought sending her away to school, like we did with the rest of you, would be enough, but the reality is, it won't be. I'd still have to drive her back and forth on free weekends and holidays, and then there are the long summer breaks. We could probably make it work for a while, but a lot can happen in a short time with this medical issue, and I just won't be able to manage it for long, William, not even if we hire help. I've decided it's best to get her settled once and for all rather than making her adjust to school and then to Canada after. It's all rather overwhelming." She blinked back what he took for tears, which surprised him. "I called George and asked him if he'd consider taking her on, and he agreed."

Will couldn't stop himself. "You didn't even consider asking me?"

"George has a more stable life than you do. His job is secure and doesn't require him to be out unexpectedly at night or in distant locales.

371

He's married, and someone is home to take care of the children when they aren't at school. I know you're hurt, but it's the best choice for her, William, it really is. You'll see that once you've calmed down enough to think it through."

"I don't need to think it through, Mother. I'm the one Lark knows. She loves her time with me. She just asked me in the car if she could stay with me. Surely that must count for something?"

"You know that you can't take on a child right now, William. I will not allow Lark into that sort of situation."

"What sort of situation? I have a stable job, too. I know you've never approved, but I'm good at it, and other people in police work manage families just fine. I could handle it."

She lowered her eyes and looked toward a window, avoiding his gaze. "I won't allow Lark to repeat the choices her mother made."

"Choices?" Realization settled in. "You mean Bronwyn and I living together, don't you?" He tried to keep the fury out of his voice, with limited success. "You think we're a bad example for her." He felt the anger overtaking him and tried to push it away. "Lark isn't Julia. She is nothing like her mother. And Bronwyn and I have a great relationship. We're committed to each other, which is a pretty nice example for Lark to be exposed to, if you think about it. We both love spending time together and with her. For us, Lark wouldn't be a burden like she will be for George. You know it's true. Just because we aren't married, it doesn't mean we can't be a good family for her."

"I won't consider it, William. End of discussion."

"How about this, then?" Desperation made him feel helpless, but he was just too exhausted with it all to think clearly. "Let me check and see if I can find a school that takes boarders nearer to us, and then I'll take her on most weekends and holidays and in the summer. That way you still get to see her, and she doesn't have to go live in a foreign country with an uncle she's never met." He watched her for a reaction, which was slow in coming. "Don't answer me now. Please, though, just think about it, okay?" He hesitated. "I know you're facing a tough time ahead, Mother. This is one way I can try to lighten your load. Please let me do this. I won't be a bad influence. I'll take good care of her."

She closed her eyes and nodded slightly. "I'll think about it, William, before doing anything final."

Outside, he slammed into his car and drove away fast. He wanted to kick something, to scream and yell, and mostly, to run away to some tropical beach or Africa or something so he didn't have to think about it all. Stress overwhelmed him. He felt hot and dizzy, and he pulled over before getting on the motorway and got out of the car, thinking to recover before getting into traffic.

He stood beside the car, one hand on the hood to steady himself. *Take a breath. You've got this.* But he didn't really feel in control, not with this on top of everything else. How dare his mother try to interfere with his personal life? How dare she try to impose her morals on him, and use Lark to do it? He kicked at the near tyre in frustration, and then let out a loud yell. He hoped no one was watching his tantrum.

Then, he stopped moving and stood still, head bowed, until he felt in control again. He'd have to make a plan so he could face it all. He had plenty of time to think during the four-hour drive back to Caernarfon. Decisions about Lark would have to wait. The backlash from the case had to be addressed first. His mother would never let Lark stay if she knew his job was in jeopardy, so trying to save his job had to be his first priority.

Back in the car, he focused his thoughts on the interrogations he'd been through since his arrest. They wanted every detail of what he and Edward had planned to do and had actually done. The way he figured it, they had four things they could charge him with. The first was insubordination. They'd try to say he'd acted on his own, without proper authorization. He'd tried to protect himself from that by confiding in Bowers, and there was also the argument that he and Edward hadn't known who all was involved in the drugs business, so they had no one they could trust to go to for authorization to investigate it. Additionally, there was the legitimate issue of the Billy Davies case. Semi-legitimate, he corrected himself. It had ceased being a reasonable inquiry once Davies' body was found. That's why they'd hidden it, which brought up the next point against him.

He signaled and passed by two lorries he'd been following for a few miles, and then he moved back in ahead of them and let his thoughts take over again. Hiding a dead body was against the law. No solicitor could argue otherwise, and Will saw no way around that charge. Not only had they moved the body to a place where it wouldn't be found as quickly, but they'd retrieved it later and used it to frame Morys Howell. None of that was reasonable or legal by any stretch of the imagination. His only chance was to hope someone would agree that extraordinary measures had to be taken in order to draw Mathews out. He didn't think it'd be a strong enough defense, though. How much time do you get for using a corpse to enable a false arrest? He had no idea what they'd even call that crime. Was that the willful obstruction Williams had mentioned? Or what else had he said Will was guilty of? Conspiring to pervert the course of justice, that was it. On reflection, it could be either charge, or both. He sighed.

Making a false police report was another charge he'd have to answer for. While the men who'd vandalized the Land Rover might have been arrested for that crime, they probably would have made bail and been back out to participate in the distribution of the drugs had Will and Edward not planted drugs in their car. The two things, combined, assured they'd be off the street for at least a few days. He'd admitted to planting the drugs. He didn't know what Edward had said. If they'd had time to plan it, maybe they'd have gotten away with saying they knew nothing about it, that the drugs must have already been there. Not knowing how long they'd been followed, though, Will thought it prudent to be truthful. Someone might have been aware of how they'd arranged it. They hadn't really filed a false report in that case, though. The men had caused their own arrest when they decided to destroy the Land Rover. As for Morys Howell, though, that was all down to them. Not only had their actions led to his arrest, but they'd used known criminals to get it done. Definitely conspiring, then.

Discouraged, he wracked his brain for other crimes they could pin on him. He couldn't think of anything, but that didn't mean they wouldn't. Scotland Yard had been leading the investigation and, thus, interviewing him, but the ethics branch of his own unit had also been present. Even if charges were dropped on the crimes he'd committed, much of what he'd done had not been up to department standards. Losing his job wouldn't be as bad as going to prison, but he'd prefer neither to happen.

He pulled over then and tried to call Edward, with no success. If he was still being confined, they wouldn't let him answer calls. If they'd let him out, he might not have had time or money to buy a new mobile, his own having been lost in the confusion. Maybe when he got back to the flat, they could connect somehow. He really needed to talk to him.

By the time he drove through the city walls and entered Caernarfon, he felt he'd gone over every eventuality and strategy he could imagine. He hoped there wouldn't be a criminal trial. He didn't know how he could ever handle that. But if there was one, he hoped it would take place in England so as to be far away from his friends in the department. He'd talk to his solicitor in the morning. Meanwhile, he'd try not to worry over it.

His flat was cold and had an empty feel to it. He opened the window to let in the sea breeze and set about cleaning it up. He and Edward hadn't bothered making the bed or washing up when they'd left, and now it suffered from the lack of care. The stink of the sea-soaked clothes he'd worn to wade through the water made his stomach churn, and a moldy half-loaf of bread on the counter didn't help. He tried Edward's mobile number again, but there was still no answer. He binned the trash and stuffed a load of laundry into the washer with copious amounts of detergent, then swept the floor and washed the dishes. When he thought the flat presentable again, he shrugged into a light jacket and went out into the late afternoon. He thought he could grab something to eat and then stop by the grocery to do some shopping. All this would keep him busy and keep his mind off things so that maybe he'd be able to sleep that night.

He accomplished the first of his tasks before he was interrupted. His mobile, his own now, sang out as he exited the building.

"Owen Gittens here. Are you back in Caernarfon?"

"Yes, I got here an hour or so ago. I was just going out to get something to eat and stock up on groceries."

"That's fine. It looks like they'll get started with the hearing in Cardiff on Tuesday. That's good news for us. There was talk of having it in London, but they decided to keep it local so witnesses could be called in more easily. There'll be sentiment on your side in Cardiff. They'll feel Mathews betrayed them."

Will felt that Gittens wanted him to say something, but he didn't know what.

After a silence that stretched too long, Gittens went on. "The three of you will all be present. They decided the cases were closely tied together, so they're just doing the one hearing. That doesn't mean you won't all get different results," he warned Will, "but they can save time and effort calling witnesses once rather than three times. You'll probably be questioned; in fact, I'm counting on it."

"I've already told them all of it."

"The magistrate won't have heard it. You aren't to have contact with either of the other two defendants until the hearing is over. You'll probably be staying in a cell, I'm afraid, until you're cleared."

Will took heart in the fact that he'd termed it 'until you're cleared.' He wondered what to tell Bronwyn. "If we are cleared, will that be it, then? I can go back to work?"

"Not necessarily. The Deputy Commissioner will also be present, as will someone from the ethics committee. They'll be hearing evidence and deciding whether to press criminal charges against any of you, as well as whether you'll still have a job at the end of it. If you do retain your position, there may be other penalties, as well."

"Suspension," Will surmised.

"With or without pay, depending on their findings." Gittens paused. "Do you need anything from me before we go to Cardiff?"

Will tried to think. "I just want it over," he said at last. And he did. Now that the threat of a trial or at least a suspension waited in the wings, the euphoria of realizing he wasn't going to die, after all, had faded. He just wanted life to be normal again, so the quicker the hearings were over, along with whatever punishment he was given, the better.

As he entered the pub he liked best in Caernarfon, voices hailed him from a table in a corner. He looked over to see Jay Mehta and Beth

Holway beckoning him over. He hadn't wanted to see any of his colleagues until things were settled, but there seemed no way to avoid them without being rude. Stifling a sigh, he strode over to the table.

"We figured you'd be in tonight," Beth told him. "Jay and I thought we'd fill you in on what we know."

"I'll get you a pint," Jay offered. "The usual?"

He nodded, humbled. He'd been afraid of their pity, but maybe that had been a false fear. "How did you know I'd be here?" he addressed Beth.

"We're detectives," she told him, smiling, proud of herself. "This is your favorite, and we figured you'd be too stressed out to cook at home."

"You got that right," he allowed as Jay handed him a beer and a shot to go with it. He held up his glass. "Cheers."

"You'll have to order your own food," Jay told him. "I didn't know what you'd want."

"That can wait. Tell me what the gossip is." He hadn't expected an opportunity to get information except from his solicitor.

Beth leaned close. "Word is that they're not going to come down too hard on you. No one knew that the chief super in Cardiff was importing the drugs himself."

"I think they realize that you and Edward didn't know who you could trust, so you went out alone to take them on." Jay's dark eyes were shining, making Will feel like a superhero. "They seem to see that you didn't have much choice, if they were to be stopped."

"Of course," Beth pointed out, "your methods were questionable, to say the least. I hear you buried a corpse in Howell's back garden so he'd be arrested when the load came in."

"That's true in a sense," Will told them. "It was actually Edward who thought of that."

"Didn't it stink?" Beth's nose wrinkled.

"To high heaven," Will said. "Bronwyn's Land Rover may never be the same again." He lifted the glass of whisky and sipped. Famous Grouse. Jay would have remembered that it was Will's favorite. "Who are you hearing this gossip from?"

"Our temporary boss likes to talk," Beth told him, "especially to the ladies."

"Is it true you were caught and nearly shot before Scotland Yard came in?" Jay wanted to know.

"Yes, it's true. We had to be rescued, and it was in the nick of time." He'd rather avoid that topic, even with them, so he tried to change the subject. "Do you know if they're going to charge me?"

"I doubt it," Beth said. "Bowers said he'd authorized everything, and your friend Edward took the blame for planting the corpse. I don't see where they can pin any actual illegal activity on you, other than buying the drugs in Liverpool and hiding the body so it wouldn't be found."

Relief made Will's hands shake. He set down the glass and folded them on the tabletop. "I don't want them taking the blame for things I did." He'd been a willing participant in it all.

"Edward may have to pay a bigger price, but Bowers should be okay. He can make the argument that someone had to get to the bottom of who was importing the drugs, and since he didn't know who he could trust other than you, he just did what had to be done. I think anyone can see that the result is worth any secrecy that went on."

"He disobeyed orders when he let me work the case."

Jay shook his head. "He had no other choice. You had the contact and the information. You had the plan. He had to ignore what Mathews said, especially since he was your main suspect, and let you investigate."

"If people had died, our people, I mean, then things might be different. As it is, your operation was a success. Bowers is taking credit for a lot of it, but we all know it wouldn't have happened without you and your friend. You didn't do much that you wouldn't have done working undercover, did you? I mean, sometimes then you had to buy illegal drugs and maybe plant them on people, right?" Beth was watching him.

"Sometimes we had no choice, but we tried to keep it legal, as much as possible. You have to do things sometimes that you wouldn't choose to do in order to be believable. This wasn't exactly the same as working undercover. We weren't trying to pass ourselves off as dealers or trying to buy our way to an inside position." He hesitated. "Do you think they'll still let me work major crimes?"

Beth's eyes were sympathetic. "That may be the sticky part. You're pretty much heroes, so firing you wouldn't be good press, would it?"

"Everyone thinks you did it right," Jay added, "except for Notley, of course."

Notley. He glanced at Beth. "I'm sorry I had to send him off on a wild goose chase, but I had to keep him out of our way." He did feel bad about it, even if he didn't like the man. Now he'd made him look the fool twice. There would be no forgiveness for that.

"He turned in his resignation," Beth said.

"What?"

Jay was nodding in agreement. "He didn't say anything. He just came in and dropped a letter on Bowers' desk, and then he walked out."

"How did you know it was a resignation?"

"Our temporary boss, Mark Ramsey, told us. I said he liked to talk. He suggested a farewell party, but Notley wouldn't show up if we did. You know how it is. He hates you the most, but because of you, he feels like we all laugh at him behind his back." Beth looked thoughtful. "I used to feel sorry for him after you made him look a fool in that churchyard case. But I see why you did it this time. The way he feels about you, he'd have thought it an opportunity to get back at you somehow. He'd have sold you out."

Will looked down at his glass of whisky. There was a casualty in this case, after all, and despite his antipathy toward Notley, he felt guilty. "I'd better get some dinner." He wanted time to digest the news. He walked up to the bar and ordered a steak and chips, and then he ordered another round of drinks for the table. He owed them that much, at least. In the end, they'd proven themselves to be his friends.

He called Bronwyn later, sitting in his chair with his glass of Famous Grouse. He'd had a bit too much after the pub drinks, but he couldn't help feeling he deserved it.

She answered, her voice soft with concern. "Are you still okay?" She'd know his being back in Caernarfon would bring it all back.

He told her about the hearing, trying to minimalize it by adding what he'd learned from Jay and Beth. "It'll be an ordeal to get through," he finished, "but I really think things will work out in my favor. I should get by with a suspension, if I'm lucky." He did feel more optimistic now, and he was glad he'd gone through it all in his mind after leaving Gloucester.

He didn't mention Lark, nor did he want to think about his mother's threats to send her off to Canada, not until the hearing was over and his future decided. He knew he could only handle one big stressor at a time, if his mental health were to recover.

"How long will it last?" Bronwyn wondered. "I was hoping you could be here for the St. Melangell's Day celebration."

"I doubt I'll make it this year," he told her, and then he remembered that she had things going on, too. "Did you tell your colleagues about the workshop?"

She launched into an excited description of their support and enthusiasm. "Reverend Wyclyff thinks we'll attract a lot more people to the centre for my guided experiences, and Janice agrees that it fits exactly into our mission, that mindfulness training will help the people who come to us with too much stress in their lives. I'm really excited about it, Will. It's something more I can do, and really, the centre paying me for coordinating should have been part-time, so now I'll feel they're getting their money's worth from me."

He smiled, although she couldn't see it. "I'm proud of you, love."

Chapter Twenty-four

"You'll ride to Cardiff with me. It'll give us time to go over your statements as we travel, and we'll decide together how we're going to approach this." Gittens had met Will at his flat on Monday morning. He was dressed in a different suit, gray with a crisp white shirt and a blue tie, and his white hair was neatly parted on one side.

"I'd rather have my car there, if it's okay," Will told him. He'd slept poorly again, falling asleep only to dream of wandering through what he guessed to be Canadian wilderness, calling out for Lark. He wanted his car. If he was let off on charges and only suspended, he could drive straight to Llangynog and sort out his future there. He suspected that Gittens thought he'd be sent to gaol on one or another of the charges, though, and then the car would be a nuisance.

"I'll drive you," Gittens repeated firmly. He eyed Will. "The beard will have to go. You'll want a professional look. What have you got to wear?"

Will showed him the suit laid out on his bed. It was his court suit, the one he wore when he had to testify in a trial. He was thankful now that he'd mostly taken casual clothes to leave at the cottage and had left his more formal attire behind in the flat. "I have several shirts I can bring, and two ties that coordinate with all of them."

"That should do." Gittens frowned over the shirts, rubbing at a stain on one of them.

"The tie covers that," Will explained, feeling overwhelmed again. He turned his back on Gittens and went into the tiny bathroom to shave.

When he came out, he'd dispelled some of the unease he'd felt earlier. If Gittens wanted to drive him, then okay, he wouldn't argue. He actually felt calmer with Gittens taking charge, as if he could push some of the worry off on the man instead of carrying it all himself. Gittens had sat down in his favorite chair and was studying Bronwyn's sketch across from it. "My girlfriend did that," he told the older man.

Gittens turned to look at him. "Will she be coming to Cardiff?"

"No, she has a job, and it's busy this time of year. There's a festival coming up that she's in charge of." He didn't want her anywhere near this ordeal. She was so happy with her new training, the last thing he wanted was to chase that joy off her face. "We have a cottage in Llangynog, in the eastern side of the district. I stay there on my free days, so this flat is just a place to sleep when I'm on duty."

"It's not a bad place," Gittens said, with a glance around. "If you're single, it's a good location for going out at night."

Will nodded. He tried to fold the clothes he'd laid out so they wouldn't be wrinkled when he wore them to the hearings.

"Roll them," Gittens advised him, walking over to supervise. "We'll hang them when we get there so the wrinkles fall out. If that doesn't work, we'll send them out to a cleaner's to be pressed."

Will wished he could warm to the man, but Gittens reminded him of his father. *It might be that both are solicitors, but they're of an age, and there seems to be an attitude that comes with it.* Somehow, the profession seemed to create an arrogance, whether due to success in the courtroom or the money that came of it, he couldn't say. Every solicitor he'd known had been self-confident to the extent of brashness, and that put him off. Still, Gittens was the man Will had to depend on now to keep him out of prison and to, maybe, keep his career intact, so he resolved to cooperate and to do everything in his power to cultivate the man's good will.

A surprise waited in Cardiff. Will and the others weren't to be confined in cells, after all, but were to be put up in hotel rooms for the duration of the hearings. Will looked at Gittens, who nodded in acknowledgement, and the man rose in Will's regard. "I didn't want to get your hopes up," Gittens explained. "We'd petitioned for it, and our request was granted. It might not have been."

Will had to surrender his mobile phone when he checked into the room. Gittens watched from across the room as he made a final call to Bronwyn, explaining that he had to be out of contact until the hearing was over and that she could follow what was happening on the news. "You'll have an update online any time of day if there's news," he told her. He didn't want her to obsess about it, but he knew she wouldn't want to be left out.

When he finished the call, he handed the phone to Gittens, who gave him a little smile. "It'll be okay," he said. "She'll still be there in a few days when this is over."

"Are you married, sir?" Will rubbed at his wrists. They were still sore from the zip ties that had restrained him, the cuts healing now but still very visible.

"Forty-three years, with two grown children and three grandchildren."

"Congratulations. That's a long time."

"We've had some fun in those years, following the boys around while they were playing sports and traveling, too. My wife made sure there was a homemade dinner on the table every night. What's she like, this girl of yours?"

He could never describe her adequately. "She's a country girl. She grew up in a little village on a sheep farm, and she's close to her family and to the earth, I guess you'd say. She's makes the crime and ugliness I see in my job seem less pervasive. We tend to think the world is full of bad people. She reminds me that there are far more good people than bad."

Gittens nodded. "Sounds like you found a good one, Cooper," and Will felt himself warming to the man even more, despite himself.

The hearing began on Monday morning. Will sat on a chair beside Gittens, while Bowers and Edward sat beside their own solicitors, separated by aisles that allowed access to the front of the courtroom. The chairs were arranged in a semi-circle facing the magistrate's imposing desk. To one side were seated the people who would hear the testimony and decide whether charges should be brought and what their actions meant for their careers. These included the head of Scotland Yard, Commissioner MacPherson, looking formidable in his uniform, and the ethics officer, a woman about the same age, whose height made her dark blue dress suit look crisp and professional. She wore black-rimmed glasses, making her look as intelligent as she probably was. A prosecutor would conduct the proceedings, calling witnesses and questioning them.

Will could see Edward and Bowers, but he had to turn his head and make it obvious when he did. Bowers looked much as he usually did, a frown of stress tugging his mouth downward, but otherwise, rested and ready to begin. Edward gave him a wide grin and a thumbs up when he came in, and Will saw that his black eye had healed to a faint bruise. He felt a surge of confidence and was glad that they could do this all at once rather than having separate hearings. He felt that might work in their favor, and he was interested to hear what the others had to say.

The testimony was to go in chronological order, so Edward was called first since it had all begun with him. He looked nervous as he was sworn in, but he relaxed as the prosecutor began his questioning and he got into his story.

It took all of the first day and well into the second for his testimony to be finished, interrupted at intervals by witnesses called to support or refute his testimony. Will listened intently as he recounted all the suspicions and incongruities that'd led him to approach Will early in his investigation, his own planned words evolving as he heard Edward's slant on things. Yes, he'd been truthful when he'd been interrogated earlier, but there were ways of making the truth look less corrosive and more necessary.

"What exactly was it that made you think someone in the drugs unit was involved?"

Edward took his time and then spoke slowly. "I've worked in drugs for a long time now, and after a while, you develop an instinct for when things are wrong. We were being sent to infiltrate smaller gangs and to intercept certain shipments, but drugs were flooding the market, and that wasn't right. Of course, we're not going to catch every shipment," he'd given the prosecutor a self-depreciating grin, "but we'd always at least caught wind of when the big ones were coming, and we had a good idea who was importing them, even if we couldn't catch them."

"But why Chief Superintendent Mathews, in particular?"

"I was being directed more than usual," Edward said. "I was being sent in the opposite direction I thought I should go. I felt I was being managed and stifled, that I was being blocked at every turn. My every move was known, so that implied someone with access to tracking information, CCTV, mobile phones, things like that. It was subtle, but it was there once I looked for it. It was logical to conclude that one or more of my bosses was responsible, so finally, I decided I had to go off on my own if they were going to be caught." He went on to detail his efforts to travel incognito, including trading his car for the motorbike and using pre-paid mobiles so as not to be tracked.

At that point, Edward was excused for the time being and three witnesses were called in turn.

The first was his partner, Jill Osbourne. Will examined her as she was sworn in. She was of medium height with an athletic build and short, curly blonde hair that was almost a match for Edward's own. She wore a black skirt with a pink blouse and flat shoes. She glanced at Edward, her mouth drawing together as if she wanted to say something, but couldn't, and her eyes were sympathetic.

"I was brought over from Dover last August," she said. "In November, I was told that my partner, Edward Smythe, was being investigated. I was ordered to report directly to Chief Superintendent Mathews, to keep a log of Edward's activities and to report anything he said that could be taken as an off-the-record remark against anyone in the department. I did as I was asked, but I couldn't see where he was doing anything unethical or illegal."

"You didn't wonder what he was being accused of?"

"No, I didn't ask. I was new to the department, and I was still feeling my way. I just reported in as I was asked to."

"And when he disappeared?"

She had the grace to look guilty. "I thought then that they'd been right, that he was dirty and had somehow found out that he was being investigated so he went underground. He'd know how to do it. We all would, doing what we do. I thought he was in hiding and he'd be found someday and charged."

Will felt cheered by her testimony, and was even more happy when the next witness reinforced her testimony and added more. A computer specialist, Andrew Yeats, had been assigned to try to find Edward after he disappeared. "I monitored cameras for a glimpse of him or his vehicle," he said, "and I put alerts out for credit card use and mobile phone tracking." He glanced at Edward. "Of course, he'd spent enough time undercover to know how to stay off the grid, even these days when there are ways to track people that not even experts can usually avoid. I mean, everybody needs money now and then." He paused, and then, lacking a prompt from his questioner, went on, "It actually started earlier, in the late fall, I'd say November or December. I was told to make a log of all the places he went, his phone calls, and his banking transactions. No one said specifically that he was being investigated, but I assumed that he was." He hesitated. "Once he disappeared, I monitored his known contacts, as well." He nodded toward Will. "Mr. Cooper was one of them. We were watching his house, tracking his vehicle, and checking his mobile records, in case Edward went to him for help. He wasn't the only one. There were more we watched."

But Edward had slipped by them and drawn Will in without their knowledge. Will drew a breath. They'd just barely kept out of sight, then.

"You never found a trace of him?"

Yeats looked at Edward again, and this time he didn't look away. "We did hear of his whereabouts from an informant he'd worked with before. My guess, considering the events that followed, is that the informant was paid more by Chief Superintendent Mathews than he was by Edward, or else he was scared enough for some reason to cooperate with Mathews. Whatever the case, I got a tip that Edward was following Billy Davies that I passed on to the chief superintendent."

A tip that led to two attempts on Edward's life. Will gave Edward a grin, knowing he'd be proud that he'd managed not only to stay alive, but to slip their surveillance after that.

386

When Edward was brought back onto the stand, he was asked about bringing Will into the operation. "I just wanted to warn him off. He was investigating the murder of Catherine Baines, which led him to Billy Davies. I knew he'd get onto Davies' drug-related activities, so I went to him and told him what I was doing. I asked him to lead his own investigation in the opposite direction., to stay out of my way. I didn't want to catch Billy Davies. I wanted to catch whoever was pulling his strings."

"How did it happen, then, that Mr. Cooper joined you in your secret investigation?"

"He's a good friend," Edward said simply. "We worked together for a long time, and we did it well. We trusted each other and could anticipate each other's thoughts and actions. He volunteered to help me, and I couldn't talk him out of it. He saw the scope of the task I was undertaking, and he knew I'd have a better chance of succeeding if I had at least one other person to work with. I was happy to have him on board, even though I didn't want to put anyone else in danger."

Things got more tense when the prosecutor turned to the subject of Billy Davies' corpse. "Did you kill Billy Davies?" he asked Edward, who shifted uncomfortably in his chair.

"No, I did not."

"Did Mr. Cooper kill Billy Davies?"

"No, sir. As you know now, Billy would have already been dead by the time Will joined me in the investigation. Will and his partner were searching for Billy at that time. If they'd known he was dead, it would have been a different sort of search."

The prosecutor paused. He glanced at the magistrate. "Do you know who killed Mr. Davies?"

Edward shook his head. "I'm guessing it was one of the guards employed by the drugs smuggling operation. He would have been instructed to shoot Mr. Davies, and probably Catherine Baines and Peter O'Connell, too, by either Morys Howell or Chief Superintendent Mathews."

"Please stick to the facts as you know them," the magistrate broke in. "We can't tolerate guesses in this hearing."

Edward glanced toward him, looking abashed. "Sorry, sir."

The prosecutor nodded. "If you didn't kill Billy Davies, how did you know where to find his body?"

Will felt his muscles tense. He'd been asked the same question when he'd been interrogated, and he'd stumbled over his answer.

"When we bought the drugs in Liverpool, the dealer was chatty. He'd heard a rumor that he passed on to us, on the off-chance it might be useful."

"He knew you were law enforcement?"

"No, sir. But he knew that there was a big player in the game who limited his inventory, and he didn't like it."

"And he told you Billy Davies' body was in that field in the middle of nowhere?"

"No, he didn't. He'd heard it was locked up in an abandoned boat on the beach in Hoylake."

The prosecutor would have already had this information. "How did it get to that remote field in North Wales?"

"Mr. Cooper and I took it there. We followed up on the tip and found the body inside a boat on a little beach isolated from the main beach by a rocky outcropping. We had to wade through the water to get to it, but we suspected it was the right boat because it would have been hard to get to. We speculated that they didn't want Davies found because they wanted Will and his partner kept busy looking for him, so the body would be in an isolated spot. We took photographs at the site, which I believe you've recovered from the mobile phones you gathered up after the raid. We carried the body back to our vehicle and drove back into North Wales, where we hid it in that field. At that point, we were worried that they knew Will was working with me, so they'd reveal the location of the body in order to draw Will out of our investigation. We felt we had to hide it from them for a while, kind of turn the game around on them to give us control rather than them."

"You have no proof of this," the prosecutor observed. "How do we know you didn't shoot Davies yourself and then hide the body in the boat, returning later to move it to the field?"

"I don't have proof. But neither do you. We admit to knowing where the body was, but you have only circumstantial evidence against us, that being the fact that we knew where the body was hidden. There's no weapon, no fingerprints."

The prosecutor smiled, a predator's smile. "But we do have them, both weapon and fingerprints."

Edward's eyes widened in shock. "Not my fingerprints, nor Will's either."

"No, not yours," the prosecutor drawled. He waited a moment for the court to settle. "Tell me about planting the body in Morys Howell's garden." His nose twitched, as if he could smell the corpse.

Edward nodded, glancing at Will. "After I saw Will on the ferry to Ireland, I decided to bury Davies' body in Howell's garden in order to get him arrested. We were pretty sure that Howell was the man running the show for whoever was in charge, so taking him out would draw out the person above him in the chain, and that's who we wanted to catch. We'd talked about planting drugs in his car, like we had with the other men, but the body seemed more of a sure thing to me. I'd put some feelers out, and I managed to draw in some help from other drug importers whose business had been hurt by this one. They agreed to help. I drove up and got the body, and they disabled Howell's cameras and buried it in his garden. When it was done, I called in a tip, and you know the rest."

"Neither Mr. Cooper nor Chief Superintendent Bowers knew you intended to do this?"

Edward grinned defiantly. "No, that was all on me."

Forensics experts were called next, two of them, taking turns. It seemed the gun that had killed all three victims was found in Morys Howell's house when it was searched after the body was found in his garden. "The gun was in a drawer in his study," one of the men said. "We bagged and tested it. Billy Davies' fingerprints were on it, smudged over with someone else's. That person had been wearing gloves, but a print taken from the plastic the gun was wrapped up in was Howell's."

The second technician, a woman, told them that the boat at Hoylake had come up clean except for a spot on the outside where someone had evidently skinned a knee while putting the body inside the boat. "The DNA from that dried blood matches a Robin McWithers, one of the men arrested at the scene of the drugs bust. McWithers has admitted that he assisted in hiding the body there, but says he had no part in killing Davies."

Will wanted to know whether McWillers had named the person who shot Davies, and whether it was the same person who shot Catherine Baines and Peter O'Connell, but the testimony ended there. He knew Howell wouldn't have done it himself. He'd have ordered one of his men to carry out that task.

When it came to how they'd known the day of the delivery, Edward said it had come down to a guess. "We knew it would be the weekend, and Saturday seemed the logical pick. We didn't know for sure. Will went over to Ireland, and he called me with the information about the lorry." When pressed, he refused to speculate as to how Will had known which lorry to follow. "I trusted that he had the right information," he told the court. "That was the kind of partnership we had: we didn't question it when one of us came up with something we needed to know." He glanced at Will. He'd leave it to Will to conjure an explanation for that crucial bit of information.

On the third day, Will was called to testify. He'd dressed in the best of the shirts he'd brought and put on his most subtle tie, and he tried to put confidence in his steps as he approached the witness stand. The magistrate, a sober older woman in her early 60s, looked down at him from her desk, studying him carefully as if assessing his guilt or innocence from his appearance. He was glad of Gitten's advice to shave and that he'd had time for a fresh haircut the day before the hearings were to begin.

Will was taken through the entire line of questioning again, although he'd already answered the same questions when he'd been interrogated in the days following the drug bust, and Edward had described their actions together during the previous two days. The goal was, Will knew, to discover any discrepancies in the answers, so he carefully stuck to the details he'd given before, now reinforced by Edward's own testimony.

"Why did you decide to join Mr. Smythe in this endeavor? Surely, you realized it would be dangerous, not only to you personally, but also to your career."

He hadn't expected that question. He thought it over and answered slowly. "I will admit it was something of an impulse," he said at last. "Edward didn't ask for my help, but I knew he wanted it. We always made a good team, and I knew he couldn't take down someone this powerful on his own. I thought I could help him, and I thought it was important that he be successful. We see a lot of drug-related crime in our work in major crimes. Taking out the source would be a big step forward." He hesitated, not wanting to sound too prideful. "If my job is to protect the people of north Wales, then trying to stop a dirty copper from importing big quantities of drugs was my responsibility. It affects all our reputations when something like this happens, and we struggle enough with our image, as it is. I just had to do it. I didn't see it as a choice."

There was a murmur around the courtroom, but he couldn't tell if it was in support or a comment on what sounded in retrospect like a high-handed declaration. He wished he could take it back.

The prosecutor frowned, waiting for the court to calm down. "You didn't see it as a bit of an adventure?"

Will shook his head. Of course, he'd thought it'd be fun to work with Edward again. There was that. And the chance to get back at Mathews for his transfer was a lure, as well. But he couldn't admit that, not in the courtroom, or he'd might as well pack his bags for prison right then and there. "No, sir, I understood the danger from the first. I like my job, and I wouldn't put it at risk unless I felt I absolutely had no choice. I also understood that Edward's life had been threatened, and mine would be, as well. Edward made it very clear that he was running scared." He shook his head again. "I never looked on this as an adventure. I knew there was a good chance I wouldn't survive it." A little exaggeration might work in his favor.

He was then asked when and how he'd decided to bring Chief Superintendent Bowers in on the operation. "It was a risk, wasn't it, if you didn't know who all was involved?"

He nodded, ready for this one. "Yes, it was a risk, and Edward had warned me not to do it. But I trusted Chief Superintendent Bowers. I'd never had any reason to question his commitment to his job, and everything I knew about him said he was a good, honest man. That was a part of it."

Silence greeted his words as the courtroom waited for him to continue.

"I needed his help, as well. Officially, I was working the Catherine Baines and the Peter O'Connell murders. I was meant to be chasing Billy Davies. Alone, I could have made it look like I was still doing that, like I'd tracked Davies to Fishguard and was checking to see if his friend Morys Howell was hiding him. Alone, I could have managed that. But I wasn't alone. I was working that case with a partner, a partner with whom I'd had a past history that led to what was really a dysfunctional partnership. In short, I didn't trust that partner not to betray me. If I was going to help Edward, I had to do it without my partner's knowledge, and I needed Chief Superintendent Bowers' support to do that. I went to him with the situation, and he gave me the freedom to work the drugs case while appearing to work the Davies case."

"What, exactly, do you mean by that?"

"I mean, he helped me, to put it bluntly, to send my partner on a wild goose chase so that I could concentrate my efforts on drawing out Chief Superintendent Mathews and whoever else was involved in the drugs operation."

"So, he was complicit in your activities?"

"He wasn't actively involved. He didn't know how we were going about it, what our activities were. He knew what our goal was and that was all."

"But he intentionally directed your partner away from your efforts in order to enable you to do what you were doing?"

Will saw no way out of that one. "Yes, that's true."

"Mr. Cooper's former partner, Sean Notley, declined to testify in these hearings, and we did not feel it necessary to compel his testimony since Chief Superintendent Bowers' testimony will be sufficient to support or refute Mr. Cooper's words on this matter." The prosecutor's words were unnecessarily complex, Will thought, but he was relieved not to have to face Notley's wrath at the hearings. It had been a sympathetic gesture not to further embarrass Notley by forcing his testimony, and he was grateful to whoever had managed it.

"Did you at any time use police resources in this venture of yours?" The prosecutor sounded insulting, and Will looked at him sharply.

"No, sir. I'd have liked to. It would have made things easier, but if law enforcement was involved, then they'd have been able to monitor my investigation. I knew that using police resources would give them access to my whereabouts and to surmise my plan of action. I resisted that impulse."

He freely admitted to buying drugs to plant on their opponents, as Edward had.

"You didn't see that as an illegal act? Buying drugs is illegal, as is framing someone for a crime he didn't commit."

"I know that, sir, but desperation calls for actions we wouldn't ordinarily consider. We didn't want to just capture the load of drugs. We didn't want to just catch the dealers, or the distributors, or even the man who was overseeing the arrival and distribution of the drugs. We wanted to draw out the person at the top of the chain, the one running the whole show. The only way to do that was to get the underlings out of the picture, and we had to take them out when the load was already on its way so it couldn't just be delayed until they were free to work again."

All of which brought up the question of the use of Billy Davies' corpse to ensure the arrest of Morys Howell. "I didn't know that was the plan, sir," Will told the prosecutor. "Mr. Smythe already said that he made that decision after I left on the ferry for Ireland." He felt like he was tossing Edward under the bus, but he had no choice but to repeat the testimony Edward had given.

"You did know where the corpse was, having helped relocate it a few days earlier?" The prosecutor's nose wrinkled again in disgust.

"Yes, that I did know. I am aware it is illegal to hide a dead body. I am also aware that doing so thwarted the investigation I was originally assigned to, so I understand that my actions could be construed as willful obstruction of that case. Again, desperate times, sir. We felt that, if the drugs gang had the body at their disposal, they could use it to get Edward and I off the streets and out of their way while the load came in. We anticipated their intent and turned it around, that's all." Will didn't feel good about his testimony on this issue. He couldn't see a way around the charges that he and Edward had obstructed justice in the deaths of Catherine Baines and Peter O'Connell by hiding Billy Davies' body.

When the final questions came, though, Will thought he was prepared. "Your partner has already explained that you guessed the date of the shipment, but what we don't know is how you decided the shipment was on that particular lorry, out of all the ones that could have crossed from Ireland. Can you walk us through that, please?"

"It's simple, really," Will told them. "I have a confidential informant who gave me exact information, the time of the shipment and a description of the lorry."

There was a loud murmur from the courtroom, and the magistrate lashed out angrily. "There will be silence."

The prosecutor waited for it to quiet. "Why haven't we heard about this informant before now?" He sounded as angry as the magistrate looked.

"I've tried to keep him confidential, as the word implies. Until the investigation is complete, it's possible more law enforcement personnel might be implicated, people with the power to retaliate against people who helped us with our efforts. We talk about the 'long arm of the law,' sir. That arm stretches in more than one direction, and I feel that revealing the name of my informant could potentially put him in danger. Additionally, I only know a street name for him, but I'd rather even that name be kept secret."

"Once the investigation is complete, you may be compelled to share that information with the court."

"I know that, sir. When I know everyone involved has been charged, it will be a different story. For now, though, I'd beg your understanding." Will could give them any name, and they could search for years and never find someone using it. Still, he felt that refusing to give a name now would lend more credence to his testimony as well as giving his imaginary informant time to 'disappear' forever.

Bowers' testimony took less time than Edward's and Will's. He'd played only a peripheral role, although he'd kept up with their efforts as well as he could without direct contact. He described Will's first approach, and revealed that he'd been instantly intrigued with the allegations.

"Some things that happened in the past six months suddenly took on a new light," he confessed. "I wasn't sure, but I thought it prudent to give Cooper and his partner a chance to prove or disprove their theory. It wouldn't be the first time someone in law enforcement took the chance to enrich himself through illegal means, although this was far bigger than anything I could have imagined."

When asked to detail what he meant by 'things that happened in the past six months,' he spent nearly an hour, consulting notes of times and dates, going over instructions he'd found baffling in light of operations underway and known trouble spots. "I listened to Mr. Smythe give his testimony a few days ago, and what he said resonated with me. It was a feeling of being misdirected. Nothing specific, but when I went back and reviewed it, there was just a feeling that I was being kept out of the way of something."

The prosecutor then zeroed in on one of the ethical issues involved: Notley. "Did you knowingly misdirect an investigation in order to keep one of your detective inspectors 'out of the way,' as Mr. Cooper termed it?"

Bowers' shoulders lifted with a deep sigh. "That is my one regret, sir, and it will be my regret for the rest of my life. Sean Notley was a good detective. He'd been with the department for more than twenty years, and he had a good close rate. My biggest fault here was that I failed as a leader in my department when I didn't negotiate a peace treaty between Inspector Notley and Inspector Cooper. They'd had a falling out, and I didn't address it as well as I should have, so by the time this issue came up, it was too late. I understood that Inspector Cooper couldn't involve his partner in this unsupported investigation and, indeed, that Inspector Notley couldn't know anything about it, if I were to protect Inspector Cooper to the fullest extent. The fewer people who knew what they were investigating, the better, if law enforcement was really involved. Reluctantly, I agreed to aid in a deception that I knew would carry deep ramifications. I did it knowingly." He paused. "I think the result is worth the cost, high as it is. As Inspector Cooper said, desperate times call for desperate measures. I regret to say that Inspector

Notley turned in his badge this past week. The cost to him personally was high. As I said, I will regret that for the rest of my life, but I did what I felt necessary. I knew the cost. I did it anyway."

Will watched steadily, his dislike for Notley fading in the face of what Notley'd suffered on his behalf. He hadn't meant for his actions to end Notley's career. He knew that Bowers really did regret what had happened, and now he'd have no chance to heal the rift that had extended from Notley and Will to include him in the end.

For Will, the most interesting part of Bowers' testimony came on the final day when he described his decision to consult with Scotland Yard about the investigation. "It had become a real investigation by then," he said, with a nod toward Will. "Even if some of their methods were unorthodox, they had uncovered a good deal of information. I could see that Chief Superintendent Mathews was trying to move our focus elsewhere, both by ordering me to stop investigating Morys Howell and by asking me to move my resources away from Anglesey. That was after telling me a big drugs shipment was coming in to Anglesey and that I should move most of my force up there to set up checkpoints and so on. I think now that he was becoming desperate by that time, that Cooper's and Smythe's actions were causing some disruption in his plans, but it was too late to stop the shipment coming in somewhere on the Welsh coast. In retrospect, his actions seemed frantic rather than ordered by that point in time."

He paused and took a moment to sip water from a glass set on the table beside him. "I didn't know whether to trust Commander Williams at that point. Mr. Smythe had raised alarms about him, too, as well as about myself, I understand. He didn't know how far the cancer had spread, who all was involved." He looked directly at the prosecutor and nodded. "From what you're uncovering now, it seems he was right to be suspicious."

Will sat up. Commander Williams was in on it, too? He'd never imagined it went that high up. He glanced at Edward, who was smiling grimly. "I knew it," he mouthed, and Will nodded.

"I called a contact I knew at Scotland Yard, as you know, James Richards. He was interested so he took it to a higher level, and he was given clearance to conduct an operation in or near Fishguard." Bowers looked at Will and scratched the back of his head. "I couldn't risk contacting Inspector Cooper, so the only option was for Scotland Yard to put a tail on him after he checked in at the station in Caernarfon. They followed him and Mr. Smythe for two days, and I don't think the two of them knew they were being followed. At least, they seemed surprised when the troops showed up at the last. That was how Scotland Yard wanted it, in case they were wrong and nothing turned up."

Later, detectives from Scotland Yard elaborated on his testimony.

James Richards was called, and he verified that Bowers had contacted him with his suspicions and that he'd gone to his superior with it. That man, a tall, stern-faced man in a black suit, went on to detail the investigation they'd launched, in the beginning to assess the potential truth of the allegations and later to form a plan of action.

"It was felt that our best move, considering the lateness of our entry to this investigation, was to create a team that would follow Cooper and Smythe and allow them to lead us to as many perpetrators as possible as the shipment arrived. Chief Superintendent Bowers was kept informed of our activities. We were aware that the two detectives had purchased illegal drugs, and we were aware that they knew the whereabouts of Billy Davies' body and used it to draw out whoever was running the operation from the top." He paused, letting that sink in. "We could have stopped them at any point, but decisions were made to allow them to proceed." He ignored murmurs of interest in the room. "When the lorry departed the ferry and they pursued it, we called in the larger team that we'd had on standby. We waited for the first load to exit the farm lane, stopped it and found that it did, indeed, contain a large quantity of illegal pharmaceuticals, and then we began our operation." He glanced at Will, and then focused on Edward. "We were unaware at that time that Inspectors Cooper and Smythe had been detained, or we might have gone in sooner. As it was, we had lost track of them and had to make the assumption that they'd stay out of a fight, if it came to that. As you know, it did. Two of the suspects were killed and two wounded before it ended with the arrests of twelve men, including Chief Superintendent Mathews. Further investigation has led us to more suspects, but it will be some time before the investigation is complete and we know for certain who all was involved."

It was Friday afternoon before the testimony was complete and deliberations could begin. The magistrate would preside in a closed courtroom as the representatives from Scotland yard, the prosecutor, and their solicitors would argue the cases. Will felt bereft once the testimony was over. This marked the end of their opportunity to argue the case in their favor, and now it would just be down to the waiting.

Chapter Twenty-Five

Their hotel rooms would remain available for them until a verdict was given, but they were no longer required to stay in them, and the ban on them speaking to each other was lifted. Will's mobile was returned to him, and the first thing he did once he'd shed his suit and put on jeans and a comfortable, old shirt was to call Bronwyn.

"It's over, love. Now we just wait for them to decide our fate."

"That must be hard, the waiting and not knowing." Her voice was sympathetic. "But it went well? I read every news report I could find about it. It seemed like everything you did was justified."

He didn't like that she knew about him buying illegal drugs, and he especially didn't like that she knew about how they used Billy Davies' corpse to their advantage. "That depends on your definition of justified. Public opinion can be very different from the law." He switched the mobile from one hand to the other, reaching out with his free hand to stuff clothes into his bag as he talked. He wanted to be ready to leave as soon as the verdicts were given. "But I don't want to talk about it now, love. It's all I've done for the past week, and either way, it's finished. There's nothing more I can do. I want to think about other things."

"Hearing your voice makes me happy. Are you coming here this weekend?"

"I don't know how long this will take. I can't leave Cardiff until they announce their judgements. I'll come to you as soon as I can." He needed to redirect her thoughts, to deflect her concern. "Are you getting any bookings yet for your new venture?"

It was slow, she told him, but they'd gotten a few bookings already and, after the St. Melangell's Day celebration, she'd go at it in earnest. "I just don't have the time right now, having been gone for a week. Summer's the best time for it anyway because we can be outdoors more easily." She then launched into a detailed description of plans she'd made for enhancing the sensory garden outside the centre, and he relaxed as he listened, allowing a smile for the first time in days. The threat was still there, his fate unknown, but at this point there was nothing more he could do but wait for the result. Meanwhile, life goes on.

Afterward, restless, he started toward Edward's room, but as he passed by Bowers' room, he stopped, gathered his courage for a minute, and knocked. Bowers opened the door, peering out to see Will, and then a real smile curved his lips. He stepped back and invited Will in, and he poured them both drinks from a bottle of single malt before sitting on the only chair in the room. "My room, my chair," he apologized. He glanced at Will's wrists, now scabbing over from the cuts he'd suffered, but he didn't mention them.

Will perched on the bed. "I wanted to thank you, sir. If you hadn't called in Scotland Yard, you'd be attending my funeral right now. We were caught, and there was nothing we could do to save ourselves. If they hadn't shown up when they did…" Words failed him, his throat closing up and threatening to choke him. He swallowed, fighting the memory of that moment.

Bowers nodded. "When I came to the conclusion that your friend was right, that Mathews was involved, I thought it was time to call in reinforcements. The two of you had little chance of stopping that operation all on your own, and I knew it. I'm glad it turned out the way it did. I understand they were almost too late."

Will swallowed again, trying to clear his throat. "That's right, sir. Another five minutes, and we'd have been dead."

"Things fell into place the way we always hope they will, but they so seldom do."

Will took a breath. "I also want to apologize for dragging you into this mess." He'd rehearsed a speech, and he wanted to get it out quickly so he'd be sure to get it right. "I'm really sorry about Notley. I was self-centered, just thinking that I needed him occupied elsewhere and not giving much thought as to how he'd feel about it when he realized he'd been played again. I didn't mean it to end his career, sir. I'm not sure why he thought he had to resign. It was my actions that were wrong, not his, and he must know that. I probably won't be working in major crimes anymore, so I wouldn't be there to remind him of what happened if he stayed. He didn't need to leave."

Bowers sipped his drink, looking off into space. "Yes, he did. It was his pride that made him resign, Cooper, not you. He could probably have faced the fact that you sent him off on a fool's errand. After all," he looked back at Will with a wry twist to his mouth, "you'd done it before. But knowing that I supported it, that's what did for him." He focused on Will. "I knew what I was doing when I approved it. I took credit for it, all of it."

"Like I said, I'm sorry about it, sir. I mean that, too. You know that Notley and I had our differences, but it wasn't fair to him to do what I asked you to do. I just couldn't see another way. If it had been Jay or Beth, or even Ian, things would have been different."

"It was just the luck of the draw that it was you and Notley who caught that case."

"That, and the fact that Mathews had requested I be sent somewhere else other than Anglesey. If he hadn't done that, we wouldn't have traded cases, and none of this would have happened."

"I'm glad it did. No matter how it turns out, Cooper, you did the right thing in taking it on."

"I feel bad about it, though. Not all of it, but about Sean, I do."

Bowers took a sip of his whiskey." Sean wasn't always like he is now, you know. He used to be an average guy with a passion for solving crime that made him an asset to us. That Sherlock Holmes thing started a couple of years before you came on to the force. At first, it was just him giving us a laugh, but," he frowned, "it got out of control. Your Bronwyn wasn't the only suspect or witness reluctant to talk to him as his quirks got more prominent. There were others."

"I guess I thought he'd always been like that. I didn't know him before."

"He wasn't different from everyone else in the beginning. Maybe something about the job got to him, I don't know. I do know it made him hard to work with."

Will nodded. "I'm also sorry I dragged you into it, sir. I didn't want to cause trouble for anyone else. I chose to get involved. You didn't."

"I'll be fine. Like you, I went to someone above me with it. That might protect us both, when it comes to retaining our jobs. We'll see. I thought the hearing went well for us, for the most part. Your pal Edward might be in the most trouble, of the three of us. He'd be guilty of insubordination, at the least, but they might just judge it justified, under the circumstances."

Will didn't know if he should ask, or if it would be beyond his clearance to know. "The commander is a suspect, too?"

Bowers acknowledged his boldness with a frown, but he answered, all the same. "I haven't been told much. I'm officially on suspension, too. I understand he's being investigated, but that may just mean they're looking beyond Mathews to see if anyone else was dirty."

"Or that Mathews gave him up."

"He'd be wanting to negotiate a deal, if he could. I notice they've kept mention of the commander out of the news, so far. I wouldn't mention it to anyone just now, if I were you."

"I won't sir." Will drank up the last of his whisky and held up the glass. "Thanks for this, sir, and for the chat. I appreciate it."

"If I get to keep my post, I'll do my utmost to keep you on, too, Cooper. Some might see what you did as walking the edge of a crime spree, but I see it as dedication to the job." He gave a theatrical sigh. "If only I can keep you within boundaries, you'll be a good investigator someday."

"I like to think I already am, sir." Will grinned and left the room.

No one answered his knock at Edward's door, so he returned to his room, not knowing what else to do. He really wanted to rehash it all with Edward, the only one who could possibly understand what Will was feeling, but it looked like that would have to wait. He wondered where Edward had gone to. Perhaps he'd just slipped out for a bottle, like

Bowers had. He hoped, if that was the case, that it was Famous Grouse he'd gone after.

He'd barely settled into his room with the news on the telly when a knock came on his door, and he opened it to see Edward standing there, grinning.

"I knocked before, but you didn't answer. Where'd you go?" he asked, pushing past Will into the room. He ran a hand through his sandy curls, pausing to scratch at a spot on the left side of his skull behind the ear. "I've been organizing."

"Organizing what?" He wasn't carrying a bag, so he hadn't gone out shopping.

Edward perched on the edge of the bed. "A welcome back celebration. I thought we'd go out on the town tonight to celebrate the end of the hearings. I've called some of your old friends from the force and a few new ones you don't know yet, and we're meeting in the Red Pony. Remember that old place?"

It had been their favorite hang-out, near enough to the station that after-hours drinks were a constant back when he'd worked out of Cardiff. He'd hoped to sit down with Edward and talk through some of what he was feeling, but obviously Edward had made other plans. "Sure, what the hell? We'd might as well celebrate today. Tomorrow the guillotine may drop." It sounded nice, actually, seeing some of his old comrades. Now that the offer was there, it was exactly what he wanted to do at the moment. He needed something to chase away his obsession with what might happen in the next day or two, and sitting in his room watching the news or re-living his terror with Edward wasn't it.

The pub was crowded with the after-work crowd. They were waved over to where two tables had been pushed together to form a larger one and supplied with drinks and pub snacks, obviously paid for by the earliest arrivals. Will looked their companions over. Most of them he recognized, the most prominent of these being his former girlfriend Lesley Dunkirk, who threw him a brilliant smile when he sat down at the other end of the table. Several didn't look familiar, so they must have come onto the force after he left.

Curious onlookers kept a watch as they recognized Will and Edward, and some even began buying them drinks, bringing them around to the table with messages of thanks. The enormity of what they'd done began to plant itself in Will's mind. He'd known intellectually that he and Edward had worked to stop powerful men from profiting by the addiction and deaths of others, but until that moment, he'd hadn't felt the impact of it all. Edward was right. They should be celebrating, no matter what the court decided.

In time, Lesley worked her way into the chair next to Will's, taking advantage of its former occupant's trip to the loo to move in. He had been unable to keep himself from watching her, trying to keep it subtle, and he was still watching her as she grabbed her drink and slid into the empty chair. She looked good, but then she always had. A sophisticated new short haircut showed off a purple streak just across the crown of her head, and either her makeup or contacts gave her eyes a brilliant turquoise blue sparkle. Lesley had always loved color, and she used it well. She wore a short dress in a flowered blue and gold design with gold lame sandals that matched her bag.

She gave him a smile and put the bag on the floor beside the chair. "It's been a while, Will." She clasped her wine glass in delicate fingers, moving it just a little side to side before lifting it to drink. "How have you been?"

Will thought of the last time he'd seen her. He'd driven to Cardiff for a Friday night date, and they'd argued at the end of it. He'd been seeing Bronwyn then, but hadn't thought that anything would come of their relationship. Still, Bronwyn had made him look at Lesley in a different light that night, and he'd suddenly realized that Lesley was all wrong for him. He'd never looked back, never regretted the decision to let her go. "I've been fine, except for this little bump in the road." He shook his head and laughed a little, to show he wasn't worried. He'd had several beers and three shots of whiskey by then, and he was beginning to feel them. "I like working major crimes."

She toyed with her glass artfully, and he didn't think she'd had as much to drink as he had. "Will you come back here, if you're invited?"

He was startled. "You think that'd happen?"

"You and Edward are heroes, aren't you?" She looked out one way and then the other, waving her free hand at the pub's patrons. "One thing's for sure, he won't be working undercover anymore, not after this."

"No, I suppose not." It was true. Edward's face – and his- had been all over the news.

"So?"

He shook his head. "I like major crimes and I like Caernarfon, so if they'll still have me, I'll stay where I'm at."

She frowned at that, and then she sipped her wine again. "Are you seeing someone?" She asked it casually, but he could hear the intensity in her voice. He guessed that she didn't want to know, but at the same time, she did.

"Yes, I am." He didn't think it necessary to elaborate. He really didn't want to talk to Lesley about Bronwyn.

Obviously, she disagreed. "Tell me about her." She kept her voice light, but there was a tightness to it, as if she were suppressing the emotion she was feeling. Edward had said she regretted their breakup. Perhaps he was right.

"She's Welsh, and she lives in a tiny village over toward Oswestry. Do you know where that is?"

She nodded, mute for a change. She had always been chatty.

"She works at a counselling centre. She's the coordinator, but she also does nature meditation exercises with groups who come in, or with individuals." Until he said it, he hadn't realized how proud it made him feel. "She's an artist, too. She sells her sketches at Bodnant Gardens."

Lesley nodded thoughtfully. "She's the one you got suspended for, isn't she?" She waited for Will's reluctant nod. "You've been dating for a while, then." She twirled her glass in her fingers and then took a larger drink.

"It was just casual at first. It didn't get serious until last fall." He paused, and then he took the plunge. "We're sharing a cottage in Llangynog, and I commute to Caernarfon when I'm on rotation."

Lesley blinked, and then she looked down at her wine glass, staring at it without seeing it. "So, it's serious." It wasn't a question, but a comment.

"Yes, I suppose it is."

Lesley turned back to him and leaned closer. "Serious enough that you'd say no to a quick fling on the side?" She smiled, and her eyes twinkled with mischief.

Will breathed in, staring at Lesley. The beer and fried food scent of the pub was strong, and he was feeling very mellow after all the drinks, but he wasn't so far gone that he had lost all his senses. Bronwyn had never been the sort of girl that'd be a casual relationship. He'd always known that, and that was why he'd resisted her for so long. But now he'd committed to living with her, and that was that. He wasn't a cheat. "I can't, Lesley."

"I had to try," she said, with a little laugh. She patted his hand, eying the healing wounds on his wrists. "I hope it all works out right for you, Will, I really do. She must be something special."

Bronwyn wasn't as sophisticated or deep down beautiful as Lesley. She certainly didn't have the fashion sense. She'd never love going to concerts or fancy restaurants or the theatre. But yes, she was special, even if he couldn't define how. She was the right choice for him, and he knew it.

Gittens came for Will the following afternoon. He waited while Will put on his suit again and adjusted his tie. Will stood for his inspection, and he wrinkled his nose in disapproval. "What did you do last night?"

Will tried to grin. His head ached and his mouth was dry. "Um…premature celebration?"

"Don't be cheeky," Gittens retorted, and he stood well back as he waited for Will to walk out the door.

The flippancy disappeared when he entered the courtroom. Suddenly, the enormity of what was coming struck him, and his knees felt weak as he followed Gittens to their seats. He nodded at Bowers and Edward in turn. They, too, were solemn this morning, sitting beside their own solicitors in readiness for the verdicts.

The magistrate spoke first. "We have spent time going over your testimonies, and also those of witnesses who were called. We have deliberated each point of potential criminal action and also each potential violation of law enforcement standards. I will first address the criminal aspects of these potential charges in all three of your cases, since you will all receive separate verdicts. Your actions, although coordinated, were all different. When I have finished, Commissioner MacPherson will address the professional standards issues. Since we expect this to take some time, I will not ask you to stand, as would be customary. You may remain seated while we give you our verdicts."

Will's nerves left him shaken. He could have stood up for a verdict, but if there were to be long explanations involved, he was grateful to be allowed to sit. It had been a complicated few days. *At least I'm alive,* he tried to remind himself. *Even if I end up in prison or unemployed, I still have that much.* It seemed little comfort at the moment.

"Before I begin, I'd first like to mention the unusual circumstances of these cases. Because of the nature of the investigation undertaken by you, William Cooper, and you, Edward Smythe, it behooves the court to consider what we call the 'court of public opinion.' Although the methods you employed were unorthodox, to say the least, the result has garnered a good deal of appreciation from the community at large. In fact, major cities in both England and Wales stand to be grateful to you for the feat you've accomplished, on your own and without police resources, and with great risk to your very lives. For that reason, this court is inclined to be lenient about crimes you may have committed in the commission of this investigation."

A surge of hope made Will's heart race. He glanced at Gittens, who gave a quick nod in return.

"We had several potential crimes to consider. The first I will address is the purchase and possession of illegal drugs." The magistrate held up his hand. "I know it isn't out of the question for an undercover agent working to infiltrate a gang to commit this type of crime under the law. However, you were not working to infiltrate this drugs operation; you used the drugs, instead, to frame some of your suspects, resulting in a false arrest." The magistrate looked at Edward and then at Will, his gaze stern. "Nevertheless, I realize that you were operating without police resources, just the two of you alone, and I understand that unusual methods were called for, both to protect you and to draw out the leadership in this criminal enterprise. Therefore, I am willing to overlook these crimes in consideration of the result obtained by you employing them."

Edward nodded at the magistrate, and Will took his lead and did the same, murmuring, "Thank you, sir." Gittens put a cautionary hand on Will's arm, and he understood that he was to behave, that celebration was still too premature.

The magistrate shuffled some papers, and then he looked up. "The more serious offense is the desecration of a corpse."

Edward started to object, but his solicitor grabbed his arm and pulled him back into his chair. Edward glared at the magistrate, but submitted to his solicitor's attempts to control his actions.

The magistrate had paused. He waited for a long moment in silence before continuing. "Perhaps the term 'desecration' is not the right one for the circumstances. I understand that you moved the body of Billy Davies twice, and neither time did you do damage to it or otherwise change the way you found it. However, I must insist that the term 'desecration' is still appropriate because of the use you put the body to. In the first instance, you hid the corpse in a field, far from the location where you found it. Not only did you fail to report that you'd found a body, but you conspired to keep it hidden until such time as you might find it convenient to report it. That, in itself, is another crime: willful obstruction of justice." He paused, looking at them sternly. "The second time you moved the body, you did so in order to, again, frame someone so that they could be arrested, resulting in yet another false police report." He paused again, frowning at Edward and Will. "Despite the reasons you had for doing these things and despite that the outcome has broad community support, I cannot overlook the fact that crimes were committed, knowingly, by you. You literally conspired to pervert the course of justice in the matters of Catherine Baines' and Peter O'Connell's deaths. Therefore, I am finding both of you, Mr. Cooper and Mr. Smythe, guilty of desecration of a corpse and willful obstruction of justice in consideration of your actions with that corpse."

He consulted the paperwork lying on the desk in front of him. "Again, taking into account what the court of public opinion might have to say on the matter, I am sentencing you, William Cooper, to time served and to one-hundred hours of community service for these crimes." He glanced at Will.

Will nodded his thanks, a great well of relief making him dizzy.

The magistrate turned his focus to Edward. "Mr. Smythe, I understand that the second moving of the corpse was your idea, and that Mr. Cooper had no part into the planning or the carrying out of this operation. Therefore, I am holding you solely responsible for it. I understand you had help in carrying it out, and we have issued warrants for your accomplices."

Those accomplices would never be found. Will knew it, Edward knew it, and the magistrate knew it.

"I am, again, inclined to be lenient considering that the outcome of your actions was that a major crime syndicate was taken out of play, and the use of the corpse to detain Morys Howell so that Chief Superintendent Mathews would be forced out of hiding led to your success in stopping more heinous crimes in the future. Therefore, I am sentencing you, Edward Smythe, to time served, plus a fine of £5000 and one hundred hours of community service for your crimes."

Edward sat forward and looked as if he were going to let out a whoop, but his solicitor pulled him around to face him and he went quiet. The fine was not insignificant, but avoiding prison time was the paramount goal. Edward had to be greatly relieved.

The magistrate allowed a small smile. "There will be no criminal trials in connection with this case. I do hope," he looked first at Will and then at Edward, "that this sort of thing won't happen again. Next time, my judgement would probably be entirely different." He glanced to his side, at the police commissioner. "This concludes the criminal portion of this judgement. I will now concede my position to Commissioner MacPherson, who will address the ethics violations that may have been committed by all three of you by your actions in this matter."

Commissioner MacPherson, a hefty man in his early sixties with a trim gray beard and a balding head fringed by gray, stood up. He wore his uniform, looking almost military in his bearing as he stood straight, looking taller than his six feet. The head of all law enforcement in the entire U.K., he carried a good deal of responsibility. He also demanded a good deal of respect.

"It is my duty to address infractions of police protocols that may have occurred during the investigation carried on by the three men we see before us today: Detective Edward Smythe, Detective Chief Inspector William Cooper, and Chief Superintendent Marcus Bowers. Any criminal complaints against them have already been addressed by this court. That leaves me with just one issue, and that is the issue of insubordination. As you know, the proper functioning of a national police force depends on a chain of command. It is expected that each person on that chain should be subordinate to the persons above them, and that anyone below them on the chain should be subordinate to them. That is how our police force functions, and it is essential that these rules be obeyed if we are to function effectively."

"Having said that, I have to add that this case presents unusual circumstances. To wit, Mr. Smythe could not carry out this investigation with the knowledge and consent of his superior. He could have gone above Chief Superintendent Mathews' head, but again, he didn't know how far the suspected corruption went. If he was determined to carry out this self-imposed mission, he felt that he had no superior officer he could report to without compromising his mission." He paused to look at Edward, who was watching him soberly. "We understand the reasons why Mr. Smythe did not trust anyone with his suspicions, but we still have to insist that some chain of command should have been maintained." He paused for emphasis, his stern gaze not leaving Edward's eyes. "I was still there, and I don't think you suspected me. You did have a choice, and you chose to turn your back on authority and to carry out this operation on your own. That insubordination cannot be tolerated. Therefore, we are imposing a suspension on Edward Smythe of one year from the force, without pay, beginning with the first day he was absent from his post."

There were gasps of surprise from the courtroom.

"I realize that the court of public opinion will object to my ruling, and you may appeal if you wish, Mr. Smythe, and ask for a trial of your peers. My other option was to demote you, but I think you'd rather keep your options open in case you decide to return to the force when the year's suspension is up."

Edward swallowed visibly and nodded. "Thank you, sir."

Will knew how much those words would have cost Edward.

The Commissioner now turned his attention to Will. He tried to breathe, terrified of what his own judgement might encompass. Edward hadn't been fired outright from the force, so he took comfort from that thought. He'd tried to protect himself more than Edward had, but was it enough? He didn't know what he'd do if he were left without a job for an entire year.

"Mr. Cooper made a different choice," the commissioner began. "Although his actions had not been assigned by his superior officer, he did them with his superior's knowledge. That choice was a difficult one to make, I am sure." He gave Will a hint of a smile. "It does honor to Chief Superintendent Bowers that you trusted him enough to go to him with this. It also saves you from your friend's fate. Mr. Cooper, I am finding you innocent of insubordination in this case. Although your actions were not actively approved or supervised, and some of them were certainly unethical, you did make an attempt to inform your chief superintendent of your intent, and you had his support in your mission. You may return to your duties as soon as you wish." He paused, and then gave Will a stern look. "However, I don't want you thinking you can go off on your own and ignore the rules whenever you decide to. You will be on probation for the next two years. We will be monitoring your activities, and any further infractions of the rules may lead to a suspension or termination. I believe you have it in you to be a good detective. These next two years will give you a chance to prove that to me."

Will nodded. "Thank you, sir," he echoed Edward's words, if not his sentiment. In his case, he meant them wholeheartedly. His head spun dizzily with relief, and he found he could breathe again.

Lastly, the Commissioner turned to Bowers. "Chief Superintendent Marcus Bowers, in your case you came to Scotland Yard with your concerns once you decided that the investigation had merit. We note that you did not do so immediately, but your position does grant you the leeway to conduct investigations as you see fit without informing your superiors unless it becomes a crime of such proportions as to be of national interest. In this case, as soon as you felt the suspicions were warranted, you reported them, as we would expect you to. Your decision about when to come to us was within the guidelines of law enforcement standards, even though the substance of the crime was such that earlier contact might have been warranted." He paused. "Like Mr. Cooper, your decision to bring us in on this case results in your being found innocent of all charges." He paused, and looked around the courtroom. "Your actions to include us on this case also resulted in lives saved, specifically those of Mr. Smythe and Mr. Cooper, and the capture of multiple high-ranking suspects, as well as a large shipment of illegal opioids. We wish you continued success in your career, sir."

Applause broke out in the courtroom.

The commissioner waited. People noticed, and they quieted quickly. "In conclusion," he said, "I want to remind the three of you that rules are there for a purpose. We cannot have rogue officers ignoring the chain of command and going off on their own investigations any time and any place they wish. We cannot have officers bending the rules or, worse, making them up as they go. This case was unusual. It will not happen again. I expect that all of you will adhere to our expectations in the future. If not, a record of this hearing will be in your personnel files. Your actions here will be remembered." With a nod at the magistrate, the commissioner left his place in the front of the courtroom and strolled toward Bowers, shaking his hand and congratulating him.

Gittens shook Will's hand. "I knew it'd go your way," he told him. "I just didn't want you over-confident. They never really had a case against you, considering the end result. But be careful in future, will you? I don't want to have to do this again."

"No, sir, I don't want that either," Will told him. "Thank you for your help. I really appreciate it."

"Don't worry too much about your friend, Mr. Smythe. If he appeals his suspension, he'll probably be successful. No one really faults him for taking on what he did."

"That's good to hear, sir." Despite his relief at his own success, he'd felt bad about Edward.

"What will you do now?"

Will grinned. "Well, first I'm off to Llangynog as fast as I can go to see that girl I mentioned. Then I'll get back to what I'm meant to do, solving major crimes in north Wales. I do love my job. I look forward to getting back to it."

Gittens offered Will a high-five. "Good luck to you." He motioned toward where Bowers still stood with the commissioner. Edward had joined them and was talking intently to both of them. "You'd better get over there and get your handshakes. It never hurts to put on a show when your bosses are around."

Will walked over, hesitant to interrupt the conversation swirling around Bowers and Edward. Edward was grinning and tossing his blonde curls away from his face, while Bowers still wore the half-smile that passed for happiness on his face. The commissioner stood with them, teasing Edward about his admittedly scruffy look.

He noticed Will and motioned him over, then shook his hand. "Congratulations, Inspector Cooper."

"Thank you, sir." Will couldn't stop smiling. "You were kind to us."

The commissioner's smile included the three of them as he leaned in confidentially. "You'll have been wondering about the investigation," he said, his voice low. "I doubt they've kept you informed, considering the circumstances."

Even Bowers was shaking his head.

"Obviously, the suspects who were on site were all caught red-handed, as they say. But there's more, a lot more. The couriers were all farmers who'd been recruited, not because they were struggling financially, but because they all had crimes of one sort or another that would be overlooked if they agreed to work for the cartel. Most of that was managed by Mathews, working from Cardiff drugs and alcohol, but there was a parole officer involved, as well. Sometimes Mathews would just make the evidence disappear if he could do so without it being noticed, but other times the parole officer approached them and arranged things."

"We suspected it was something like that," Edward told him.

"I talked to the parole officer, and things just seemed a little off about him," Will added. "It wasn't anything we could pin down, but he seemed to evade our questions, for the most part."

The commissioner blew out a breath. "Billy Davies was a different situation. Mathews helped some by manipulating evidence, but Billy was recruited by Morys Howell, who had himself been recruited by Mathews when he committed a double homicide. Somehow, the evidence disappeared on that case, and even most of the file was wiped clean."

"We found that file, sir," Will interrupted. "I showed it to Bowers and one of our techs. None of us could understand how even the names of the investigating officers on the case had been deleted from the file. It made us suspicious of Howell. We thought then that he'd be someone important to the organization, more than just a courier or a guard."

"You were right to be suspicious. He was the man in charge of pretty much everything. Mathews recruited him by making that homicide case disappear, and then Howell gathered in farmers to transport the loads and men to provide security. He had the responsibility of meeting the loads off the ferry and overseeing the distribution to various cities across England and Wales, even up into Scotland. Additionally, there is enough evidence to implicate Howell in the deaths of Catherine Baines and Peter O'Connell, although witnesses to those crimes, who are themselves suspects, tell us that Howell ordered the murders but didn't actually pull the trigger. He had a man under his thumb who was willing to do that in order to avoid a serious previous rape charge."

"Why were they killed, though?" Edward wanted to know. "Wouldn't that draw unwanted attention to Billy Davies that might be traced back to them?"

The commissioner gave Edward an appraising look. "That's what brought you to them, wasn't it?"

Edward nodded.

"Howell isn't talking, but some of his men are. It looks like Billy Davies was skimming off the top, and they figured it out. He was meant to take his loads to Liverpool, but he had a friend who lived near there. That was Peter O'Connell. He would head for Liverpool so CCTV cameras would show him taking that route, then he'd detour and drop some of the load at O'Connell's in Wirral before finishing in Liverpool. Someone noticed the load was short, and Catherine Baines was killed to scare Davies into compliance. We're pretty sure Davies didn't kill her himself. We think he was made to hold the gun so they could threaten to frame him for it if he didn't comply with their orders. He loaded up his trailer and headed north on their instructions after that, but at some point, he must have decided to run for it. He turned off onto back roads to Wirral. We think he planned to leave the whole load there and arrange for O'Connell to get some of the profits from it to him later. Mathews, or Howell, was onto him, though, and both he and O'Connell were killed." He looked at Will. "They knew by then that you were searching for Davies as a suspect in Baines' murder, so they hid his body in order to keep you looking and away from their operation. I don't know how you found that body, but it didn't really matter, did it? By then, Smythe had contacted you and you had been drawn into his investigation."

The commissioner paused to catch his breath and think for a minute. "The investigation is still ongoing. One of the security men suggested that there was involvement higher up than the chief superintendent. We don't know if that information is accurate yet. For now, we are not letting that news out and nor will we until the investigation proves that one way or another. You know how the media is. If someone is named as a suspect, his life is over whether he's actually guilty or not." He gave them a commanding look. "Bowers will be kept informed, and he will pass on any information we feel you need to know. I know I can trust you to keep it to yourselves."

Will turned to look at his chief superintendent. "You're back to work right away, sir?

"I've heard that my replacement likes to gossip," he said. "I need to get things back in order." He gave Will an assessing look. "As for you, I'd like you to take a couple of weeks off, and then I'll expect you back at the station, ready to work. I'm guessing you need some recovery time to get your head back together after coming so close to being killed that night."

"I could use that time, sir." Will still couldn't remember those moments without terror welling up and leaving him trembling. He didn't know how effective he'd be until he got that under control, nor how long it would take for that to happen.

"You'll qualify for some counselling," Bowers told him. "We'll arrange it for when you get back. Meanwhile, go see Bronwyn and make up for the time you've spent away working this case. Celebrate your success, relax, try to get your head around it all. Be thankful that the court saw it as a success in the end."

"I will, sir." Suddenly, the room seemed lighter and the future brighter. He still had Lark's future to figure out, but that could wait for another day. This day was for celebrating the reprieve he'd been given, for allowing his mind to take in the fact that, not only was he not going to prison, but he still had a job to return to. Today, life was good. Tomorrow was soon enough to tackle everything else.

Chapter Twenty-Six

Will declined Gittens' intention to drive him back to Caernarfon, opting instead to accept Bowers' offer of a ride. Despite that the man had proven himself effective in the outcome of the hearings, Will still felt as if he were trying to make small talk with his father when he was with Gittens. Bower would no doubt be better company, even if he was Will's boss.

As they wound their way north through central Wales, Bowers looked over at Will. "You can talk about it if you want to."

Will knew he was referring to the case, not to his relationship with Bronwyn. He didn't want to re-live it yet again, but he supposed Bowers was entitled to the details, considering his role in it all. "I really just want to put it all behind me, sir," he started, "but there are details that didn't come out in the hearings that you should probably know."

"I won't tell you that I'm not curious," Bowers glanced at a lorry in the next lane, "but I won't push you about it if you aren't ready." He signaled and sped up. "I understand it was a traumatic experience."

Will took a breath and started at the beginning, forcing a description of Edward's paranoia when he showed up at the cottage that night, paranoia that they now knew to be justified. "I didn't know what to think," Will told him. "I knew Edward, and I didn't want to think the job had gotten to him, that he was seeing villains where there weren't any. But what he said made sense, at least to me. Maybe I wouldn't

417

have been as suspicious as Edward was, maybe I wouldn't have thought my chief super," he met Bowers' eyes in the rear-view mirror, "was bent, but when Edward pointed out what had led him to his convictions about Mathews, and maybe others, it made sense to me." He paused, thinking. "It must be tempting, sir, when you're working in drugs and alcohol, I mean, to realize that you have the ability to become richer and more powerful than the men you take down. Mathews must have felt himself invincible."

"Until he realized the two of you were onto him," Bowers observed drily.

"Even then, he thought he could pull it off." He thought for a moment. "He nearly did."

"Was it as close as you made it out to be?"

Will closed his eyes and took a deep breath. "I don't know about Edward. We haven't had a chance to talk about it, not really. I don't know if we ever will. But I can say, for me, it felt like the end. I'd given up hope after they brought Edward in. As far as I knew, there was no one to rescue us." He glanced at Bowers in the mirror. "Truthfully, sir, I was terrified. I always imagined that, if I knew I was about to die, I'd be accepting, that I'd just brace myself and wait for it. But it wasn't like that at all. I was shaking, I was so scared. I just wanted time to slow down, to have just a few more minutes." He wouldn't mention that his last thoughts were of Lark and Bronwyn. Some things had to remain secrets. "I'd rather not talk about it, if you don't mind, sir." He shook his head. "I just can't, not right now, not that part of it."

"Counselling will help. The memories will fade in time, and you'll be able to go on."

"You aren't speaking from experience?"

"No, I'm not. I was threatened a few times back when I was on the streets, but I've spent more time solving puzzles than I have worrying about dying." Bowers tapped the speed control and sped up, readjusting it. "This was a one-time thing, Cooper. It isn't going to happen like that every time you take a case."

"I was knocked unconscious a year ago and woke up in hospital," Will pointed out, "and then I was stuck with a needle full of heroin in the fall. I came out okay both times, but I seem to put myself into situations where my life is more at risk than is usual in this career. Is it just me, or am I unlucky?"

"You run toward danger rather than away," Bowers observed. "It's part of what makes you good at the job."

Will thought about that for a few miles. Beside him, Bowers drove in silence, moving in and out of traffic, watching the road.

"I'd like to tell you about Billy Davies," Will said after the silence had stretched too long. He thought it a safer subject, that he could now look back on that part of the operation with a bit of humor. He picked up his mobile phone and looked at the screen. No new calls or texts waited to distract him. He took a breath and launched into a vivid description of their wading through the sea to get to the boat, of floating the body back to the other side, where they could load it into the Land Rover. "We were lucky to have the fog that night. We didn't have to worry so much about being seen." He grinned. "The smell, though, sir. I don't think I'll ever get it out of Bronwyn's car. That poor old Land Rover took a beating, between carrying the corpse around and being beaten in by those thugs from the pub." But at least they'd gotten it back. That was sheer luck, given that the guys who'd borrowed it could probably have retrieved the Citroen and kept it, as well.

"You were lucky to have it. Poor Billy Davies wouldn't have fit into that little sports car of yours."

Thankful for the opening, Will let Bowers' comment launch them away from Will's illegal and unethical adventures into a safer discussion of cars. They talked about which were more practical and why Will's little MGF wouldn't suffice for long if he wanted to continue the commute between Llangynog and Caernarfon. That topic took them nearly all the way to Caernarfon, to Will's relief. He really didn't want to think about the past three weeks any longer, at least not for the next few days. He was exhausted with it all, and now was the time to try to let his mind heal.

Bowers dropped him by his flat with instructions to take at least two weeks off and then to check in by phone to let him know if Will was ready to return or not. "Don't let it be too long," he said with a stern

419

shaking of his forefinger. "Don't get so comfortable with the domestic life that you keep putting off your return to work."

"No, sir." Will grinned. "I've already taken too much advantage of your good will. I won't want to look like I've forgotten my place."

Bowers smiled and rolled the window of his car up.

Will walked up the stairs and into his flat. It was late-afternoon. He could be in Llangynog by dinnertime if he left right then, but he had a few other things he wanted to accomplish first.

He called Bronwyn to tell her he was back in Caernarfon and that he'd be in late. "I know you have to work tomorrow, love. Don't wait up for me."

She protested, telling him she'd have dinner waiting for him, but he gathered himself to be firm about it. "I'll be there for at least two weeks. You'll have plenty of time to feed me and to get tired of me hanging around, I'm sure. I really do have things to get done here before I can leave again."

"I'll have to work most days while you're here," she warned him. "I have only just over a week until the festival."

A sudden thought struck him. "Is it too late to register for the pilgrims' walk? Maybe I could pick Lark up from school on Friday, and she and I could do the walk on Saturday."

"I'll be busy running things," she told him. "I won't get to spend much time with her. She may not get a ride on Hobbs."

"It's okay. I can take her to see him by myself on Saturday after the walk, if she's done enjoying the festival by then. She knows how to saddle him now. You and I can take her home on Sunday afternoon."

"I should be free by then," she conceded. "I'll have earned a day off."

"Unless you don't want me to get her," he added then, worried that he'd pushed Lark on her too often of late.

"No, I think it's a brilliant idea," she told him. "I love that the two of you will be a part of my big event this year. You could bring Daisy on her leash, too. I'll see about adding just two shirts to my order. It shouldn't be a problem."

That conversation ended, he took a breath and called his mother. *Might as well get it over with. At least this time I won't have to cancel at the last minute.* "Mother?" he said when she answered. "I'd like to invite Lark for next weekend. There's a pilgrim's walk at St. Melangell's, where Bronwyn works, and I thought she'd enjoy doing it with me."

Unfortunately, his mother sounded more like her old self. "I'll let her go with you this time, but don't think this is how you'll manipulate me into letting her stay with you. I can see right through that ploy, William."

Couldn't she just see that he loved spending time with Lark and that at the moment he had time available to do just that? "I'm not manipulating you. I just have time off right now, so it's easier for me to have her without the possibility of having to cancel at the last minute. We don't need to talk about her future yet." But soon, he'd have to tackle that subject, too. He had a lot of thinking to do, and not just about the events of the past weeks.

"You didn't tell me you were involved in that big drug bust, William."

Of course, she'd have seen it on the news. "I played a minor role, Mother. It's my job."

"The news media is treating you as a hero in the whole affair."

"It's exaggerated, I'm sure." While he'd like her to think he'd done something really important, knowing the details would probably only encourage her disdain for his job in law enforcement. It definitely wouldn't help his case for taking Lark if she knew the danger he'd put himself in. "I'll just get her from school on Friday, and we'll bring her back on Sunday evening." If he picked Lark up from school, he wouldn't have to see his mother alone, and Bronwyn would be with him on the Sunday. It was the best way he knew to avoid another confrontation, at least until he'd had time to figure out a plan.

"Don't bring her home too late," she warned him. "She'll have school on Monday."

"We'll be there by five, but we'll have to take right off again. It's a long drive back to Llangynog, and Bronwyn will have to work the next morning, too." He'd figured out the timing of it carefully so as to avoid another disastrous dinner with his parents. Bronwyn would thank him for that when it came time.

Phone calls done, he grabbed his wallet and keys and headed out the door. He had some shopping to do, and he hoped he could find what he needed in Caernarfon. If not, he'd have to make a stop elsewhere; maybe he could try Betws y Coed. If all else failed, he could drive to Wrexham one day while Bronwyn was at work. It was a bigger city and would have more shops to browse. He'd stop by the Tesco, as well, and load up on groceries for the next two weeks' meals. It'd take a while to plan some meals around Bronwyn's vegetarianism, but he didn't like to think that she'd be buying everything they'd need during his time at home when her budget was so tight. His was tight, as well, at the moment. He'd spent a lot on his adventure with Edward, and he doubted he'd ever see a penny of it reimbursed. Still, he could afford the few things they needed.

An hour and a half later, satisfied with his efforts, he parked his little car in the station car park. Sooner or later, he'd have to walk back inside and face his colleagues, this time without a Scotland Yard escort, and he'd might as well get it over with. The last time he'd been inside, he'd tried not to catch anyone's eye, embarrassed by his unethical activities and subsequent arrest. It would take courage to walk in again now.

He got out of his car, locked it, and forced confident steps to the back door, the employee entrance. Taking a breath, he opened the door and walked steadily inside. A duty clerk was watching the door. She eyed him, smiled, and waved him by. "Welcome back, sir."

He nodded at her, smiling his thanks at her welcome, and strode past her desk, past the employee break room, the locker room, and finally, into the main room where he and his colleagues worked. Someone had been watching the door rather than working, probably checking the hour since it was nearly six o'clock. A mumbled exclamation swiveled heads, and then a hush fell as eyes all over the room turned to where Will had stopped in the doorway to gaze into the room.

The long moment of silence stretched into what felt like an hour, and then Will's head swiveled as one pair of hands started to clap slowly.

It was Quigley, standing by his desk and slapping his hands together loudly, a grin on his face. As Will watched, Mehta stood up and joined in, and then others quickly followed suit, standing and applauding, some shouting out cheers or congratulations or whistles. Will swallowed as emotion brought tears to his eyes, but he lifted his chin, determined not to let them see.

He screwed his mouth tight, and then he forced a grin and held up a bag. "I've brought pastries by way of apology for my behavior."

"Pastries!" a voice called out disdainfully. "Where's the booze?" It was Ian O'Flynn, one of the DCIs, and he jeered as others in the room joined the fun.

"I've got that," barked a voice Will recognized well, and he turned his head to see Bowers looking out his office door. "Break room, now, all of you."

There was a scramble as chairs were pushed aside and Will's colleagues hurried to crowd into the break room. Will looked past them to Bowers, who nodded and held up a bottle of whisky. Sometimes a bottle came out to celebrate the end of a particularly difficult case, and Will supposed this one qualified.

It was just after nine in the evening when Will parked his MGF beside the cottage and met Daisy, who'd come out to greet him. He'd thought he'd arrive later, but things had gone more quickly than he'd estimated. His shopping had been accomplished to his satisfaction, he'd used the excuse of the long drive to evade offers of more drinks from his colleagues, and light traffic on the roads had allowed him to make the drive in record time. Despite being really tired of take-out food, he'd picked up a sandwich to eat on the road, and the time passed quickly as he mused on the unexpected reception his colleagues had offered. Maybe it was true that none of them liked working with Notley. Certainly, no one had mentioned him as they'd pressed him for details about the case, most of which he'd dodged. He was glad now to be given time to get away from Caernarfon and thoughts of what had happened during the past few weeks, even to let the accolades settle. He needed the time to get his head together again before another case came up.

The door opened and Daisy ran out into the light drizzle that had begun. He stooped to ruffle her ears, smiling as she rubbed against him, tail wagging furiously. He pulled the passenger door open. "Come help me with the groceries," he called out.

He could see Bronwyn pulling on her wellies in the doorway, and then she ran out, stretching up to kiss him. "You brought groceries?"

"Lots," he confirmed, feeling proud of himself. "I'm going to be here for at least two weeks, and the last thing I want is for you to worry about feeding me when you've got St. Melangell's Day to organize. I am going to take over all the domestic duties for the time being." He liked the idea; it gave him a feeling that the cottage was really home, that he wasn't just a weekend guest. He lifted a carrier bag out and handed it to her, then added a second one. "I can carry the rest." He gathered up three more bags.

"There won't be room in the fridge for all of this," she told him. "We do have local shops, you know."

"But no time to visit them, with you working all hours," he pointed out. "I want you to relax when you're done working for the day. Let me take care of you."

"You're going to spoil me." She opened the door with her free hand, hefting the two bags in the other. He could see she was pleased. "I have chores lined up for you to do, by the way." She stepped inside, letting Daisy rush past into the little entryway. Holding onto the wall for balance, she kicked off her wellies, one at a time.

"Chores! This sounds serious." He followed her inside and set his bags on the floor so he could remove his own boots. "I'm beginning to regret my decision to come."

She smiled, and he followed her into the kitchen, where she set the bags on the counter. "The door handle on the back door is loose. I called the landlord, and he said he'd knock off £100 this month if we can fix it ourselves." She looked at him earnestly. "That's a lot, Will. He doesn't want to have to drive all the way here to do it. We'd have to buy a new handle, and then you'd put it on."

He looked back at her. "You're trusting that I'm capable of such a task." He had no idea how he'd go about it, but maybe at the shop they could give him some instructions when he bought the handle.

She nodded. "And then there's my fence. I really want to get the garden planted next week after the celebration is over, and Maddock never did make it over to help you with it."

"You're saying I have to tackle it all by myself?" Now she was talking a serious challenge. "Do we even have tools?"

"No, but you can borrow what you need from my dad. I'll call ahead, and he'll have it all ready for you, the fencing, the posts, and the tools, too."

"So, you're saying I'm going to be kept busy, with no time to dwell on my troubles," he pointed out, smiling. *I'm a smart man. I can figure this out.* It'd probably be just as well. He'd been worried that while she was at work, his mind would be busy re-living what he'd thought the last moments of his life. Being busy would be good for him.

"After this week is over, I can ask for a day off, and I can get off work most days earlier, too, once the celebration is done. Then we can go hiking in the evenings, if you want."

He reached out for her. "I do want."

She gazed up at him, a question in her eyes. "What is it you want right now?" she asked softly. "Your new chair and a glass of Famous Grouse?"

"Not tonight," he told her, his voice suddenly husky with spent emotion. "Tonight, I just want you."

The days fell into a rhythm. After Bronwyn left for work, he tidied up the cottage, and then he called to Daisy and took her for long strolls up the lane and partway up the footpath toward Pennant Melangell. Daisy knew the path and foraged ahead of him, but he took his time, stopping for the view and trying to work up his stamina again for when Bronwyn could join them. She'd always been a better hiker than he had, and that embarrassed him more than he wanted to admit.

One day he drove into Oswestry to buy the door handle from a shop.

"It's easy to install," the cashier had told him. "Just follow the instructions, and you'll be fine."

He wasn't fine. The old handle dropped out easily enough, but the new one wouldn't fit. No matter how many curse words he muttered or how hard he tried to squeeze the shank through the opening, it was too short to fasten on the other side. It just didn't fit. Finally, he determined that he'd bought the wrong handle. Without a handle, the door couldn't be shut, so he closed it as best he could against the rain that had settled in and called to Daisy to come with him.

She sat in the passenger seat as he made the half hour drive to Oswestry, back to the shop, where the nice cashier showed him that the shank could be expanded to fit the door.

Another day, he traded Bronwyn vehicles and drove over to the farm, where he picked up a roll of fencing, some metal posts, a shovel, a mallet, and some zip ties. Feeling confident, he laid everything out around Bronwyn's garden patch and set to work. The post holes he dug easily enough, since the posts themselves were pointed on the bottom and easy to insert into the rain-softened soil. He put them in deep, reasoning that it would make the fence sturdier that way. Proud of himself, he then set to work on the fencing. This wasn't quite so easy. The material wanted to fold in on itself into the roll. He stretched it as well as he could, held it with one hand, and tried to fasten the zip ties with the other. This, he couldn't do. He swore at the fence and tried again, managing to fasten one zip tie around the center of the fencing. He stepped back to look. It was too high, so he tried to push the fencing down, but the tie was too tight. He thought about it for a minute, then fastened another zip tie in the same spot, leaving it looser, and cut the first one off. He was then able to adjust the height of the fence to just above soil level. After that, it was easier.

When he'd made it all the way around, he stepped back and admired his work. It was a little bowed in places where he'd left it too loose, and it dipped in places where he'd fastened it too high or too low, but overall, he thought it a roaring success.

A half hour later, he went outside to walk Daisy down behind the cottage, and a rabbit blinked at him from inside the fence. It had managed to push the zip-tied fencing up on the post high enough to slip beneath. He shook his head and examined the damaged spot. That's when he saw the notches on the post, which were obviously meant to be hammered down over the fencing to hold it in place. He went back inside, got a hammer, and, two damaged fingers and a few curses later, he declared the fence a triumph of inept labour.

When a day stretched too long and his memories began to take over again, Will left the cottage and drove to the farm in an attempt to banish them. He wandered out into the pasture and offered to help Bronwyn's dad and Maddock with the sheep, thinking it wouldn't hurt to make the offer, even if he didn't particularly like the noisy animals, nor their smell. It didn't take long to get the idea of spraying the sheep with insecticides to keep insects off, which took most of the day, even with the three of them working at it. At the end of the day, bruised from wrestling the ewes into submission, he was given cardboard mailing cards and shown how to collect fecal samples to be sent to a lab for analysis. He left the farm near dinner time exhausted and feeling that perhaps it was easier to fight off his memories than it was to be a sheep farmer. He treated Bronwyn to dinner at the Tanat Inn that night.

Another day, he went back to the farm and declined Bronwyn's dad's offer to teach him more about caring for the sheep. He took Daisy across the pasture and through the forest land to Bronwyn's rock. He sat there, thinking not just about the case, but also about Lark and about Bronwyn, too. He looked into the pool of water and tried to imagine what it would be like to see things in it, like she did. He wondered how she'd known the date of the ferry crossing, and the time, but his mind didn't want to go there. In the end, he laid flat on the rock with Daisy beside him and looked up at the tree branches overhead, taking time to close his eyes and listen, smell, and feel nature. He wasn't as good at it as Bronwyn was, but it left him relaxed and feeling that he could face whatever came afterwards.

"Look up, Will. Make a wish."

He looked up. The dark sky was brilliant with stars, the moon a sliver just over the horizon. It never looked like that in the city. It was Sunday night, the day after the St. Melangell's celebration, and Bronwyn had a rare day off. They'd left early to return Lark to Gloucester and returned mid-afternoon, relieved to finally have some quieter time together before Will had to return to Caernarfon. "Okay," he mumbled, "I'm wishing for…"

She shrieked and put a finger across his lips. "You can't say it out loud, or it won't come true. Close your eyes and wish it in your head."

Obediently, he closed his eyes as he felt her finger drop away. It was superstitious nonsense, of course, but if he had a wish, the only thing he could think of would be to keep his life exactly as it was at the moment.

He opened his eyes and looked at Bronwyn, a shadow in the dark standing within touching distance. He reached for her and started to pull her close for a kiss, and then thought better of it. "Marry me," he said gruffly.

She was close enough that he could see her eyes widen in surprise, despite the dark. Not dismay, though, was it? No, he was sure of that.

"You're drunk, Will," she said softly. They'd shared a bottle of wine with dinner. But her voice revealed a yearning he seized on.

He dropped to one knee, holding her hand. "I want to do it properly," he muttered, trying to appear steadier than he felt. "You're right. I've had more to drink than was sensible, but this isn't down to the drink. I've been working up my courage for this for a while now." He didn't tell her that the courage was for himself, to help him face the commitment, rather than fear that she'd turn him down. "Bronwyn," he started, and then the words came fast, "I am happier now than I've ever been, and I don't want anything to change. Please marry me so that I can know that this is not just for the next few months or years, but for the rest of my life." He paused, and then he knew what was expected next. "I love you. Please say yes," He looked up at her, waiting. It hadn't been the most elegant of proposals, but he'd stumbled through it. "I bought you a ring, but it's inside."

She pulled him up and stepped closer, inches from his face. "Yes, that's what I want, too," she said softly, and he relaxed.

He was committed now. No turning back.

Two days later, he made it official. They'd enjoyed dinner with Bronwyn's parents, an invitation that had come unexpectedly on a

Tuesday evening when they'd stopped by after Will picked Bronwyn up from work. His first week off had gone by fast, and he didn't want to put his obligations off any longer. He'd managed the proposal; now it was time to observe the customs.

Bronwyn followed her mother into the kitchen carrying a stack of dishes. Will stood up and reached for a platter, ready to follow Bronwyn's dad with his own handful of dishes, when suddenly he realized this might just be the moment he'd been waiting for.

He plunked himself back into his chair, settling the platter on the table in front of him.

Bronwyn's dad stopped, looked at Will, and then pulled his own chair back out, his expression neutral. "Something on your mind, son?" He settled back into his chair. "I expect it's okay if I call you that?"

"Yes, sir," Will responded, feeling his cheeks grow hot. He wasn't usually prone to blushing, but this situation had him unsettled, for sure.

Bronwyn's dad waited, his face now reflecting growing relief, mixed with amusement.

Will took the plunge. "Sir, I hope you know that I've never taken my relationship with Bronwyn lightly." He eyed Bronwyn's dad, who said nothing to help him along. He took a breath. "I know she's not the kind of girl you date casually, and if it looked like I wasn't as committed to her as you'd have liked, I didn't mean for it to. The thing is, I wasn't looking for a serious relationship when I met her, but now I can't imagine my life without her."

Bronwyn's dad nodded briefly, an acknowledgement more than anything.

"I know we have some things to work out. It's not an easy commute between Caernarfon and Llangynog, for one thing, but we're managing it for now. I've found I like living in a small village, and I like having family close by, too." He felt he was babbling on. *Time to wrap it up.* "The thing is…we're ready to commit to each other, and we'd like your blessing, if you'll give it. I've asked her to marry me." He stopped, feeling that he had no more to say.

Bronwyn's dad smiled then, an odd little half-smile that had Will wondering if he'd handled the asking well enough to suit. "Her mother and I would like that," he said, his quiet voice even quieter than usual.

"She fancies you a great deal, and we want to see her settled and happy. You make her happy, son."

"Then we have your blessing?" Will needed to hear the words.

He inclined his head. "You do, indeed."

Later, Maddock and Mai stopped in with the children.

The others had just finished a cherry tart and were still at the table, chatting.

"Let's go into the sitting room," Bronwyn's mother suggested. "I'll get you some dessert." She inclined her head toward Maddock and Mai in a question, and they nodded.

As they entered the larger room, Mai looked at Bronwyn, her eyes bright. "What's that on your finger?"

Bronwyn held out her hand, her smile shy. She'd waited to put her ring on until after Will had talked to her dad, wanting to give him the time to ask before they made the announcement.

"It's about time." Maddock grinned at Will, and then he grabbed him in a bear hug. He was surprisingly strong, Will thought, as he struggled to free himself. Then something hit him from behind – Griffyn – grabbing onto his back legs and tugging. Now the struggle turned into a tussle as Will tried to stay upright and shake them off while they all laughed fit to lift the old ceiling.

Maddock let go suddenly, leaving Will to fall on his rear. He managed to direct his fall so as not to crush Griffyn beneath him, but he fell awkwardly, sprawled on the floor.

Maddock stood above him and offered a hand, pulling him to his feet. "Griffyn, I think us Bagley men have a better way to welcome someone into our family, don't we? This bloke is going to be your Uncle Will now."

Griffyn scrambled to his feet and held his hand out to Will. "Welcome to the family, Uncle Will," he said gravely.

Will took his hand and shook it firmly. "Thank you, Griffyn." A sense of belonging made him grin uncontrollably.

He'd never in his life felt as much a part of a whole as he did at that moment. No one could predict the future, but now he wouldn't have to face it alone. He'd have Bronwyn at his side to share the good times and bad, to come home to at the end of a hard case, to make his life richer. Maybe she *had* put a spell on him somehow. If so, he was grateful.

Janet Newton

Printed in Great Britain
by Amazon

Over the

Whales' Road